Mark Billingham has twice won the Theakston's Old Peculier Award for Crime Novel of the Year, and has also won a Sherlock Award for the Best Detective created by a British writer. Each of the novels featuring Detective Inspector Tom Thorne has been a *Sunday Times* bestseller. *Sleepyhead* and *Scaredy Cat* were made into a hit TV series on Sky 1 starring David Morrissey as Thorne, and a series based on the novels *In the Dark* and *Time of Death* was broadcast on BBC1. Mark lives in north London with his wife and two children.

*Also by Mark Billingham*

*The DI Tom Thorne series*
Sleepyhead
Scaredy Cat
Lazybones
The Burning Girl
Lifeless
Buried
Death Message
Bloodline
From the Dead
Good as Dead
The Dying Hours
The Bones Beneath
Time of Death
Love Like Blood
The Killing Habit
Their Little Secret

*Other fiction*
In The Dark
Rush of Blood
Cut Off
Die of Shame

# MARK BILLINGHAM

# Cry Baby

Little, Brown

LITTLE, BROWN

First published in Great Britain in 2020 by Little, Brown

1 3 5 7 9 10 8 6 4 2

Copyright © Mark Billingham Ltd 2020

The moral right of the author has been asserted.

*All characters and events in this publication, other than those
clearly in the public domain, are fictitious and any resemblance
to real persons, living or dead, is purely coincidental.*

All rights reserved.
No part of this publication may be reproduced, stored in a
retrieval system, or transmitted, in any form or by any means, without
the prior permission in writing of the publisher, nor be otherwise circulated
in any form of binding or cover other than that in which it is published
and without a similar condition including this condition being
imposed on the subsequent purchaser.

A CIP catalogue record for this book
is available from the British Library.

Hardback ISBN 978-1-4087-1241-2
Trade Paperback ISBN 978-1-4087-1242-9

Typeset in Plantin by M Rules
Printed and bound in Great Britain by Clays Ltd, Elcograf S.p.A.

Papers used by Little, Brown are from well-managed forests
and other responsible sources.

Little, Brown
An imprint of
Little, Brown Book Group
Carmelite House
50 Victoria Embankment
London EC4Y 0DZ

An Hachette UK Company
www.hachette.co.uk

www.littlebrown.co.uk

*For Claire. Twenty years on. Still chocolate . . .*

Halfway up the front door, where the shit-brown gloss is not worn away or flaking, he can see a scattering of handprints. He lets out the breath he's been holding and leans closer. That clammy palm he had felt pressed hard against his own the previous day at the station, the calloused thumb and thick fingers; the shapes of them are all marked out perfectly against the paintwork, in brick-dust and blood.

He puts his own, far smaller hand inside one of the prints, and pushes.

The door swings open and he steps inside as quickly as always.

He stands for a few seconds in the semi-dark.

He listens and sniffs.

The music he can hear in one of the rooms further down the hall – tinny, like it's coming from a cheap radio – is the same as he'd heard the day before leaking from the station locker room. That Eurythmics song about angels and hearts. The smells are familiar too, though a little trickier to identify immediately.

Something ... burned or boiled dry in the kitchen. Mould blooming behind the textured wallpaper or perhaps in the bare boards beneath his feet ... and a far richer stink that drifts down from the upper floor, growing stronger as he stands and sweats and puts an arm out to steady himself, until he can swear that he feels it settling on his face and neck like soft drizzle.

Rotting meat and wet metal.

In contrast to the hallway, the stairs are thickly carpeted and,

1

when he takes his first step up, he feels his foot sink deep into the pile. He looks down and sees a viscous, grey-green liquid oozing up and into his shoes, then quickly lifts his head and fixes his gaze on the top step when he feels something slithering against his ankles. By the time he's reached the landing he's out of breath, his socks are sodden and things are moving beneath the soles of his feet. In turn, he pushes each foot hard against the floor, feels something flatten, then burst.

The bile rises into his throat and he grabs for the banister. Just for a moment it's as though he's about to fall backwards and tumble down the stairs behind him.

It would be all right to fall, he thinks, to keep falling. The pain would be done with quickly enough and blackness would be better than this.

Blankness.

He forces himself to take a step, turns right and moves towards the door at the far end of a corridor that narrows before it curves around the foot of a second set of stairs. There's a converted attic above him and he knows that the three small beds it contains are neatly made, identical. There's no point looking, because he knows too that there's nobody up there. Time is precious, so he can't afford to waste it.

Three plump and empty pillows, that's all. Three pairs of furry slippers with eyes, and ears and whiskers. Three freshly laundered pillowcases, the initials embroidered in red, blue and green.

*L, S, A-M.*

He keeps on walking towards the big room at the front of the house, the *master*. There are several other rooms on this floor, plenty of other doors, but he knows exactly which one he's meant to walk through.

He knows where he's needed.

It's twenty feet away, more, but it's as though he reaches the door in just a few steps and it opens as he stretches his hand

2

towards the doorknob. A hand that he moves immediately to cover his nose and mouth.

The man sitting, legs splayed out across the hearth, looks up, as though blithely unaware that much of his face is missing and most of his brain is caked like dried porridge on the mirror above the mantelpiece. Unaware that, by rights, he should not be seeing anything. The man gently shakes what's left of his head, a little miffed to have been kept waiting.

He says, 'Oh, *here* you are.'

On the bed opposite, lying side by side, the three small figures are perfectly still. Their hair is washed and brushed, their night-dresses spotless. They're asleep, that's all, they *must* be, though it's strange of course that the gunshot hasn't woken them.

Wanting attention, the man in the hearth clears his throat and it rattles with blood. It's hard to imagine he has any left, judging by the amount that's dripping down the wall, soaking his vest, creeping across the tiles around his legs. He raises his arm and proffers the gun. Dangles it.

'Always better to be sure,' he says. 'And I know how much you want to.'

There was hesitation the first time, the first few times, but now he just steps forward to calmly take what he's being offered and leans down to press the barrel hard against the killer's fore-head. He watches it sink into the tattered white flesh, pushing through into the hollow where the man's brain used to be.

'Belt and braces, Tom,' the dead man says. 'Belt and braces . . .'

He closes his eyes and happily squeezes the trigger.

As he recoils from the explosion, he feels the warm spatter across his cheek and his ears are singing when he turns to look towards those six white feet in a line at the end of the bed. It's odd, of course, because he can barely hear anything, but that voice grows louder suddenly; the music that's still coming from the kitchen below, the song about angels. No odder than

3

anything else, all things considered, but still, he's always aware how strange it is and how perfect.

He's come to suppose that it's simply because the song provides the perfect soundtrack for that moment when the youngest of the girls moans softly, then opens her eyes. When, one by one, the three of them sit up and look at him, wide-eyed, blinking and confused.

Thorne did not wake suddenly on mornings like this. There was no longer any gasping or crying out. Rather, it had become like surfacing slowly towards the light from deep under dark water, and everything stayed silent until his stubble rasped against the pillow, when he turned his head sharply to see if his wife was next to him.

Of course, she wasn't.

Better, he thought, that Jan was no longer there, his wife in name only. He was well aware of what she'd have been likely to say, the tone of voice when she said it. He'd have heard concern, obviously, but something else that would have let him know she was weary of it and starting to run out of patience. With all sorts of things.

*Same dream?*

*Not exactly the same.*

*Ten years, Tom.*

*It's hardly my fault—*

More *than that . . .*

He got dressed quickly and went downstairs. He turned on the kettle then the radio and stuck a couple of slices of bread in the toaster. Grabbing butter and Marmite from the fridge he found himself humming 'There Must Be An Angel', though by the time he was pouring milk into his tea he was singing along tunelessly with those two comedians from *Fantasy Football League* whose song seemed to be on the radio every five minutes. It was starting to get on his nerves to be honest and it didn't help that one of them was a bloody Chelsea fan. Thorne wasn't altogether sure that football was coming home or that thirty years of hurt was likely to end any time soon, but he was undeniably excited about the three weeks ahead.

Provided other things didn't get in the way, of course.

Jan, and the wanker she was shacked up with.

Murder.

He'd talked to a couple of the lads at work, tried to switch his shifts around so he could watch England v Switzerland in the opening match of the tournament that afternoon, but his DI was having none of it. Thorne had done his best not to look too annoyed, but was sure it was because the man was Scottish. He guessed the miserable arsehole would be rooting for Switzerland, anyway. If things were miraculously quiet, there was always the possibility of nipping round the corner to the Oak, watching the game in there. He could find a radio, worst came to the worst.

By then, he might have stopped touching a hand to his cheek to wipe away spatter that wasn't there, and the smell he imagined was clinging to him might have faded a little.

Not that it mattered much.

He wasn't kidding himself.

The memory of what had actually gone on in that house was always there, of course, and, however stubbornly it might linger, the dream was very different. The wife rarely featured for reasons he couldn't fathom, strangled downstairs in the kitchen he never ventured into. The girls had actually been found in a small bedroom at the back, side by side on the floor between bunk beds and a mattress. And crucially, of course, people did not die more than once.

Thorne carried his dirty plate, mug and knife across to the draining board. He turned off the radio. He picked up his bag and leather jacket from the chair he'd dumped them on the night before, then stepped out into the hallway.

He raised a hand, placed it flat against his front door and

thought how small it looked. Those prints on *that* front door had been a new addition, the slimy stuff on the stairs, too. All as unpleasant as ever, but nothing he couldn't live with, would not prefer to live with. He opened the door, squinted against the sunshine and watched for a minute as the man who lived opposite struggled to attach a flag of St George to the aerial of his car.

The man looked up and waved. 'Easy win today, you reckon?'

Thorne said, 'Hope so.'

Thinking: *Belt and braces* . . .

The dream was always so much better than the memory.

Because, in the dream, he saved them.

# PART ONE

## Hide and Seek

# ONE

'Sweet,' Maria said.

Cat looked at her. 'What?'

'The pair of them.' Maria leaned back on the bench and nodded towards the two boys in the playground. Her son, Josh, had just landed with a bump at the bottom of the slide and Cat's son, Kieron, was hauling him to his feet. The boys high-fived a little clumsily, then ran towards the climbing frame, shouting and laughing.

'Yeah,' Cat said, grinning. 'They're proper mates.'

'We can still do this, can't we?' Maria asked. 'After you've gone.'

'Haven't gone anywhere, yet.' Cat sipped the tea bought from the small cafeteria near the entrance. 'Might all fall through, anyway.'

Maria looked at her, as though there might be something her friend hadn't told her.

'I mean, these things happen, don't they? All I'm saying. Some form not filled in properly or whatever.'

'Presuming it doesn't, though,' Maria said. 'It would be such a shame if we can't still bring them here.' She looked back towards the playground, where the two boys were waving from the top of the wooden climbing frame. The women waved back and, almost in unison, they shouted across, urging their children to be careful. 'They do love it.'

'Well, it's not like I'll be going far.'

'I'd hate that,' Maria said.

Cat smiled and leaned against her. 'You can always bring Josh over to the new place. Put your lazy arse in the car. There *are* decent parks in Walthamstow.'

'This is our special place though,' Maria said. '*Their* special place.'

An elderly woman they often saw in the wood walked by with her little dog and, as always, the boys rushed across to make a fuss of it. Cat and Maria sat and listened while the woman talked about how nice it was to get out and about, now the warm weather had kicked in, and told them about the campaign to install new bird-feeders and bat-boxes. She stayed chatting for a few minutes more, even after the boys had lost interest and gone back inside the playground, before finally saying goodbye.

'How's Josh doing at school?' Cat asked.

Maria shrugged. 'Could be better, but I think things are improving.'

'That's good.'

'Kieron?'

'Well, he's still missing Josh. Still saying it's unfair they can't be at the same school.'

'It *is* unfair.' Maria shook her head, annoyed. 'You know, a neighbour of mine went out and bought one of those measuring wheels. Walked it all the way from her front door to the school gates, trying to persuade the council she was in the catchment area. A hundred feet short, apparently. It's ridiculous . . .'

'He shouldn't be there for too much longer anyway,' Cat said.

'Right.'

'Fingers crossed.'

'What about schools near the new place?'

'Yeah, pretty good. Best one's only fifteen minutes' walk from the flat, but it's C of E.' Cat shuddered. 'Got to convince them I'm a full-time God-botherer if he's going to get in there.'

'You must know a few hymns,' Maria said.

'"All Things Bright and Beautiful", that's about my lot. Not sure I can be doing with all that stuff, anyway. When I went to have a look round, one of the other mums had a moustache Magnum would have been proud of.'

'What?'

'Something about not interfering with what the Lord had given her, apparently.'

'You're kidding.'

'Mental, right? Anyhow, there's another school a bus-ride away, so it'll be fine. It'll all work out.' She stood up and brushed crumbs of blossom from the back of her jeans. 'Right, I'm desperate for a pee . . .'

'Pizza when you get back?'

Cat stared across at her son and his best friend.

The boys were walking slowly around the edge of the playground, in step together and deep in what looked like a very serious conversation. Josh raised his arms and shook his head. Kieron did exactly the same. They were almost certainly talking about *Rugrats*, but they might have been discussing the Mad Cow crisis or growing tensions in the Middle East.

Cat smiled. 'Sounds like a plan,' she said.

'I'll round them up.'

Maria watched Cat walk away through the trees towards the toilets by the café, then turned back to watch their children playing. It had been more than chit-chat, because she would certainly miss Cat when she moved, miss seeing her as often. They were unlikely friends. They said as much to each other all

11

the time. Maria was five years older and lived in a nice house in Muswell Hill, while Cat's place in Archway was somewhat . . . rough and ready, much as she was.

The odd couple, she'd heard people say that.

*Best* friends, however much they might seem mismatched to others. Well, Cat was probably Maria's closest friend, at any rate, and Maria found herself becoming a little jealous if Cat talked about any of her other mates for too long. Maria had lost touch ages ago with the girlfriends she'd met at university and she wasn't particularly close to anyone at work. Most of the women she'd thought of as friends up until a few years before had mysteriously melted away after the divorce. Almost all had been one half of a couple, so perhaps they'd simply wanted to avoid any awkwardness, though Maria preferred to believe that they could not really have liked her very much to begin with, so told herself she was better off without them.

That she still had time to make new friends. True friends.

Now, Josh and Kieron were racing one another around the playground perimeter. They pulled faces at her as they flew past. They reached the far side, then stopped to get their breath back, before Kieron whispered something to Josh and went tearing away into the trees.

Maria shouted across, warned her son not to go too far, then watched him run off to follow his friend.

She and Cat had met five years earlier, at a mother and toddler group in Highgate, no more than a mile or so from where she was sitting now. Each of them had remained immune to the charms of the po-faced 'group facilitator'. Both had laughed at the petty one-upmanship of some of the more competitive participants. They had agreed that, as far as refreshments went, wine – or better yet whisky – would have been far more conducive than herbal tea and Hobnobs, and had quickly made arrangements to remedy the situation in their own time.

They had been equally delighted to discover just how much

they had in common. The important stuff at least. The pair of them single, for a kick-off, if for very different reasons.

Maria glanced up and saw Josh moving quickly through the trees behind the playground; a flash of his bright yellow coat. She smiled, remembering the look on his face when she'd brought it back from the shop.

'I'll look like a big banana, Mummy.'

Cat had been right, of course – she usually was. The brave one, the sod-it-who-cares one, the one whose glass was always half full. There was no reason why anything should change, nothing that mattered, anyway. There was no need to worry. So, the four of them might not be able to come to the wood quite as often as they did, as they had been doing for the last couple of years, but it wasn't as if Cat and Kieron would be miles away. *And*, of course, there was always the possibility they might not be moving at all; hadn't Cat said that herself? However things panned out, the most important thing was that the boys stayed close, saw each other as often as possible.

Important to Maria, too.

She reached into her bag for cigarettes and lit one. She never smoked in front of Josh, but could not resist seizing the opportunity for a quick one while he was out of sight. A habit she'd quit at her husband's insistence, taken up again when he became her ex-husband.

One with a glass of wine in the evening. Several with several glasses.

She sat back, closed her eyes and let the smoke out slowly, then looked up when she heard one of the boys shout from somewhere in the wood. She couldn't hear what he was shouting, and it was hard to tell which one it was anyway, but then they were alike in so many ways. Same size and shape, same colour hair. Maria had lost count of the times she'd taken Kieron's hand by mistake, walked away with him.

'You're welcome to take both of them if you really want to,'

Cat had said, the last time. She'd laughed, even though she'd made the same mistake herself, several times. 'I'll hop on a plane to Majorca for a couple of weeks.'

As soon as she glanced around and saw Cat coming back towards the bench, Maria stubbed the cigarette out, but the look on her friend's face made it clear she had not been quite quick enough.

'Thought you were going to pack those in.'

'Trying,' Maria said. 'It's been difficult, you know.'

'I'll pretend I didn't see it if you give me one.'

Maria reached into her bag again and offered the Silk Cut across. Cat took a cigarette and turned to look for the children. 'Where are the boys?'

'They're messing around in the woods,' Maria said, pointing. 'I just saw Josh . . .'

Without waiting for a light, Cat began walking towards the playground.

Maria stood up. 'I heard them shouting—'

Cat moved quickly through the playground towards the exit on the far side, calling her son's name, oblivious to the stares of other parents whose kids stopped what they were doing to watch. Maria hurried to catch her up and they both stopped dead when Josh appeared suddenly and came running from the trees towards them.

His yellow coat was streaked with mud and he burst into tears the instant he laid eyes on his mother.

'Josh?' Maria leaned down and took her son's face in her hands. 'You OK?'

'Where's Kieron?' Cat asked, looking towards the trees. 'Josh, where's *Kieron*?'

The boy began wailing and buried his face in his mother's stomach.

The unlit cigarette fell from Cat's hand and she began to run.

# TWO

When it came to the more traditional superstitions, Thorne had no truck whatsoever with any of that walking under ladders or lucky/unlucky black cats nonsense, but like most coppers he knew, like almost anyone working in one of the emergency services, he was extremely serious when it came to never saying the Q word. There were not too many rules he swore by, but that was certainly one of the few, unwritten though it might be. It was a word only ever uttered by masochists or mental cases and would usually earn any idiot stupid enough to say it a light thumping or at the very least something nasty in his tea.

You said 'Q', simple as that. Just . . . Q.

You *never* said . . . the *word*.

Which was why, half an hour before, sitting in the Oak, when the shit-for-brains DC – with whom he'd been happily discussing what kind of team Terry Venables was likely to send out – leaned across, rubbing his hands, and said, 'Lucky it's a nice quiet shift, eh?', Thorne had known his chances of actually watching the England game live had just gone down the toilet.

True to form, his pager had bleeped within five minutes.

He'd downed what was left of the Guinness he'd been about to top up, then used the phone behind the bar to ring through to Control. Scribbling down the details, he'd glared across at the DC who was now getting it in the neck from everyone else at the table and wondered if he could possibly make it through what was suddenly sounding like a very long day without hearing the result. It would be like that episode of *Whatever Happened to the Likely Lads*.

Thorne parked behind a line of marked squad cars on Muswell Hill Road and walked back up the hill to the entrance at Gypsy Gate. He was stopped by a PC who looked even less happy to be there than he was, and told, in no uncertain terms, that the wood was currently closed to the public. Thorne showed the man his warrant card and trudged inside, along a path baked hard by a week or more of fairly constant sunshine. Walking past one of the Keepers' Cottages and cutting left towards the playground, he could imagine an overexcited John Motson saying, 'Perfect playing conditions this afternoon, here at Wembley . . . '

Thorne knew Highgate Wood a little, had been here once or twice with Jan. He had never been any great fan of walking, unless there was a pub at the end of it, and on those unfortunate occasions when Jan had managed to drag him out of doors, they'd usually gone to Highbury Fields which was close to the house, or ventured across to Waterlow Park, a mile or so south between here and Archway.

Maybe her *lecturer* liked walking, Thorne thought.

He swatted a branch aside.

Maybe that had been the big attraction.

Perhaps the spineless arsehole was a *rambler*.

Thorne exchanged a nod with a DC he vaguely knew who was lugging around one of the top-of-the-range portable telephones that were now being issued to select squads, usually

16

for use in remote locations. The thing looked like something a metalwork student had cobbled together: a misshapen grey box with a rudimentary handle, a rubber aerial and a handset attached. Thorne could see why they were a good idea, because they were certainly handy in an emergency if the nearest phone box was miles away, but on the few occasions he'd had cause to use one he'd been unable to get any sort of signal.

Recently, he'd started to see more of the genuinely portable ones. He'd spotted several ageing yuppies braying loudly into what looked like giant walkie-talkies, and he'd been in a few cars in which a phone had been wired into the centre console. He could see that these things were likely to become increasingly commonplace – smaller too, probably – but having clocked the price of one in a Dixons window, he seriously doubted that anyone pulling in less than several hundred thousand a year would ever be able to afford one.

A fancy toy for twats and the seriously minted, that was all.

By the time Thorne could see the top of the climbing frame ahead of him, he'd shown his ID to another half a dozen PCs or WPCs and spotted at least three times that number moving slowly through the trees or pushing their way through dense undergrowth. It was no great surprise. He knew that the immediate response from any uniformed officers first on the scene of a missing child would be to draft in as many of their colleagues as they could possibly summon up. It would only be if the child stayed missing for more than half an hour or so that CID would be brought in.

Unless that had been because of something the other kid had said, something he'd seen.

The kid who wasn't missing.

Coming out onto more open ground, and skirting the edge of the cricket pitch, Thorne could see the crime-scene tape that had been wound around the playground's perimeter and now criss-crossed both its entrances. He raised a hand, seeing one or two more faces he recognised, and thought that, however many bodies had been drafted in to help look for the missing boy, they would have their work cut out – middle of June or not – to search the entire wood thoroughly before the light went.

A child who felt like it could stay hidden a long time in seventy-odd acres.

A body, even longer.

'Tom . . .'

He looked up to see his senior officer urgently beckoning him across. Thorne nodded acknowledgement and picked his pace up. In over five years as a detective sergeant, he had worked under a good many DIs, but Gordon Boyle was the one he liked the least, and not just because of his intransigence over the football. The Scotsman was a little too fond of pulling rank when a job went well and of passing the buck when it didn't. A little too fond of himself, truth be told.

Five years . . .

Depending on who you talked to, Thorne had been too lazy to take the inspectors' exam or too worried that he might fail. Too scared, perhaps, that he might actually pass it. If he were being honest with himself, Thorne would have admitted that there was something in each of those theories, but Jan, thank goodness, had given up nagging him about it, once she'd seen that the increase in pay had not been incentive enough.

'I'll get round to it,' he'd said, the last time it had come up in conversation. Back when they'd still been having conversations.

Thorne walked past DC Ajay Roth, who was talking to an old woman holding a small dog, pen poised above notebook. He threw Thorne a look which suggested it was not the most productive of discussions.

'In your own time,' Boyle shouted over, then went back to the conversation he was having on his radio. Half a minute later, when Thorne arrived at his side, he leaned close to mutter, 'Glad you could join us.'

Thorne said, 'Sir,' like he meant it, like there wasn't beer on his breath, though he knew that Boyle could not have beaten him to the scene by very much.

The DI led him across to the edge of the playground and Thorne shook hands with a uniformed inspector named Bob Docherty he had met once or twice before, who was clearly there to coordinate the search. 'Could do with another fifty bodies, if I'm honest,' Docherty said, quietly. He sucked in a breath, then the three of them walked across to the bench a few feet away, where a small boy in a yellow coat was sitting between two women.

Boyle looked a little uncomfortable, as though unsure which expression was needed. Serious, but not too serious? Relaxed, as if there was no reason to panic? Stick the man in an interview room with an armed robber and he was right as ninepence, but dealing with members of the public, especially those who were scared or suffering, had never been his strong suit.

'Right you are, then,' he said.

These days, Thorne tried not to think too much about whether it was *his* strong suit, either. Empathy, or his own version of it, had done enough damage ten years earlier. Still, it was at least fairly obvious which of the women in front of him was the mother of the missing child. She was shaking her head and crying, knuckles wrapped around the edge of the bench, while the other woman stared straight ahead and the boy looked at his feet, swiping a broken branch through the sandy ground in front of him.

Boyle made the introductions.

Maria Ashton, the older of the two women, looked up, the ball of sodden tissues still pressed to her face. 'I only took my eyes off them for a few seconds, I swear.' She lowered her hand and turned to her friend. 'A few seconds, that's all.'

Thorne saw immediately that he'd read it wrong, that the younger of the women was actually the one whose son they were currently combing the woods for. She said nothing, her face a mask, though now Thorne could see the terror barely held in check, and a hint of something else around her eyes. A fierceness.

'Nothing to be gained by blaming yourself,' Boyle said.

'Absolutely not,' Docherty said.

Thorne stepped towards Maria Ashton and nodded at the boy. 'Did your son say anything when he came back?' He leaned down close to the seven-year-old, but the boy kept his eyes fixed on the ground, on the stick with which he was now poking it harder.

The woman stifled a sob and shook her head.

'Nothing at all?'

'Josh was upset.' She reached to take hold of her son's hand. 'He was hysterical.'

'And he's said nothing since? Maybe—'

Boyle raised a hand to cut Thorne off. 'Let's leave the uniforms to do their job.' The inspector nodded his agreement. 'We need to interview Mrs Ashton and Mrs Coyne as quickly as possible. Highgate station's obviously our best bet.'

Instantly, the younger woman became animated. She looked up at Boyle as though he was insane and snapped at him, 'I'm not going anywhere.'

'Right,' Boyle said.

'I mean it.'

Boyle raised his hand like he was surrendering. 'Obviously you're upset, but it's important to get your statements while the memory's fresh in your mind.'

Catrin Coyne shook her head. 'No way. Not until every inch of this place has been searched.' She looked up at Docherty. 'Why can't I go and help them?'

'We could both help,' Maria said.

20

Cat was still staring at Docherty. 'I know the wood and I know which bits of it Kieron likes the best.'

'You've already given us that information,' the inspector said. 'It was hugely helpful.'

'Trust me.' Boyle leaned forward and laid a hand on her shoulder. The woman looked as though she'd been scalded. 'The best thing is if we get you down to the station. I promise you'll be the first to know if we find anything.'

Thorne saw the shadow pass across Cat's face and watched the hand fly to Maria's mouth. He glanced at Boyle and saw that the DI had realised exactly what he'd said. How it sounded.

'Anything' did suggest something . . . inanimate.

'We'll take my car,' Boyle said, quickly. He turned to Thorne. 'Tom, you can follow on with DC Roth. I've radioed through and the guvnor will meet us there.'

A few minutes later, they were all walking slowly in a ragged group towards the gate through which Thorne had come in. There seemed to be even more uniforms on display than before, though several seemed to be doing very little and he glimpsed one having a sneaky cigarette behind a tree. Lagging ten yards or so behind Boyle and the women, Thorne was talking quietly to Ajay Roth.

'They'd have found him by now.' Roth eased a finger beneath the edge of his turban and scratched. 'Don't you reckon?'

'It's a big place.' Thorne was watching the trio ahead of him. He saw that Gordon Boyle was doing his best to keep the two women moving forward; that Maria Ashton and Catrin Coyne exchanged a long look before staying a good distance apart from one another.

'Even so,' Roth said.

They were no more than a few yards from the gate and Thorne had already got his car keys in his hand when the group in front of him stopped suddenly. He watched Catrin Coyne spin on her heels, turn back to the wood and shout out her son's name. Before the echo had died, Josh Ashton planted his small feet and began to do the same, screaming for his friend until it sounded as though his lungs were about to burst, and his mother began to cry again.

# THREE

With cases such as this – like the one it could well become – taking the necessary steps as quickly as possible would always be the top priority at this stage of the game. Boyle had suggested Highgate, next door to Haringey Magistrates' Court, as it was the nearest station to the scene.

Andy Frankham was waiting for them at the desk.

He looked keen to get into it.

As detective chief inspector on the local major incident pool, operating out of Islington, he was the *de facto* SIO on the case and would have begun setting up the operation before Thorne had left the pub, putting together a team while extra uniforms were still being drafted into Highgate Wood, in the hope, if not the expectation, that it would never be needed.

Frankham introduced himself to the two women, softly spoken, but all business. Maria Ashton stepped forward to shake his hand, her son moving with her, clinging to her coat.

Catrin Coyne simply nodded, looking past the DCI towards the uniformed officer behind the desk.

'I'm not stupid enough to tell you not to worry,' Frankham

said. 'I've got kids myself. But I just want to assure you that I'm going to use every resource available to find Kieron.'

'Thank you,' Maria said.

Thorne saw Catrin Coyne glance at her friend, caught a flash of something that seemed like resentment.

*It's not your son that's missing.*

He saw understandable anger in the way the younger woman stood frozen to the spot, heard it in her breathing.

*If you'd been watching them, like you were supposed to . . .*

'Right now, it's important that we get some initial statements, fast.' Frankham nodded towards the boy. 'Most importantly, from Josh.'

Maria drew her son close. Said, 'Joshy? You want to tell the policeman what happened in the wood?'

The boy lurched away, as if he was sulking about something. He wandered over to a noticeboard and stared up at it for a few seconds, his back to them, before edging across to a row of moulded plastic seats and dropping into one.

'He's upset,' Maria said. 'It's understandable.'

Now, Catrin Coyne turned and stared at her.

'Absolutely,' Frankham said. 'Only natural. Right, I'll leave you with Detective Inspector Boyle and the others for the time being. If you feel you need to talk to me at any time, about anything at all, just let one of them know.'

Maria nodded, reddening as Catrin continued to stare at her.

There was a somewhat awkward hiatus, before a WPC came out of a side door to show the two women and the child through to the interview rooms.

Frankham watched them leave, then turned to Thorne and the others. He said, 'Let's get this done on the hurry-up, all right? I'm heading back to the office to make sure everything's set up and I'll let you know when I've arranged somewhere we can get the evidential statements.'

'Right you are, boss,' Boyle said.

'We'll need a social worker,' Roth said. 'Video suites, what have you.'

'Thanks for that, Ajay.' Frankham's tone was polite enough, while making it perfectly clear he knew exactly what was needed. With his slight frame and thick glasses, the DCI had the air of an academic and reminded Thorne of a geography teacher he'd had at school. Thorne would not have wanted to cross him, though.

'Let's have you then,' Boyle said. 'I'll take the mum . . . Ajay, you talk to the friend.' He pointed to Thorne. 'See what you can get out of the kid, Tom. What you can *glean*.'

Roth smiled.

Thorne could easily imagine crossing his immediate superior. Though in this instance, *crossing* was a polite word for it. The fantasy usually consisted of staring down at Gordon Boyle in some dimly lit back alley while the Scotsman spat out several teeth.

'Sir,' Thorne said.

A minute or so later, on their way to the interview rooms, they passed an office where a group was gathered in front of a TV set. Boyle put his head round the door and asked the question. He closed the door and the three of them carried on walking.

'One nil to your lot,' he said, looking less than thrilled about the situation. He muttered the offending name as if it were that of a notorious serial killer. 'Shearer.'

'Please, Mrs Ashton.' Thorne saw Maria Ashton open her mouth to speak again and raised a hand. She had already given her own brief statement to Ajay Roth, but clearly had plenty more to say. 'Please.' He had warned the woman before they'd entered the room that, at this stage, they only needed to hear from Josh; that she was simply there to put her son at ease and that any prompting or encouragement on her part could easily affect what he told them and harm the investigation going forward.

'Sorry,' Maria said. She leaned towards the portable

twin-cassette recorder on the table. She said 'Sorry' again, then sat back, shaking her head at her own idiocy.

Thorne nodded to let her know it was OK, then looked back to the boy.

'So, why did you and Kieron go out of the playground?'

From statements given earlier at the scene, it was clear that the boys had left the play area at the far side and run into the part of the wood that bordered the underground tracks. Rather more disturbingly, it was no more than fifty yards from an exit onto the Archway Road.

'There's nowhere to hide in the playground.' The boy was kicking the table leg every few seconds and fiddling with a toy car that he'd dug from his pocket when they'd sat down.

'You wanted to play hide-and-seek?'

Uniformed officers had already begun house-to-house enquiries on the stretch nearest the exit and posted hand-drawn appeal boards asking for information. It was a very busy road.

'No.' Josh shook his head firmly. 'Kieron wanted to play.'

'Kieron ran off to hide, did he?'

Another shake of the head, as though Thorne was being silly. '*I* did.'

'Oh ... well, hiding's more fun, isn't it?'

'I'm a better hider than he is.'

'OK. So, where did you hide?'

Josh glanced up then went back to his car. 'There's a big tree you can get inside. I've been in there before.'

Maria Ashton began to cry again. Thorne gently pushed the box of tissues towards her but kept his eyes on the boy. 'Did Kieron find you?'

Josh shook his head. More slowly this time.

'Do you think he *couldn't* find you?' Thorne waited. 'Or do you think he wasn't looking?'

Josh shrugged, chewed his lip.

'I mean, it sounds like a fantastic hiding place.'

26

'Yeah, but Kieron knows that's where I hide sometimes, and I didn't even *hear* him.' The boy grunted and raised his arms in a gesture of delayed amazement. 'Like, you can always hear someone when they're looking, because of the branches and the crackly leaves and everything. But when I was inside the tree it was really quiet.'

Thorne could feel the eyes of the boy's mother on him, sense her efforts to make as little noise as possible as she cried. 'How long do you think you waited, Josh?'

'Like a *long* time.'

'OK.' He thought about the location of the area where Josh had been hiding. He leaned across the desk. 'Did you hear any trains go past?'

A slow and solemn nod. 'Yes.'

'How many?'

The boy scrunched his face up, trying to remember. 'Two, I think.'

Thorne knew that trains ran up and down that stretch of the Northern Line regularly. 'So ... five minutes, maybe? Something like that?'

Josh nodded. 'It was ages.'

'Then what did you do?'

'I came out of the tree and tried to find Kieron. I was shouting him and I ran back to where he was when he covered his eyes and started counting.' The arms were raised again, and he widened his eyes, suitably mystified. 'He wasn't there. He wasn't *anywhere.*'

'That's when he came out of the woods,' Maria said. 'When Cat and I went looking.'

Thorne ignored her. 'Did you see anyone else in the woods, Josh?'

'There were *lots* of people,' Josh said. 'The funny old lady with the smelly dog. Loads of people.'

'In the trees, I mean. After you left the playground.'

The boy shook his head.

'Are you sure?'

Maria leaned forward. 'He said all this back at the wood.'

'Did you see Kieron talking to anyone?'

'He told that inspector before you arrived.'

'Can we go home now?' Josh asked.

Thorne reached across and turned off the cassette recorder.

Having finished his interview with Catrin Coyne, Boyle was waiting with Ajay Roth in the corridor outside. He said, 'Interesting.'

'What is?'

'Turns out the mum's old man is currently at Her Majesty's Pleasure and not for the first time. Did eighteen months for GBH seven years ago and he's currently doing a ten-stretch in Whitehill for attempted murder.' He shook his head. 'Right nasty piece of work by the sounds of it. Beat seven shades of shit out of some bloke who cut him up on the North Circular.'

'Nice,' Roth said.

'So?' Thorne asked.

Boyle looked at him.

'You think he might have escaped from a Cat A prison and abducted his own son?'

'I said *interesting*, that's all.' Boyle stuck a finger into his mouth, began working at something stuck between his teeth. 'Because it is.'

'Did Mrs Coyne say anything to make you think it's something we should be looking at?'

'*Ms* Coyne,' Roth said. 'His name, but they're not actually married.'

'Living in sin.' Boyle had finished his probing and turned his head quickly to spit something out. 'Well, they were, until he got banged up.'

'Did she?'

'Look, I was just trying to find out what happened in the woods,' Boyle said. 'Same as you were. She happened to mention his name, so I ran it through the PNC upstairs.'

'Fair enough,' Thorne said. 'Good to know, I suppose.'

Boyle seemed irritated suddenly. 'I tell you what, Tom, why don't *you* take *Ms* Coyne's evidential statement?'

'The boss rang through ten minutes ago,' Roth said. 'It's all set up for the social services centre behind Upper Street. The cars are waiting for us outside.'

'Yeah, if you want,' Thorne said. He clocked the DI glancing conspiratorially at the DC. He knew that he was meant to clock it.

'I don't know . . . maybe you can shake her hand.' Boyle gave up trying to conceal the smirk once he saw the look on Thorne's face. 'See what you *know*.'

# FOUR

There was no need to go over what had happened four hours before at Highgate Wood. Thorne knew by now that Catrin Coyne had seen nothing. He knew, equally well, like someone gnawing at a mouth ulcer, what she would almost certainly be imagining.

What *might* have happened.

The worst, always the worst.

Now, the job compelled Thorne to dig away at her most terrible fears and drag them out into the light. To ask, with all necessary sensitivity, the very questions that would give them credence. He felt like he was whispering through a loud-hailer and tiptoeing around a worst-case scenario in size ten Doc Martens.

'So, was Kieron . . . OK?'

'OK?' The woman stared at him. 'What does that even mean?'

Half an hour into it and she had clearly had enough. Perhaps she craved some time alone to process her agony in private or else wanted to share it with friends and family of whom Thorne was, as yet, unaware. With a few hours of light left,

30

she might well just be desperate to get back to Highgate Wood and join in the search. Or maybe she simply failed to see how answering stupid questions would be of any use in getting her son back and did not understand why this detective was asking them again.

'Were there any problems at school?' Thorne asked.

'Not really.'

'So, some problems, then?'

Thorne had done his level best. Before they'd started, he had explained that this second round of more in-depth interviews was crucial, without spelling out exactly why. He had told her that their conversation was being recorded – like those being conducted elsewhere in the building with Josh Ashton and his mother – because it might prove important later on. That this was just the way it had to be done. The woman was not stupid, Thorne could see that, but all the same he took care to avoid specifying that these were *evidential* interviews and would be the ones presented in court, if and when her son's disappearance resulted in a person or persons being brought to trial.

On . . . whatever charge.

That necessary sensitivity again.

'He had a bit of trouble settling in, but that was a couple of years ago.' Catrin Coyne had seemed fired up back at the woods, ready to fight. Now she looked washed-out and weary. Thorne knew she was not quite thirty, but right now she might have been ten years older. She tugged at her short, dark hair; shrank down inside the Puffa jacket she had kept on, though the room was far from cold. 'He didn't like not seeing as much of Josh, that was all really. Still doesn't like it.'

'Where's the school?'

'In Tufnell Park. I tried, but I couldn't get him in to the one Josh goes to.'

'That's a shame,' Thorne said. 'They're obviously close friends.'

31

'Yeah.'

'And you're close friends with Josh's mum.'

She let out a low, short hum. She looked away and shook her head, though it seemed to Thorne like a gesture of confusion or disbelief rather than a hard denial. He understood that, in situations such as the one she now found herself in, it was natural to lash out and look for something – or better yet some*one* – to blame. Watching her eyes close as she shrank a little further into her big, blue coat, Thorne guessed that the anger she had felt towards Maria Ashton was subsiding a little and that she had begun to blame herself for trusting someone else – however close – to watch her son.

A seeping wound that, in time, would give her a nice, fat scab to pick at.

Thorne glanced up at the clock, at the red light glowing on the video camera mounted next to it. He said, 'Is there anyone you can think of who might want to hurt your son, Catrin?'

Her eyes snapped open. '*What?*'

'Sorry, but I do need to ask.'

'He's a seven-year-old boy.'

'OK . . . is there anyone you can think of who might want to hurt *you?*'

She sat back and folded her arms, stared at him for a few seconds. 'No.'

'Nobody at all?'

'Nobody.'

'Tell me about Kieron's father,' Thorne said.

She nodded, sighed as though she'd been waiting for this. 'Do I really need to? I mean, you obviously know all about him already.'

'I'd like you to tell me.'

'Look, Billy's a really good dad, all right?'

Thorne tried to maintain a blank expression, but clearly he didn't quite manage it.

'Yeah, OK, obviously he's not around now, but when he was. He loves Kieron to bits ... loves both of us.'

'He clearly has a capacity for violence, though. So, I hope you can understand why we'd want to find out a bit more about him.'

'He lost his rag that one time.'

'It was more than one time, Catrin.'

'That first one was nothing,' she said. 'The GBH, so-called. One too many in the pub, that's all, and it wasn't him that started it. The road-rage thing was stupid, I grant you. He knows that.'

'So, never anything like that at home?'

'I told you—'

'With you, or ... ?'

'Billy's never raised a hand to me and he would never touch Kieron.' She shook her head and sat back hard. 'Never.'

'Understood,' Thorne said. 'Thank you.'

'I don't get it, anyway.' Suddenly, the woman looked fired up again. 'I mean, the poor sod's sitting in his cell right about now, so how can this be remotely useful?'

Thorne nodded. Wasn't that more or less what he'd said to Boyle? 'Like I told you, I have to ask.'

There was a sharp knock on the door and Ajay Roth poked his head around. He needed a word. Thorne suspended the interview and told Catrin Coyne that he'd be back as soon as he could.

Outside, Roth said, 'I've already told the boss, but I thought you should know, we've had to knock it on the head with Josh Ashton.'

'Because ... ?'

'Poor little bugger's wiped out. It's like talking to a tiny brick wall.'

'Has he been given something to eat?'

'Yeah, course. Social worker made sure he had a sandwich

before we started, but she still doesn't think he's up to it. Doing more harm than good, she reckons.'

'Maybe he needs some chocolate or something.'

Roth nodded. 'Yeah, that's what I thought, get some sugar in him. Couple of cans of Fanta or whatever, but his mum said he's not allowed fizzy drinks.'

'Orange juice?'

The DC shook his head. 'Him and his mother are already on the way home, mate. She says she'll bring him back first thing in the morning.'

'Right.' Thorne stepped back towards the door of the interview room.

'How's it going in there?' Roth asked.

'Yeah, well, I thought she was starting to shut down a bit as well, but she's perked up. So we'll see.'

Before Thorne had a chance to open the door, Gordon Boyle came bowling round the corner, slurping from a plastic cup of coffee. He looked at his watch. 'How much longer d'you reckon?'

'Another hour, maybe,' Thorne said.

'Right,' Boyle finished his coffee, looked around for a bin. 'I'll get a car organised to take her home. Find someone to go with her.'

'I'll do it.' Thorne turned to Roth. 'Fancy coming?'

Roth said he didn't have anything better to do.

'Up to you,' Boyle said. 'Usual procedure when you get there though, yes? You know what we need.'

'Let's be gentle.' Thorne looked at Roth. 'All right?'

'As a baby, mate.'

Thorne turned back to the door.

'It's a shame,' Boyle said.

Thorne stopped. 'What is?'

'That Swiss equaliser.' He shook his head. 'Don't think a draw is the start your boys were after.'

'It's how we started in sixty-six,' Roth said. 'Nil-nil against Uruguay.'

Thorne had stopped listening and was already reaching for the door again. He was thinking about his conversation with Catrin Coyne; about how animated she'd been just before they were interrupted, and what she'd told him about the father of her missing child.

Perhaps Boyle had been right to flag that up, after all.

That slight hesitation.

*He . . . loves both of us.*

# FIVE

With one arm stretched out to brace herself against the granite-topped island, Maria hummed with pleasure as the first mouthful of wine went down. It was quickly followed by another and she immediately reached for the bottle and poured herself a second glass. She could not remember when she had needed a drink quite this badly.

She was still shaking.

She had been thinking about that open bottle of Pinot in the fridge all the way home from the station and from the moment she had seen the squad car drive away and closed the front door behind her. Thinking about it when she'd shucked off her coat and ushered Josh towards his bedroom, helped him undress and watched him climb silently into bed. As she'd wiped away the tears that came when she'd crept towards the door, and while she'd told him to be brave, because everything was going to be all right.

Told *herself*.

He'd grizzled for half an hour before she'd finally felt able to leave him and go back downstairs. To get what she needed. Now, lifting herself on to one of the leather barstools, letting out a long breath and lifting her glass, she felt ashamed, because even then – his warm, wet face pressed into her neck – she had felt a stab of resentment towards her son for keeping her from this.

*Mummy's medicine.*

She set down the glass and told herself that she was being ridiculous, that if ever there was an excuse . . . no, not an excuse, a *reason* to need a drink, it was this.

What a miserable, *horrible* day. From everything ticking along, being perfectly normal; from all of them being happy to . . . *this*, in what, just a few seconds? It couldn't have been much longer than that. Time to smoke a cigarette, that was all, to close her eyes for just a few moments.

It wasn't her fault.

A wash of shame moved through her again as she thought about Cat, for the first time since she'd walked through the front door, if she were being honest.

She wondered if Cat was back at home yet and, if so, what she was doing.

She wondered if she should call.

Maria took another drink and decided that it was probably not a very good idea. She'd call first thing in the morning. It wouldn't be an easy conversation, she knew that, but it had to be done. She wanted to help, to let Cat know she was there for her and that she'd do whatever she could.

*I think you've done enough already, don't you?*

*Please don't say that. You need to try and stay calm.*

*You wouldn't be saying that if it was your kid . . .*

No, not an easy conversation at all.

She sat and tried to imagine how she might be feeling if it *was* Josh they were searching for, if she'd been the one coming home alone to an empty house. It was impossible, though, and not just because she was starting to feel a little light-headed. Swallowing another mouthful of wine, she realised that she hadn't eaten since breakfast. *I can't imagine*, that's what people always said when something terrible happened and it was the simple truth, because you couldn't even get close. Grief, she decided, that might be about the nearest thing to it. The same coldness, the shutting down, she had felt when her father had died.

Or when Jeffrey had left.

That had been a kind of grief too, of course; a deadness that had lasted longer, if anything. Looking back, she should not have been surprised. There had been a distance, an oddness. Try as she had, she had clearly never been what he'd wanted, but still ... when he'd finally come out and told her he wanted a divorce, like he was telling her he'd run out of socks or quite fancied lamb for dinner, it had been a sucker-punch.

It had been months before she'd felt she could breathe again.

All very civilised now, of course. Ancient history. They both had lives to get on with and obviously there was their son to think about, especially of late when he'd seemed so unsettled. She remembered ducking Cat's question in the park earlier, about how Josh was getting on at school. There were still problems that were becoming harder to ignore – outbursts of aggression and bad behaviour – and the bedwetting was now an almost nightly occurrence.

Christ, what was she thinking?

It was all a million miles away from what Cat must be going through. Her son's things scattered around, the smell of him all over the house and the thought of him being alone in those woods or ... wherever else. Even worse, the thought of him *not* being alone.

Maria reached for the bottle again, but it was empty.

*It wasn't her fault.*

'Mummy ...'

She let out a gasp of surprise, then turned to see Josh standing in the doorway. He looked on the verge of tears again, his fat bottom lip quivering, an expression that, until today, might just have meant that he wanted something. Another story, usually.

He said, 'I think I'll sleep better if I come in your bed.'

That wasn't something he'd asked for in a very long time.

'Come on then, chicken,' Maria said. 'Let's get you tucked up.'

As they walked towards the stairs, Josh took her hand and said, 'I've been thinking about it, and maybe Kieron just got confused. About whose turn it was to hide.'

'Yes, maybe that's it,' Maria said.

The boy nodded, satisfied, as though he'd solved a big mystery. He held up his free hand for a high-five, which, after a few seconds, Maria stooped to return. 'He's still hiding, that's all.'

# SIX

Catrin Coyne lived a few minutes south of Archway tube station, in a two-bedroom flat on the sixth floor of Seacole House, a twelve-storey block off the Holloway Road.

A mile from Highgate Village and a world away.

Stepping into the lift, she turned and said, 'I really don't see why you need to come in. I'll be OK on my own.' She had not spoken a word on the drive from Islington, hunched in the passenger seat of Thorne's Cavalier and staring intently out as though she might catch a glimpse of her son on the darkened pavements.

Thorne pushed the button and the doors began to clatter shut. 'Best if we do.'

'I promise I'm not going to throw myself out the window.'

'Glad to hear it,' Roth said.

Nobody spoke again until a few minutes later, when Catrin led them into her living room. She stood with her back to the wall-mounted electric fire and stared at them. 'So?'

'Is it OK if I have a quick look round?' Roth asked.

'What?' Catrin looked from Roth to Thorne and back again. 'Why?'

The DC cleared his throat and shifted a little awkwardly from foot to foot. There was a job to be done but clearly he was paying heed to what Thorne had said about being gentle. 'It's just what we have to do. It's not—'

'You think Kieron's found his way home?'

'No.'

'You think he's hiding under the bed?'

'It's a box we need to tick,' Thorne said. 'That's all.'

Catrin looked at him, her eyes narrowed. 'Or maybe you reckon I've made the whole thing up. That we're all just pissing you around and Kieron's been here the whole time.'

'Of course not.'

'Fucking . . . tied up in a cupboard or something.'

Thorne could see that Catrin Coyne was becoming agitated and he could hardly blame her. He had no more idea where Kieron Coyne was than she did, but he knew for certain that he wasn't here. That said, there *had* been cases where parents had reported their children missing maliciously. There had even been occasions when they had done so with rather more sinister motives, to cover up the fact that the children had been hurt, or worse, during incidents at home, which was why such possibilities needed to be dismissed as soon as was practicable.

He said, 'It's just a box.'

'I promise I'll be quick.' Roth backed slowly towards the hallway. 'I won't make a mess or anything.'

Catrin nodded and he stepped out.

'It's ridiculous.' She moved away from the wall and dropped on to a leather sofa.

'Most of it's about covering our arses as much as anything.' Thorne walked across to the chair opposite. She grunted permission, so he perched on the edge of it and leaned towards her.

41

'And some of the other stuff might not seem too . . . sympathetic, even when it's got to be done.'

She nodded again and sat back. She looked even more exhausted than she had done back in the interview room.

'It's best in the long run, you know?'

'I don't *want* there to be a long run,' she said. 'I want it sorted. I want one of your lot to ring the bell right now with Kieron in his arms.' She looked close to tears but pushed them back with the heel of her hand. 'I want him here. I want him home.'

'Course you do.'

'The long run's what scares me.'

Thorne could hear music – the stuttering drone of a bassline – from the flat above, and Roth moving about in one of the bedrooms. 'We need to ask you for a DNA sample.'

She sat up fast. 'What the hell do you need my DNA for?'

'A sample from Kieron.' Thorne saw the spasm of horror on her face, that glimpse of what might be there at the end of the long run. 'Would you mind if we took his toothbrush?'

She leaned down to unlace her boots. 'Do what you have to.'

'A recent photograph would be useful too, if you have one. Something we can get up on the appeal boards, in the newspapers.'

Catrin kicked her boots off, dragged herself to her feet and left without a word to fetch the things Thorne had asked for. She passed Roth in the doorway. He stepped into the living room and shook his head to let Thorne know he'd found nothing to be concerned about.

Box ticked.

'She's gone to get the stuff.' Thorne lowered his voice. 'Listen, you might as well get on your way and I'll see you back at the office.' He saw the question on Roth's face. 'I think I'll stay here for a bit.'

'Really? I don't see the need—'

'All the same.'

When Catrin returned, Roth took the photograph and the toothbrush which she'd put into a plastic sandwich bag. He thanked her and told her to take care of herself. He told Thorne he had Ms Coyne's phone number and would call if anything came up.

Thorne followed him to the front door.

'Get the toothbrush over to the lab and make sure the media liaison boys get cracking on that photo.'

'Running all the way.' Roth moved across the landing and stabbed at the button to call the lift. 'Listen ... I meant to say.' He turned and took a few steps back towards Thorne. 'All that stuff with Boyle, that shaking hands business, the digs about what you'd *know* or whatever. It's all just a wind-up. You get that, right? Nobody means anything by it.'

Thorne looked at him. He said, 'It's probably too late for tomorrow, but we need the boy's picture in the papers on Monday.'

The DC nodded, embarrassed suddenly, as though he wished he hadn't said anything. 'I mean, everyone's heard the story, that's all.'

Thorne said nothing and, when the lift arrived, he wasn't sure which of them was the more relieved.

When Thorne came back into the living room, he and Catrin stood looking at one another for a few seconds. The thumping bassline seemed to have got louder. 'Can I make you a cup of tea or coffee?' he asked. 'Something stronger?'

'There might be some heroin in the flat next door.'

'I'll pass that on.'

'Please don't,' she said, quickly. 'I'd rather not piss my neighbours off. They watch Kieron sometimes ... and before you ask, not the one doing the smack.'

'I'm kidding,' Thorne said.

They looked at one another again.

Thorne cast an eye around the room. The sofa and armchair

took up most of the available space, but the carpet and glass coffee-table were spotless, and everything seemed well organised. There was a large plastic box filled to the brim with toys in one corner and a stack of videotapes sitting next to the TV. *Animaniacs, ChuckleVision, Mike & Angelo.* He walked across to the window, stared down at a main road that was still busy at quarter to nine at night. He guessed it was always busy.

He turned back into the room. 'It's nice.'

'No, it isn't.' Catrin chewed at a fingernail. 'That's why we're moving. Well, supposed to be moving.'

'Where to?'

'Council flat in Walthamstow.' She nodded towards the window. 'I mean it's OK round here, been perfectly happy and all that, but nowhere this close to the Holloway Road is ever going to be *nice*. You can feel it in your chest, you know? Black snot, all that.'

'Lower Highgate,' Thorne said.

'What?'

'I've heard estate agents say that about Archway. Trying to make it sound a bit more fancy. Upmarket.'

'Wankers.'

'You're not wrong.' With Jan determined to sell the house, Thorne was desperately trying to put off his own inevitable dealings with them.

'Actually, round here, we prefer to call it Highgate's Bollocks,' Catrin said. 'That's definitely got more of a ring to it.' Seeing Thorne smile she began to laugh, high-pitched and almost hysterical, but it quickly caught in her throat and became a sob.

'Don't,' Thorne said.

He watched her reach out an arm and for a second or two he thought she was going to fall. Thorne said her name, and stepped quickly across, just in time for her to collapse into his arms.

# SEVEN

It was after midnight by the time Thorne got home to the house in Highbury, half past when he carried a few slices of cheese on toast and a can of Kestrel through to the living room. He sat down in front of the TV. He had not banked on the day being quite as full-on as it had turned out to be, but, anticipating the worst, which was generally his default position, he'd set the video recorder just in case. Belt and braces. He watched the game as he ate and the can emptied, the remote in one hand to fast-forward when necessary. It was hard to summon any more than a passing interest, though, and not just because – thanks to Gordon Boyle – the result was hardly going to come as a surprise.

He'd left Catrin Coyne asleep on her sofa.

For over an hour, he had held her while she'd wept, feeling more than a little awkward with her head against his shoulder, feeling as though it should have been someone else's job. A friend's. Under normal circumstances, it would probably have been Maria Ashton doing the comforting, had relations between them not been as understandably strained as Thorne guessed they currently were. He hoped for both their sakes that they were able to move past their ... situation.

On screen, the Shearer goal went in and, predictably, the crowd had begun to sing 'Three Lions'.

It took a damn sight less than a missing child to sour a relationship, Thorne thought. He swallowed the last of the lager. It didn't take much to kill the magic.

The smallest lie, a selfish remark.

Almost any little incident could do it.

Coming home to find his wife being shagged by her creative writing teacher had done the trick very nicely.

Her desperate protestations. His hairy fucking back.

There had been two messages from Jan waiting for him when he'd walked through the door. A piss-perfect end to the day. That blinking red light on the answering machine almost always meant bad news of one kind or another, but lately Thorne had found himself hoping it had been a colleague calling with post-mortem results or to tell him he was needed at a crime scene, as opposed to some accountant or, God forbid, a solicitor.

He could handle murder.

Instead it had been Jan's voice he'd found himself listening to, while he'd stood in the kitchen and watched his bread browning under the grill. Polite enough, because they were grown-ups and had stopped shouting at each other a long time ago, but with an edge he could have grated his cheddar on.

'We have to get the sale of the house organised, Tom ... it's just sitting there ... we're both in limbo.'

Thorne wondered how long *limbo* had been defined as 'shacked up with a randy lecturer in Cockfosters', but he knew what his wife was getting at. His wife legally, if in no other respect. Having both agreed on a sensible way forward months before when Jan had left, she had said she was very happy to leave all the arrangements to him. Not because she was remotely shamefaced at walking out on him after twelve years, but because Thorne, being a police officer, might have a 'bit more clout with estate agents and the like'. While Thorne had not argued, because he was certainly not going to let Jan or her new boyfriend take charge, he'd been unable, as yet, to muster enough enthusiasm to do anything about it.

A hundred and seventy-five grand she reckoned they could get for this place, enough for each of them to get a decent flat. A hundred and seventy-five grand and they'd only paid sixty thousand for it. Property was changing hands for bloody silly money these days.

He thought about what he'd said to Catrin Coyne in that tower block.

*Nice . . .*

The spiky response he had so thoroughly deserved.

He sat back and looked at a room in which there was a lot more space than Catrin and her son had. He was definitely rattling around in the place, rather more noisily since Jan had come over to collect her stuff in a van the lecturer had hired for the day. It wasn't as if they'd had that much of anything to begin with.

It had all been so different a dozen years before.

Thorne's old man had salted away a reasonable amount which he'd been happy to donate and, together with the money Jan's mum and dad had thrown into the pot, there'd been enough to put down a decent deposit. The house was handy for the area Thorne's team was working and the school Jan was teaching at. It was rather too close to the Arsenal ground for Thorne's comfort, but there was a nice park and Highbury tube station was on the doorstep. Married less than a month, the pair of them could not have been more excited to move into a place which seemed so perfect; to settle down for a year or two, stick a bit of money away, then try for the baby they both wanted.

Try for a while, fail for a while.

Pretend to forget they'd ever actually been trying.

47

Carry on like it didn't really matter.

Thorne hit fast-forward, smiling in spite of himself at the comic spectacle of players chasing the ball around like lunatics, before he stopped to watch the late Swiss penalty. He didn't take a great deal in after that, just sat feeling restless and, strangely, not nearly as tired as he was sure he should be. He *was* sure that one can of weak lager was never going to cut it, so he got up and went through to the kitchen to fetch another.

He wondered if Catrin Coyne had come to the same conclusion that he and his colleagues had reached several hours earlier. It had been unspoken, and would probably remain so until tomorrow at least, but the team was already working on the assumption that Kieron Coyne was not simply going to turn up any time soon.

That he was not lost and he was not hiding.

That they were now looking for a missing child and the person or persons who had taken him.

It was Catrin's assumption, too, Thorne guessed that. He thought he'd seen it back at her flat, in that moment when he'd mentioned DNA and the fight had gone out of her. *Felt* it, as she'd pressed her face against his jacket and clutched at the cushions on her sofa.

Thorne walked back to the living room and stopped in the doorway. He leaned against the frame, opened the can and stared across at the TV. Happy to watch from where he was.

He'd stood in the same spot a few months earlier and watched the unbelievable scenes on the news after Take That had announced they were splitting up. The wailing and the hysterics, the calls to suicide helplines. He shook his head now, remembering it. If that was the worst pain any of those young people were ever going to feel, they could count themselves seriously lucky.

In the studio, Des Lynam and the besuited pundits were busy jabbering, while behind them in the stadium, the crowd, clearly not downhearted by the result, had begun to sing that bloody song again.

It was all just noise.

Thorne stood for a while, and drank, and thought about Catrin Coyne; the agony settling in and making itself almost comfortable, until it just became something she lived with. How that life, such as it was, would pan out if they did not catch the person who had taken her son. If she never saw Kieron again.

Thirty years of hurt.

# EIGHT

The incident room had been established on the second floor of Islington station. Narrow and windowless, the space was serviceable enough under normal circumstances, but now it was home to a team of thirty detectives and had, overnight, become decidedly cramped.

'Barely room to swing a bloody cat.'

The moaning DC – who had arrived for the Sunday morning briefing with moments to spare and brown sauce on his tie – was about to elaborate, before glancing across at the large whiteboard at one end of the room and thinking better of it. At the photograph of the missing child's mother, her name and its diminutive scrawled underneath in felt-tip pen.

He sat down with everyone else and took his notebook out.

A dozen or so workstations had been pushed closely together, a handful of the desktops dominated by bulky computer terminals and a couple more home to fax machines. One corner of the room was dedicated to the Home Office Large Major Enquiry System that would serve as the administrative hub of the investigation. It was into the HOLMES computers that every statement would be logged, each report and piece of intelligence filed and from which actions would be raised, indexed and subsequently cross-referenced. The system ensured that, at all times, the investigation's left hand knew what its right was doing, providing the capacity to link other forces into the inquiry when necessary and to give any and all information the appropriate significance. Most importantly, the system had been designed specifically to eliminate the kind of headless-chicken incompetence that had come to light fifteen years before, at the end of the Yorkshire Ripper inquiry.

HOLMES would be each detective's bible.

Their prayer book.

At nine o'clock on the dot, Ajay Roth shouted, 'OK, everyone,' and DCI Andy Frankham stood up to preach.

'I'm hoping this is the one and only time I have to do this,' he said. 'That none of us has to be here very long. I'd be over the bloody moon if we could pack this room up tomorrow and get back to other cases, but however long *this* case goes on, we never forget what it's about. Not for one second, all right? *Who* it's about.'

Frankham turned and pointed to the biggest photograph on the whiteboard. A blown-up version of the picture Catrin Coyne had given Roth the evening before.

The DCI waited a good few seconds, let them look.

It had been mentioned by Catrin or Maria or perhaps both the day before, but Thorne was struck again, as he had been when he'd first seen the photograph, how very much alike Josh Ashton and Kieron Coyne were. It was no wonder they were friends, he thought.

They might have been brothers.

Frankham spoke for another minute or two about the urgency and dedication which they needed to demonstrate on a crime-in-action case such as this one. He told them how confident he was that they wouldn't let Kieron Coyne and his

51

mother down. Then he called Gordon Boyle up and told him to crack on.

The Scotsman had jobs to dole out. He quickly allocated various roles to those working full-time with HOLMES. Receiver, action allocator, analyst, statement reader. One detective was assigned to intelligence and two more were tasked with assisting the forensic teams who were now working in a targeted area of the wood between the playground exit and the Archway gate. After announcing that both mothers would need be re-interviewed, he told a couple of DCs to drive up to Milton Keynes and pay a visit to Catrin Coyne's partner in HMP Whitehill.

'For those of you who don't know, that place was specifically designed to take some very dangerous men,' he said. 'Men with issues. So it can't hurt to check Billy out. Check out the people he's in there with while you're at it. Let's see if he's upset anyone who might want to take revenge by targeting his family.'

'What about the bloke he almost battered to death? Poor sod might fancy a spot of revenge himself.'

'Right, I was getting to that.' Boyle pointed at the officer who'd asked the question. 'Dig him up and find out what he was up to yesterday afternoon.' He glanced down at his page of scribbled notes. 'Now, goes without saying that we're already putting together a list of known sex offenders, so we need to start working through that and we need to prioritise. Top of the list is anyone who's ever snatched a child. Anyone who's so much as looked at a child, all right? So, start knocking on doors and getting movements accounted for, and don't worry about being too polite about it.'

There was no shortage of volunteers.

Boyle had yet to talk about what was likely to be the most significant line of enquiry, but he'd obviously been saving it. Now he looked keen to pass on the news he'd already shared with Thorne half an hour before.

'So, a witness rang through first thing in response to one of our appeal boards, to say that yesterday afternoon, just about the time that Kieron Coyne went missing, he saw a man and a boy around Kieron's age getting into a car on the Archway Road.' He watched Ajay Roth as the DC moved through the room handing out pieces of paper. 'As you can see, we've got no number plate, nothing much as yet in the way of detail, but even so, this is obviously massive for us. Most importantly, as far as this witness could tell, the child was getting *willingly* into the car.' He let that sink in for a few seconds. 'We obviously need to ask ourselves if this man was someone known to the missing boy.'

A detective near the back said, 'One more good reason to talk to the father.'

'Bang on,' Boyle said. 'Could this man have been a friend or associate of the father? Someone the boy might have met before? So, obviously, this car is what we're going to be focusing most of our effort on.'

A hand was raised at the front of the room and Thorne became aware that more heads than might otherwise have done so had turned to look. DS Paula Kimmel was the only female detective on the team – one more than on the last major case Thorne had worked. Like many others, he had thought that TV series a few years earlier with Helen Mirren would herald a marked increase in the number of women rising through the ranks. Maybe it was happening in uniform, but Thorne had yet to notice any significant change in CID.

'Are there any CCTV cameras on Archway Road?' Kimmel asked.

It was a question Thorne was hearing asked by colleagues a lot more often these days, though he had yet to hear an answer that meant any kind of positive development. Cameras had now been installed in many city centres nationwide but were still there largely to target minor offences such as burglary and illegal parking. Those in favour of the scheme claimed it was useful in stamping down on drug use and other antisocial behaviour, while many believed that those intent on committing serious crimes would simply up sticks and commit them somewhere else.

'Sadly not,' Boyle said.

The officer sitting next to Thorne shook his head and said, 'Never one of those things where it can do any good, is there?'

Thorne knew there were plans afoot to change that. John Major's government had just announced that three-quarters of its entire crime prevention budget for the year would be spent on installing more cameras, but Thorne remained sceptical. The people producing the equipment were clearly going to make a killing, but he couldn't see the day coming any time soon when CCTV would replace old-fashioned nous or shoe leather when it came to solving any major investigation.

'We need way more on this car,' Boyle said. 'We know it was red, we know it was small, a hatchback possibly, might be a Fiesta or a Golf . . . so, those of you with a high boredom threshold can enjoy the next few hours on the phone to the DVLC getting us a list of all possible vehicles.' He nodded, seeing the looks exchanged. 'Aye, I know it's going to be one hell of long list, but boo-hoo, there you go. The rest of you get up there and re-canvass that stretch of road. We do the house-to-house all over again and make sure we speak to everyone who wasn't at home yesterday. Mention of this car might jog a few memories. Oh, and if you need something to anchor the time in people's heads, you can always mention that football match yesterday.' He could not resist a smile. 'Anyone remember the score?'

He nodded through a few seconds of predictably sweary heckles then raised a hand to silence the cat-calls.

'Same thing when you go back to all the people who gave statements yesterday in the wood. The description of the bloke's every bit as vague as the car, but again, it might shake something loose . . . and as of now, that's what we're about.' Boyle pointed out the officer who had been given the role of action allocator.

'Right, Terry's got all the specifics.' He glanced across, looking for the nod from Andy Frankham who was leaning against the wall, then turned back to the team, many of whom were already shifting in their seats, keen to get on it.

'Now, get fucking shaking.'

Thorne walked out into the corridor and along to the small office he would be sharing with a fellow DS seconded from a local team. Russell Brigstocke was a broad six-footer, with thick black hair and thicker black glasses that made him look like Buddy Holly on steroids.

'Chances?' Brigstocke asked.

'What, of this having anything at all to do with Catrin Coyne's old man?' Thorne shook his head. 'I can't see it.'

'Me neither, but I suppose we need to cover all the bases.' Brigstocke looked at him. 'Not what I meant, though.'

Thorne looked at him, well aware he hadn't answered the question Brigstocke had actually been asking. By now, on a relatively straightforward murder case, someone would have almost certainly opened a book on the sly; adjusting odds according to the team's progress and taking bets on the chances of a good result. Same again if anyone was ever brought to trial, tens and twenties piling up in a biscuit tin, a little extra 'mustard'.

But not when kids were involved.

Not since the James Bulger case three years earlier and certainly not since the murders of sixteen children in Dunblane only a few months before.

Superstition or sentimentality? Coppers were prone to both, but Thorne didn't think it mattered much either way. As far as he was concerned, when it came to the way things might turn out, it didn't do anyone any good to think about their odds for very long. Least of all those to whom the result would matter the most.

'God knows,' he said.

Brigstocke nodded, and they both turned when Gordon Boyle appeared in the doorway. 'What's this, then? Mothers' meeting?'

Thorne tried to look as if he'd found the DI's comment funny, to plaster on the appropriate expression, but he wasn't sure he'd managed it.

It was mothers he was thinking of.

# NINE

As she had done several times already that morning, Cat took a deep breath and said a silent prayer to a God in whom she had not one iota of faith. She felt every muscle in her body tense in those few, breathless moments before she walked across the room and snatched up the phone.

'Cat? It's me . . . '

Maria. *Fucking* Maria.

Cat felt a surge of relief that this was not the call she had spent a sleepless night dreading, then another – stronger still – of despondency, because it was not the one for which she had desperately been hoping. Both gave way quickly to anger, that Maria was wasting her time, *distracting* her; that she was using a phone line that Cat needed to keep clear.

That the woman was calling at all.

Cat said, 'This isn't really a good time.'

'Oh, OK.'

Like that was a shame, like she was . . . disappointed. Put out. Yes, perhaps it might be best to leave it for the time being and Cat could suggest a time that was a little more convenient.

'I need to keep the line free.'

'I just wanted to see how you were holding up.'

*Seriously? Take a wild stab in the dark.* 'How I'm *holding up*?'

'Sorry. Stupid thing to say.'

'It's ...' Cat swallowed, searching for words and suddenly feeling a twinge of something like sympathy for the woman, despite herself. Nothing that was going to make much difference in the long run, but just enough to be irritating.

'Do you want some company?'

'I don't think so.'

'I can be there in fifteen minutes.'

'Like I said—'

'Maybe I could bring some food over or something. My mother can watch Josh—'

A silence then, which to Cat's mind did her friend some small degree of credit, at least. The woman stopping dead, all too aware of the hideous weight her own son's name now carried. The son who was still there, who'd got up and had his breakfast with her, who was probably playing just a few feet away.

Cat could not stop the terrible thought squeezing its way in.

*The one who should be missing.*

She said, 'I don't think it's such a great idea.'

'Of course. I wanted you to know, that's all ... anything you need. Just pick up the phone, OK?'

Cat thanked her automatically and instantly regretted it. She was not going to rant and rave like a madwoman but, by the same token, there was no way she was going to let Maria off the hook. She was not going to console her or say everything was all right and she was certainly not going to reassure her that she was not to blame for what had happened.

Why should she? How the hell *could* she?

'I take it you've not heard anything?'

Cat bit her tongue, resisting the urge to apologise for not giving Maria an update every half an hour. She said, 'No,' but all she could think of was Maria's expression the day before, when she'd come back from the toilets. Sneaky and sly, then shame-faced because she'd been caught out. Far more concerned with hiding the fact that she was smoking than with keeping an eye on the boys, on *her* boy.

No, not sneaky. *Guilty . . .*

For a few seconds there was nothing but a crackle on the line and the noise of an argument in the flat upstairs. Then Maria said, 'I'm sorry, Cat. I can't tell you . . . I'm so sorry.'

The woman sounded on the verge of tears.

'I know,' Cat said. She listened to the sniffles and wondered if now was a good time to ask exactly what Maria was sorry for. Sorry for what had happened, or sorry for the fact that she was responsible? Was it actually an apology or just a declaration of sadness at how perfectly terrible everything was?

For *both* of them.

There was not much point, Cat decided, because however the situation panned out, things between them could never be the same. Even if a copper came bowling through her door right that minute with Kieron loping in after him, hungry and covered in mud, confused as to what all the fuss had been about, she could not see herself trotting off to the park with Maria again any time soon. Meeting for lunch, trips to the pictures together, all that.

No friendship could survive this, could it?

That's if they had ever really been friends to begin with, as there had been plenty of times when Cat couldn't help but suspect she was just around to provide light entertainment or chosen as a last resort; when Maria was bored or just desperate to get out of the house and other people were busy.

'Cat? You still there?'

She wondered if Maria had only ever been slumming it.

Cat was still struggling for something to say, to decide if there was anything else worth saying, when she heard the knock at the door.

59

She gasped and said, 'I've got to go.'

'Oh . . .'

'There's someone at the door.'

'Right,' Maria said.

The word thrown away; disdainful almost, as though poor put-upon Maria didn't believe her. Sulky, like the spoiled princess she was, because being so sophisticated and super-bright she *knew* that the knock at the door – which could mean news about Cat's missing child, for Christ's sake – was just an excuse to get rid of her.

Like she was the victim here, tortured and hard-done-by, the one who was actually suffering.

Cat put the phone down and walked across to the door.

Dry-mouthed and all but panting, she opened it.

She looked at the woman standing there, slowly lowered her head and shook it. Then both of them burst into tears.

# TEN

Felix Barratt lived on the ground floor of a Victorian semi in Wood Green. He worked as a housing project manager for the local council – 'It's not the most exciting job in the world, but it suits me fine' – and lived alone with only a cat for company, because, he'd told Thorne almost immediately, that was the way he preferred it.

'I love the ladies, don't get me wrong,' he'd said. 'Too much, sometimes, if I'm honest. But I don't want someone telling me what I can and can't do. What I can watch on the television, what to wear.' He'd shuddered theatrically and grimaced. 'No, thank you very much.'

They were sitting in a fastidiously kept front room with crowded bookshelves, a collection of ornamental birds in a glass-fronted case and a view of the treelined street through a large bay window, at which Barratt glanced every few minutes.

He had brought tea through in china cups. There were biscuits on a plate.

'When you called in, you said you'd been in the woods yourself a little earlier.'

'Correct,' Barratt said. 'I'd left the woods an hour or so before I saw the car. Nipped up to Muswell Hill, just to potter around the shops for a bit. I was walking back to my own car when I saw the man with the boy.'

Though he was somewhere in his early forties, Barratt dressed like someone a good deal older. He wore brown corduroy trousers and highly polished brogues, a shirt and tie under a tweed jacket. Sunday best, Thorne thought, or perhaps he'd smartened himself up a little because there was a police officer coming round. Thorne was well aware that some people were like that, though in the end he decided that Barratt was probably not one of them. As someone who only ever looked smart when he absolutely had to, Thorne could never quite fathom those who did so as a matter of course.

'Why all the way up to Highgate Wood?'

'Sorry?

'Well, I'd've thought Alexandra Park was a lot closer, that's all.' Thorne turned and pointed through the window. 'It's what . . . five minutes away?'

'Oh, the wood is *so* much nicer,' Barratt said. 'It's a lot older, a lot more *established*. There are great spotted woodpeckers and nuthatches. Treecreepers, now and again. Seventy-one different species, all told.' He nodded towards the glass-fronted case. 'I like birds.'

'See any good ones?'

'Good ones?'

'Any good birds, yesterday morning?'

'Oh yes, but sadly, nothing I haven't seen before.'

Thorne wrote it all down. 'And can you remember which shops you went into? When you were pottering about?'

Barratt sipped his tea. Thorne thought the man looked a little irritated, but if he was wondering why he was being asked so many questions when he was the one trying to help, the one who had come forward with important information, he kept it to himself. 'Not really,' he said. 'A couple of the charity shops. I popped into Woolworths, I think.'

'Thank you,' Thorne said, scribbling again. 'This is all very helpful. I'll come on to what you saw in a minute, but we do need all these details, I'm afraid.'

'Of course, fire away.' Barratt took another sip of tea, glanced towards the road again.

'Did you buy anything?'

'Where?'

'From Woolworths? Or anywhere else?'

'No.' Barratt smiled. 'I was just killing time.'

Thorne wrote that down and underlined it. 'Why were you killing time?'

'Well, the weekends can be quite boring, tell you the truth. Yes, I generally prefer my own company at home, but we can all get on our own nerves at times, can't we? I'm actually happiest when I'm working.'

'Right.'

'What about you?' Barratt studied him across his teacup. 'Looks like you enjoy your job.'

'Some days are better than others,' Thorne said. He lowered his notebook for a moment. 'I can't say that this case is what I'd call enjoyable.'

'No, of course not. Not until you catch him, anyway. This man ...'

Thorne watched Barratt lean down to stroke the ginger cat who had come padding into the room; he made kissing noises as he rubbed its ears. 'Well, let's hope that you coming forward with this information helps us do that.'

Barratt sat up again and smiled. He raised his cup as if in a toast. 'Amen to that.'

Felix Barratt's name had been run through the Police National Computer as a matter of course. Thorne knew that nothing so much as a parking ticket had turned up and his name was certainly not on their current list of known sex offenders. All the same, he was not drinking tea in Barratt's front room solely in an attempt to flesh out the somewhat sparse descriptions the man had provided over the phone.

It would not be the first time an offender had insinuated himself into an investigation or had attempted to muddy the waters by helpfully providing false leads for the likes of Thorne to chase up.

A conveniently placed vehicle. A suspect who had never existed.

'I was wondering if you'd remembered any more about this car since you rang in,' Thorne said. 'Red, you said.'

'Yes, that's right. A *bright* red, like a post box, and very clean.'

'OK, that's useful.'

'As I told the officer on the phone, one of those little ones, like a Golf.'

'Or a Fiesta?'

'Yes, that's right. I'm not great with cars, but something a bit sporty.'

'Anything else? Any marks on the car? Dents or scratches?'

'Not that I could see,' Barratt said. 'I was on the other side of the road.'

'And what about the man you saw getting into the car?' Thorne glanced down at his notebook, at the description Barratt had given when he'd called the appeals line. 'Medium height, dark jacket . . . any idea if he was dark-haired, blond . . . ?'

'He was wearing a hat,' Barratt said. 'I don't mean a woolly one or anything, I mean it wasn't particularly cold, was it? More like a cap, but not a baseball cap or anything like that.' He paused, searching for the right word. 'Jaunty, that's it.'

'If you had to guess at an age?'

Barratt puffed out his cheeks. 'I'm really not sure. Forties, perhaps?'

'And what about the boy?'

Barratt leaned back. The cat was still nosing around his ankles. 'Well, like I said, he was six or seven, I think. It's hard to be sure, isn't it? Some children are taller for their age than others, aren't they?'

'You still can't remember what he was wearing?'

'No and I've been racking my brains. It's funny, but the man stuck in my mind and the boy just ... didn't.'

Thorne said it was fine, that people always remembered certain details while failing to take in others. He did think it was a little strange that Barratt could not remember the distinctive-looking tartan anorak with a furry hood the missing boy had been wearing. But then there was always the possibility, of course, that the boy Barratt claimed to have seen had been wearing something rather more nondescript, because he wasn't Kieron Coyne.

'It was all just in passing,' Barratt said. 'I hardly took it in, really ... didn't even think about it until I saw that board appealing for information.'

'Right.'

'I thought they were related in some way, I remember that, because the boy was holding the man's hand.' Barratt leaned forward. 'They knew one another, or looked as though they did, at any rate. That must be significant, surely?'

Thorne stood up and thanked Barratt for his help, for the tea. 'So, just to be clear, you saw our appeal board when you went *back* to the wood first thing this morning?'

Barratt stood up and watched his cat skitter away. 'As I told you, weekends can get a bit dull. Sundays are even worse than Saturdays.'

On his way to the door, Thorne took one last look at the glass-fronted cabinet and made a mental note to find out just how many species of birds there were to be spotted in Alexandra Park.

# ELEVEN

The woman, who sat Catrin down on the sofa and passed her a small pack of tissues from her bag, was tall and slim, with spiky blonde hair that was dark at the roots. She wore skin-tight stone-washed jeans and a black bomber jacket over a denim shirt. Her high cheekbones and delicate features were every bit as striking as always, but the absence of make-up revealed the shadows beneath her wide eyes and what were usually called 'laughter lines' like brackets around her mouth, though she was not generally a woman who laughed a great deal.

Fifteen years earlier, in a different world, she might have been a model, but in north London in 1996 the closest Angela Coyne came to the catwalk was the pictures in *Cosmopolitan*, while she made her living selling cut-price household goods from a market stall in Shepherd's Bush.

'Did Billy tell you?' Cat had put a call through to the prison the night before and Billy had rung her back half an hour later. She dabbed at her eyes. 'He sounded so upset.'

Billy Coyne's big sister nodded. She had already stopped crying, sucking up the snot as she'd marched in and wiping her face with the back of her hand. 'Yeah, he called a couple of hours ago, but I knew before that. The police were at the stall first thing asking me questions. When did I last see Kieron, what was I doing yesterday lunchtime, all that.'

Cat looked up at her. 'I'm sorry, Ange. That's so stupid.'

Angela shrugged. 'Makes sense, when you think about it. At least it shows they're doing this properly.' She held up a plastic bag, clanking with beer cans. 'Right then.' She walked out to the kitchen to put four cans in the fridge and brought the other four back to the table. She sat down next to Cat and opened one for each of them, took cigarettes from her bag and offered the pack.

Catrin took one and leaned across for a light, but she struggled to keep her hand steady, remembering the last time she'd held a cigarette between her fingers. The morning before, in that playground. Josh in tears and her starting to run.

She stifled the sob that rose up suddenly, smiled when it turned into something like a hiccup, then laughed when Angela did. She said, 'It's good of you to come, Ange.'

'Don't be daft. Why wouldn't I come?'

'All the same.'

'He's my nephew, isn't he?'

'Yeah.'

'I'm his Auntie Ange, right? And you're more like a sister than a sister-in-law.' She took a fast drag and hissed out the smoke. 'I mean, I know we're not, really, but you know.'

Cat nodded. 'Good as,' she said. 'And yeah, more like sisters.'

The woman turned to look at her. 'I always wondered why you and Billy never tied the knot. I was thinking about that the other day.'

'I wanted to,' Cat said, 'but Billy seemed to think we'd be better off not bothering. Something about benefits, about it being easier if we weren't married. I don't know.'

'Yeah, he's usually pretty clued up about all that stuff and how to work it. Shame he doesn't think about some other things a bit more.' Angela swallowed beer and shook her head. 'My baby brother doesn't know his arse from his elbow most of the time.'

Cat grinned, but the laugh died in her throat. 'I do miss him, though.' She brushed a worm of cigarette ash from the cushion and her voice dropped to a whisper. 'I wish he was here right now.'

Angie leaned to lay a hand on her arm, dug long fingernails in. 'I know.'

They sat close together on the sofa, drinking and smoking, and said nothing for a minute or more. The old woman downstairs had her TV cranked up and they could hear the closing moments of whichever horse race she was watching, the voice of the posh commentator rising up a notch right at the end.

'I hope the old girl's won a few quid,' Cat said. 'Last time she backed a winner she brought Kieron some sweets.'

Angela swallowed what was left in her can, smacked down the empty and opened another. 'When they catch whoever's done this . . . '

'What?'

'The mongrel's life won't be worth living . . . won't be worth *anything*, wherever he ends up.'

'Is that what you think?'

'It's what happens to that sort inside, isn't it? They're targeted.' Her mouth tightened, those laughter lines deeper suddenly, and dark. 'Well, *you* know that.' She nodded, bringing the can to her mouth. 'Something, I suppose.'

'I mean, do you think someone's got him? Got Kieron?'

'Well, Christ, I hope not . . . but it doesn't do any good to kid yourself, babe.' Angela Coyne stubbed out her cigarette, reached into her bag for another and let her head drop back against the thick leather cushion. 'I mean, they'd have found him by now, wouldn't they?'

# TWELVE

'Thanks for coming,' Maria said. 'I'm a bit . . . all over the place, if I'm honest.'

Her ex-husband walked into the kitchen, dropped his jacket across one of the barstools and sat down, clearly still comfortable in a house he'd lived in until five years before. 'Why on earth didn't you call yesterday, when this happened?'

'I was hoping it would have sorted itself out by now.' Maria sat down opposite him, at the other end of the island. 'That he'd have turned up, you know?'

'How's Joshy doing?'

'He's in bits. Well, of course he is.' Maria hopped off the stool and moved to the door. 'Let me tell him you're here.'

Jeff Ashton waited, listening to his ex-wife's feet on the stairs as she ran the two flights up to their son's room. She was back a few minutes later and if she thought it strange to find him casually opening and closing cupboard doors, as though checking to see how well the contents had been organised in his absence, she didn't say anything.

'He'll be down in a minute.' Maria sat down again and her shoulders dropped. 'He's still really upset.'

Ashton looked up and shouted his son's name. He waited, then raised his arms in exasperation.

'It's understandable, really.' She watched him as he sauntered back across the kitchen. 'You know how sensitive he is.'

Ashton nodded, as though he knew only too well. He sat down again, looked at her. 'What's he been like? Before this, I mean.'

'The same, really. He can't settle. He bit a little girl at school last week.'

'Why didn't you tell me?'

'I thought they were going to suspend him.'

Ashton leaned towards her. 'Listen, why don't I take him for a few days?'

'No.'

'Give you a break. I mean, this has obviously upset you.' He waited until she looked back at him. 'You look frazzled.'

'I'll be fine.' Maria sat up straight and pushed back a hank of hair that had fallen across her face. 'Let's stick to the arrangement.'

'I'm only offering to help, Mazz—'

'I know, but ... you take him the weekend after next. Last thing he needs is for his routine to get messed up on top of everything else.'

Ashton nodded, as though he could see the sense of it. He stood up again, walked to the fridge and helped himself to a small bottle of water. 'How's your friend? What's her name again?'

'Cat,' Maria said. 'Her name is Cat.'

Jeff had never liked Catrin very much, Maria knew that. Among his many faults, he had always been something of a snob and had clearly wondered why, how a GP's wife could be friends with a woman who seemed content to live on state hand-outs. Whose partner was in prison, let's not forget that. Maria had tried to explain and, while not going as far as reminding

70

him that she wasn't exactly overburdened with close friends any more, had pointed out that *she* wasn't contributing a great deal to society either. Not while she was living in a house that someone else had paid for; a lady who lunched and went to the hairdresser once a week, *scraping* by on the money Jeff doled out to her every month. She and Cat, she had told him, had a lot more in common than he, or anyone else, liked to believe.

'It must be horrible for her,' he said now. 'Makes me go cold, just thinking about it.' He sat down again. 'If it had been Josh, you know?'

'It's what I thought, too.'

They talked for a few minutes about standing orders for utility bills, about when Maria's car might need servicing and about some mortgage-related accountancy issue that Maria was far too stressed to take in properly. When they had run out of domestic matters to discuss, she asked him how he was.

He looked at her.

'Seriously. How are things?'

'Well, there isn't anyone else, if that's what you're asking.'

'It wasn't.'

'I'd tell you if there was,' he said. 'Too bloody busy at the surgery, apart from anything else. What about you?'

She barked out a laugh. 'No chance.'

'That's a shame,' he said. 'Really, it is.'

'Actually, I did go out for a drink with someone.' She smiled, seeing his eyebrows rise. 'Spent hours getting dolled up in a brand new outfit, then got to the restaurant and spent an hour and a half jabbering about Josh. Poor man couldn't get out of there quickly enough.'

'Well, he's an idiot.'

Maria was embarrassed and a little annoyed with herself when she felt blood moving to her cheeks. 'Listen, you fancy staying for an early dinner?' She moved those errant strands of hair again. 'Wouldn't take me long to knock something up.'

It seemed as though he was considering the offer, but finally he said, 'I think I'll head back once I've seen Josh. The drive's always a pig on a Sunday.'

They sat in silence for a minute or more. Ashton glanced towards the ceiling, but all was quiet above him. 'Do you think that spending so much time with you is possibly making him over-sensitive? You know . . . a bit soft?'

'Sensitive is not soft,' Maria said.

'I'm just saying.'

'Try telling the parents of that girl he bit that he's soft.'

Ashton nodded, taking the point. 'Sorry, this is all just a little . . . ' He shook his head. 'You will call me as soon as there's any news?'

'Course I will.'

'Or if you change your mind about letting me take Josh for a while.' He flashed what he'd always thought of as a winning smile and said, 'Oh, and tell Cat I'm thinking about her.'

Maria grunted. 'Right now, I don't think she wants to talk to me.'

'She thinks it was your *fault*?' He looked horrified. 'That's so unfair.'

'She's lost her child, Jeff,' Maria said. 'I mean maybe lost him for good. That must have crossed her mind by now.'

'Even so.'

'Like you said, what if it had been Josh? How would you be feeling?'

Ashton lowered his head slowly, and when he raised it again just a few seconds later there were tears in his eyes.

Maria smiled. 'Right, and I'm the one who's making Joshy soft.'

# THIRTEEN

When Thorne stepped into the lift, there was a smell he could not remember from the night before. He looked around but couldn't see any evidence of what he presumed to be the cause. A young man shouted and ran across the lobby to join him just before the doors closed. He screwed up his face and shook his head in disgust.

'Bloody kids.' The man had an accent; Polish, Thorne guessed, though he couldn't be sure. 'Dirty bastards.'

Thorne asked which floor the man wanted and pressed the button for him.

He found it hard to believe that anyone who lived here would piss in their own lift, but he was equally bemused at the idea that someone who didn't might be desperate enough to pop in off the street to . . . use the facilities.

'Filthy,' his companion said.

Thorne had given up wondering why people did certain things a long time ago, but in the minute or so it took him to reach the sixth floor he couldn't help but speculate.

Were the lift-pissers marking their territory? Homeless people getting out of the cold and doing it in their sleep? Perhaps it was a natural reaction for those with a pronounced fear of confined spaces. By the time the doors opened and he could breathe through his nose again, Thorne was leaning towards the conclusion that people did it just because they could.

He had put away a good few murderers with motives no more complex than that.

Catrin Coyne opened the door and said, 'Oh.'

Seeing the colour drain from her face, Thorne reached quickly into his bag for the photograph he'd placed in a stiff-backed envelope, to let her know as quickly as he could exactly why he was there. 'I thought you'd want this back as soon as possible.' She stepped back and turned, and he followed her inside. 'It'll be in the papers tomorrow.'

Walking into her living room, Cat said that she was grateful to have the photograph back, that it was good of Thorne to bring it round. She took it from the envelope and placed it on the narrow mantelpiece above the electric fire. She stood looking at it, her back to Thorne, and he couldn't hear what she was saying.

'Sorry?'

She turned, tearful. 'Any news?'

'We're following up a few leads,' he said.

Thorne had spent the afternoon at the office. He'd typed up a report on his interview with Felix Barratt, while others reported back from their trip to HMP Whitehill. Billy Coyne, they said, was 'predictably upset' and though they would talk to anyone who'd been in to see him over the previous few months, nobody on his approved visitors list had rung any alarm bells. The officer who had tracked down Coyne's attempted murder victim announced that they could rule him out. The man had been in Leeds, where he now lived, at the time Kieron had gone missing, though they would, of course, be paying a visit to all his close friends and relatives.

There was plenty to do.

Everyone was busy.

In Thorne's case, this had meant a fruitless hour on the phone trying to talk to someone, anyone, from local bird-watching groups or ornithological associations. Nobody had been available on a Sunday, so he had left several messages. He'd told Boyle what he was doing, how he'd felt after the conversation with Barratt that it would be worth checking out.

The DCI had been predictably dismissive.

'Got a funny feeling about him, did you?'

Thorne had said nothing, just sat and imagined kicking a few more of the Scotsman's teeth out.

Cat sat down and stared up at him. 'What sort of leads?'

'People have been calling in. Hopefully there'll be a lot more when the papers come out in the morning.'

'Calling in to say what?'

'Possible sightings,' Thorne said. 'We're looking into every one of them and if there's anything positive we'll let you know. I promise we won't keep you in the dark.'

She nodded, then kept on nodding. She muttered, 'In the dark,' then looked at him. 'He's still scared of it, you know? Wherever he is, I just hope there's some light.'

Even if he had not seen the half-dozen empty Harp cans on the table, Thorne would not have needed to stretch himself professionally to work out that Catrin had been drinking. He'd smelled it on her when he'd walked in and he could hear it in her voice. It was not so much the words – nothing slurred or stumbled over – but the spaces between them; uneven, out of kilter. He could tell she was a little drunk because he saw how hard she was trying to appear sober. He remembered reading somewhere that it was a trick actors used.

He nodded towards the empties, scattered around a saucerful of cigarette butts. 'You've had some company then, anyway?'

Cat managed a smile. 'Billy's sister was over.' She reached to

75

stand up two cans that were lying on their sides. 'I mean I like a drink, but even I couldn't do that lot on my own.'

'It's good to have family around,' Thorne said.

'You want one?' Cat stood and gathered up the empty cans, stepped towards the door. 'I'm going to, so . . .'

Thorne didn't take too long to say yes. He was heading home after this, anyway. 'Keep you company,' he said.

Half a minute later, she was back with a couple of the cans Angela had left in her fridge. They opened them, touched them together as though they had something to celebrate, or perhaps in the hope that they soon would.

'What about your mum and dad?' Thorne asked.

'Dad left when I was sixteen,' she said. 'No idea where he is. Mum died a few years back, not long after Kieron was born.'

'Sorry,' Thorne said.

She shrugged, the pain of it negligible suddenly. 'You?'

'Yeah, mine are still around. I should really go and see them, actually, but . . .'

'You're a bit busy right now. Sorry about that.'

'Don't be daft.' Thorne took a decent drink and then another. 'Have you spoken to Mrs Ashton?'

Cat took a drink of her own. 'Well, she called, but it wasn't great. I wasn't exactly friendly.'

'It's natural to look for someone to blame,' Thorne said. 'Doesn't really do any good in the long run, though.'

They both stared at their drinks for a few moments.

'You do a bit of social work on the side, do you? Samaritans, something like that?'

He laughed. 'I can't even sort my own life out.'

'Yeah?' Cat watched him drink, took another swig of her own.

Thorne wondered if hearing about someone else's problems might take Catrin Coyne's mind off her own. He quickly thought better of it. Jan, the house, the shit he was still getting

76

from certain people at work ten years on from what had happened with Frank Calvert.

All of it so unimportant.

'You reckon someone's got him?' she asked. '*Keeping* him?'

'I really don't know,' he said.

'It's fine to tell me, if that's what you think.' She waited. 'If someone's got him, it means he's still alive, right?'

Thorne knew that the vast majority of those who abducted children killed them relatively quickly – within a day or two, usually. He did not want to go down that road, and certainly not the one that was darker still and led to those who kept children alive for reasons nobody would want to think about for too long.

'Truth is, I don't know what to think.' She turned her head towards the window and talked quietly to the blackness beyond it. 'Either he's already gone . . . or he's out there somewhere, scared to death in the dark, shouting out for me. One minute I'm thinking one thing, then I jump the other way and it doesn't really matter, because both of them are like a knife in me. You know?'

Thorne nodded and finished what little beer was left in the can. He held it up when she turned back to him. He said, 'I don't suppose you've got another one of these.'

# FOURTEEN

He might have been six floors up and more than a few beers to the good, but Thorne had decided to do his olfactory system a favour and take the stairs. He was on his way to the scarred metal door next to the lift when he clocked that he was being watched. Peered at. He could not see much more than a man's pinched, pale face – a long nose with oversized nostrils and fat lips which were moving quickly and silently – staring at him around the front door that was one along from Catrin Coyne's.

'Can I help you?'

Thorne saw panic flash across the man's face a second before the door was closed. He walked across and knocked. Waited, then knocked again.

'Hello?' The occupant, who was clearly standing on the other side of the door, was softly spoken and sounded a little nervous.

Thorne leaned close and lowered his own voice. 'Can you open the door, please? I'm a police officer.'

A few moments later the man behind the door opened it, but no further than it had been when Thorne had first become aware of him. Once again, he peered out; at Thorne, then – craning his neck a little – at the empty space around and behind him. Thorne held up his warrant card, which very swiftly seized and held the man's attention.

'Is everything all right, sir?'

The man nodded, his lips moving rapidly again, though it took a few moments before they produced any words. 'What's going on?' The voice was flat and accentless, barely above a whisper. Long fingers bristling with rings snaked around the door and he pointed in the direction of the flat from which Thorne had just emerged. 'With Catrin. I saw all the police here last night, that's all. I saw the comings and goings.' The hand moved back and he began scratching at his neck.

'Do you know Ms Coyne?'

He looked surprised, almost offended. 'Well, of course I know her. Is she all right?' He stared at Thorne, pupils like pinpricks. 'Is Kieron all right?'

Thorne moved back a few paces and curled a finger. 'Would you mind stepping out for a few moments?'

The man blinked slowly and retreated a little. He said, 'Well, it's very late.'

'Please.'

The low mutterings before the door was fully opened and the man stepped out were indecipherable, but there was no mistaking the smell – sharp, vinegarish – that followed him. A lot less unpleasant but every bit as distinctive as the one left behind in the lift. Thorne remembered what Catrin had said to him the night before. Her concerns about upsetting certain neighbours.

Thorne took out his notebook. 'Can I ask your name?'

'Yes, you can.'

Thorne waited. 'I *am* asking.'

'Grantleigh.'

'Well, Mr Grantleigh ...' Thorne stopped, seeing the man smile. He smiled back. 'Something funny, sir?'

'Grantleigh is my first name. I didn't know we were being formal.'

'So . . . ?'

'Figgis. My name is Grantleigh Figgis.' He turned slightly and nodded back at his front door. 'I'm presuming you don't need to ask my address.'

He was very tall and extremely thin, the bones in his wrists and at the top of his shoulders as pronounced as the sunken eyes and the hollows in his cheeks. He wore a tight, sleeveless pullover, somewhat incongruous above a pair of grubby grey tracksuit bottoms and the kind of furry slippers more usually associated with old ladies. Thorne looked at him – the mop of greasy blond hair, those dry lips smacking together again – and a description he'd once heard his father use about someone the old man had worked with popped into his head.

A proper funny strip of piss.

'How well do you know Catrin?'

Figgis cocked his head and thrust his hands deep into the pockets of his tracksuit bottoms. 'We're not intimate or anything.'

Thorne was always interested when people answered questions he had not asked them. He waited.

'We're neighbours, so . . . you know.' The hands came out of the pockets and were waved about a good deal as he spoke. 'A cup of sugar here, a spare loo roll there. I might lend her my lawnmower once in a while.' He smiled, showing just how bad his teeth were. 'Mostly, we just bitch about some of the other residents, to be honest.'

'What about Kieron?'

Figgis looked at him, very still suddenly. 'What about him?'

'You see much of him?'

'Yes, obviously, because he's always with his mum and I see quite a lot of her.'

'So, Kieron's always with his mum, is he? When you see him?'

80

'Yes, of course, but it's not like he's ever in the way or anything. Kieron's a lovely boy. Very *polite*.' He began scratching at his neck again. 'You still haven't said what this is about.'

'No.' Thorne tucked his notebook away. 'I haven't.'

'Has something bad happened?'

'I'm afraid I can't go into details, but it might be best if you could give Catrin a little . . . space for the time being. That OK? Maybe get your cup of sugar somewhere else.'

'Absolutely,' Figgis said.

'I'd appreciate that.'

'Whatever you think.'

'And thank you for being so helpful.'

'Well, if you say so . . . you're welcome.'

Thorne walked across to the lift, then remembered and veered away towards the stairs. When he turned, just before heading down, he could see that Catrin Coyne's neighbour had moved fast and was already safely back behind his front door again.

Still watching.

Thorne was on his way back to the car when he spotted the phone box on the other side of the road. He waited for a gap in the traffic, reached into a pocket for his phonecard, then jogged across.

It couldn't hurt, could it?

Stupid, because he knew that it could, that it *had*.

Five minutes before, halfway up that tower block, chatting to an amiable, if unusual, individual whom Thorne had no reasonable excuse to suspect of anything, it had been a feeling he had recognised; unwelcome, insistent. A nagging pain that was all too familiar. Impossible to ignore however much he might want to, yet equally hard to describe in a way that anyone would understand.

Only the dreams made any sense of it.

No, *not* a pain. Not to begin with, anyway.

81

Stepping into the phone box, Thorne felt something close to real agony and told himself he was an idiot for not using Catrin Coyne's toilet when he'd had the chance. He was suddenly bursting. He slammed in the phonecard and dialled, gritting his teeth.

'Come on. Jesus . . .'

He knew that, when caught as short as he currently was, there were those who would make use of the nearest phone box, if there wasn't a lift available, but he was not quite that desperate. Yet.

Ajay Roth answered, full of it.

'Just talking about you,' he said. 'One of your twitchers rang back.'

'What?'

'People who look at birds. Anyway, he reckons there's over a hundred different species in Alexandra Park. Including dunnocks and mealy redpolls, whatever the hell they are . . .'

Thorne resisted the temptation to tell him that they were almost certainly birds and said, 'Listen, Ajay, I need you to run a name through the PNC for me. Have you got a pen?'

'Yeah, somewhere . . .'

'Grantleigh Figgis.'

'Bloody hell. Where did you dig him up?'

'He lives next door to Catrin Coyne.' Thorne spelled the name out. 'You got that?'

'OK, might take me a few minutes. Can I call you back?'

Thorne wondered if he had enough time to nip out and find somewhere to piss, then decided against it. It wouldn't take very long, however bad Roth was with computers, and Thorne did not want to miss his call.

He moved gingerly from foot to foot and tried not to think about it.

A couple came and stood close to the phone box. The woman looked at her watch and stared in at him. Thorne found a small

area of the window that was not obscured by ads for local prostitutes and pressed his warrant card against the glass until the
couple wandered away, swearing.

He snatched the phone up the instant it began to ring.

'Jackpot,' Roth said. 'This bloke's a neighbour, is he?'

'Go on.'

'Well, I wasn't too excited at first, because he's not on our
list, but there's a very good reason for that. The charges were
dropped before it ever got to court. So, never convicted. Oh, and
for what it's worth, he also happens to be a fairly major-league
smackhead.'

'Yeah, I caught a whiff earlier.' Thorne had forgotten all about
needing to piss. 'What charges?'

'Two years ago, Grantleigh Ralph Figgis was arrested for
sexually assaulting a minor.' Roth left a suitably dramatic pause.
'Sounding good so far?'

There was a prickling at the nape of Thorne's neck, soft fingers moving through the fine hairs. He shuddered. 'Very good.'

'I haven't even got to the best bit yet,' Roth said. 'Once I
found out about the sex offence, I checked with the DVLC
and guess what? Your Mr Figgis drives a red Volkswagen Polo.
Very similar to a Golf, don't you reckon ... if you were on the
other side of the road and you didn't know your way around
cars? Tom ... ?'

'Yeah, I'm here.'

'Hang on, the boss wants a word.'

There was a clatter as the phone was laid down on a desk, and
a few seconds later Gordon Boyle was on the line.

'Well, I think we can forget all about your dodgy birdwatcher,'
he said. 'Fucking ... *dunnocks* or not. I've spoken to Andy
Frankham about this bloke you've pulled out of a hat, and he
reckons that on a crime-in-action like this one, we've already
got enough to nick him.'

'Right,' Thorne said.

'So, I've already been in touch with local uniform and they're sending a car to pick him up. Where are you, by the way?'

Thorne told him.

'Perfect. You stay exactly where you are and, when uniform arrives, you can be the one to put the cuffs on. Fair enough?'

Thorne said nothing. He was thinking about the look of alarm on that pinched, pale face, and how tight those handcuffs would need to be around Grantleigh Figgis's thin wrists.

'Good work, Tom,' Boyle said. 'Really good, mate.'

Thorne was happy to wait in his car, but knew he had to empty his bladder before doing anything else. He hurried back down Holloway Road towards the side street where he was parked, searching desperately for somewhere suitable, before uniform arrived and things got serious.

He ducked into a darkened passageway between a bookies that was closed and a branch of McDonald's that wasn't. As traffic roared past, he unzipped quickly, then thought about the DI's unusually generous words while he relieved himself.

*Good work.*

He groaned with pleasure as he pissed against the wall, buzzing with excitement. He leaned back, arcing the jet as high up the brickwork as he could manage, the same ridiculous way he and his friends had done when they were kids.

Before things got serious.

# FIFTEEN

Maria wasn't sure she'd managed any sleep at all by the time Josh began to thrash and moan next to her. She shushed him as he kicked and cried out and she could feel the heat coming off him when she pushed the duvet down and saw that his little fists were tightly clenched. His hair was plastered to his scalp and his pyjamas were soaked in sweat.

Maria laid a hand across his clammy forehead until the cries faded to whimpers. 'It's OK, Joshy ... come on.'

It had been clear for a while how badly her son had been affected by the divorce, by the fallout from it. Just when she had begun to think that things might be settling down, they would ramp up again. A tantrum at home for no reason, a screaming fit in the car, an 'incident' at school. She turned to look at Josh as he rolled away from her, snivelling. Now, things looked as though they were only going to get worse because of what had happened to his best friend.

'I'm here, chicken.'

His *only* friend, truth be told. Something she and her son had in common, Maria thought, lying there in the dark, though there was at least a reason why *he* was struggling to form meaningful friendships. Josh had always been something of a loner anyway, happy enough to play on his own, but it would never be easy to get close to anyone when your first instinct was to shout at them, or worse.

*I'm sorry, Mrs Ashton, but I have to take the feelings of the poor girl's parents into consideration. It's left a very nasty mark and the fact is we simply can't allow this sort of behaviour to continue . . .*

Though neither she nor Jeff had ever resorted to biting, it was perhaps her own memories of shouting, and worse, that made her think about her ex-husband. *His* first instincts, and her own. Scratchy-eyed and staring at the shape of the lamp above her, Maria decided that it had been nice of him to come round earlier.

Thoughtful, which was not a word she associated with him that often.

It had not been at all unpleasant.

Seeing how very much he cared for Josh, how upset he'd been just before he'd left, had . . . moved her a little. An old-fashioned word, but right then she couldn't think of any other. She would not have gone as far as to say it had rekindled feelings she'd long since thought dead and buried – that would be ridiculous – but at the very least it was a reminder of why she'd once loved him. Why, despite the selfishness, the snobbery and the rest of it, she was still fond of him.

Josh aside, they still had a connection.

She kicked the duvet off completely and found herself wondering what might have happened if Jeff had stayed for dinner. Had he secretly wanted to? He certainly seemed keen to let her know he wasn't seeing anybody.

Josh moaned and wriggled close to the edge of the bed.

Maria told herself that she was being very stupid and *very* selfish. She slid across and gently drew her son back towards her. She wrapped an arm around his hot, skinny waist and kept it there.

Reminded herself that there was only one man in her life who mattered.

Catrin opened her eyes and sat up, uncertain about what had woken her so suddenly, but very clear as to the reason she was reaching immediately for the clot of used tissues on her bedside table. She pressed it to her face, every bit as angry as she was upset. Frustrated and furious at whatever had dragged her from Kieron, or at least some dream of him. It was already fading, water swirling quickly away in a sink, but the details didn't much matter. She could not even swear that he had been there, next to her or even close, but in the dream, at least, she had been happy.

A dream of before.

When there had been no terror.

No stone, hard and heavy at the centre of her.

She heard a bang, then a metallic clattering from the hallway outside her front door and knew it was the noise that had woken her. Someone kicking at the lift door, it sounded like. Kids, probably; someone coming home pissed.

She got out of bed, pulled on an old T-shirt and knickers.

Now, someone was knocking on a nearby door. She could hear voices raised and others raised still further above them. Bastards . . .

She all but ran towards her door, ready to let rip. She was buzzing with it suddenly and relishing the opportunity to tell whoever was out there exactly what she thought of them, to scream away a little of her pain. To slap and punch and claw it away if that's what it came to.

The weight of that stone.

She flung open her door and watched a man in a white plastic suit carrying a heavy metal box towards the doorway of a neighbouring flat. It clattered as it was laid down. Not the lift

87

door, she thought as she watched it judder open and saw two more figures in plastic Babygros step out with more metal boxes. She turned when she heard the knocking and saw a pair of uniformed coppers banging on doors, quickly moving along to bang on a couple more while they waited for their heavy knocks to be answered.

One of the coppers noticed her and froze. She wrapped her arms around herself, self-conscious suddenly, half dressed on the landing. The copper turned away, stepped smartly across and muttered something to his colleague.

There was a quick glance in her direction but no more than that, then the pair of them stood close together looking gormless and uncertain. Guilty, despite the uniforms.

Catrin stared at them, waiting, but they couldn't look at her.

# SIXTEEN

It was past midnight by the time Grantleigh Figgis had been planted unceremoniously in an interview room to answer some direct questions from Gordon Boyle and Ajay Roth.

Heroin aside, nothing of significance had been found during the initial search of his flat and nothing that so much as resembled the 'jaunty' cap Felix Barratt had described seeing. By now, though, Thorne knew that a forensic team would be inside looking for evidence invisible to the naked eye and, perhaps more important, another would be examining the arrested man's VW Polo every bit as carefully. If Barratt was to be believed and Kieron Coyne had been driven away in that car, they would almost certainly find the DNA traces to prove it.

Hair, skin, fibres from a tartan anorak.

Blood.

At the same time, as many uniforms as could be spared by the local boys would be swarming all over Seacole House, searching electrical cupboards, waste-disposal areas. Anywhere the missing boy might have been hidden. They would be attempting to gain access to every flat on each of its dozen floors. Every flat except Catrin Coyne's, of course.

Thorne grabbed a much-needed coffee and, for five minutes or so, lurked in the corridor outside the interview room. As soon as he was sure that he wasn't being observed, he leaned close to the door.

'*Just tell us where he is, Grantleigh.*'

'*How can I?*'

'*Is he alive? Tell us that much.*'

'*This is ridiculous. I swear, I thought you were the drugs squad.*'

When it became clear there was to be no instant revelation, that Boyle was not about to come crashing out of the interview with Kieron Coyne's whereabouts, Thorne wandered back into the incident room.

'Where do you reckon he's put him?'

Thorne had already marked DC Russell Brigstocke down as the type to call a spade a spade and it was clear that he had not been wrong. He knew that when Brigstocke said 'him' he really meant 'his body'.

He shook his head.

'Top marks, by the way.'

'Come again?'

'Finding Figgis.'

'He found me,' Thorne said.

They walked into the small office they shared and, when Thorne sat down, he saw a number of curling Post-it notes stuck to his desk. A CPS lawyer wanted to talk to him about a domestic murder case Thorne was keen to push to trial, but on which the CPS were still refusing to bite. The key witness to an arson attack wanted to let him know she wasn't quite as certain about what she'd seen as she had been the week before.

Catrin Coyne had called him four times.

Leaning back behind his own desk, Brigstocke told Thorne that he'd been the one to take the messages, that the woman had sounded keen to speak to him. He watched as Thorne dialled.

'She'll be pleased you've got some good news for her,' he said.

She wasn't.

'The fuck's going on?'

'I'm sorry I wasn't here when—'

'There's coppers everywhere.' It was hard to tell if it was panic or anger that was colouring Catrin Coyne's voice. 'Loads of those ones in plastic suits like on *Silent Witness* or something. There's stuff happening in the flat next door.'

'I should tell you that we've made an arrest,' Thorne said.

'You *should* tell me? Why the hell haven't you already told me?'

Thorne tried to explain why he'd been more than usually tied up when she'd been trying to contact him. Why this was the first chance he'd had to call her back. He didn't get very far.

'Grant? You've arrested *Grant*?' She laughed, but there was no trace of humour in it. The laugh of someone who's just been given a terminal diagnosis. 'Why would you think . . . ? Grant's just a bit weird, that's all.'

'We haven't arrested him because he's a bit weird.'

'He's a smackhead, you do know that, right?'

'Yes, but—'

'A harmless junkie.'

'I'm afraid there's a bit more to it than that,' Thorne said. 'He drives a car that matches one spotted by someone at the woods yesterday morning. A child matching Kieron's description was seen getting into it.'

There was another laugh – somewhat more nervous, *dislocated* – and now, she wasn't coming back at him quite so fast. 'A *car*? That's the reason there's coppers dragging everyone out of bed?'

'He was arrested before,' Thorne said. 'For a sexual offence.'

The pause was even longer this time. 'What kind of offence?'

'I'm sorry, but I really can't go into the details just yet.' As Thorne listened to Catrin's breathing, ragged suddenly, he saw that Brigstocke was still watching him. 'Right now we're conducting what's called an urgent interview, and with a bit of luck we'll know a lot more by the time that's finished.' He turned, hearing Boyle's voice in the corridor, and watched Brigstocke get up and head out to see what was happening. 'OK?'

'A bit of luck,' she said. 'Right.'

'Look, I know it's frustrating, but I'm hoping I'll be able to let you know more very soon.' Thorne looked up as Boyle appeared in the doorway, Roth and Brigstocke arriving behind him. Brigstocke caught Thorne's eye and shook his head. 'Catrin . . . ?'

'Worth a try, but sweet FA,' Boyle said.

Thorne moved the phone to his chest and put his hand across the mouthpiece.

'So, we'll let him get some sleep. We'll bring a doctor in to give him a shot of methadone, make sure Mr Figgis is nice and relaxed first thing tomorrow and have another crack at him. Sound like a plan?'

'Spot on,' Roth said, nodding.

Thorne brought the phone back to his ear, but Catrin Coyne had hung up.

'He'll give us what we need tomorrow,' Brigstocke said. 'He's just figuring out the best way to play it, same as they always do.'

Boyle yawned theatrically, spreading his arms wide, then nodded at Thorne. He said, 'You best get your head down as well, while you can.'

Thorne wasn't sure that getting his head down was an altogether good idea, knowing it would only give the thoughts that had begun rattling around inside it a chance to settle and take hold. Right then, keeping busy felt like the safer option. He said that he was happy to stay on a little longer. He offered to supervise the suspect's medical visit, but the DI wasn't having any of it.

'I *think* we'll manage without you for a few hours.' Boyle was smiling as he turned to leave, yawning again, the two DCs in tow. 'Now, bugger off home.'

*

There was a somewhat tetchy message from his father on the machine when Thorne got back to the house. The old man wanted to know why Thorne hadn't been across to see them over the weekend like he'd promised, when his mother had cooked specially. Why he hadn't so much as bothered to call to let them know he wasn't coming and what the hell was wrong with common courtesy.

The two messages from Jan were even more bad-tempered.

'*You can stall all you like, Tom, but this isn't going to go away. We need to do something about the house and you can't just put your fingers in your ears and pretend it isn't happening, same as you always do. I thought we were going to be reasonable about this . . .*'

Thorne thought he heard the lecturer chipping in, or trying to, just before Jan had hung up. He rewound and listened to the tape again, but he still couldn't be sure. Just the word 'come' maybe.

*Come on, why bother even trying to talk sense to him.*

*Come here, and tomorrow we'll just call an estate agent ourselves.*

*Come back to bed, darling . . .*

Thorne stabbed at the erase button. 'Twat.'

In an effort to delay putting his head down as long as possible – knowing that the rattling was now going to be that little bit louder – Thorne slid a Johnny Cash CD into the stereo and prowled from room to room for a few minutes. When he finally dropped on to the sofa, it was clear that he wouldn't be able to fight the exhaustion for very long.

He wondered how much sleep Grantleigh Figgis was likely to get, or Catrin Coyne.

Within moments, he was desperate for it.

Thinking about what Boyle had said in his office, and a few minutes later, just as Thorne had been leaving. Boyle and Roth outside in the car park, laughing and smoking, the job as good as done.

'Go on, get yourself home and put your feet up, mate. You've earned it.'

Lying there fully dressed and wanting more than anything for sleep to swallow him up, Thorne was not sure he'd earned anything. For reasons he could not explain and did not want to think about for very long, it felt more as though he owed somebody something.

# SEVENTEEN

Kieron thinks the man must have gone out somewhere. He can't hear him when he's upstairs, but he's already used to the scrape when the door opens and the slap of the man's feet on the steps when he's coming down. That happens a lot, but it's been a long time since Kieron heard anything at all.

A really long time.

Hours and hours . . .

He doesn't like it when the man comes down, but now he's starting to get scared in case the man's gone away and won't ever be coming back. He's still got plenty of crisps – a whole box of them – and chocolate and biscuits and cans of Coke, but he's trying to decide if he should start to eat everything a bit more slowly. Make things last longer. Half a biscuit a day maybe and one can of Coke, because he doesn't know if there's going to be anything else to eat.

He sits on the mattress and wonders how many days he could go without eating a single thing. How long it would take before he started to look like one of those sad African children he's seen on the TV. When they're asking people to send money or old clothes.

Like, a week, or something?

The room's starting to smell really bad, too. Up until the last time he'd gone to sleep, the man had been down a few times to take him up to the toilet, but that was ages ago, so he's had to start going in the bucket by the door. He'd tried to hold it in for as long as he could, but it had really hurt after a while and now he's started to worry about what's going to happen if the man doesn't come down again and the bucket gets full up.

He holds his breath for as long as he can.

He pulls his anorak over his head to try and block the stink out.

He knows the time would go faster if he was doing something, it always does, but he's pushed all the toys and books into one corner, because he doesn't want to play with them any more. He can play for ages with Josh, all day sometimes, but he doesn't want to touch those stupid cars or the Game Boy again, because the man bought them and the man lied to him.

Lied to him a *lot*, and that's bad.

The man told him this would be like a holiday. *Better* than a holiday. Told him they could eat pizza with pineapple on and watch TV together; that he had loads of channels, probably way more than Kieron had at home. Kieron had told him that was really expensive and his mum always says there are better things to spend money on. The man had said the money didn't matter and Kieron remembers thinking that was funny.

He remembers laughing, and the man laughing, too.

Now, Kieron feels like he's going to cry, but he breathes hard and wraps his arms around his chest until the feeling goes away. He doesn't want to do that any more, either. He cried quite a lot to start with, *way* more than he ever does at school or anything, because he doesn't like being on his own, especially in the dark. After a while, though, he didn't want the man to keep coming down, so he's been trying to stay quiet. Now, he only cries when it's impossible not to, like when he thinks of things that make him miss his mum and because he's fed up waiting for her to come and get him.

The man said she was coming. Promised him.

Then suddenly he thinks, *that's* where the man's gone and as soon as he thinks it he knows it has to be true, and begins to feel a lot better. He reaches for a bag of crisps, tears it open and starts to eat, getting happier with each mouthful. He smiles, not bothered about the dark and the smell quite so much any more, because that *must* be what's going on.

Like a surprise, Kieron thinks, because he's been such a good lad and done what he was told.

The man's gone to fetch his mum.

# PART TWO

## What's The Time, Mr Wolf?

# EIGHTEEN

It was not as if he'd been given much chance to make himself presentable when he'd been arrested and taken from his home the night before. Certainly not enough time to pick out a suitable outfit.

But even so . . .

Grantleigh Figgis had on the same sleeveless pullover he'd been wearing when Thorne had first spotted him lurking in the doorway of his flat, those same grey tracksuit bottoms. A far cry from the Sunday best of Felix Barratt and his finicky ilk. Thorne struggled with the temptation to 'accidentally' drop a pen, then lean down to see if their suspect was still sporting the furry slippers, which – unless there was a specialist Nan Unit of which Thorne was unaware – were certainly not the favoured footwear option of too many being questioned by a murder investigation team.

Though of course they knew very well that it was not the first time that the man sitting across from them – anxious and fidgety, next to a somewhat bored-looking duty solicitor – had been inside an interview room.

And they were not counting the previous evening.

Boyle told Figgis he was being interviewed under caution, then said, 'Tell me about Kevin Scott.'

Figgis groaned and stiffened a little in his chair. 'That little shit.'

'Right,' Boyle said. 'That little shit you sexually assaulted two years ago in a public toilet.'

Suddenly, Jeremy Prosser, the duty solicitor, looked a little less bored. He sat forward. 'Accused. My client was accused of sexually assaulting Mr Scott. The charges were quickly dropped, as you very well know, Detective Inspector.'

Boyle shook his head. 'Slip of the tongue.'

'The charges were dropped because they were entirely malicious.' Figgis looked at Prosser and then at Thorne, perhaps believing, albeit mistakenly, that of the two detectives in front of him, Thorne was the softer touch. 'Scott was the one who ended up getting done, later on.'

Boyle waved it away. 'No worries.'

'Tried it on once too often—'

'OK, well we'll leave all that for now, shall we?' Boyle turned over one of the sheets of paper in front of him. 'Let's move on.'

Boyle was an insufferable arsehole, but this was unquestionably an arena in which he thrived and Thorne knew exactly what the DI's game was. Happy to acknowledge his oh-so-innocent mistake and to move on, having lodged the memory of a painful incident, however legally insignificant it might prove to be, front and centre of his suspect's mind. Figgis looked every bit as shaken as Boyle wanted him to be, though he had hardly been a picture of poise or confidence to begin with.

Watching him sit down fifteen minutes earlier, Boyle had leaned across and muttered to Thorne; delighted with himself as he summed up the man's appearance with his usual pith and wit.

'He's shitting it.'

Thorne had been unable to argue.

Though far from being an expert, Thorne wondered just how much of a substitute methadone could ever be for heroin. He wasn't convinced that, if he was desperate for a pint or three of Tennent's Extra to stave off the heebie-jeebies, a can of Shandy Bass would do the trick, and Figgis certainly did not look as if he'd had a comfortable night in any sense. His face looked paler than it had done the previous evening, his hair greasier. He was wide-eyed and jittery, and that voice – soft and well spoken – had a catch in it.

Walking into the room, he'd looked like a man being poked towards the edge of a cliff.

'Let's talk about Kieron Coyne.' With the subtlety of a flying mallet, Boyle glanced across at the pile of morning newspapers he'd laid on the table before the interview had begun. Each had been helpfully opened at the story dedicated to the search for the missing boy and the individual responsible for his disappearance. The photograph provided by Catrin Coyne was prominent on every page, and though the stories varied in style and emphasis, depending on whether the paper had a red top or not, there were certain words common to almost all of them.

*Hunt. Snatched. Nightmare.*

Figgis did exactly as Boyle had been hoping and looked across at the newspapers. He tentatively reached across as though to pull one towards him, stretching out his thin fingers, before drawing his hand back at the last moment. He swallowed hard, said, 'What do you want to know?'

'Anything that might help,' Boyle said.

'I want to help,' Figgis said.

Boyle leaned back. 'Well, we shouldn't have a problem then.'

Thorne picked up the cue. 'How well did you know Kieron?'

'Pretty well, I suppose. I'm closer to his mum, obviously.'

'You were close, then,' Boyle said.

'Sorry?'

'To the boy?'

'Not in the way you're suggesting.'

'I'm not suggesting anything.' Boyle shook his head as though disappointed at being so terribly misjudged. He looked at Thorne. 'Just asking questions.'

Prosser sighed. He was doodling.

'Has Kieron ever been inside your flat, Mr Figgis?' Thorne asked.

'No ...'

'You sure about that?' The forensic team was still working in Seacole House and, though they had not discovered any evidence immediately damning, they would certainly be able to match any DNA found in the flat to the sample provided by Kieron's mother. If Figgis was lying, it would be easy enough to prove.

'Well, he might have run inside once or twice, just for a few seconds when I was talking to Cat by the front door.'

'Right.'

'Maybe he came in with his mum once. I can't really remember.'

'But he's never been in your flat on his own.'

'No.'

'Just the two of you, I mean.'

'No, never.' Figgis had been hunched over in his chair and staring down, as his finger traced a pattern in the metal tabletop, but now he straightened up and looked at Thorne. 'Absolutely not.'

Boyle turned over another sheet of paper, studied the page for a few seconds. 'How's your memory this morning, Mr Figgis?'

Figgis looked at him and shrugged. 'Fine.'

'Because last night you told us that on Saturday morning, when Kieron went missing, you were at home in your flat with a man you'd met the previous evening.'

'That's right.'

'I only ask because last night you couldn't really remember very much about him.'

104

Figgis sighed, scratched at his neck. 'No, because I didn't *know* much about him. Because I'd only met him on Friday night.'

'Alan, you said.' Thorne waited until Figgis looked at him. 'His name was Alan.'

Figgis nodded, closed his eyes as he repeated the story he'd told them the night before. 'Alan, correct. I met him Friday night at the Astoria and he came back to mine. We had sex—'

'Did you take drugs together?'

'Well, I can't see what that has to do with anything, but yes, we did.'

'Just trying to get the picture,' Boyle said.

'We had sex, we went to sleep, I made him a late breakfast the next morning, and he went home. That's it. I don't know his second name, I don't know what he does for a living, I don't know where he lives. I know nothing about him.'

Boyle could not suppress a smirk. 'Just what he likes to get up to in bed.'

Figgis stared back. 'That's the way it is.'

Boyle let out a long breath, like he was shocked. 'Is it?'

'This is . . . ' Figgis stopped and breathed deeply for a few seconds. For the first time he looked more irritated than frightened. 'It's ridiculous. Why the hell would I want to hurt Kieron? Or Cat? She's my friend and he's . . . well, he's a lovely boy.' He looked to Prosser, who immediately dug into his pocket for a handkerchief and passed it across.

'Take a moment if you need to,' Prosser said.

Figgis dabbed at his eyes with a hand that was visibly shaking and, when he spoke, his voice was cracked and whispery. 'It's ridiculous. It's just not . . . *fair.*'

'Was Kevin Scott a lovely boy?' Boyle asked.

Prosser rolled his eyes. 'Oh, for heaven's sake.' The solicitor was about to continue, but Figgis cut him off.

'Yes, he was.' There was a degree of power in his voice suddenly. 'At least I thought he was.'

Boyle nodded. 'See, I'm just the old-fashioned sort, a bit of a romantic, I suppose you'd say. I can't help wondering why you'd be hanging around in a public toilet trying to have sex with a seventeen-year-old boy?'

Prosser said, 'That was never proved,' but Figgis did not seem to be listening.

'Because I'm a homosexual.' Figgis said the word slowly, relishing it, but at the same time imbuing it with the disgust he presumed it would instil in the Scotsman, that he had presumably seen it instil in others like him. 'It's what some of us do, now and again, if there's no other way. It's very risky, of course, because the likes of Kevin Scott can take advantage. On the occasion you seem so very keen to talk about, I was offered sex, by a boy I firmly believed to be older than seventeen.' He leaned towards Boyle, the handkerchief now balled in his fist. 'He made it very clear what he wanted, but as soon as I reciprocated, he backed away and announced that he was only seventeen. He said he wanted money and that unless I gave him everything I had on me he was going to call the police and tell them I'd . . . molested him. I told him to go right ahead, so that's exactly what the little bastard did. He laid it on nice and thick and I was arrested. The police officers, who I should say were rather more assiduous than you, worked out what was going on rather quickly, and after a good deal of unpleasantness the charges were dropped. All's well that ends well, right? Except of course it doesn't end, because that arrest is still a matter of record. A stain that doesn't go away. Because the likes of you are still able to drag it up whenever it suits them and do their utmost to use it against me.'

Thorne watched as Figgis leaned slowly away, dropped his head back and raised his eyes to the ceiling. Heavenwards. He'd seen no indication that the man was remotely religious, but it seemed, at that moment, as though he might have concluded that divine intervention was his best and only hope.

'That's all very helpful, Mr Figgis,' Boyle said. 'So, thank you.'

Now, Thorne watched Boyle gather his pieces of paper together then tap the edges against the tabletop to get them good and straight. He knew the way the man worked, the strategies that he believed would yield results, especially when he believed wholeheartedly that the person he was dealing with was guilty. Get them rattled, then wear them down.

Boyle said, 'Right. Let's start again, shall we?'

An hour later, Figgis on his way back to a cell, Thorne stood with Boyle next to the coffee machine. The DI was fired up and full of it, happy with his game.

'He's sharp,' Boyle said. 'Give him that much. All that business about how Kieron *might* have popped into his flat once or twice. He knows full well that if and when we find the boy's DNA in there, he's covered, because he told us about it. The car's a different matter, though. We find evidence in there, he's not got a leg to stand on.'

'Maybe he just told us that because it was the truth,' Thorne said.

Boyle looked at Thorne as if he'd just suggested the Earth might actually be flat. He brandished his sheaf of notes. 'Right, I'm away to get this lot typed up.'

There was plenty of material. Over the course of a two-hour interview, they'd talked in further detail about the nature of Figgis's relationship with Kieron Coyne, enquired about the movements of his red VW Polo, and tried without success to elicit more information about the mysterious Alan.

'So, what's next?' Thorne asked.

'Let's bring your birdwatcher in, shall we? Try to put a few holes in Figgis's so-called alibi.'

'Sounds good.'

'Should just about put the tin lid on it, I reckon. Then we go back at him, find out what he's done with the boy.'

'We should see if we can find this bloke he picked up.' Thorne stuck a few coins of his own into the drinks machine. '*Says* he picked up.'

Boyle nodded, looking at something in the notes. 'Yeah, obviously.'

'Get someone down to the Astoria, find out if anyone there knows him or can remember seeing Figgis leave with anyone.'

'No bother,' Boyle said. 'I'm on it.'

As Boyle was about to leave, Thorne said, 'If some woman came on to *you* in a public toilet, you'd be up for it, wouldn't you?'

'What would a woman be doing in a men's toilet?'

'Come on, you know what I'm saying.'

But Boyle was already turning away, grinning.

# NINETEEN

At the same time as Gordon Boyle was strategically laying out a selection of the Monday morning papers in an interview room at Islington station, a single copy of the *Daily Mirror* was being set down rather more forcefully on the sixth floor of a tower block two miles to the south; slapped angrily on to the coffee table in Catrin Coyne's living room.

'Were you going to tell me?'

'There were other people needed telling first,' Cat said. 'His father.'

'*I'm* his father.'

'No.' Cat sat forward and shook her head, but took care to keep her tone nice and even because she was stating what she considered to be a self-evident truth. 'You're not. Kieron has a good father.'

'Good?'

'I know exactly what Billy is, but he loves his son. And I love him.'

The man was pacing back and forth between the sofa and the window, the ash from his cigarette falling to the floor as he waved his hands around. 'Oh yeah, I get it. All that "Stand By Your Man" bollocks.'

'As opposed to standing by your child, you mean?'

'I would have done.'

'Yeah, right.'

'Course I would, if you'd given me the chance.'

'Rubbish. I knew it the minute I told you I was pregnant, knew you wanted nothing to do with it. The look on your face.'

'I was surprised, that's all.' The man looked hurt at Cat's suggestion. 'I mean, we only did it a couple of times.' He sat down on the arm of the sofa, pretended not to notice as Cat inched away from him. 'Can't help it if I've got balls loaded with the good stuff, can I?'

'Why are you here?' Cat asked.

He pointed towards the paper on the table. 'Why do you think I'm here? That's my flesh and blood that's missing and I only get to find out when I read the fucking paper.'

'So, all of a sudden, you care. That what you're telling me?'

'I've always cared.'

'What's his favourite food?' She looked at him and waited. 'When's his birthday?'

The man swore and got to his feet again. He leaned down to stub out his cigarette then immediately reached into his pocket for the packet. 'I was doing you a favour. Keeping well out of the way, you know, to make things easier for you. You seriously trying to tell me that's not what you wanted?'

Cat knew there was little point in trying to deny it.

'Yeah, so.' He pointed. 'What *you* wanted. Doesn't mean I wasn't thinking about him, does it? Doesn't mean I didn't wonder how the little bugger was doing every day or that I didn't worry about him.' He lit another cigarette then reached down and picked up the newspaper. 'Turns out I was right to worry.' He shook his head as he read the story again. 'I mean, Christ, Cat . . . how could you—'

110

'Don't you fucking dare.' Cat scrambled to her feet and reached across to try and slap the newspaper from his hands. When he stepped back and lifted it above his head so that she was unable to reach, she grabbed fistfuls of his shirt instead. 'Don't you dare.'

'I wasn't trying—'

'You've got no right.'

'OK, easy . . . '

She held on tight to him, pressing her forehead against his chest and they stayed that way for half a minute or so, Cat clinging to him, while he stared over her head, blew out thin streams of smoke and made reassuring noises.

'Come on, now.'

He watched her turn to walk slowly back to the sofa and lower herself on to it like a woman three times her age. He said, 'Look, I didn't come here to start a row or anything.' He waved the paper again. 'It's in all of them, you know, what's happened. Every single one. The papers and the telly, they'll be all over this now, looking at all the . . . angles or whatever, so I thought you might need a bit of support, that's all. And like I said, I have got a . . . vested interest, or whatever you call it.'

Cat looked up at him, expressionless.

'I mean I'm not daft. I wasn't expecting you to put flags out, anything like that.'

'What *were* you expecting?'

He smiled and shrugged, looked at his watch as though it made a difference. 'Well, a drink might be nice for a kick-off.'

# TWENTY

Roth and Brigstocke seemed content to stand, so Thorne took the seat next to Boyle in front of the monitor and pressed the necessary buttons. The screen flickered into life, displaying the live feed from a room two floors below them at Highgate station. A black and white image which, at first glance, might have been a still, had not one of the eight men sitting on plastic chairs leaned back suddenly and yawned.

A voice off-camera: 'Shouldn't be too much longer.'

Boyle pointed at the screen, ran a finger along the line. 'Got to hand it to whoever rounded this lot up.' The finger moved again, jabbed at the man sitting second from the left. 'Can't have been easy finding seven blokes who looked anything like this freak.'

'Best detective work I've seen in ages,' Roth said.

Thorne leaned forward and looked at the 'freak' in question. Though Grantleigh Figgis – after a brief consultation with the duty solicitor – had given his permission several hours before to the identity parade, he now looked as though he might be regretting his decision. He sat, straight-backed, palms flat on his knees, his lips moving as though he was giving himself a last-minute pep talk. Like the seven men lined up alongside him, he wore a flat cap he'd been given in the hope it might make the job of the man tasked with identifying him easier. All of them had been asked to push the caps back so as not to shield their features and, though the lighting was basic and the image hardly pinprick sharp, the tension etched across Figgis's face was clear enough.

'He's a worried man,' Boyle said.

Thorne heard a cigarette being lit behind him, turned when a hand was laid on his shoulder. 'So he should be,' Roth said, squeezing. 'If Tom here likes you for something, well . . . it's a done deal, right?'

'That's what they reckon,' Boyle said.

Thorne turned back to the monitor. He was every bit as fired up as Boyle and the rest of them, but now he sat and watched Figgis talking to himself and wondered if the man he'd been responsible for bringing in was as nervous as he was, or had slept any worse. It didn't much matter, either way. Thorne knew exactly what *he* was afraid of, but he'd been in similar situations many times before and reminded himself that a scared suspect was not necessarily a guilty one.

Innocent or otherwise, Figgis would be terrified of being picked out.

The men in the line-up had begun to fidget.

'What's taking them so long?' Brigstocke asked.

Thorne knew that in an adjacent room, a uniformed inspector who was unconnected with the case and had been appointed as identification officer for the day would be running through the procedure with Felix Barratt and with Prosser, the solicitor. Though he had already declared himself happy with the set-up, Barratt would once again be offered the option of attempting the identification from behind a one-way mirror. The men on the chairs had already been given their instructions, but it was important that the man who would try to pick one of them out was equally comfortable with what was about to happen.

113

They could only hope he was as good at identifying people as he claimed to be with birds.

'Here we go.' Boyle slapped his hands against his thighs.

The ID Officer led Barratt and Prosser into the room and the uniformed officer already present instructed the men on the chairs to raise the numbered pieces of paper they had each been given.

Grantleigh Figgis was number two.

Thorne watched as the inspector stepped close to Felix Barratt. 'I'm now going to ask you to look at a group of people, one of whom may or may not be the man you claim to have seen on Saturday afternoon, getting into a car on Archway Road.'

Barratt straightened his tie and tugged at the hem of his tweed jacket. He said, 'I understand.'

'Could you please walk along the line and back again? Take all the time you need . . . '

Barratt did as he was asked, walking nice and slowly, stopping for several seconds in front of each candidate, before turning to the inspector. 'Could you ask them to stand up?'

'Oh, for Christ's sake,' Boyle said.

'It might make it easier,' Barratt said.

The inspector asked Prosser if he had any objections. The solicitor shook his head and the men were instructed to stand. Barratt moved along the line one more time then walked back to stand next to the inspector.

He said, 'OK.'

'Is the man you saw on Saturday afternoon in this room?'

Boyle leaned closer to the screen. 'Come on.'

Barratt lowered his voice, as though wary of being overheard, but the sound was clear enough to those gathered around the monitor. 'Number two,' he said.

Boyle pumped his fist. 'You fucking beauty!'

'Well, I think it *might* be number two.'

'Oh shit,' Roth said.

Boyle was on his feet, his excitement having instantly given way to irritation. 'He *thinks*?'

'It might be number two.' The inspector stared at Barratt, then made a careful note on his clipboard. 'But you're not sure.'

Thorne was watching Grantleigh Figgis.

His eyes were closed and he was breathing heavily.

The piece of paper with his number on slipped from his fingers and floated to the floor.

'Not *sure*, no,' Barratt said. 'The man I saw was on the other side of the road. I was very clear about that when the officer came round.'

Boyle turned to look at Thorne, as though the pointless farce being played out for them on screen was somehow all his fault. Thorne looked right back at him and said, 'Everything Barratt told me was in my report.'

The DI had clearly seen and heard enough and Roth was quick to follow him as he stalked from the room.

'*I* read your report,' Brigstocke said. He joined Thorne at the monitor and they watched Felix Barratt being led from the room before another officer moved forward to escort Grantleigh Figgis back to his cell. 'Let's be honest, it was never really on the cards, was it?'

'Boyle's a born optimist,' Thorne said.

Brigstocke smiled. 'One word for it.'

They caught up with Roth and Boyle in the corridor.

' ... would have clinched it, no worries,' Boyle said. 'But there's no chance he'll go for it now.'

Thorne did not need to ask who or what the DI was talking about. A positive identification might have persuaded the superintendent that, though there was not yet enough evidence to charge Figgis, they certainly had grounds to extend the custody period. Now, barring a last-gasp confession or the miraculously fast return of positive DNA results, they would have no choice but to release their suspect within the statutory twenty-four hours.

There was not much time left.

'So, we make it work for us,' Boyle said. 'If life gives you lemons, all that.'

Roth grunted his enthusiastic endorsement.

Thorne looked at them both, waited. Roth studied his shoes and, when Boyle deigned to reveal his plan of action, he spoke as if explaining something blindingly obvious to a seriously remedial cadet.

'His sort are always the same, aren't they?'

Thorne kept his mouth shut, though if he knew anything with certainty it was that Boyle was talking nonsense. Half a dozen of that 'sort' selected at random were unlikely to have much more in common than any other group.

'Like dogs returning to their own vomit.'

'I've never had a dog,' Thorne said.

'Dead or alive, he'll want to go back to wherever he's left the boy.' Boyle left a second or two for acknowledgement of his genius then pressed on when it was not forthcoming. 'I'm telling you, he won't be able to resist. So, we cut him loose and we watch him. Let him do our job for us.'

Thorne thought that, as cunning plans went, it was up there with Baldrick's best, but chose once again not to speak up, knowing that others would.

'Sounds bang-on to me, boss,' Roth said.

At that moment, the identification officer stepped into the corridor and walked towards them. He shrugged, brandishing the clipboard he'd used a few minutes earlier to record the result of the ID parade.

He said, 'I can't put it on here for obvious reasons and it's no use to us officially, but for what it's worth, Barratt told me after we'd left the room that he thought it probably *was* number two.'

116

'That's helpful of him,' Thorne said.

'But that he wasn't sure the man he saw was quite that tall.'

Boyle muttered, 'Twat,' before turning away to confer with Roth about surveillance arrangements.

Thorne could not be sure who the insult had been aimed at, but guessed that was exactly what Boyle had intended.

# TWENTY-ONE

Once her unwanted visitor had drunk all the booze in the flat and she had finally managed to get rid of him, Cat decided that she needed some air. She walked down the main road, then cut into Whittington Park and sat on a bench at the corner of the football pitch. It wasn't somewhere too many locals would go after dark unless they were looking to buy drugs or fancied being robbed, but it was nice enough when there were people about.

She sat and enjoyed the warmth of the sun on her face.

She tried to blot out the shouts of children from the playground.

She thought about Billy.

It was hard to imagine just how bad he would be feeling banged up in there, how helpless. How much worse than the way she knew he felt every minute of the day. Bored shitless, killing time, the stink of his cellmate's farts every night and slopping-out every morning.

It was all there in his letters.

Missing her. Missing their boy.

He was a silly bastard but still, she had lied to him. Done the dirty behind his back, which was unforgivable. No, he hadn't been around back then when she'd needed him, needed *somebody*, and it was only those couple of times when a few drinks had done what they did, but all the same she knew how she would feel if he'd been the one playing away. How badly she'd have wanted to hurt him.

They had Kieron, though, which had always made everything OK.

They hadn't made him, but they had him.

She felt the tears come, laid her head back and let the sun dry them. They *used* to have him . . .

It wasn't like she'd never thought about any of this before, or didn't feel like a whore every single time she looked at her son, but the man bowling through her door that morning had made a shitty situation so much worse, and it wasn't as if she didn't know that he was up to something. She wasn't buying the father-suddenly-choosing-to-care act for a moment. Even if she hadn't seen him for the best part of ten years and had no real idea what he'd been up to since Kieron was born, she knew him well enough.

The likes of him usually had an angle.

People like Billy. People like *her*.

She wandered back on to the main road, bought a bottle from the off-licence to help her sleep, a pasty from the brand-new Greggs and trudged back up the hill. She tried to eat and tried every bit as hard to keep her head down, telling herself not to stare whenever a child walked past, alone or with an adult. Unable to help herself, she looked hard at every single one.

One woman stopped, yanked her child back and glared. Said, '*What?*'

Fifty yards from the entrance to the block, Cat saw that she had another visitor. Leaning against the grubby glass doors and looking at her watch, like she was waiting for a bus. Cat didn't break stride as she dropped what was left of the pasty into a bin and tried to decide if she should run headlong into the woman's arms or slap her stupid.

'I'm sorry,' Maria said. Cat was still half a dozen paces away, so the older woman waited. 'I probably should have phoned.' She glanced hopefully past Cat, towards the lifts. She opened her mouth and closed it again, set herself.

Cat had made her mind up. She wasn't going to slap her, but she wasn't going to invite her up for tea and cake either. 'Yeah?'

'Only I saw the papers this morning, and thought, well . . .'

*Another one,* Cat thought. 'I might need some support?'

'Yes, of course.' Maria shifted from foot to foot. 'I mean, whether you'd want it or not was another question, but actually, there was a journalist hanging about here when I arrived.' She raised an eyebrow. 'Well, we shouldn't be very surprised, I suppose.'

Cat ignored the *we*, looked around.

'Oh no, don't worry, he's long gone. I've been here a while.'

'Did you speak to him?'

'Only to tell him to piss off,' Maria said.

Cat smiled in spite of herself and Maria smiled, too.

'Cheeky so-and-so asked me if I knew where you were, when you were coming back. He asked me if I was a friend of yours.' She looked away. 'I didn't say anything, obviously.'

The implication would have been clear enough, even without the woman's somewhat sorry-for-herself expression.

*I didn't say anything because I didn't know the answer.*

Cat wasn't sure she could be much help.

She said, 'They've arrested someone.'

'*What?* I mean . . . who?'

'I'm not supposed to say.'

'Well, that's good.'

'I suppose.'

'You must be so relieved.'

Cat felt anything but relief. It took a good deal of effort to stop

120

herself shouting: *I don't give a toss who they arrest as long as they find out where Kieron is.* She could see that Maria was waiting for more; hoping for it. Cat said, 'I don't know what's happening. They haven't told me.'

'I'm sure you'll be the first to know when there's news,' Maria said.

Cat nodded and stared at the woman who, under normal circumstances, would have been the second to know. A woman to whom she'd been so close until two days before, who knew almost everything about her.

Maria looked tired.

She still looked stylish, of course, but had not made the usual effort.

Cat wanted so much to tell Maria Ashton the one thing she didn't know, but that could never happen. Not while Cat still had the urge to throw her to the pavement, to pull out her glossy hair at the roots and scratch every inch of make-up off her face.

It was an ugly urge, Cat recognised that. Shameful and pointless. But it refused to go away.

'How's Josh doing?' She waited, watching Maria's eyes fill, watching small white teeth gnaw at a trembling lip.

'Oh, Cat.'

'Look, I need to go.' Cat marched across and opened the doors, then turned. She said, 'Just so you know. So you can tell Josh. Wherever my Kieron is, he's missing him.'

# TWENTY-TWO

'About bloody time,' Jim Thorne said. 'Thought you'd lost the number.'

'Yeah, sorry. It's—'

'Work . . . course it is. Don't worry, I'm only winding you up.'

Thorne had carried the phone through to the sitting room. He pulled his feet up, kept one eye on the highlights of the Netherlands v Scotland match from that afternoon.

'Your mum worries, that's all.'

'I know,' Thorne said.

'Well, you never stop worrying about your kids, do you? Doesn't matter how old they are.'

'I know,' Thorne said.

'Especially now.'

'Right.'

*Now everything's gone to shit. Now your wife's buggered off and there's a divorce to get sorted. Now you're starting again.*

'So, everything good?' his father asked.

Thorne almost laughed. His old man had never been the

most tactful or socially aware of souls. Always more comfortable around machines than he was with people. 'Yeah, ticking along,' he said. 'Just got a big case on, so . . . '

There was a short silence before his father said, 'Righto.'

Thorne could hear his parents' TV in the background. His dad was watching the football, too.

'I meant to say, your mum went to see the quack about her blood pressure this morning. Had to nag her, mind you. Reckons it's still a bit too high for his liking.'

'Has he put her on something?'

'Oh, she's been on tablets for ages. What d'you call them . . . the red and white ones. Now, he's told her she needs to sort her diet out and she's not very happy about it.'

'You need to make sure she sticks to it,' Thorne said.

'This is your mother I'm talking about.'

'OK, well maybe you could do a bit more cooking.'

'I *cook*.' His father sounded put out. 'Sausage and mash or whatever. Big breakfast on a Sunday.'

'Yeah, but something a bit healthier wouldn't hurt now and again. The odd salad or whatever.' Even as Thorne was suggesting it, he knew that it would hurt a good deal and that he was probably the last person from whom anyone should take nutritional advice. 'All I'm saying.'

His father grunted. 'Anyway, I'll put her on. We going to be seeing you any time soon? This side of Christmas would be nice.'

Thorne began to answer, said that he'd do his best, but it all depended on . . . then he heard his dad shouting his mother's name and knew there was little point carrying on.

'Maureen! He's on the phone.'

Thorne turned to the TV. Nil-nil at Villa Park and, having checked the result already, he knew he wasn't going to be seeing goals any time soon. He looked at his watch. Grantleigh Figgis was probably being bailed at that very moment; shortly to return to a home that had been extensively 'redecorated' in the way that only half a dozen Scenes of Crime Officers and a full forensic team could manage.

Thorne had never been inside Figgis's flat, but found it hard to imagine it had been a tasteful picture of order and calm before it had been turned upside down. Not too many junkies lived in show-homes.

'Hello, love . . .'

He chatted happily to his mother for a few minutes, content to put heroin addicts and missing children to the back of his mind for as long as he could manage. He asked her what the doctor had said and she told him she was fine. She said that if anything was responsible for putting her blood pressure up it was his father and that there was no way on God's green earth she was going to eat bloody rabbit food three times a day.

She was always keen to talk about eating.

'Have you got plenty in?'

'I'm not going to starve, Mum.'

'Plenty of stuff in the freezer, I mean.'

'Yes—'

'You can't live on takeaways.'

Thorne did not want to tell her that most of the stuff she'd brought round and put in the freezer for him the week after Jan had left was still there. Shepherd's pies and casseroles, an enormous moussaka her friend Arianna had made. He said, 'I'm fine, I promise.'

'So, have you seen her then?'

'Who?

'Jan. Who else would I be talking about?'

His mother was as socially awkward as his father was, but in a rather different way. She was hard-wired to broach subjects that should by rights have been off-limits, to say the unsayable; to tell someone that they'd put on weight while all those around her were talking about kids or dogs or weather.

124

'We've talked,' Thorne said. 'Well, we've exchanged messages. But I haven't seen her for a while.'

It wasn't strictly true. He'd seen her coming out of the lecturer's house early one morning. On several mornings, in fact, watching her from his car parked on a side street opposite. She'd looked tired, he'd thought – his mother would have told her as much to her face – and he'd spent the drive back to Highbury imagining each and every gymnastic thing she might have been doing the night before to wear herself out.

'Well you should,' his mother said. 'Get all this squared away.'

'Yeah, I will,' Thorne said. 'Just got a lot on at the minute, with work.'

'I know, love.' She let out a long, rattly sigh. 'I suppose that means we won't be seeing you for a while?'

'I was telling Dad, I'm going to try and get over as soon as I can.'

'Oh, that's good,' she said. 'I'll cook you something nice and maybe you can spend the night.'

Thorne's pager sounded on the table next to the TV. He got up to look and told his mother that he needed to go, that it was a work thing.

'Make sure you bring back all my bowls and casserole dishes.'

'I will—'

'When you come over.'

'OK, I'll call at the weekend.'

She said, 'You stay safe.'

As soon as he'd hung up, Thorne rang through to the incident room and a sergeant on the night team told him that Catrin Coyne was trying to get hold of him. She'd left several messages.

'Right.' Thorne remembered how angry the woman had been when he'd called her the night before. The dressing-down she'd given him, after they'd arrested Figgis.

'She sounded like she'd had a drink,' the sergeant said.

When Catrin answered the phone a few minutes later, Thorne

could hear at once what the man had been talking about.

'I need to see you.' Before Thorne could respond, she said it again, more slowly, as though she wasn't sure she'd said it right the first time.

'OK,' Thorne said. Whatever she wanted to see him about, she didn't sound angry.

'Can you come over first thing in the morning?'

'Is everything all right?'

It took her long enough to answer for Thorne to start thinking that she'd wandered away from the phone to fetch herself another drink, or even fallen asleep.

Finally, she said, 'Thing is, I haven't been completely honest.'

Cat was woken an hour or so later by a soft, persistent knocking. She swung her legs off the sofa and blundered out into the hall, dry-mouthed and groggy. The man at the door looked every bit as terrible as she felt, but she sobered up quickly enough to push the door quickly back towards him, those all-important few inches, to make it clear there would be no invitation to come inside.

The hostile reaction – she'd heard herself say 'No' as she'd wrapped both hands around the edge of the door and shoved – had been instinctive, but Cat was still a little alarmed by how unfamiliar it was.

How unlike her.

Figgis took a step back and said her name.

'It's late,' she said.

'I know.' Figgis shoved one hand into the pocket of his jacket, clawed the fingers of the other through his hair, as though there were things in it that were making him uncomfortable. 'They've only just let me come home.'

'You probably shouldn't be here,' Cat said. '*Here*, I mean.'

She stared at him, while he looked at the wall to the side of the door, at the letter box, at his shoes. Someone was shouting on the floor above and the lift clanked and growled as it passed them on its way down.

He said, 'I'm really sorry about Kieron.'

Cat said nothing because there was nothing to say.

'I didn't do anything.' Figgis lifted a foot off the ground, as though to take a step towards the door, then planted it slowly back where it was.

He looked like a big lost bird, Cat thought.

'I didn't *do* anything.'

'I'm tired, Grant.' She leaned her head against the edge of the door, moved forward with it. 'I'm so fucking tired.'

Now, it was really kicking off on the floor above. Someone was a *selfish wanker* and someone else was telling both of them to keep it down.

Just before she closed the door, Cat said, 'You look like shit, by the way.'

# TWENTY-THREE

Kieron thinks his dad looks like a soldier.

It's hard to remember *exactly* what he looks like, it's been so long, but he remembers how strong his dad is. He remembers how easily his dad can lift him up, like he hardly weighs anything, and when he closes his eyes to try and see his dad's face, he *thinks* he had a beard like someone he saw on TV once, in a programme about the army his mum was watching.

A soldier with a scraggly beard, who was brave and good at fighting.

It was ages ago when he first met his dad, and ages and ages since he last saw him. He remembers how excited he was, that first time. His mum had been telling him for weeks that his dad was coming back. She knew exactly which day the job he'd been doing was going to finish. She put up balloons and everything. There was a big party and his dad got a bit drunk which was really funny, even though his dad looked really sad after everyone had left.

Kieron tried not to cry when his dad had to go off to do his job again, because his mum told him to try and be a big boy,

128

even though *she* cried a lot. He could hear her through the wall of his bedroom. She doesn't know exactly when he'll be back this time, though. She says it depends on all sorts of different things; that it's complicated.

He'll be amazed at how tall you are, she always tells him that. He won't hardly be able to believe it. What a big strong lad you've become.

He says he can't wait to see you.

Kieron knows that's true, because his mum shows him those bits in his dad's letters, but Kieron thinks his dad probably won't be *that* surprised at how much he's grown, because his mum's been sending photos. Loads and loads of photos . . .

Now, Kieron's starting to think that because there's no definite time for his dad to come back, because it's *complicated*, that maybe his dad will be coming here instead of going home. Coming here specially, to take him away from the man upstairs.

He could lift the man up easy, Kieron thinks.

The man had come back eventually, but not with his mum like Kieron had been hoping. He'd tried his hardest but hadn't been able to stop himself crying, however much the man told him not to.

Same thing with the food. He'd been trying to make it last when the man was away, but eventually he'd got so hungry that he'd almost finished it by the time the door opened and the man brought him some more down.

More crisps and biscuits and Coke. Chocolate.

The man told Kieron how sorry he was that he'd been gone for such a long time and that he wouldn't do it again. It was a work thing, he said, something stupid he couldn't get out of. The man had missed him very much, he said. He hoped Kieron had missed him, too.

Kieron said that he had, because he could tell that was what the man wanted him to say.

It made the man happy.

Same as when they went out into the woods behind the house. The man says it's important to get some fresh air every couple of days, that it's good to have a bit of exercise. It was almost dark when they went and really quiet, not like the woods he goes to with his mum, but he doesn't like to think about that place any more. The man held his hand and told him there was nothing to be scared about and told him exactly which kind of owl was making the 'to-whit-to-whoo' noise in the trees. He said it would be silly trying to run off anywhere because there was nowhere to go, and that there was no point in shouting, because there wasn't another house for miles and nobody could hear. Only the foxes and badgers and things. He told Kieron to try, kept saying, 'Go on,' and laughing about it. So Kieron had shouted as loud as he could and screamed until his throat had started to hurt.

The man had said, 'See?' and then they'd walked back to the house.

He doesn't really want to do what the man says, but he knows it's better if the man is smiling and isn't shouting. His mum always says that if someone is doing something mean it's best not to fight back, because that usually only makes things worse. He knows what happens when people lose their temper. He doesn't want the man to get angry and turn the light off. He doesn't want him to not empty the stinky bucket on purpose or take any of the food away.

He's tired, so he lies down on the mattress.

Kieron decides that when he sees his mum, he'll tell her that he remembered what she'd said about people being mean. He'll tell his dad too, even though he doesn't think his dad exactly agrees with his mum about not fighting back and all that. He was only three, or three and a half, but he remembers them arguing about it, shouting when he was upstairs. His dad telling his mum that the only way to deal with bullies was by teaching them a lesson.

Something like that.

Sticking up for yourself.

He closes his eyes and tries to imagine what his dad would say if he came into the room right then. Smashed the door open like the Incredible Hulk and ran down the stairs. It's hard though, and Kieron cries just a bit, because he still can't get his dad's face right, like it's a blurry picture on the TV.

# TWENTY-FOUR

They met just after eight on Tuesday morning, at a café on the south side of the Archway roundabout; a busy little Turkish place where Thorne had eaten several times before. Thorne was hungry and ordered a Mediterranean omelette, with feta, spinach and spicy sausage. Feeling the need for a jolt of caffeine, he asked for a can of Coke to go with it.

Cat drank tea and ate toast while she told him all about a man called Dean Meade.

'We went to the same school.' She turned and pointed. 'Just over there, in Hornsey. So, he'd always been a mate, sort of . . . part of the gang. We didn't see a lot of each other for ages after we left, then hardly at all after me and Billy got together. Just in the pub now and again, sort of thing.'

'Then you started seeing him again after Billy went inside.'

'Not the way you mean,' she said. 'Yeah, I saw a bit more of Dean after Billy got sent down that first time. He'd come over to the flat for a beer and a catch-up or maybe we'd go the pictures or something. It was a bit of company, that's all. He had a girlfriend then, anyway.'

'So, what happened?'

Cat pushed her plate away, picked up her mug with both hands. 'Yeah, I suppose there'd always been a spark, or whatever. We'd messed about a few times when we were kids, and he was still decent enough looking. I know it's not much of an excuse to say I was pissed. That we were both pissed.'

'You don't need to make excuses to me,' Thorne said.

'I'm just telling you how it was,' she said.

'Fair enough.'

'A few too many beers one night and we got silly, that's all.'

'One night? You were unlucky then.'

She blinked slowly. 'It was a few nights. So, I was mad with Billy for being so stupid and I was miserable. I was still trying to get my head round the fact that any time I wanted to see the bloke I'd thought I was settling down with, it meant schlepping all the way down to Wandsworth prison. I was all over the place and Dean was a shoulder to cry on, I suppose.'

Thorne ate and waited.

'Once I found out I was pregnant, I decided I'd have to come clean with Billy. I knew it wouldn't be easy and I knew how he'd react because it was fair enough and I'd have been exactly the same . . . but he wasn't going to be out for a while, so it seemed like the best thing to do. Then, once I told Dean and it was obvious that he wasn't too keen on sticking around, I couldn't see much point in telling Billy anything, except . . . he was going to be a dad.'

'What about the dates?'

'Well, there was only a couple of weeks in it and Kieron came a bit early anyway, so there were never any questions. All Billy cared about was having a son. So, that was it. Dean couldn't get away fast enough, I had Kieron, then eventually, I had Billy back as well.'

'Happy ending,' Thorne said.

'Happy as I was ever going to get.'

'So, why has the charming Mr Meade decided to come back?'

Cat half-smiled at Thorne's description, then grunted her distaste. 'Oh, because of what's happened to Kieron, he says. Because he cares about him . . . he's *always* cared.'

Thorne pushed sausage and cheese on to his fork and lifted it. 'Cares enough to have taken him, you think?'

'*Dean?*'

'Well, let's say he *does* care. A few years go by, he sees his son growing up . . . thinks he can do a better job of raising him than you can, but knows that you're in the way. Knows that Billy's very much in the way, even if he isn't around. So, maybe Dean decides he wants his son and does something stupid. He wouldn't be the first absent father to snatch his child.'

Cat was shaking her head well before Thorne had finished. 'No chance,' she said. 'And even if he did, which he didn't, why come knocking on my door a couple of days later?'

Thorne chewed, well aware that, even though his line of questioning had been the obvious one to pursue once Cat had come clean, she had a good point. He swallowed. 'You should have told us straight away.'

'Don't you think I know that? I almost called you half a dozen times, even before Dean showed up.'

Thorne knew why she hadn't spoken up, of course; what she'd been afraid of. Whatever Cat chose to tell the inquiry would – theoretically – be treated in the strictest confidence, but some teams were . . . leakier than others and there could never be a cast-iron guarantee that information would not get out somewhere along the line. Cat had not wanted to risk that happening and word reaching HMP Whitehill. Whatever she had told Thorne about there never being any violence at home, it was obvious what Billy Coyne was capable of.

Who knew how a man like that would react to finding out that the child he'd believed to be his own for seven years was not?

'Anyway, why are you even asking about Dean? What about *Grant?*'

'Well, until anyone is actually charged—'

'He came to see me last night. When he got back.'

Thorne leaned forward. 'What did he say?'

'What do you think he said? That it isn't him. It was really bloody awkward.'

'It's a tricky situation.'

'What, me living next door to the bloke you arrested for abducting my son? Yeah, just a bit. Going to be a bag of laughs standing next to him in the lift.'

'I'm sorry,' Thorne said. He knew that under normal circumstances steps would have been taken to avoid a situation that was at best uncomfortable and at worst potentially dangerous, but he understood why Boyle – however misguided his masterplan was – hadn't chosen to take them. The last thing he wanted was to have Grantleigh Figgis stashed away in a safe house. He needed the suspect somewhere he felt relaxed, somewhere he could come and go while being watched at all times. 'We could make sure there's always a couple of officers outside, if it would make you feel safer.' Like they wouldn't be there anyway. 'Move you somewhere, maybe.'

'I don't feel unsafe,' Cat said.

'That's OK, then.'

'I can't speak for him.' She drained the last of her tea. 'Why did you let him go, anyway?' She stared at him. 'There was a witness, you said.'

Thorne knew that – especially considering Catrin Coyne's proximity to the suspect – he should trot out the same old line about an *ongoing inquiry*. Tell her he was *unable to go into details at this stage*. But he could see how desperately this woman needed to know what was happening, and he knew that she, above everyone else, had a right to.

He sat back and said, 'We didn't have enough, simple as that. We need a bit more time to gather evidence.'

'What did he say when you had him?'

'Same as he told you.'

'Do you believe him?'

Thorne had changed his mind several times in the previous twenty-four hours. Yes, there had been something close to certainty when he'd first encountered Catrin Coyne's strange neighbour, but Thorne was all too aware how dangerous that feeling was. That same certainty he'd felt shaking hands with a man at a police station ten years previously. An unasked-for *knowing*, that still fuelled smirks and sarky comments from Boyle and the rest of them.

Ten years ago when he'd been right, but it had all been ultimately useless.

*Three freshly laundered pillowcases, the initials embroidered in red, blue and green.*

*L, S, A-M.*

'He fits the bill,' Thorne said.

'So, what about this witness? The one who saw the car.'

'The witness didn't pick Figgis out of a line-up,' Thorne said.

'Well ...'

'What?'

Thorne looked away and signalled for the bill. 'He didn't pick him out.'


Halfway back to Cat's place, Thorne's pager sounded and he asked if she would mind letting him use her phone to make the necessary call.

'You paid for breakfast,' she said.

Less than a minute later, they caught sight of the small crowd at the entrance to the tower block and Thorne understood why someone at the office was urgently trying to get hold of him.

'Oh, shit,' Cat said.

A dozen or more men and women with large cameras and flash guns.

Others scribbling in notebooks, while some – clearly

136

colleagues or rivals – chatted animatedly to one another, excited to be gathered together once again on the front line, waiting for their moment.

'There was one here yesterday.'

'No worries,' Thorne said. 'I'll get you inside.'

Then Thorne noticed the front page of a newspaper being read by a man at the back of the scrum. He saw the headline and the photo beneath, and he knew it wasn't Cat they were after.

Some teams were leakier than others.

# TWENTY-FIVE

By the time Thorne got back to Islington station just after ten o'clock, he'd missed the official heads-up/call to arms/mass bollocking meted out by DCI Andy Frankham. The less-than-gentle reminder about regulations surrounding professional conduct and the promise of retribution to those who had chosen to flout them.

Brigstocke ran him through the highlights while Thorne sat and looked at the front-page story in the *Sun* that had caused all the trouble.

**IS THIS THE MAN WHO TOOK KIERON?**

The story not only named Grantleigh Figgis, but revealed him to be a neighbour of the woman whose son had been snatched. It reported that the suspect – a known drug user – had a history of sexual offending and that police and forensic scientists were examining a motor vehicle owned by the suspect which they believed was directly linked to the abduction of seven-year-old Kieron Coyne.

There was a small photograph of Kieron, grinning in a West Ham shirt, and a far larger one of the man the paper was as good as accusing of snatching him. A photo of Grantleigh Figgis – taken on a long lens from a distance away – as he was being led from Seacole House to a police car two nights previously.

Figgis looked alarmed, certainly, and disorientated, yet the expression on that thin face – pale beneath the shock of hair – could just as easily have been seen by those with an agenda as nervous or shifty. There was something like anger in the eyes, too, if you were looking for it. A flash of that same irritation Thorne had glimpsed in the interview room.

Figgis looked unbowed yet also, strangely . . . unworldly.

*A proper funny strip of piss . . .*

He looked guilty.

It wasn't hard to see why the DCI had been so furious. 'Smoke coming out of his ears,' Brigstocke had said. For their suspect to have had his picture taken moments after his arrest could only mean that the paper had been tipped off by a member of the team.

Thorne knew how it worked.

Nobody ever joined the Met for the money, but while making ends meet wasn't usually a problem for most, any unexpected drain on wages could easily put the average copper under pressure. Alimony, a serious drink or drug problem, gambling debts. Some just racked up as much overtime as they could manage and there were more than a few who had second jobs, working as private security guards or manning all-night car parks. Others found easier and more lucrative ways to beef up their salaries, and passing information to people who were not supposed to reveal their sources often proved too tempting to resist.

Not that too many of the journalists Thorne had met were burdened with any more scruples than those to whom they passed envelopes stuffed with twenty-pound notes.

Ethics . . .

For some, it was just the way people with a lisp pronounced the name of that county where all the girls wore white stilettos.

Boyle and Roth wandered in, looking rather less rattled by the turn of events than they ought to have been.

'Pain in the arse, all this, but there you go,' Roth said.

'Yeah, there you go,' Brigstocke said.

The DI shook his head. 'I've already had the head of the surveillance team on the blower to tell me they're wasting their time. Can't get anywhere near Figgis while every arsehole with a camera's hanging around. Still, look on the bright side ...'

Seeing the man smile suddenly, Thorne wondered if Gordon Boyle had any unsuspected drains on his wages. A taste for high-class prostitutes maybe, or a secret second family. Mind you, imagining even one willing to put up with him was a bit of a stretch.

' ... we don't need a surveillance team to tell us what Figgis is up to, because the papers will do it for us.'

'Save us the trouble,' Roth said. 'Probably save us a few quid an' all.'

'Does that mean we can finally buy a new kettle?' Brigstocke asked.

'Yeah, but even if you're right about Figgis leading us to Kieron,' Thorne said, 'he's hardly likely to do that with the press watching him night and day.'

Perhaps it was the *even if* that wiped Boyle's smile away. 'They'll find something else to write about in a few days and lay off him. Meantime, we just get on with it and see how Mr Figgis handles the pressure.'

'Not very well so far,' Roth said.

'Listen, I talked to Catrin Coyne first thing,' Thorne said.

'Oh, yeah?' Boyle waited.

'She told me that Billy Coyne isn't Kieron's real father.'

'Interesting,' Brigstocke said.

'Thought we should probably have a word with the man who is.'

'Fair enough.' The DI looked as if he was already thinking about something else. 'Just write it all up and I'll have a look when I've finished dealing with all this Figgis business.'

Thorne turned to Roth. 'What did you mean about him not dealing with the pressure?'

'Oh, just that he's already been on the phone twice today.' Boyle held up two fingers, either to illustrate exactly what *twice* meant or to emphasise how pleased he was with the way the situation was panning out. 'First to moan about the fact that he couldn't get out to go to work, then half an hour later to tell us that work had called and told him not to bother coming in anyway.'

'Jammy sod's got himself a day off already,' Roth said.

'Right, but we haven't.' Boyle clapped his hands and rubbed them together, mustard-keen. 'So, let's crack on.' He stopped at the door, turned to look at Brigstocke and Thorne. 'Oh, and don't think it means that when all this is done and dusted, I won't be going after the twat who leaked the information and having his balls for breakfast.'

Roth smiled and rubbed his belly, as though he quite fancied the leavings from his master's plate.

When Boyle and Roth had gone, Brigstocke said, 'Crack on with what, exactly? Forensics won't be coming back any time soon and there's nobody else in the frame.'

Thorne picked up the paper again. Kieron Coyne's toothy grin. Figgis, like a rabbit trapped in the headlights.

'We've spunked all our money away on one horse.'

'Right,' Thorne said.

'I know he's the favourite, but still.'

Thorne nodded and tossed the paper into the bin next to his desk.

The failure of the Yorkshire Ripper inquiry might have led to a shake-up when it came to cross-referencing intelligence, but other bad habits still lingered, fifteen years on. More than once,

Thorne had been swept along by the dangerous tendency of some colleagues to focus exclusively on one theory, one suspect, while choosing to ignore any evidence that might run counter to that. To stop looking for it.

The Ripper killed because of a hatred for prostitutes.

The Ripper was from Wearside.

How many women had died because of those fixations? Half a dozen?

None of this was to say that Boyle wasn't right, of course. The horse he'd backed. There were compelling reasons why their prime suspect was exactly that. But it would also mean Thorne had been right, that he would bear responsibility if things did not work out well, whether anyone thought he deserved it or not. So, for as long as he turned the lights out still fearful of dreaming about three dead girls, he would kick against it.

Thorne grabbed his leather jacket from the back of the chair. 'Come on, you heard what he said.'

'Where are we going?'

'Let's have a chat with the World's Best Dad.'

# TWENTY-SIX

As soon as he heard the letters slapping on to the hallway floor, he hurried to open the door, keen to catch the postman. He held up the bundle, mostly junk mail of course, and waved it. He recognised the Asian with the bike and the red shoulder-bag, who always seemed genial enough, though they had never actually spoken.

'It's getting later and later,' he said.

The postman turned at the bottom of the path, peered at him through thick glasses. 'I know, but it's hard to keep it regular,' he said. 'These out-of-the-way routes.'

'All the same. It's virtually lunchtime.'

'Some places are lucky if they get their mail before teatime.' The postman smiled, oblivious to the fact that he was being told off, or simply not caring a great deal. 'They always get it, though.'

'OK, well. Just thought I'd mention it.'

'No problem. I'll have a word at the office, see what I can do.'

'It's a bit inconvenient, that's all.'

The postman had begun sauntering back up the front path,

seemingly happy to chat. He pointed towards the hanging baskets on either side of the door and said, 'These are doing very well.'

'Yes.' The man nodded and reached up to check the soil was damp enough. 'I'm very pleased with them.'

They stared at each other for a few moments.

The postman hoisted his bag up on to his shoulder and said, 'I meant to say . . . is your son all right?'

'Sorry?'

'I presume it's your son?'

The man blinked and began thinking furiously, his face a mask.

'Only I heard him crying yesterday morning.' The postman shook his head and smiled. 'Well, more like *lunchtime*, obviously . . . anyway, not sure you were here. So, I just thought—'

'He's got—'

'He sounded really upset.'

'He's had terrible earache.'

'Oh. That can be nasty.'

'Absolutely,' the man said. 'That's why I'm keeping him off school.'

The postman pulled a face. 'Yeah, I remember when my youngest had it. She screamed the place down. You got Calpol?'

'Oh yes. Calpol and plenty of treats. Don't worry, he's getting good and spoiled.'

'The best way,' the postman said.

The man took a step back and drew the door towards him. 'Well, thanks for, you know . . . '

'Not a problem. I'll see what I can do about getting here a bit earlier from now on.'

The man closed the door, stared out through the frosted-glass panes and watched the postman get on his bike and ride away. He stayed there until he felt his breathing start to settle down.

He would clearly need to do something, quickly.

He had thought that the room was far enough below ground, but obviously those eggboxes weren't doing the trick in terms of soundproofing. He would go out and get what he needed straight away, pick all the stuff up from that DIY megastore on the trading estate and get to work.

It wouldn't take very long.

Putting his jacket on and trying to remember where he'd left his car keys, he wondered if maybe he could let the boy out into the garden while he was doing the work in the cellar. He was fairly confident that the boy wouldn't shout or scream or try to climb over the fence, and even if he did, there was nowhere close he could get to very quickly. On second thoughts, it would probably be less stressful for both of them if the boy stayed put. Maybe the boy could help him. They could make a game out of it.

He would like that and he guessed that the boy would like it, too.

Anything that brought them closer.

Even if it was the two of them messing about with tools and whatever else, turning that room into something more like a prison cell. He hated to think of it in those terms, even though he wasn't an idiot and knew that's more or less what it was. It wasn't how he wanted the boy to see it, not if he was going to be there for a while.

He wanted the boy to feel safe down there, to feel at home.

He wanted the boy to know he was loved.

# TWENTY-SEVEN

Dean Meade was the assistant manager of a tile showroom in Palmers Green and had a badge to prove it. He appeared to be the only member of staff working there, however, and even though there was only one customer in the place – a woman browsing sullenly through a display of cut-price laminates – he announced that he was busy. As soon as the browser had wandered out of the shop, Brigstocke turned the sign on the door to closed.

'It's just a quick natter, Dean,' Thorne said.

Muttering about his boss having his 'guts for garters', Meade led them to a small, musty-smelling office in the back where boxes of tiles and large tubs of grout took up most of the available space. Brigstocke and Thorne squeezed on to plastic chairs behind one side of a desk-cum-hot drinks station. Meade took a seat opposite them and leaned back, a little happier suddenly, like someone who rarely got to sit in the big comfy chair. He saw Thorne staring at the calendar behind his head and turned. A Formula One car, on which a pneumatic blonde in a string bikini was perched holding a chequered flag as though it was the most natural thing in the world.

'Nice, right?' Meade said.

'The car or the girl?' Thorne asked.

'Well, they go together, don't they? Sort of . . . complement each other.'

Brigstocke opened his notebook. 'Why did you go to visit Catrin Coyne yesterday?'

'Are you serious?' Meade looked from one to the other.

'We know that you're Kieron's father,' Thorne said.

'Well, how come you're asking, then?' Meade was skinny, in a collar and tie, which he tugged at, jutting out his chin, like it was too tight. His dark hair was streaked with what Thorne always thought of as 'bird-shit highlights' and had been styled into a series of long strands which hung over his forehead like spider's legs. 'Obvious, I would have thought.'

'You'd have thought,' Brigstocke said.

'Tell us anyway,' Thorne said.

'I read about what had happened, didn't I?' Now, he began fiddling with the stud in his left ear. 'I thought I should be there for her. For Cat.'

Thorne looked at him. A Jack the Lad who wasn't a lad any more. 'You wanted to *be* there?'

'Yeah.'

'A bit ironic, isn't it? Considering you hadn't been there since Kieron was born. I mean, as far as I'm aware, you've never even seen him.'

'Did a runner before he was born,' Brigstocke said.

'I didn't do a runner,' Meade said. 'It wasn't like that. I . . . stepped away.'

'Considerate,' Thorne said. 'And you haven't seen Cat for what, seven years?'

'Something like that.' Meade folded his arms. 'But my son's never been abducted before, has he?'

'So, you thought it was time to put in an appearance.'

'Yeah, I thought I should,' Meade said. 'I thought it was the decent thing to do. Like I told Cat, it's not like I never cared about him.'

'So, seeing as you cared about your son so much,' Brigstocke said, 'I presume you kept up with what he was doing?'

'Well . . .'

'Did you know what school he was going to?'

'Yeah, I knew that. I'd heard something in the pub from one of Cat's mates.'

'Did you send cards on his birthday?' Thorne asked.

'Well, I wanted to, but it didn't seem like a good idea. I mean, it wouldn't do anyone any good to have certain people asking awkward questions. Definitely not Cat.'

'Certain people being his father?'

'I'm his father.'

'Fair enough, but don't you think the man who *believes* he's Kieron's father might start asking questions now?'

'Maybe. If he finds out.'

'But that wasn't going to get in the way of you doing the decent thing.'

Meade shrugged, still fiddling with his earring. 'Billy Coyne can ask all the questions he likes, can't he? What's he going to do, stuck in Whitehill?'

Thorne nodded, but he knew people like Dean Meade were well aware how easy it would be for Billy Coyne to get others to ask those questions for him. Well aware, too, of just how awkward they might be.

'What kind of car do you drive, Mr Meade?'

'Fiesta Cosworth.' He nodded up towards the calendar. 'Doesn't go quite as fast as that, mind you.'

'What colour?'

'Sorry?'

'Your Fiesta?'

'Blue. It's dark blue.' Meade looked concerned suddenly. 'Look, what's my car got to do with anything?'

They would check to see if Meade owned any other vehicles, of course, but Thorne guessed that the car had got the missing boy's biological father off the hook. All the same, he could not help wondering again about their public-spirited birdwatcher and if they were giving his story too much credence.

Had Felix Barratt seen anything at all?

It would certainly suit the guilty party to be regarded as a friendly witness, but then, if Barratt did have something to hide, why hadn't he confidently picked Figgis out at the ID parade? Why hadn't he picked *anyone*? That would have done him a favour, surely.

Meade opened a drawer and took out a folded and well-read copy of the *Sun*. 'Now, here's the one you should be talking to.'

'We have talked to him,' Thorne said.

Meade flattened the newspaper out and stabbed at the picture of Grantleigh Figgis on the front page. 'State of him.' He shook his head, disgusted, sat back and loosened his tie again. 'I mean, you can just see it with some people, can't you? Like Fred West, or whoever. Like all those sick thoughts have leaked into their faces. Let's hope this one does us all a favour, same as that piece of shit did.'

Fred West, who had killed himself in Birmingham prison the year before.

What had Boyle said yesterday?

*His sort are always the same.*


It was just shy of going-home time and Thorne had almost finished typing up his report on the interview with Dean Meade when Boyle gathered the senior members of the team together. With an index finger working busily at something inside his ear, he announced that, unfortunately, his plan to let the ladies and gentlemen of the press do the surveillance job on Grantleigh Figgis for them would need to be . . . amended.

'Bang goes our new kettle,' Brigstocke said.

'Didn't go down too well with the brass, apparently.' Boyle removed his finger and studied the end of it. 'Seemed to think it was making us look bad.'

'By which, of course,' Roth said, 'they mean making them look bad.'

It was not often that Thorne had cause to inwardly applaud a decision taken by the powers-that-be. Most of them were closer to being politicians than they were to being coppers, but he guessed that every so often, just statistically, they were bound to get something right.

Monkeys, typewriters, Shakespeare.

All that.

'So, we do what we *can* to clear that mob of journalists away from the tower block.'

Thorne knew that Boyle was choosing his words carefully.

'We all know that some of these journos can be very enterprising when they choose to be, so we might not be able to get rid of every single one. I mean, we haven't got the manpower, have we?'

'We'll have a good go at it,' Roth said.

'That's all I'm asking for, Ajay. So, I want a team of officers at the entrance, day and night, making sure that the only people who get inside Seacole House are people who should be getting in.'

'You mean the residents?' Thorne asked.

'Well, obviously.'

'How's that going to work in practice, though?' Brigstocke asked.

'There's probably upwards of three hundred people living in that block,' Thorne said. 'What about friends? Family?'

Others were quick to voice their concerns.

'Will every single resident need to produce ID?'

'Do they have their names ticked off a list or something?'

Boyle raised a hand until there was silence. 'Look, I'm not going to draw it all out in crayon for you,' he said. 'Obviously, the last thing we want to do is stop people going about their everyday lives and I'm not saying this is going to be a piece of piss. Just ... we must do what we can to make sure that things in that block get back to normal.'

Thorne almost laughed.

How could things ever get back to normal for Catrin Coyne? For the man living next door to her, come to that?

'So that *if* Mr Figgis chooses to get out and about to take the air, he is free so to do. That's when the surveillance team start earning their money again.'

'And if he puts a foot wrong,' Roth said, 'we've got him.'

Walking out into the car park fifteen minutes later, Brigstocke said, 'I'm not sure if I fancy Figgis for this or not.' He veered away from Thorne towards his car. 'I'm pretty sure he isn't stupid, though.'

'*He* isn't,' Thorne said.

# TWENTY-EIGHT

The phone sat on the floor next to the sofa, which, barring necessary trips to the kitchen and bathroom, was where Cat now spent almost every waking hour indoors. She grabbed it before it had rung twice, not because she thought it might be news about Kieron, but because she knew it was Billy. Oddly, she almost always knew when it was him calling, but she didn't usually tell him. He'd just have said she was being daft as usual or taken the piss out of her for being witchy.

'Jesus.' He laughed, and it was the most wonderful sound Cat had heard in days. 'You must be sitting on the phone or something.'

She lifted the phone on to her chest. 'I need to keep it near, you know.'

'Yeah, I know.'

'Just in case.'

'How are you doing, Kit-Cat?'

It was what everyone asked, in one way or another.

Sometimes there was a hand laid gently on the arm. Usually a cocked head or a gentle nod and always some kind of sad, awkward smile. The stuff people normally saved up for funerals. Cat wanted to step close to these people and shout in their silly, concerned faces. *How the hell do you think I am?* But coming from Billy it was different. Especially now, since that chancer Dean had come out of the woodwork. Hearing Billy ask that simple question stopped her breath for a few seconds, and when it came back it brought a strangled sob with it.

'Don't,' he said.

'Sorry,' she said.

'I can't be long. You know how it goes.'

Cat knew exactly how it went, because Billy had explained, way back when he went inside the first time. Whenever he'd call, there'd always be a line of men behind him waiting for their turn. Men he'd prefer not to fall out with if he could avoid it, even if most of them were rather more worried about upsetting *him*. All of them wielding phonecards as though they were weapons, which of course, with a little prison handiwork, they could easily be.

'Those few minutes of contact with the outside, that's what you think about all week,' Billy had told her back then. 'You can't afford to waste them.' There was simply never time for meaningful silences or drawn-out declarations of longing. It was why he always talked fast whenever he called her, gabbling because he had to, like he was speeding or something.

But not this time.

He said, 'I saw the paper.'

'Yeah, I guessed you would.'

'Everyone saw it,' he said. 'Passing it round, giving me funny looks. One or two of them making offers, you know?'

Cat asked what he meant, though she knew very well.

'That animal won't last five minutes once he gets sent down. Not once the word goes out.'

'Will *you* put the word out?' She waited. 'Billy . . . ?'

Now, there was a meaningful silence. Eventually he said, 'Do *you* think it's him?'

'I thought I would know,' she said. 'That I'd be able to see it. I thought that if I ever got the chance to look whoever took Kieron in the eye, I'd know.'

'So?'

Her mouth was dry and she struggled to swallow. 'What I do know is that our boy's still alive.'

Cat heard laughter in the background, a door clanging, somebody shouting something. Then Billy. A low whisper, like he was pressing his mouth close to the phone. 'Yeah?'

'I always thought that was rubbish,' she said. 'I've seen it with other people who've . . . lost kids, whatever. On those documentaries. They always say that, don't they? That they can feel it, somehow, feel that their child's still out there somewhere, because of that . . . bond or whatever. How strong it is. But it's not rubbish, Billy. I *know* Kieron's still out there and I know he's waiting for me to come and get him. Sometimes I don't even know if I'm awake or not and I can hear him crying. I know it sounds mental, and I swear the first couple of times I thought I'd just been dreaming it was him, or that *I'd* been the one crying in my sleep. But it isn't that, I know it's not. I know it's him.'

There was another silence. Ten, fifteen seconds of breathing and sniffing before Billy said, 'I need to go, Kit-Cat.'

Cat said, 'How are *you* holding up? Is everything . . . ?'

But there was only noise, then Billy's raised voice, just a word or two of curses at someone or other, before the line went dead.

Somebody else's turn.

Cat hung up and cradled the phone to her chest for a few minutes. She was as calm suddenly, as *light*, as she could remember feeling since that terrible morning in the woods. The constant noise in her head, like a low moan just audible below a screaming hiss, had died down a little. It had felt amazing to say those things to a man she loved and trusted. To share her thoughts with someone who, whatever had happened and however things turned out, would never judge her.

She lifted the handset from its cradle.

She needed to do it again.

Anything to keep the noise down . . .

'Oh, babe,' Angie said, when she answered. 'I'll have to be quick, I'm just on my way out the door.'

'Sorry. It doesn't matter.'

'Don't be daft.'

'Just wanted a natter, that's all. With everything that's going on.'

'Yeah.' Angie's voice was low, almost a growl. 'Soon be over, sweetheart.'

'Not until I know where Kieron is.'

'Course,' Angie said. 'But even if that fucker doesn't tell them, sits there and gives it the whole *no comment* bit or whatever, it's something, isn't it? Some comfort, anyway. Knowing they got the man who took him.'

Thorne was relieved to see that the release of their prime suspect hadn't made the local news, though he guessed it wouldn't take them too much longer to cotton on. Instead, two months on from the official announcement that Mad Cow Disease was now killing people, he watched footage of cattle being dumped on to enormous bonfires, while a grim-faced reporter revealed how much the ban on British beef was costing the meat industry and said that as many as two farmers a week were committing suicide.

He wondered what had happened to that chinless Tory idiot who'd fed his daughter a burger a few years back, to prove just how safe it was. He hoped the daughter was safe and well, but mostly that she'd grown up and come to realise how much of an arsehole her father was.

He turned off the news and skimmed through highlights of Italy beating Russia at Anfield, then went to the kitchen to grab something to eat in advance of the Turkey v Croatia game.

155

Thorne wondered if the mob of journalists had been cleared from outside Seacole House. How Catrin Coyne and her next-door neighbour were coping with it all. He thought about Felix Barratt's certainty that Kieron had known the man who had led him from the woods and asked himself just how many people the average seven-year-old knew.

Family members, neighbours, teachers?

He sat and ate what was left of the meat-feast pizza he'd had delivered the night before and thought about those suicidal farmers and the ways they might have chosen to end it all.

A roast-beef sandwich would probably have done the job nicely.

When the game had finished and he'd washed up, he decided to bite the bullet and call Jan back. It was getting late. He was already six tracks into *Hank Williams: Moanin' The Blues*, and he thought that she and the lecturer might well have already gone to bed. With a hot milky drink perhaps, or a good book each, or a variety of sex toys.

He would almost certainly be waking them.

He marched into the hall to fetch the phone.

Cat pressed the first six buttons automatically, her finger tracing a pattern of numbers she had dialled countless times. She stopped, poised over the final digit, and stared at her bitten-down fingernail for almost half a minute before letting out the breath she'd been holding and pressing.

Maria sounded as surprised to be answering the call as Cat was to be making it. She said, 'Oh, God . . . *hello*. How are you?'

That question again. Cat almost laughed, thought about hanging up.

'Sorry. Why do I always ask that ridiculous question?'

Cat told her exactly how she was. She told her about the crowd of journalists and photographers that had been gathered on the street outside, the reporters who had been calling every ten minutes for most of the day. 'I'm feeling a bit trapped, to be honest. I could do with a bit of peace.'

'Why don't you come and stay here?'

In different circumstances, it would have been the first place Cat would have headed, her chosen refuge. She had stayed with Maria while she was having the flat painted and when Billy and his sister had taken Kieron down to Kent for the weekend. For a few days when she'd been low for no particular reason and had just fancied getting the hell away from Archway.

'I don't really think—'

'Josh would so love to see you. *I'd* love to see you. Properly, I mean.'

'Thanks, but I'm sure it'll get easier,' Cat said. 'I just need—'

'And having *him* right next door. I mean, how the hell can the police let you go through that?'

'I told them I'd be all right, that I didn't feel unsafe.' Cat had been wondering if she'd done the right thing in saying that to Thorne ever since she'd started slamming the phone down on reporters; swearing at several of them when they'd begun talking about what they'd be prepared to pay for an exclusive interview.

'You don't get brownie points for being brave, sweetie,' Maria said. 'Nobody should have to put up with what you're going through, with that man so close.'

'Well, they've let him go, haven't they? I mean, officially he hasn't done anything.'

Maria hummed her doubt, her disgust. 'I met him once, when I came over. We got in the lift together. Remember?'

Cat didn't.

'I thought even then that he was odd. Out of the ordinary somehow. I wasn't awfully surprised when I saw the newspaper, put it that way.'

Despite what she'd said to Thorne when he'd first told her about the arrest, Cat asked herself for the hundredth time how surprised, or otherwise, *she'd* been.

She still didn't like the taste the answer left in her mouth.

'So, how's tricks with you, anyway?'

'Listen, Cat, you don't—'

'*Yes*, I do,' Cat said. 'I really do. I have to try and kid myself that the world hasn't just stopped. For a few minutes, anyway. So . . . ?'

'Well, I'm . . . Josh is still off school.'

'He's still upset,' Cat said.

'Yes, but he wasn't doing awfully well before. He's not really been himself for a while and I'm still not sure if there's something going on at school. I've asked him if he's being bullied, but he says not, so I just don't know. I mean, he says he wants to go back, but I think it's best if I keep him at home for a while longer.'

'Sound like that's best,' Cat said.

'Aside from anything, I'm a little worried about the press myself. Who knows what kind of information they've got? I mean, look how easily they got hold of your phone number. I really don't want them hanging around outside Josh's school, anything like that.'

'No, you're right.'

'Oh . . .' Maria stopped, but it sounded like the necessary pause she usually left before delivering a particularly juicy morsel of gossip. Cat had heard it a good many times before.

'Come on, spit it out.'

'Well, my ex popped over the other day.'

'OK.'

'Only because he was concerned about Josh. After he'd seen that first story in the paper. Anyway, I found myself inviting him to stay for dinner.'

'*What?* Jeff?'

'I know.' Maria barked out a laugh. 'Who would have thought? I've no idea what it means, but I suppose something like this happens and you just start thinking differently about all sorts of other stuff. Reconsidering all manner of things; looking at yourself.'

Cat said nothing. Thinking: *Counting your blessings, right?*

'It changes you,' Maria said.

'Yeah, it does,' Cat said.

Half an hour later, she dragged the thin duvet over herself and thumped the cushions on the sofa into a more comfortable shape. She reached for the remote and flicked through the channels until she found an old Clint Eastwood film she'd seen several times before. The one with the monkey.

She turned the volume up.

The walls in the building were paper-thin and Cat had become well used to hearing all sorts, the fucking and the fighting, but some things she could simply not bear to listen to. Not now. What she'd said to Billy was true, but now she was wide awake and knew exactly who was doing the crying.

Wiped out, but knowing her chances of sleep were slim, she nudged the volume up a little higher. Higher still, until the brawling and the roaring of engines on screen drowned out the sound of Grantleigh Figgis sobbing.

# TWENTY-NINE

St Mary's was a large, state primary school half a mile in the wrong direction from the Holloway Road. Thorne knew that fifteen minutes' walk away there were sought-after schools in Tufnell Park and Crouch End whose pupils lived rather more comfortably than Kieron Coyne. A fair few kids with mums and dads who had high-end jobs in the city or flourishing careers in the arts. Thorne didn't know a lot about how catchment areas worked, but even though St Mary's was yet to open its doors for the day, he doubted very much that any of the parents he'd seen gathered near the gates when he'd arrived had comparable incomes.

Not too many bankers or novelists among them.

Elspeth Gibson, the head teacher – younger and dressed rather less formally than he had been expecting – was waiting for Thorne at the door. After a few muted words of welcome, she led him to her office and Thorne moved quickly to the important questions. Had anyone at the school noticed strangers hanging around? Had any of the children mentioned anything out of the ordinary happening? Gibson said that she would, of course, talk to all her staff, but as these things would normally be reported to her immediately she was certain that no such incident had occurred.

'Everyone's very vigilant,' she said. 'Well, you have to be, don't you?'

Thorne thanked her, and once he had politely said no to tea or coffee, she offered to escort him to Kieron Coyne's form room.

They walked briskly along a corridor that had just been freshly mopped and smelled like it. Drawings and collages adorned almost every inch of the walls and a brightly coloured map of the world had been painted on the floor at the entrance to the assembly hall.

'I've never had to deal with anything like this,' Gibson said. 'I had a child die when I was at a school in south London a few years ago.' She glanced at him. 'Meningitis. That was terrible, obviously, but this is somehow worse. How's his mum doing?'

'She's coping amazingly well,' Thorne said.

The Head nodded. 'That's good. I know she doesn't have it easy at the best of times. Her partner and everything.'

They walked past the cloakroom area. Rows of labelled plastic baskets with hooks above. Thorne wondered which basket was Kieron's; which hook would still be empty after the children had arrived.

'Here we are.' Gibson knocked on a door, opened it and stepped aside so that Thorne could enter. A man in his early thirties was laying out workbooks. He looked up and nodded, having clearly been pre-warned and knowing very well who his visitor was.

'Simon Jenner,' Gibson said. 'He's Kieron's form teacher.'

Jenner was shortish and well built – compact, Thorne thought – and wore a red polo shirt over jeans and trainers. He dropped the workbooks on to his desk then stepped across to shake Thorne's hand.

'OK, well, I'll leave you with Simon.' Gibson opened the door.

'No worries,' Jenner said.

'He knows Kieron better than anyone here.'

Once the Head had closed the door behind her, there were a few slightly awkward moments as, without saying anything, the two men tried to decide where best to position themselves. The chairs were obviously too small for adults to sit on and, in the end, they both remained standing. Jenner leaned against his desk and Thorne moved across to stand by the window.

'This is just horrible,' Jenner said.

'Yes, it is.'

'Kieron, I mean ... not talking to you. Mind you, it's never particularly nice talking to police officers, is it, because it's almost always because something bad has happened?' The teacher shook his head and smiled. 'Sorry, I'm gabbling ...'

'Don't worry.' Most people were a little twitchy in these situations, even those who had done nothing wrong. In Thorne's experience they were often jumpier than those who had something to hide.

Nerves were rarely a reliable indicator.

He asked Jenner the same questions he had asked the headmistress and Jenner gave the same answers; the answers Thorne had been expecting. He doubted very much that the man responsible for taking Kieron had been watching him at school. There were always too many people around. Still, he had to ask.

'So, you think he's definitely been abducted then?'

'We can't know for sure,' Thorne said. 'But three days is a long time to stay lost in the middle of London.'

'He'd ask if he was lost,' Jenner said. 'Kieron isn't exactly shy. He's actually a pretty confident kid.'

'Trusting, you think?'

'You talking about strangers?'

Thorne said that he was, though he had not forgotten what Felix Barratt had told him. The man and the boy, hand in hand.

162

'Well, they're all told about talking to strangers. We do it in school certainly, and . . . well, at home too, I'm sure.'

'You know what some kids are like, though?'

Jenner waited.

'You tell them not to climb up on a roof, it's the one thing they most want to do.'

Jenner grunted and reached behind him to straighten some folders on his desk. 'They're at a funny age.' He nodded out towards the arrangement of empty chairs. 'Kieron and his class-mates . . . an "in-between" age. They don't want to be babied.' He laughed. 'Certainly not the boys and definitely not in front of their mates. But every now and again you see how desperately some of them still need a cuddle. You know?'

'Was Kieron like that?' Thorne glanced out of the window, saw that the playground had filled up. 'Did he need a cuddle?'

'He got upset sometimes.'

'What about?'

'I don't think he's ever quite settled in. Well, not as well as some of the other kids, anyway. It was a lot to do with his best friend, I think.'

'Josh?'

'He goes to a different school, right?'

'Up in Highgate.'

'Right. Very nice.' Jenner clearly knew the kind of school Thorne was talking about. 'Look, we see this quite a lot every year. Boundary lines kicking in, friends getting separated. It's a shame, but there's not a lot anyone can do except encourage kids like Kieron to make new friends.'

'Did he?'

'Yeah, he's got plenty of mates. He's . . . popular, but he and this other boy were obviously very close. He talked about him a lot. I think Josh was as upset about it as Kieron was.'

'Did Kieron talk about his dad much?'

'Yeah, a bit. His dad's . . . away, right?'

Thorne understood that the teacher knew exactly where Kieron's father was. 'For the time being.'

'That's a shame,' Jenner said. 'A lad needs a male role model around. An older brother . . . someone. Without that, it can be—' He stopped when a bell rang outside, and they both turned towards the window. 'Right then.' Jenner moved around his desk and picked up his workbooks. 'The stampede is imminent . . .'

Thorne thanked the teacher for his time. On his way to the door he reached into his jacket for one of the cards on which the incident room contact details were printed. He'd scribbled his home number in biro at the bottom. 'If you think of anything,' he said.

'Yeah, of course.'

'Or I might pop back.' Thorne opened the door. 'If *I* think of anything.'

Jenner took a step towards him. 'The truth is, you don't always connect with kids. It doesn't matter how hard you try, but I was getting there with Kieron.' He tucked the card into the back pocket of his jeans. 'I was definitely getting there.'

# THIRTY

Thorne had only been back an hour or so when he was summoned by one of the team at the front desk. He could hear the commotion as he jogged down the stairs and, though he wasn't sure what was happening, he guessed the shouting could be heard by pretty much anyone in the station. Anyone on the neighbouring streets, come to that. It felt more like a full-moon Friday night than a Wednesday mid-morning that had, up until now, been mercifully Q.

It wasn't until he pushed through the door into reception that Thorne could see who was doing the shouting.

'No, I will *not* bloody well calm down.' Grantleigh Figgis struggled against the two uniformed officers who had set themselves at either side of him and had each taken hold of an arm. 'I should not have to put up with this. This is intolerable.'

Thorne came around the desk. Looking past Figgis towards the glass doors, he could see the ruck of cameramen that had gathered outside, most still snapping away and a few shouting about 'press freedom' as three or four officers ushered them back towards the road.

'Come on now, sir . . .'

'Tell them to let go.' Figgis struggled harder, the officers gritting their teeth, looking to Thorne. 'Tell these animals to get off me.'

Thorne gave the nod and the officers stepped back.

Figgis immediately lurched forward, slammed both hands down on the desk and leaned towards the stony-faced sergeant. 'I want to speak to whoever's in charge. *Really* in charge, I mean. I demand to speak to a . . . superintendent or whatever.'

The sergeant reached calmly for whichever form he was duty-bound to fill in. 'What's the nature of your complaint, sir?'

'My complaint?' Figgis shook his head, breathing heavily. 'Where do you want me to start?'

'Wherever you like, sir.'

'Just get me the most senior officer in the building.' He was screaming suddenly, hoarse and close to tears. '*Now.*'

Thorne stepped close to him. 'I think you'll have to make do with me for now,' he said. 'That OK?'

Figgis stared at him for a few seconds as if it was anything but OK, as though he were about to spit in his face. Instead, he turned and waved a hand towards a handful of the most persistent reporters who were still outside taking pictures, fighting a rearguard action against the officers trying to move them away from the station. He cried out and took a step backwards when two of the reporters broke free and rushed towards the door shouting his name before being dragged back.

'Look at them,' Figgis said. 'Parasites.'

Thorne didn't see much to argue with. 'You're safe in here.'

Figgis wheeled round. 'You think? If I'd never been here, this wouldn't be happening. This is what you wanted, though, isn't it? If you can't prove I did anything, the very least you can do is make me suffer afterwards. You lot must be rubbing your hands in glee—'

'Mr Figgis . . .'

166

Thorne turned at the sound of Boyle's voice, saw the expression of concern on the DI's face. Like make-up applied by a blind man.

'Have we got a problem?'

'Well, *I* certainly have,' Figgis said. 'And I'm here because I fully intend to make it your problem as well. I'm . . . ' He stopped, flagging suddenly, and leaned back against the desk. He tried to summon up a last volley of indignation, but his voice cracked. 'I'm at my wits' end. Truly . . . '

Boyle nodded. He came round the desk and laid a hand on the man's shoulder. He was looking at Thorne as he spoke. 'Come on, why don't we find somewhere a little more private where we can sit down and talk about this?'

Outside, one of the reporters shouted, 'What have you done with Kieron Coyne?'

'We'll see what we can do to help you,' Boyle said.

As an officer led Figgis behind the desk and through into the corridor, Boyle stopped Thorne at the door. 'How did it go at the school?'

'I was just typing it up,' Thorne said. 'Nothing very much to get excited about. I talked to the headmistress and to Kieron's form teacher.'

'He or she?'

'A bloke, and I've already checked him out. There was a caution back when he was a student. The big CND march in eighty-three.'

Boyle curled his lip. 'Oh, one of those, is he?'

'Other than that . . . ?'

'Talking of "one of those" . . . ' Boyle nodded towards the small window in the door, through which they could see Figgis still remonstrating with the officer, 'let's go and see how the noncey neighbour's doing, shall we?'

There were no red lights winking this time, nothing being recorded, but sitting in a room in a non-secure part of the

167

station, Grantleigh Figgis looked every bit as uncomfortable as he had when they'd interviewed him two days earlier.

'You've no idea what it's been like,' he said. 'They were outside the flats, dozens of them. Some of them were *inside*, banging on my door, pushing notes underneath.'

'Not since last night, though,' Boyle said. 'We took steps to have them removed yesterday.'

'Oh, is that right? Because the minute I left home this morning they just appeared out of nowhere. Like they'd been lurking in the bushes or waiting in cars. They were all over me, shouting and taking pictures. They came after me on to the Tube, followed me all the way here.'

Figgis lowered his head and began clawing at his hair as if he was trying to drag it down across his eyes. Thorne imagined him doing much the same thing on the way here, struggling to get to somewhere he thought he might be protected, the terrible irony of that having long become meaningless. A man with nowhere to run, hemmed in on a crowded underground train with cameras in his face. Trying to keep his head down or hiding behind his hands like a child playing hide and seek.

Like Josh Ashton, four days before in those woods.

'Why are you here?' Boyle asked. 'I mean, obviously I'm very sorry that you're having to put up with this ... intrusion, but beyond doing everything we can to keep the press away, I don't see that there's much more—'

Figgis looked up. 'I've lost my job.' He nodded. 'The college called first thing and told me not to bother coming in at all until further notice. You know ... *under the circumstances*.'

'They can't do that,' Thorne said.

'You want to call them up and tell them?'

'I'm sorry,' Thorne said.

'That doesn't help me, but thank you.' Figgis nodded mock-graciously at Thorne, like someone accepting a compliment. 'So ... the neighbours look at me like something somebody brought in on their shoe, I'm a prisoner in my own home, I've got the press all over me and now I'm out of work.' He stared at Thorne. 'So, what? Am I supposed to just trot down to the dole office?'

'It's what people do,' Boyle said.

'I'm not people though, am I?' Figgis turned to Boyle and smiled sarcastically, a flash of yellowing teeth. 'I'm not *normal* people. How can I declare myself available for work when I can't go anywhere? More to the point, how many people do you think would be willing to give me a job right now? What can I do, I wonder? School caretaker, do you think? Maybe a nice job at a nursery?'

Thorne knew that, on top of everything else, no job meant Figgis would have no way to buy the drugs he needed, and he wondered how long it had been since the man had been able to score. For all his obvious discomfort, Figgis didn't look as though he was withdrawing. The heroin found when they'd searched his flat had been confiscated, so Thorne could only assume that Figgis had sorted something out for himself as soon as he'd got home. Had his gear delivered, like pizza. Thorne knew that most drug dealers wouldn't mind having to dodge a few journalists if there was cash waiting for them at the end of it.

'Maybe you should talk to the papers,' Boyle said.

'Excuse me?'

'Give them what they want ... if you're short of money. I'm sure they'd be willing to make it worth your while. More than worth it.'

Figgis looked from Boyle to Thorne and back. 'Are you serious? Talk to them? My side of the story, just like that?' He looked as though he might be sick. 'It would be like tossing raw meat to a pack of wolves.'

Thorne wondered what game Boyle was playing. Having suggested that Figgis might conveniently lead them to Kieron Coyne, did he now seriously believe that his prime suspect

169

would crack with a few hundred quid on the table and confess everything to the *Daily Mirror*? In the end, seeing his boss's barely concealed smirk, Thorne guessed that, for want of anything better to do, the Scotsman was merely twisting the knife.

'I don't know what else to suggest,' Boyle said.

'You need to do something,' Figgis said. 'They've got my address and my phone number. I don't feel safe.'

'There are officers stationed outside the block.'

'Oh, right, and suppose one or two of them believe what the papers are all implying? Suppose they think the same way you do? I'm damned sure they wouldn't mind seeing me get a good kicking, or worse.'

'We rely on evidence,' Boyle said. 'No officer under my command is going to let personal feelings or opinions get in the way.'

Thorne felt his fists clenching beneath the table.

'What about a safe house or something?'

Boyle raised his hands, helpless. 'I'm sorry, but strictly speaking they're for witnesses who need protection. We don't usually make them available to people in your position.'

'Suspects.' Figgis sat back and nodded, breathing noisily through his mouth. He drummed his thin fingers on the table-top. 'I mean, I am still a suspect, aren't I?'

'You could always come back here,' Boyle said. 'It's a bit out of the ordinary, but I'm sure we could provide a bed for a few nights if you arrived voluntarily. Not five-star, of course.'

Figgis was still nodding, as though he might be considering the offer, but Thorne could tell he had stopped listening. He had shrunk into his chair, and now he closed his eyes and began muttering inaudibly to himself.

'Look, I'm sure we can run to a car to get you home safely.' Boyle pushed his chair back and stood up. 'Other than that, there's not an awful lot we can do.'

'I'd be happy to go back with him,' Thorne said. 'There's probably still plenty of press around.'

'If there's nothing else you should be doing,' Boyle said.

Figgis did not move. He looked as though he wanted nothing more than to be left alone in that room to drift away for a while, as though his own mumbled words were the only ones that would make any kind of sense; that he could trust. Thorne could not take his eyes off the man as he hummed and tutted. The suspicious manner, the peculiarities that had rung so many alarm bells just a few days before, were now blanked out by despair. Where once he had seen a curiosity, Thorne now found himself staring at someone who simply appeared . . . absent.

A shell, broken and unreachable.

'I'll get that car organised.' Boyle stepped towards the door. 'Oh, and I wouldn't worry too much anyway, Mr Figgis. I don't know if you've had a chance to look at a paper this morning, but you've been knocked off the front page.'

# THIRTY-ONE

A journalist – Maggie, or Mary – had called first thing, her voice a little too hushed and thick with concern as she'd asked Cat what she thought of the article and if she had any comment. Having provided one that was almost certainly not printable, Cat had quickly thrown a coat over her pyjamas, run down to the newsagent to pick up a copy of the newspaper and read the story for herself.

He looked smart but suitably mournful in the photograph, clutching a teddy bear that had almost certainly been provided for him. A touching, faraway look on his face and a simple enough, four-word headline:

**KIERON IS MY SON.**

Now, Cat understood exactly what it was that Dean Meade cared so much about.

He declared that he was 'sick with worry'. He revealed exclusively that he'd been 'cut out' of his son's life and though he bitterly resented being 'sidelined' and denied access to a child he had never stopped loving, it was now time for Kieron's *real* family to pull together. 'It's only at times like this,' Meade had said, 'that you realise what's really important.'

Cat screwed the newspaper up and pushed it down hard into the kitchen bin. Thinking: *Yeah, right – the money they're paying you, that you might be able to squeeze out of a few more papers and magazines, the fat fees for TV interviews and all the rest of it . . .*

She carried tea across to the sofa and set her rage to one side, because it would be there to draw on when she needed it. Because Dean Meade meant less than nothing and because, right then, it was hard to think of anyone else but Billy.

He would know by now, of course, the paper left outside his cell by a helpful screw. He would have done his best to deal with the crude comments over breakfast. The snide remarks from inmates and guards alike about his shortcomings in the bedroom and the gleeful insinuations about the woman he stupidly believed was waiting faithfully for him.

*Her.* His two-timing slag of a girlfriend.

*'It's not news in here, mate. We've* all *had her.'*

*'More cock than KFC . . .'*

*'They'll have to bury your missus in a Y-shaped coffin.'*

Would Billy have risen to the bait and lashed out? Or would the anger be something that built up slowly; that festered? She knew the temper he had on him. It was something the two of them had in common. One minute she imagined him banged up in solitary already, nursing bloodied knuckles, and the next lying on his bunk, hollowed out by her betrayal.

She knew she would have to call and try to explain.

She would take whatever he handed out, had every right to hand out, and do everything she could to make him understand that he was Kieron's dad in all the ways that mattered. That her and Dean Meade had just been something stupid that only happened because she'd been so messed up at losing Billy.

173

Cat lay down and cried for a while, because she knew how mealy-mouthed she would sound saying all this, coming clean now only because she'd been rumbled. Making it worse by trotting out a piss-poor excuse when what she'd done could never be excused.

*It was just because I missed you.*

*I was thinking of you, I swear . . .*

Then Angie rang, so Cat said it all to her instead.

'Calm down,' Angie said. 'Look, I'm not going to say I'm happy about it, because I'm not, but for good or ill, it's all out in the open now, so everyone's just going to have to deal with it.'

'I think I should talk to Billy.'

'I'm not sure that's a good idea just yet.'

'I should go and see him.'

'I'll do it,' Angie said. 'If he *is* going to kick off, it might be best if I deal with it first. Take some of the flak, yeah?'

'You sure?'

'Let me . . . pave the way or whatever.'

Cat was grateful, if a little taken aback. Angie had always been close to her brother and Cat would not have been surprised if the woman had let her have it with both barrels. That temper ran in the family.

Instead, Angie said, 'You've got more important things to worry about right now. You *and* Billy. This shit about you in the news is going to blow over soon enough.'

'Yeah?'

'Tomorrow's fish and chip paper, babe.'

Cat knew that, despite how wretched and guilty she felt now and however much it seemed like she'd ruined everything, Angie was probably right. She and Billy would survive this, because they'd been through plenty already and what had happened with Kieron would only make them stronger. They were a team, always had been.

'Just sit tight and don't do anything stupid,' Angie said.

174

'I'll come over after work and we can talk about it. Open a bottle, yeah?'

'Open several bottles,' Cat said.

When she'd finished talking to Angie, Cat felt a powerful urge to get out of the flat for a while. She needed to get some air, to talk to people. She decided that she'd go and sit in Whittington Park for a while, try and clear her head.

She got dressed quickly. She tidied up her hair and put on some make-up for the first time in several days. She hadn't noticed any press types knocking around outside when she'd gone out for the paper, but even if there were a few down there by now, she would deal with them in one way or another.

She would spit on their lenses and swear at them or she would smile sweetly and answer all their questions like a good girl. Perhaps she would just keep her head down and her elbows out and knock them aside like skittles as she ran.

She would see how she felt when the time came.

Before she left, Cat picked up the phone and left a message on Dean Meade's answering machine.

'I hope you're pleased with yourself, you spineless wanker. You are a worthless piece of shit and I thank God that Kieron doesn't have an *ounce* of you in him. You don't deserve to live.'

# THIRTY-TWO

Jan had suggested the Pizza Express in Muswell Hill and Thorne hadn't argued. Looking around a room they'd both been in many times before, he could see now that it was the ideal choice. Nice enough, but not stupidly posh or anything, not a venue for any sort of special occasion. Bright and buzzy. The kind of place that would quickly smother any wildly misplaced romantic notions that either party might still be kicking around. Food was always reliable, too.

You knew where you were with Pizza Express, and it never let you down.

After a meal there, one or other of them would usually come out with some version of that shared homily and, looking at her now across the table, Thorne could tell that Jan knew more or less what he was thinking.

*Shame you can't say the same about a marriage.*

'You're not going to get all maudlin, are you, Tom?'

'God forbid,' Thorne said. 'Never felt cheerier ... but you know me, I love a pizza.' He leaned back as a waitress laid their meals down. A Margherita and sparkling water for her, American Hot and a large Peroni for him. 'On top of which, this hasn't been delivered on the back of a moped, so it's like I'm eating at the Ivy or something.'

She smiled and he smiled back. They began to eat.

'Is that how it's been, then?'

'What?'

'Home delivery pizza?'

'Not had a lot of time to cook,' Thorne said. 'Work's been full-on.'

'It always is,' Jan said.

Thorne did his best to take that as a comment on the crime rate as opposed to a less-than-subtle dig at his commitment to the Job. His inability to leave it at the door. A niggle which had grown to become a major bone of contention as their marriage had gone on.

*Dragged* on . . .

'I like your hair, by the way,' Thorne said. 'What you've had done.'

The moment he'd sat down he'd thought how great she looked and, fifteen minutes on, he was still asking himself if that was just the way it went once you'd been dumped. He remembered being fifteen and fancying the pants off Fiona Lomax *way* more after she'd got off with that knob-head from the rugby team on New Year's Eve and subsequently chucked him. Or was it that his wife had simply made more of an effort because there was a new man in her life? Now there was someone who might actually appreciate it?

'I'm not sure I like it.' Jan moved her hands through hair that was shorter than it had been the last time he'd seen her and streaked with reddish highlights. 'I think the hairdresser went a bit over the top.'

Thorne looked at her. 'Why can you never take a compliment?'

'What?'

177

'You never could. You always had to turn it into something else ... I don't know, I was thinking about it the other day, that's all.'

Jan laid down her cutlery, though she had barely eaten anything. 'Is that why you think I wanted to get together? So we can sit here and score points off each other?'

'No ...'

'You really want to go over it all again, drag everything up and talk about what went wrong? You need reasons?'

'I'm just talking.' Thorne bit into a slice and wiped the grease from around his mouth. 'Something we never did enough of, apparently.'

'Oh, for heaven's sake, Tom.'

'You *said* that.'

She leaned towards him and lowered her voice. 'So, you want me to explain, *again*, why I ended up feeling shrivelled up and ... shit. How I had no self-esteem at all. You want chapter and verse on why I fell out of love with a man who seemed like he couldn't give a toss and could only show his emotions if he was screaming at a rapist or being threatened by a serial killer?'

Thorne swallowed and shrugged. 'Well, I was thinking more along the lines of why you jumped into bed with a beardy twat who wears sandals, but I suppose it's the same thing.'

Jan sighed, leaned back slowly. She said, 'I'm not going to do this. I've got nothing to feel guilty about. We should be past all this now and moving on.' She pointed. '*You* should be moving on.'

'You say it like it's easy.'

'I know it's not easy,' she said. 'But nothing worth having ever is, is it?'

Thorne finished his meal and watched Jan finish hers, the perfect ring of crust that she always left on the plate.

'I'm doing my best, I swear,' he said.

She nodded. 'Have you found a solicitor yet?'

'No.' He saw the look on her face and raised a hand. 'But I will.'

'What about the house? Have you sorted estate agents out?'

This time Thorne decided it would be simpler to lie. 'I've got a couple coming round next week.'

'That's good. Let me know what they say and remember they always tell you it's worth more than it is.'

'Yeah, I know.' The waitress came back to collect the plates and Thorne asked for another beer. He said, 'Oh and so you know, it hasn't just been home delivery pizza.'

She waited.

'My mum brought me some stuff to put in the freezer.'

She laughed, in exactly the same way she had when he'd passed out of training college at Hendon all those years before, when she'd seen him in the tall hat for the first time. Thorne watched her laughing now, and it killed him.

Figgis tried to ignore the knocking, praying that whoever was outside his door would go away. After half a minute's silence, he presumed they had given up and he crept close to the door, only for the knocking to start again and drive him cowering back into the hall. The police had told him that no more reporters would be allowed past the entrance downstairs. They had promised, but he'd been doubtful to put it mildly and he wasn't very surprised that one had mysteriously wormed their way inside.

Slipped one of the coppers a few quid, probably.

He was padding quietly back towards his bedroom when he suddenly wondered if it might be Cat outside and felt something like a smile begin to tug at his lips for the first time in days. He understood why things between them were so weird, but seeing that look on her face when he'd tried to talk to her two nights before had been unbearable, nevertheless. She *knew* him, knew what he was like, so he'd thought that she, of all people . . .

Catrin wasn't herself though, how could she be? He balled

his fists and pushed his nails into the flesh of his palm; berated himself for even daring to think that his own situation, awful as it was, could even compare to what she must be going through. How did he even have the nerve to stand there and worry about *himself*?

He was just the *worst* friend anybody could have . . . the *stupidest* . . . the most hideously *selfish* bastard that ever drew breath, and not very much better than those newspapers said he was.

He walked back to the door, leaned a sweaty forehead against it and said Cat's name.

'Listen, I only need a minute.'

Not Cat, but a voice he thought he recognised.

'Who are you?'

'A friend, OK? Open the door, Grant . . . you'll be glad you did.'

Figgis listened and heard only his own rasping breaths. Felt the pulse ticking in his neck. It didn't sound like a reporter and, even if it was, what could they possibly do to him that would make things any worse?

He opened the door a few inches and peered around it.

A face he recognised, too.

Hands were raised, seeing the concern on Figgis's face. 'It's OK . . . I don't want anything.'

'Everybody wants something,' Figgis said.

'I know what you want, Grant.'

He waited, watching the hand that slipped inside a jacket pocket.

'Well, what you need, at any rate.'

If the face was only vaguely familiar, Figgis knew exactly what was inside the small plastic bag that was being dangled in front of him. His eyes followed it as it swung gently. 'Why, though?'

'Because I know what's happened to you and you don't have to be a genius to work out how shit that must be. Because I reckon you could do with cheering up and every once in a while it's good to do something nice for someone.'

180

Figgis looked from the bag to the face of the person offering it.

'Because I can, OK? Look, it's up to you . . . '

The bag was slowly withdrawn.

Figgis reached out quickly for it.

Outside on the pavement, Jan said, 'Thanks for that.'

'No problem,' Thorne said. He had volunteered to pay the bill even if he could not have explained why, though when handing over his credit card he had not been able to stop himself wondering just how much money the lecturer earned.

'I mean it.'

Thorne knew that she wasn't thanking him for her pizza. She was grateful because she understood how hard the evening had been for him, and why – subconsciously or not – he'd been doing everything he could to avoid the sort of conversation they'd spent the latter part of the meal having.

The nuts and bolts of their separation.

The arrangements.

'I'll get it all sorted,' he said. 'As soon as work eases up a bit.'

Jan seemed content with that, or at least accepting of the fact it was as much as she was going to get. They hugged, a little awkwardly, and moved away from the door. Things quickly became more awkward still when it became clear that, at least until Thorne turned into the street where he'd parked, they'd be walking in the same direction.

'Is it the missing boy, this case that's taking up so much time?'

Thorne nodded.

'Horrible. That poor woman.'

A young couple, arm in arm and clearly the worse for wear, weaved towards them. Thorne and Jan stepped apart to let them through.

'It's all gone mad in the papers.'

'That's our fault,' Thorne said. 'Somebody on the team taking a backhander.'

Jan winced. 'Be good to find the boy before that gets out. Or find out what happened to him, anyway.'

Thorne stopped at the corner and pointed. 'I'm down here . . .'

'Right.'

They hugged for a second time and Thorne held on a second or two longer than he probably should have. He wanted to catch just a hint of the perfume she always wore, some vanilla stuff from The Body Shop. He could smell nothing and wondered if the lecturer wasn't a fan, or just preferred the way she smelled naturally.

When they separated, Thorne said, 'I know we went through this and we're moving on and all that . . . but do you think things would have been any different if we'd had a baby?'

'Come on, Tom—'

'It's a simple question.'

Jan considered it. 'No, I don't think so. It would just have made what's happening now even more difficult.'

'Fair enough,' Thorne said.

'Don't you think?'

Thorne looked at the pavement for a few moments. 'Well, I'll call when . . . you know.'

They both nodded and walked away from one another. After a few steps, Thorne turned when Jan called out to him.

She said, 'Just so you know, *I* can't stand those bloody sandals either.'

Grantleigh Figgis lay back, knowing full well what was going on, and thought, *God, it's so quick.*

Over the years, it had happened to people he knew – not well, but friends of friends – because now and again it was unavoidable, but he'd never imagined it would be like this, that it would hurt quite as much and happen so bloody fast.

Like being hit by a truck.

He'd always thought it would be more peaceful somehow, that there would be . . . drifting and *time*.

One second the sheer joy of the warm, syrupy smell that always meant something wonderful was coming; the flat thick with it, the anticipation of that blissful nothingness he needed so very much. A moment or two of quiet as he waited for the hit to spread and then . . . *fuck*! As if someone wearing size twelve boots had jumped on his chest.

Just a few faces after that, like he was looking down at them through dirty water: his poor, put-upon mother; a kid from school he thought he'd forgotten; the first boy he'd kissed, whose mouth had tasted of fags and the Remy Martin they'd stolen from his father's drinks cabinet. Last thoughts then and the strange comfort of knowing they were last thoughts. That it didn't matter what anyone thought of him, that they could piss all over his memory if that's what they fancied and write what they liked, because he wouldn't be there to see it.

That Cat would be all right and, please God, her little boy.

And that life, even as you lost it, was full of surprises.

# THIRTY-THREE

Angie came bowling into the living room at a little after five a.m. Half-past stupid, still dark outside for pity's sake yet she somehow managed to look fabulous, like she'd had a full night's sleep and an hour to get herself ready. Obviously she was used to getting up early with a market stall to prepare, but even so.

Cat felt like shit, even if she was starting to get used to it.

The night before, once it had been decided that she'd stay the night, Angie had tried to persuade Cat that *she* should be the one sleeping on the sofa, but Cat wasn't having it. It was something else she'd been getting used to. The sofa part, at least.

It had been the only thing they'd argued about.

Yes, she'd been OK on the phone, but with most of the day for Angie to mull over Dean Meade's sleazy revelations in the newspaper, Cat had been fully prepared for a row. A stiff talking-to at the very least. Instead Angie had turned up with a bag of booze, and, more amazingly still, sympathy.

'Look, I do understand,' she'd said. 'Not like it's that unusual, under the circumstances.'

When Cat had tried to explain how terrible she felt for doing the dirty on Billy, Angie had been quick to stop her. 'Trust me, I know how you feel, babe.'

'What?'

'Well, a few of the blokes I've been involved with weren't exactly angels, put it that way.'

'So?'

'Went down the same road my brother did, a couple of them, and I wasn't always a good girl while they were away.'

Cat was shocked. Over the years Billy had made one or two knowing remarks about Angie's 'complicated' love-life, but it was still a surprise to discover those complications ran to boyfriends getting banged up and her cheating on them when they were inside.

'They call it cheating, because that's what it is,' Cat said. 'Not playing by the rules. Me and Billy talked about it before the trial, and even though we both knew it would be difficult, Billy said that there was one rule I could never break.'

Angie looked at her. '*Billy* said?'

'Yeah, OK . . . but I agreed with him. It was the right thing to do. Two cheap bottles of fizzy plonk and Dean Meade making it obvious he was up for it and that number one rule went straight out of the window.'

'Right.' Angie had sat Cat down then, looked hard at her. 'But it wasn't like Billy stuck to his word either, was it?'

Angie had a point. After that first time, Billy had sworn he was never going back inside again; he'd made her a promise. For Kieron's sake, he'd said.

Now, Cat struggled up off the sofa and into a dressing gown and asked Angie if she wanted coffee or something.

'You're all right.' Angie put on a black leather jacket, checked her face in the mirror by the front door. 'I'll grab tea and a bacon roll when I get to the market. Nice to have a natter with the lads, you know.'

Cat showed her out and walked across the hall with her to the lift.

'Thanks for last night. You've no idea how much I needed to hear that.'

'No worries. I'll call you later.'

'I mean, I still feel like a dirty cow and I do need to talk to Billy about it, but it really helped.'

Angie turned to hug her, then nodded over her shoulder. 'Hello . . .'

Cat turned and they both stared at the half-open door to Grantleigh Figgis's flat.

'He never leaves the door open,' Cat said. 'Especially not now.'

Angie sucked her teeth. 'Yeah, well, if I was him I'd put a few extra padlocks on it.'

'It wouldn't be open if he'd gone out.'

'Actually, forget extra locks. I'd just leave the fucking country.'

Cat was already walking towards the open door.

Angie shouted after her. 'What are you so bothered about him for?' She sighed and followed Cat back across the hall. 'Just leave it . . .'

Cat said, 'Grant?' and nudged the door open with her slippered foot.

Then she said, 'Oh Christ.'

An hour later, back at Cat's place, drinking sweet tea with a generous shot of whisky in it, Angie looked up from the sofa at DC Ajay Roth as if he was an idiot and said, 'Do you not think I know what a body looks like?'

'I'm just trying to find out what happened right before you called us.'

'Listen, it was obvious he was dead.'

'You could tell that from looking round the door?'

'He was blue, for God's sake.'

In the kitchen, Thorne was talking to Catrin Coyne. She pulled

186

her dressing gown a little tighter across her chest and nodded towards the living room. 'When we found him, Angie said, "You don't need to be Sherlock Holmes to work out why he's topped himself".' She leaned back against the worktop. The shadows under her eyes were almost black. 'You think she's right?'

'Well . . .'

'Guilt.' Cat was staring down. 'Couldn't live with himself probably, that's what she meant.'

'We don't know anything yet.' Thorne saw her look at him and realised how that had sounded. *We don't know why Grantleigh Figgis is dead, we don't know if Grantleigh Figgis took your son, we don't know what happened to your son. We don't know our arse from our elbow.* As things stood, he could hardly blame her for thinking they were clueless about everything. 'Hopefully we'll have a better idea when they've finished next door.'

'Right.' Cat nodded slowly. 'A better idea.'

Behind her, in a glass-fronted cupboard, Thorne could see a mug with a bright cartoonish K on the side. The fridge was all but covered with the boy's paintings and drawings. 'Obviously I'll let you know as soon as we've got any more information—'

A uniformed PC wandered in looking a little sheepish and apologised for interrupting. He said, 'We've got the pathologist on the phone and there's a problem.'

Thorne told Cat he'd be back as soon as he could and followed the PC outside. 'What problem?'

'Him,' the PC said.

'Who?'

'The pathologist. He sounds like a right stroppy sod. Says he isn't coming over.'

Walking back into Figgis's flat, Thorne could see that the body had yet to be moved. Figgis lay half on and half off his sofa, one arm crooked against the carpet, a thin red belt tied tight, just above the elbow. A dried trail of blood snaked down the arm from the spot where the needle had gone in. The syringe was

187

on the floor – having presumably fallen out when the arm had dropped – and lay alongside the bent and blackened spoon, the disposable lighter, and the plastic bottle of lemon juice he had used to cook the heroin.

'Here we are again.'

Thorne looked up and recognised one of the SOCOs who had been there three days earlier when they'd examined the flat after Figgis's arrest and who was now dusting a small plastic bag for fingerprints. Before he could respond, Thorne saw Russell Brigstocke waving him across to the corner of the room, his hand clamped across the mouthpiece of a cordless phone.

Brigstocke thrust the phone towards him. 'Good luck.'

'This is DS Thorne. Who am I speaking to?'

'Hendricks,' the man said. A nasal, northern accent, Manchester by the sound of it. 'With a CKS, not an X like the guitarist, yeah? Are you going to be as much of a pain in the arse as your colleagues?'

Thorne was momentarily speechless.

'Now, like I tried to explain to the last bloke, there's really no need for me to come over there.'

'You're the on-call pathologist, aren't you?'

'Quite right, and here I am on a call, but you're looking at a bog-standard overdose, right?'

'Appears that way,' Thorne said.

'Spoons and shit, a needle knocking about, yeah? I mean, I don't want to tell you your job or anything.'

'That's good,' Thorne said. 'Because I wouldn't want to lose my temper.'

'I'm just saying, there's no point me hauling my arse up there to tell you what you already know. Sound reasonable to you?'

'Not really, no.' Thorne moved closer into the corner, aware that everyone in the room was looking at him. 'This death is connected to a serious and ongoing inquiry that is anything but bog-standard.'

'Oh, right. Sounds exciting, but not really my problem.'

'*What?*'

'Get your dead junkie over here and I'll do what I do. Until then, any idiot can tell you he's dead, have a stab at when he might have popped off; I mean, it's not difficult. So there's no need to panic, is there?'

'Nobody's panicking.'

'What it sounds like.'

'We're just trying to be professional.'

'Well that's a bonus, because I wouldn't want to work with amateurs, would I?'

Thorne looked round at Brigstocke. He shook his head and made the universally recognised gesture to indicate that the man he was talking to was somebody who overindulged in self-love. 'PM as soon as though, right?'

'Definitely. I'll be ready to carve him up for you first thing tomorrow morning.'

'Sorry,' Thorne said, 'but that's not going to be soon enough. We need this one done on the hurry-up.'

'Best I can do, mate.'

'Are you trying to piss me off?'

'Listen, you're welcome to shop around, see if there's anyone else who can do it sooner – and best of British with *that*, by the way – but I'm up to my elbows right now. Literally, as it happens, in some bloke whose wife caved his head in with a steam iron. Nine o'clock do you?'

Brigstocke was waving, mouthing. *What's going on?*

'I'll have to make some calls and let you know,' Thorne said.

'Up to you, mate.'

Thorne listened to the dial tone for a few seconds and muttered, 'Arrogant twat.'

'Sounds like someone needs a slap,' Brigstocke said.

Thorne thought the pathologist needed several, though it would have to wait until the following day. All being well, once the post-mortem was out of the way, he wouldn't have to see the bloke again, because it was a long time since he had come across anybody he'd taken a dislike to quite so quickly.

# THIRTY-FOUR

Josh shakes his head and says, 'The Hulk would *smash* blue Power Ranger. He'd smash him into little pieces.'

'What about Blue and Red Power Rangers together?' Kieron asks.

A nod, slow and certain. 'Yeah, the Hulk could smash both of them.' Josh grins as he demonstrates with his fist, pounding it against the floor. Smash, smash, smash . . .

'Are you sure?'

'He's the Hulk.'

'But they've got super-speed and super-strength,' Kieron says.

Josh shrugs, unimpressed.

'I bet he couldn't smash the Power Rangers and the Ninja Turtles if they *all* tried to fight him. Like, in a team.'

'Yeah, he could,' Josh says.

'All of them?'

'The Hulk would just crush every single one of them. He'd squash every turtle, easy.' He squeezes his fist and roars. 'Like a grape.' He roars louder and sticks his chest out.

That makes Kieron laugh and he doesn't really care any more

which one of the super-heroes would win in a fight. It usually ends up like this. Once, they were arguing about who would win out of Ant Man and Spiderman and Josh said that Ant Man would just crawl up Spiderman's bum and then go normal size, and he acted it out with all the noises, and that made Kieron laugh until he thought he'd wet himself.

Josh does the grape's squeaky voice. 'Please don't squash me!' Then the Hulk's low growl. 'Die, you stupid little grape-turtle . . . '

Kieron laughs again, but it sounds strange, now there's all that new stuff on the walls. Black and rubbery.

'Like the stuff Batman has,' Josh says.

'Yeah.'

'Maybe you should pretend this is the Batcave.'

Kieron tries, but he can't manage it, because he knows the Batcave would be bigger than this and not as cold and it wouldn't smell as bad.

Josh is wearing the same yellow coat he'd been wearing when Kieron had last seen him, when they'd been playing hide and seek in the woods. Josh always says the coat makes him look like a giant banana, but it's what he usually wears, except when they're playing inside at his house, or at Kieron's. If Kieron had the choice, he'd always prefer to be round at Josh's, because Josh's mum does amazing tea and there's a TV in the kitchen and a garden with a trampoline and a football net. He thinks his mum prefers it, too. If Josh and his mum ever come round to the flat, his mum is always smiling too much and sometimes she's a bit bad-tempered afterwards.

Kieron closes his eyes and tries to think about what Josh might say next.

Something funny . . .

'If *you* were Ant Man, you could crawl up the man's bum, the next time he comes down.'

Kieron tries to laugh, but it doesn't seem like such a funny idea this time.

'What would be the best superpower to have?' Josh asks.

'To be able to go invisible.' Kieron answers quickly, because he's thought about it. 'So the man can't find me. So when he comes down he'll think I've gone, then he'll leave the door open and I can get out.'

'I'd be the Hulk,' Josh says.

'You *always* want to be the Hulk,' Kieron says.

'Because he's the best.'

'Yeah, he *is* the best,' Kieron says.

Josh nods down at the shackle around Kieron's ankle. 'If I was the Hulk I could snap that stupid chain like it was made of jelly.' He roars again and grabs the chain that's attached to the wall. Kieron grabs it, too, and the pair of them pull and pull until they're out of breath.

There's nothing much they can say to each other after that.

Or, at least, Kieron is too tired to imagine what else they might say.

There's just a boiler rumbling in the house above, water sloshing through pipes somewhere and the noise of a fly that's stuck down here with him.

Kieron doesn't know if it's morning or night, but he lies down anyway.

Wonders if the Hulk ever cries; if his tears would be green.

He says goodnight to Josh and to his mum and tries to sleep.

# THIRTY-FIVE

Initially at least, things had threatened to go every bit as pear-shaped at Hornsey mortuary as they had done the previous day on the phone. Worse, in fact. Thorne was not predisposed to getting along with the bolshy pathologist anyway, but it hadn't helped that he'd immediately mistaken Dr Phil Hendricks (FRCPath) for one of the mortuary assistants.

Fortunately, the pathologist seemed a little less bolshy today.

'Understandable,' Hendricks said. He was fastening his plastic gown over tight black jeans and an equally tight black T-shirt with the fluorescent outline of a ribcage on the front. 'I suppose.'

'I just thought . . . ' Thorne was gesturing, vaguely. Then he pointed straight at Hendricks. 'I wasn't expecting you to look like . . . that.'

'Thought I'd be older?'

'Yeah.'

'A tad more conventional?'

'You know.' Thorne was still staring, waving his hands again. 'All of it.'

Hendricks was a few years younger than Thorne and looked

like someone who worked out regularly. He had what Thorne would have called a buzz-cut, but that seemed almost conformist compared to the alarming array of piercings on display. There were studs of various sizes running the length of each ear, rings through both nostrils and eyebrows, and a fearsome-looking spike protruding just below his bottom lip.

*How can this weirdo kiss anyone*, Thorne wondered, *without stabbing them in the face?*

Then there were the tattoos: Celtic rings and crucifixes; skulls, flames and hearts impaled on barbed wire. A snake curled down from the sleeve of his T-shirt and, when Hendricks turned round and asked Thorne to do his gown up for him, Thorne saw some hideous creature with scaly wings climbing the back of his neck.

'Last bloke I saw in here was wearing a bow tie,' Thorne said.

'Oh, I used to have one of them.' Hendricks was continuing to dress, snapping on nitrile gloves, pulling on bootees. 'One of them ones that spins round, you know?'

Thorne could not be sure he was joking.

'It upset the relatives, though.' He put on what appeared to be a pink plastic shower-cap and said, 'Shall we get stuck in?'

Thorne pointed to the shower-cap. 'You seriously wearing that?'

'Says the bloke in the cheap leather jacket and old man's Levi's.' Hendricks tied up his mask and pushed through the swing doors into the pathology suite.

Thorne swore beneath his breath, smeared a thick streak of Vicks across his top lip and followed.

Phil Hendricks may have looked like a bouncer at a Sisters Of Mercy concert, but he worked with as much skill and something like tenderness as any pathologist Thorne had ever seen. Or at least as tender as it was possible to be with a skull-saw and rib-cutters. Murmuring into a hand-held Dictaphone, in that flat accent which had so annoyed Thorne the day before, he moved around the slab like a dancer. Graceful, if almost certainly dangerous. He fingered the mottled and discoloured flesh as though wary of bruising it and gently set the dead man's organs on the scales, in stark contrast to many Thorne had seen slapping down livers and lungs like butchers weighing out cuts for Sunday lunch.

'Your man here was pretty healthy, all things considered,' Hendricks said, towards the end.

'Really?'

'I mean, not now, obviously.'

'Obviously,' Thorne said.

'But . . . you know. For a junkie.'

Thorne nodded, amazed as always by how much more you could tell from examining someone's innards than you could from looking at them when they were still walking around. How slicing carefully through a brain could reveal a truth you might never get to by asking questions of its owner. A face, clothes, whatever, only told others what you wanted them to know. Those things could lie, if you so chose; they could pretend. However we elected to present ourselves to the world, furred-up arteries or blotches on a pancreas always told the real story.

It worked the other way too, of course, he knew that. To some degree or other, everyone was guilty of judging people based purely on their manner or appearance. They made assumptions.

Books, covers, all that.

Thorne stared down at what remained of Grantleigh Figgis . . .

'You been enjoying the games?'

'What?' Thorne said.

'The Euros, mate. Thought the Dutch looked pretty tasty last night.'

'Didn't see it.' Thorne nodded towards the slab. 'All this to deal with.'

'Big one tomorrow.'

Thorne nodded. With England set to take on Scotland the following afternoon, bragging rights within the hate/hate relationship between Thorne and his boss were well and truly up for grabs. Thorne was desperately hoping he could find time to watch it somewhere. He looked at Hendricks, said, 'You're Manchester, right?'

Hendricks nodded and grinned. 'Blackley boy, mate.'

'So, what are you? City or United?'

'Neither. Only one team worth talking about.' He placed a bloodied, gloved hand across his chest, like he was swearing an oath of loyalty. 'And that's Bruce Rioch's mighty Arsenal.'

'You are joking, right? You're a bloody *Gooner*?'

Hendricks saw the look of horror on Thorne's face and his grin widened. 'You're Spurs? Bloody hell, no wonder you're so miserable. How many places above you did we finish?'

'It was two points,' Thorne said. 'That's all.'

Hendricks was laughing as he finished up. He checked that the organs were properly bagged, that the necessary blood and tissue samples were correctly labelled, then called in one of the assistants to close up Grantleigh Figgis's body. He lowered his mask as he and Thorne walked slowly towards the doors.

'It takes a big man to admit he was wrong,' Hendricks said. 'I'm big enough where it counts, so . . . maybe not quite as bog-standard as I thought it was.'

'An overdose, though?'

'Oh, yeah. *Seriously* over.'

'If you're going to top yourself,' Thorne said, 'you might as well get there doing something you enjoy, right?'

Hendricks stopped and looked at him. A half-smile, as though he'd been waiting for the right moment. Waiting, because he wanted to make the most of it. 'Who said anything about topping himself?'

'Come again?'

'It was done *for* him. Well, as good as. Matey boy over there was murdered, simple as.'

Thorne turned instinctively to look back at the slab, where the mortuary assistant was already busy with his thick needle and thread, sewing up the chest cavity. He stared, as though Grantleigh Figgis might nod in agreement or raise a thumb to confirm what Hendricks was saying.

'How the hell can you tell that before you've run any tests?'

'Piece of piss, my dear Watson.'

Hendricks wandered across to where the dead man's clothes lay, gathered into separate plastic bags. Thorne recognised the jogging bottoms and sleeveless pullover, the slippers that now simply looked sad. Hendricks took out a smaller plastic bag from inside another and held it up as if it were evidence of something other than simply his genius. Thorne noticed that the pathologist, having disposed of the gloves he'd used for the PM, was now wearing a fresh pair, presumably to avoid leaving prints.

'All you need to know, right there.'

Stepping closer, Thorne saw a small wrap of waxy paper inside the bag, the brown powder that had spilled from it gathered in the creases of the plastic.

'Where d'you find that?'

'In the pocket of his joggers,' Hendricks said.

Thorne stared at the bag, shook his head. 'Am I missing something?'

'Trust me, mate, any self-respecting junkie, if they were trying to OD, would take everything they could lay their hands on ... *everything*. They'd do the lot, I'm telling you. Soon as I found this, I knew he hadn't killed himself.'

'You *knew*?'

'Hundred per cent. Junkies tend to be a bit greedy with the smack, know what I mean?' He shrugged. 'What's the point in leaving any?'

'This based on ... specialist knowledge, is it?'

'Let's just say I've known some interesting people.' Hendricks looked at Thorne, whose expression still suggested that he was dubious. 'Don't worry, the toxicology tests will prove it. Street heroin, which is what you would have expected him to take if he'd scored it himself, has all sorts of impurities from the opium, the most obvious one being noscapine, yeah? So, if the tests show up 6-monoacetylmorphine or 6-MAP, which is what diacetylmorphine metabolises into when it's injected, and they also show noscapine, we're looking at run-of-the-mill smack. Shout up if this is too much science for you?'

'Go on,' Thorne said.

'But I'm betting we find plenty of 6-MAP but we *won't* find noscapine, which means that whatever he took was very pure. Medical-grade morphine near as damn it, and certainly a damn sight pokier than this poor sod was used to or that his body could stand. Something given to him by someone who knew exactly what they were handing over and exactly what the outcome would be. So, there we go.' He sniffed. 'You're welcome.'

'Right . . .'

Thorne had already forgotten the potted chemistry lesson, but he was busy trying to process its basic conclusion: Hendricks's assertion that Grantleigh Figgis had not taken his own life. Wrestling with the implications for the inquiry and those who were orchestrating it.

The damage limitation that would almost certainly be needed.

Hendricks laid the small plastic bag carefully back inside the larger one before they walked back out into the locker room and he began to get changed. He dumped gown, mask and boot-ees into the hazardous waste bin and sat down to put on some serious-looking boots. Buckles, straps and more studs, metal hooks instead of lace-holes.

Like he might be going mountaineering.

Nobody's idea of a *strip of piss*, Thorne thought. But definitely *proper funny*.

'To answer your earlier question,' Hendricks said. 'That "specialist knowledge" I might or might not have? Yeah, I've popped a few pills in my time, got mashed on a bit of other gear now and again, but no . . . I have never taken heroin.' He stood up and opened a locker, took out a heavy-duty biker's jacket and shook his head sadly. 'Shame really, because I gather it's quite more-ish.'

# THIRTY-SIX

Trudging back up the Holloway Road towards home, Cat wondered why clean clothes always seemed that much heavier than when they were dirty. Stepping aside to avoid two teenage boys cycling on the pavement, she exchanged a look with the officer who had accompanied her to the launderette; a smile that was not returned. The WPC was as friendly as she needed to be but had kept conversation to a minimum since clearing a path through the crowd of reporters waiting outside Seacole House. A firm instruction for Cat to keep moving, a word or two in the launderette as she'd helped Cat find the right change for the machines.

The woman was just doing her job, Cat guessed.

No room for sentiment, or judgement.

Cat had known there would be renewed press interest because a body had been discovered, and the questions shouted at her as she'd struggled through the mêlée with her bags of dirty washing an hour and a half before had made it very clear they already knew whose body it was.

*'Why do you think he killed himself, Cat?'*

'*Was there a note?*'

'*Are you glad he's dead?*'

Cat was happy enough to ignore the questions, because she didn't have an answer for any of them.

Now, she shifted the bin bag from one shoulder to another, felt the weight of the clothes, soft against her back, and felt a little better. A little more normal than she had done in a few days.

Happy with the deal she'd made with God or fate or whatever.

For almost an hour the night before, she had sat slumped beside the laundry basket in her bedroom, soaking up the tears with her son's dirty clothes and bed linen. Breathing in the sweat-sweet, glorious smell of him on stained sheets and Power Rangers T-shirts, on his favourite jeans and his smart blue school jumper. She had pressed each item to her face, all too aware that if she washed them, that smell would be lost for ever, the last trace of him.

Cat had wept, because she could not decide what to do, what to believe.

She knew that if she chose not to wash Kieron's dirty things, it was only because some part of her had accepted that he was not coming back. That this might be all she had left. It was stupid, she knew it was stupid, it was only a bit of washing for Christ's sake, but ... if she refused to acknowledge that terrible possibility and washed his clothes like she always did, couldn't that just as surely mean that one day he'd be home safe and sound to make them dirty all over again?

Like avoiding the cracks on the pavement.

She would take any sign, clutch at any straw.

In the end, Cat had decided that hope was all she had left to hold on to and that she would be picking up her beautiful boy's stinky socks and grubby pants for a long time to come, so she had stuffed them all into the bin bag, swearing that she would never moan about having to do it ever again.

That she would never moan about anything.

The WPC moved a few steps ahead as they approached the tower block, a couple of her colleagues coming to join them, ready to run intercept. The dozen or so reporters surged forward and were blocked with stiff arms and harsh words from the police officers. Cat was once again told to move as fast as she could towards the entrance, but then she recognised the face of a man waving at her and stopped. Seeing that he had Cat's attention, the man stepped towards her and an officer barred his way.

'It's OK,' Cat said. 'I know him.'

The man was allowed through and, even though Cat's reaction had made it obvious that she knew who he was, he said, 'Simon Jenner. From St Mary's?'

'Yeah, I know.' Cat felt herself redden slightly and struggled for something to say next. *Nice to see you? Thank you for coming?*

'I was just—'

'Shit . . . I never called the school. To say that Kieron wouldn't be coming in. I'm sorry—'

The teacher laid a hand on her arm. 'Don't be silly. We all read about what had happened . . . and the police came in to talk to us.'

'Oh, I didn't know. Was that . . . OK?'

'Yes, fine. Just all the questions you'd expect them to ask and obviously everyone was eager to help.'

The WPC was ushering them both forward, still keen to get Cat inside.

'Do you want to come up?' Cat asked.

In the lift, Cat gabbled a little; the white-hot chaos of those first few days, the police and the reporters, her complete inability to think straight. 'Didn't know if I was coming or going,' she said. 'Still don't, sorry.'

'Please stop apologising,' Jenner said.

Cat hoped she had stopped blushing.

The young teacher – well, a few years younger than she was

anyway – was someone Cat had noticed on Kieron's first day at school and had more than happily run into several times since. He had short, sandy hair and very blue eyes. A shy smile. He wore a denim jacket over a yellow T-shirt and one of those funny corduroy caps that John Lennon used to wear. He looked more like a student than a teacher, Cat thought. It was harmless, of course, but there had been moments, late at night or on dull afternoons, when she'd found herself imagining a parent/teacher relationship that was highly inappropriate for a good many reasons. It was fine, of course, because she didn't believe for a minute that she was the only woman Billy ever thought about in that way. There had even been one or two desperate occasions, before the arsewipe had actually reappeared in person, that Dean Meade had crept into her fantasies.

*That* would certainly never be happening again.

Cat could not be sure how much Simon Jenner knew about the most recent events, but when they stepped out of the lift there was no ignoring the crime-scene tape that criss-crossed the door next to her own.

'There was a body found,' she said.

Jenner stared as they walked towards Cat's flat. 'Was it the man that's been in the papers?'

'Yeah,' Cat said. 'The man in the papers.'

'Must be awful for you.'

'Relative, isn't it?' Cat shrugged. 'Hard to remember when everything *wasn't* awful.' She dug keys from her bag and opened her front door. 'Do you want some tea?'

A few minutes later, once Cat had shifted her bedding from the sofa and they'd sat down with tea, Jenner said, 'I just wanted to come over to let you know that we're all thinking about you.'

Cat nodded.

'All of us at the school.'

'Thanks,' Cat said.

'We're all missing Kieron.' The teacher reached into the

leather satchel he'd brought with him and produced a large card. He passed it across. 'Everyone signed it. All the kids . . . the teachers.' He watched Cat open the card and read it, then quickly went back into the satchel for tissues. 'Sorry . . . '

'Now you're the one who's apologising.'

Seeing Cat smile, Jenner smiled himself and shook his head. 'It's so hard to know what to say. There's nothing you *can* say, is there?'

'Not really,' Cat said. She held up the card. 'Thank you for this. I'll put it on the sideboard, so it's there waiting for him.'

Jenner nodded, drank his tea.

'He *is* coming back.'

'Course.'

'Back home and back to school.'

'I know,' Jenner said.

'And you know how bright he is, right? So he won't have any problem catching up.'

'He won't have missed very much, anyway. There's never very much happening once we get close to the summer holidays.'

'Tell me,' Cat said.

While they finished their tea, Jenner told her about the teacher who had just started at the school and a couple of new kids who would be coming the following term, one of whom would be in the same class as Kieron. He talked about some new equipment they'd be having installed in the playground and the head teacher's ideas for a couple of school trips later in the year: a city farm in Vauxhall, a boat trip along the Thames.

'Kieron's going to love that,' Cat said. 'He's mad about boats.'

Jenner thanked her for the tea and picked up his satchel. He moved towards the door. 'Anyway, like I said, I just wanted you to know we were thinking about you.'

'Hope you manage to get through the mob downstairs,' Cat said.

'Don't worry.' He hung the satchel over his shoulder, lingered at the door. 'When you have to handle thirty-something seven-year-olds every day, that lot's a doddle.'

Seeing that he was ready to leave, itching to get out quite probably, Cat knew that she should get up and see him to the lift, but suddenly she didn't have the strength. Not an ounce of it. She clutched the card Jenner had delivered to her chest and it was as though its simple message of love and support, the multicoloured jumble of childish signatures, was pressing her down on to the sofa.

# THIRTY-SEVEN

Detective Sergeant Paula Kimmel leaned back against the wall of the cramped tea station and nursed her Cup-a-Soup, one eye on Thorne as he mashed his teabag then hunted in the fridge for the sole carton of milk that hadn't yet become cheese. She grunted – just loudly enough, Thorne reckoned, for him to hear and so clock that she was happy enough to chat, you know ... if he fancied it. The signal wasn't needed. Thorne had already begun to wonder why the woman hadn't immediately taken her drink back to her desk the way she usually did, why she had hung around.

Thorne blew on his tea, held up the paper cup. 'This is the only reason I got into the job,' he said. 'The glamour.'

She smiled, ran fingers through short dark hair with an undisguised smattering of early grey at the roots. 'Right.'

Kimmel was a good copper, Thorne had decided, better than good, but up to this point, based on the couple of snatched conversations they'd had, she'd been all business. Almost certainly because she had to be, he thought. Because choosing to get her nut down and not waste time on bullshit and banter might be

207

the only way to get ahead – or even to stay on something like level terms – when she was the only member of the team without a penis.

Thorne smiled back.

Gordon Boyle *probably* had a penis, he thought, but it was almost certainly only visible with the aid of an electron microscope.

'Somebody's put the cat among the pigeons,' Kimmel said.

Thorne looked at her. Sipped his tea. He knew that by *somebody* she meant him.

'I'd heard you were pretty good at that.'

'I wasn't the one doing the post-mortem,' Thorne said.

'Don't shoot the messenger, you mean?'

'Something like that.' Though shooting might have been going a little far, even for Boyle, the DI's expression had visibly darkened when Thorne had passed on what Hendricks had told him. He had certainly looked as though he wouldn't have minded giving Thorne a good kicking. A Glasgow kiss, at the very least. 'You think it's bad news, then? That Figgis was murdered?'

Kimmel poured what was left of her soup into the sink and turned on the tap. 'Bad news for somebody.'

Thorne knew who *that* somebody was, too. Whoever had leaked Grant Figgis's identity, and almost certainly his address, to the newspapers. 'Hope whoever it was had a decent payday,' Thorne said. 'Enough to last them through an early retirement.'

'They might not have time to spend it,' Kimmel said. 'There's a case to be made for bringing charges, I reckon.'

'For what, though?' Thorne took another mouthful of tea and considered it. 'Accessory's probably pushing it. Perverting the course, maybe.'

'What about just ... "being an arsehole"?' Kimmel smiled again, steely. 'I know the CPS might not go for it, but worth a try.'

'If we ever find out who it was,' Thorne said. 'And *if* the powers-that-be decide to air the Met's dirty linen.'

The silence that fell between them was enough to acknowledge that both ifs were sizeable and was only broken when Ajay Roth leaned around the corner.

'DI's office,' he said. 'Now.'

Thorne had never been very good at dissembling, at keeping his thoughts from being eminently readable on his face. Roth's reaction made it clear that what was going through Thorne's mind at that moment might just as well have been flashing up in neon on the wall behind him.

*I don't much appreciate what sounded a lot like an order being barked at me by an officer I outrank. Fair enough, Ajay? Certainly not one whose tongue is usually so far up his guvnor's fat arse that I'm always amazed when he manages to say anything at all.*

Kimmel was looking at the floor, but Thorne knew that she'd seen it, too.

'Just . . . passing that on,' Roth said.

Boyle had been at his desk, head down over paperwork, when Thorne and Kimmel arrived to join Roth and Brigstocke in the DI's office, but now he stood up, walked round and leaned back against it. He appeared casual, confident even, in the wake of an urgent meeting with DCI Andy Frankham and the chief superintendent, which everyone on the team had presumed would be tricky to say the least.

A prime suspect released then hand-fed to the mob.

A man murdered inside a building with officers stationed outside, only hours after begging the police for help.

A plutonium-grade cock-up.

'So, a confirmed overdose, then,' Boyle said.

'An overdose, for sure.' Thorne looked to Brigstocke for a little support.

'Not self-inflicted, though,' Brigstocke said. 'Not by the look of it. The heroin, for a kick-off.'

Thorne sat forward. 'Pure morphine, basically, and if not

209

actually administered by a third party, supplied in the full knowledge of what would happen when Figgis shot up.'

'Right,' Boyle said. 'According to this new weirdo pathologist we've been lumbered with.'

'Hendricks,' Roth said.

'His theory.'

'Which he's certain will be confirmed when the toxicology results come back.' Thorne sat back again. 'Yeah, he takes a bit of getting used to, but he knows what he's talking about, I can promise you that.'

'Well, it's certainly worth bearing in mind,' Boyle said.

Thorne looked to Brigstocke again, then to Paula Kimmel, then back to Boyle. 'We *are* opening a murder investigation?'

'Obviously, if that's what it turns out to be, but let's not get ahead of ourselves.'

'Don't we want to get ahead of the game?'

Boyle's manner wasn't quite so casual any more. 'Come on, Tom. What did Russell say a minute ago? Not self-inflicted by the look of it.' He nodded at Brigstocke. 'Right?'

Brigstocke hesitated.

'A suspicious death,' Kimmel said. 'That's what he meant. So surely—'

'I don't understand.' Thorne took care to keep his voice down, his tone nice and even. He understood completely, but there was little to be gained in a shouting match, especially when he knew Boyle would give as good as he got. 'If we'd found Figgis with half his head splattered up the wall and a gun in his hand we wouldn't take it at face value, would we? We'd still check the gun for prints or whatever, look for signs of forced entry. We'd still do a proper job. So why is this any different?'

'It's not.' Boyle raised his hands, helpless. 'We're stuck waiting for toxicology results. Not sure there's a lot more we can do.'

'We could talk to Billy Coyne,' Thorne said. 'He's got to be pretty high on a list of suspects. He's just found out he's not

Kieron's dad. He's all over the place, probably; every chance he's going to lash out, I would have thought.'

Boyle shook his head. 'Too early, you ask me. I've already sent officers to interview him once, the day after the boy was taken, so let's hold fire on that for now.'

'Hold fire?'

'OK, we can call and check Coyne's visitors' list, for now. Look, I've already spoken to Andy about this. Made sure he's up to speed about everything – your pathologist's theory included – and we're on the same page. Fair enough?'

*Andy?* As if Boyle and Frankham were best mates, suddenly. It was becoming clearer by the moment that the meeting had been less about upgrading the inquiry and more about damage limitation. Boyle seemed keen to move on, but Thorne didn't want to let him.

'I just think, seeing as you seem so bothered about how things *look*, we shouldn't forget that we all thought Figgis *looked* guilty.' Thorne jabbed a finger to his chest. 'Me especially. It looked like he was the man we're after, but we couldn't find a single piece of evidence to back that up and the only witness we had turned out to be useless. Figgis looked so *very* guilty that the papers, with a bit of help, pretty much told everyone he *was*, and that was obviously good enough for whichever upstanding member of society decided to handle things personally and give him enough top-of-the-range smack to kill an elephant.'

Thorne stopped and glanced around. Brigstocke was look-ing at Boyle, and Roth sat with his arms folded, like he had somewhere better to be. Thorne caught Kimmel's eye just for a moment and she gave him the smallest of nods.

Boyle said, 'Noted, Tom.' He walked back around his desk and sat down again, then looked to Ajay Roth. 'How are we getting on with the parents?'

They had, thus far, been unable to trace Figgis's next of kin, with no mention of parents or siblings to be found on any official

211

documents, as though they had deliberately been omitted or even expunged. In the end, with no one else available to do what was required, they had asked a work colleague to provide the official identification of the body.

'Finally managed to track down the mother.'

Roth revealed this breakthrough as though it was the result of many hours of dogged police work, when Thorne had overheard him an hour or so earlier describing the difficulty in contacting anyone close to the dead man as a 'decent bit of luck'.

'The dad died a few years ago,' Roth said. 'After they both moved to Australia.' He described the steps he'd taken to locate Margaret Figgis, her current whereabouts and circumstances. 'I spent a good while on the phone with her, passed on condolences, all that, but I've got to say she didn't seem massively upset. She never mentioned a funeral, asked for more information, anything like that. I don't think they were close.'

Another bit of luck, Thorne thought. Nobody to make a fuss or hold them to account. Nobody to go after the newspapers that put Grantleigh Figgis on trial alongside the horoscopes, the competitions to win holidays or free booze for the weekend, and the 'Starbirds' with their tits out.

'Good work, Ajay,' Boyle said. 'Never an easy conversation to have, we all know that.'

While the DI said a few more things designed to bring his team back together, to gee them up as they resumed the push to find a missing boy, Thorne found himself thinking instead about a middle-aged woman living alone in a suburb of Adelaide. Not all families were like the Waltons, he knew that. Brothers and sisters, mums, dads and kids fell out for all sorts of reasons and minor disputes could easily escalate, most especially between those who were supposed to be close. The estrangement between Grantleigh Figgis and his parents sounded more than usually serious, though.

Had it been his decision to cut them out of his life, or theirs?

'Right then,' Boyle said. 'Moving forward . . . '

Thorne wondered what had happened between them. Something simple and stupid, probably. Or perhaps Margaret Figgis and her husband had not liked the way their own son *looked* any more than everyone else.

# THIRTY-EIGHT

Laying down the Roald Dahl book, an hour or more after she'd first brought Josh upstairs, Maria sat at the end of his bed and watched her still wide-awake son snuggle tight to a stuffed bear called Snowball, which he'd had since birth. One of many presents from Jeff's passive-aggressive mother, if she recalled. Maria had washed the grubby white bear and stashed it away in a cupboard a few years ago, once Josh had replaced it with toy cars and superhero figures, but it had been quickly brought out of hibernation and Josh had been keeping it close – tearful if he so much as lost sight of it – since Kieron had gone missing.

Before then, now that Maria thought about it.

The friction at home and then the divorce; problems of some sort at school. Maria still couldn't put her finger on exactly when or why things had started to become difficult for her son.

'I want to go back to school,' Josh said, pulling the bear closer.

'I don't think that's a very good idea, chicken.'

'You said I could.'

'Of course you can go back to school, but not just yet, that's all. It's been horrible for you. With Kieron and everything.'

'I *want* to go.'

There was a vehemence in his voice Maria didn't much like the sound of, but she comforted herself with the thought that his wanting to go back so badly had to be a good sign. That he was on the mend, that perhaps he hadn't been lying when she'd asked if anyone was being horrible to him at school. If Josh was being bullied or if there was a teacher he was frightened of for whatever reason, surely he'd be keen to stay away.

'Well, why don't we wait and see how things go over the next couple of days?' Maria said.

'Why can't I go back tomorrow?'

'Because it's Saturday tomorrow.' She squeezed his foot through the duvet. 'Silly.'

He groaned in frustration, then growled as he grabbed the edge of the duvet and pulled it up over his face.

'If you still feel OK about it on Monday, maybe you can go back.'

Josh's face reappeared slowly and he nodded, serious. 'I don't want to wear my yellow coat.'

'Oh.' Maria had washed the mud off the coat as soon as they'd got back from the woods that terrible afternoon. He'd never much liked it, but she guessed that now he was associating it with his missing friend. She told him it was fine, that she'd buy him a new coat. One that didn't make him look like a banana. 'You should try and go to sleep now,' she said. 'You look ever so tired.' She stood up, leaned down to kiss him and moved towards the door.

'Don't turn the light off,' he said. He turned his face away so that she couldn't see it. 'Snowball doesn't like the dark.'

Maria half-closed the door, walked downstairs and opened the bottle she'd been thinking about through three chapters of *George's Marvellous Medicine*.

Hers was even better.

She sat down and turned on the TV, became quickly annoyed

by what seemed like wall-to-wall football coverage, so switched to the VCR and began to watch an episode of *This Life* that she'd taped a couple of nights earlier. She didn't much like Anna and thought Egg was a bit soppy, but the actor playing Miles was unquestionably dishy. He reminded her a little of Jeff actually, of a younger Jeff, anyway, and she found herself wondering what he was doing on a Friday evening, who he might be with.

She poured herself another glass of wine.

Now Warren, the gay one, was flirting with a motor-cycle courier.

She turned down the volume and picked up the phone.

'I suppose you're watching the bloody football,' she said when he answered.

He took a few seconds. 'Is everything OK?'

'Everything's fine.' Maria swirled the red wine around in her glass, took a quick mouthful. 'There doesn't always have to be a problem. I know that if I'm calling you it's usually because there *is*, but we can just . . . talk. That is allowed, you know.'

Jeff laughed. 'Right, but you must admit it's normally because you need money for something.'

'I don't need any money. Honestly.' She was smiling as she lifted her feet up on to the sofa; flirting, she supposed, the way she'd done with that younger Jeff ten years before. When they were Miles and Anna. 'Obviously if you want to send me some just because you feel like it, I'm not going to say—'

'Or it's a problem with Josh. Is he all right?'

'He's fine,' she said. 'So come on then, who's playing?'

'Italy versus the Czech Republic.'

'Sounds gripping.'

'Not a bad match, actually.'

'You don't even like football.'

'*What?*'

'Not really.'

He laughed again. 'Yes, I do.'

216

'Well, you definitely prefer rugby. I don't remember you ever going to watch a game.' She waited for him to come back at her, enjoying the cut-and-thrust of it. She took another drink and leaned down to pick up the bottle.

He said, 'You were a bit quick before.'

'What?'

'When I asked if Josh was all right. And you changed the subject.'

Maria poured herself some more wine. 'He's still upset about Kieron. Still a bit fragile.'

'Right,' Jeff said. 'Of course he is.'

'Clinging on to that bear like it's his only friend in the world.'

'Snowball? Blimey, I thought he was way past that.'

'He's keen to go back to school, though, so that's a good sign. Don't you think?'

'Listen . . . have you ever wondered if it might be something else? These problems he's having?'

'Such as?'

She heard him swallow and there was silence for a few seconds. 'Such *as*, Jeff?'

'You know what I mean, Mazz.'

'You're being ridiculous.'

'I don't know who he sees, do I? Friends of yours.'

'I don't *have* any bloody friends,' Maria said.

'Sorry—'

'Well, not very many, and none that you need to be concerned about.'

'I just don't think we should ignore the possibility that . . . somebody's doing something to hurt him. Oh, God, I don't know.'

'It's this business with Kieron, that's all. On top of the divorce. All that upheaval.'

Ashton grunted. 'I wish you'd let me take him for a bit. I'd really like to spend more time with him.'

217

'It's fine.'

'Well, yes, it's fine for *you*.' There was an edge to his voice suddenly. 'It suits you perfectly ... same as the fact that he's always loved you more than he loves me.'

'Now you're being really stupid,' Maria said.

'We don't *have* to stick to our arrangement, that's all I'm saying.'

'I know we don't, but—'

'Especially when something awful like this happens.'

'I just don't think now's a good time to change things.'

'No, you're probably right.'

'His routine, you know? It's important.'

She heard him sigh. 'Next weekend then?'

'He's looking forward to it.' She reached to try and smooth out a crease in her skirt, rubbed at it. 'It'll be even more of a treat than usual.'

'So, how are *you* doing?'

On screen, Warren and the motorcycle courier were kissing, their hands all over each other. Hungry.

'Oh, you know me,' she said.

'Yeah, you were always good in a crisis.'

'Was I?' The wine like acid suddenly, her tongue coated with it, thick and heavy in her mouth. A man who had drifted so far from the one she had fallen in love with, who she had finally begun to glimpse again, describing a woman she no longer recognised.

Lost, lonely and ashamed.

He said, 'I just miss him, you know ... ?'

Maria closed her eyes, feeling the tears brimming. 'I know you do.'

# THIRTY-NINE

It was a warm night, and George Jones singing about heart-break and helplessness provided a particularly appropriate soundtrack as Thorne sat outside in one of the rarely used garden chairs, leafing through the property-for-sale section of the *Evening Standard*. Once he'd got over the extortionate price of everything and started thinking realistically about the sort of place he'd be able to afford, the process became marginally less unpleasant.

Horrible as opposed to straight-up hideous.

He looked at the details of a flat he quite liked the look of in Kentish Town. It was handy for the Tube and there was an Indian restaurant just around the corner he'd heard good things about. Taking into account stamp duty, solicitor's fees and the like – if he didn't mind doing without food and furniture for a while – he reckoned he *might* be able to afford it, once the house was sold and he'd taken his share.

Then he blinked and that memory jumped into his head again. Jan laughing at him. Passing out day in Hendon.

His mum and dad had been there, too, dressed up to the

nines, and they'd laughed along with her. They'd always loved Jan, still did as far as Thorne could tell. They certainly kept strangely quiet whenever he said anything negative about her and he nursed an uncomfortable suspicion that they thought the divorce was all his fault. That perhaps he had devoted more time and attention to the Job than he'd done to his wife. That maybe he was the one to blame for what she and the lecturer had been getting up to while he was busy working overtime shifts.

Right . . .

Clearly, he'd as good as begged her to sneak round to the lecturer's flat wearing brand-new underwear. To unbutton the creepy bastard's denim shirt and climb into his bed. Candles burning in wine bottles, almost certainly, and a red cloth draped over a lamp, with some tuneless sixties shit playing while they were at it . . .

She'd been taking a picture, that blazing afternoon at the Police Training College, and had struggled to keep the Instamatic straight because she'd been laughing so much.

*'What . . . ?'*

*'Nothing. Just . . . you in your massive policeman's helmet, that's all.'*

*Saying the words 'policeman's helmet' made her laugh even more.*

*'Just hurry up and take it, love. I'm roasting in all this.'*

*'Why d'you have to wear those stupid white gloves, anyway?'*

*'How should I know?'*

*'Are they so your helmet stays nice and shiny?'*

*She'd laughed a whole lot harder later on, once she'd watched him trying to march.*

Thorne opened the paper again and drew a circle around the Kentish Town flat. It was all academic anyway; looking at places he might be able to buy once the house in Highbury had been sold when the house hadn't even been put on the market yet. He would do it, because he'd promised Jan, because he knew it was the right thing to do, but not quite yet.

220

Talk about putting the cart before the horse. It was like . . . opening a murder investigation before you'd got toxicology results. Thorne muttered to himself, a cod Glaswegian growl. *'Let's not get ahead of ourselves.'*

Presuming they did open a murder investigation, he wondered – bearing in mind the degree of responsibility the team could be seen to have had for the death – just how thorough any such inquiry would be. How hard would they really try to catch the person responsible for the death of Grantleigh Figgis?

Probably about as hard as they'd be looking for Kieron Coyne.

Seven days missing, there was an unspoken understanding that, whether Figgis had taken the boy or not, they were almost certainly looking for a body. They wouldn't stop, but they wouldn't waste unnecessary effort, either. Preservation of life was the number one priority, always would be, but once that seemed futile . . .

Manpower shortages, fresh cases, back-burners.

Of course, once in a blue moon, someone would wander into a police station somewhere and announce that they were Child X or Teenager Y who had gone missing many years earlier. It was always a huge story because it was so unbelievable, so extraordinary. It didn't take long on the job before you came to see just how extraordinary such things were, because day to day you dealt with crimes that, however terrible, were perfectly, *shockingly* ordinary.

You understood that such things were run of the mill.

You hoped, but you tried not to be stupid.

You played the odds.

Thorne tossed the paper on to the garden table, picked up a mug of coffee that had gone cold and wandered back inside. He moved aimlessly from room to room, thinking about Catrin Coyne. He thought about the individual tasked with identifying Grantleigh Figgis's body and tried to imagine how much harder it would be if the body you were staring down at was your child's.

If. When . . .

On cue, George Jones began to sing 'He Stopped Loving Her Today' which was, Thorne thought, just about the saddest song he'd ever heard. It was one the great man had nearly not recorded because he'd thought it too miserable, famously describing it as a 'morbid son of a bitch'.

Thorne guessed that, right then, it was exactly what he was. It was hard to know if this was just something he'd learned – a grim default position, adopted once hope had given way to expectation – and by the time the song had finished he was still trying to remember if he'd been like this all those years before.

Full of piss and vinegar on that blazing afternoon.

In a stupid hat and spotless white gloves.

# FORTY

The IRA were not in the habit of doing the Metropolitan Police any favours, and certainly not four months earlier, when a bomb in Docklands had killed two people and injured over one hundred more. Today, though, there were some officers in their debt, even if most would not dream of saying such a thing out loud. Not to anyone who wasn't a fellow football fan, anyway.

Thorne had overheard one such officer talking quietly to an Irish colleague and saying: 'I owe your boys one.'

The Irishman, who happened to be from Dublin, had smiled thinly and said, 'Not my fucking boys.'

News of a serious explosion in the centre of Manchester had begun to come through just after eleven thirty a.m. and, though details were scant, the headlines did the job: a massive blast; widespread damage and countless injuries, but, thanks to a tele-phoned warning and a well-organised evacuation, no fatalities.

A large-scale terrorist incident on the day of a major football international inevitably resulted in a shift of priorities. While anti-terror units were immediately placed on high alert and security measures ramped up in advance of the three o'clock game at Wembley Stadium, the focus was temporarily taken away from those tasked with investigating serious crimes that were not politically motivated.

A degree of leeway had been created.

On the second floor of Islington station, calls were made to the top brass, schedules were hurriedly rearranged and an accommodation reached before the smoke had settled. Any officer who was happy to work an extra hour at the end of their shift could take a slightly later and somewhat longer lunch if they so wished. It was no great surprise when a decent number opted to eat their lunches between two forty-five and four forty-five in the nearest pub and it didn't hurt that the DI was as keen to see the England/Scotland game as anybody.

'I hope football *is* coming home,' Boyle said, several times. 'Just so we can break in this afternoon and nick it.'

Now, five minutes before kick-off, the main bar of the Crown on Penton Street was rammed, and though many were keen to stay up to speed with developments in Manchester, a cheer went up when the channel on the big-screen TV was changed and the serious face of a newscaster was replaced with the lush green of the pitch, an undulating wall of flags and the two teams of players lined up and itching to get going.

Venables looking nervous in the dug-out.

The pundits making last-minute predictions.

The cheering turned quickly to boos, in the pub as well as the stadium, when 'Flower of Scotland' was played. Boyle, at a table with a handful of fellow Scots, turned, grinning, to raise a finger and someone at the back of the room – clearly more concerned with impressing his mates than getting promoted any time soon – began to chuck peanuts at him.

'Here we go, then . . .'

Thorne looked up from his seat at the table he was sharing with several others, including Paula Kimmel who, it turned out, was a rabid Crystal Palace fan. Phil Hendricks had somehow managed to commandeer a spare chair and now he was struggling to squeeze it in next to Thorne's.

'Sorry about the smell,' the pathologist said. 'It was either shower or miss the kick-off and I'm probably only a *bit* . . . corpsey.'

'Bloody hell,' Kimmel said.

'You get used to him,' Thorne said, shifting his chair sideways.

Hendricks rubbed his hands together. 'Right, who wants a drink?'

Thorne stared glumly down at a glass of Diet Coke. 'I'd love one, but I'd better not.' A good few of those around him, Kimmel included, had decided that the leeway extended to a pint with their late lunch, though they were well aware that their boss might not be quite so prepared to look the other way if Scotland went three goals down.

'Well, I'm having one.' Hendricks tugged gently at the spike beneath his lip. 'Only got one more job on this afternoon and the gentleman concerned is hardly likely to smell it on my breath, is he?'

He began pushing his way towards the bar and the officer on the other side of Thorne leaned over, rolling his eyes. Muttered, 'Who's your friend?'

'His name's Phil,' Thorne said.

Hendricks was back at the table just as the players were taking their positions in and around the centre circle. He laid down a pint of Guinness and several bags of crisps, then shrugged off his leather jacket to reveal a vintage Arsenal shirt. There were more than a few jeers, from Kimmel and others.

'Oh, spare us,' Thorne said.

Hendricks sat down, shaking his head. 'Don't be like that. We put our petty rivalries to one side when England are playing, don't we?'

'Are you OK?' Thorne asked.

Hendricks looked at him. 'Yeah, I'm good, mate. What?'

The accent would have made it obvious to anyone who'd ever seen an episode of *Coronation Street*, but Thorne remembered exactly where Hendricks had told him he was from.

*Blackley boy* . . .

'The bomb,' Thorne said.

Hendricks nodded. 'Oh, yeah.'

'Just wondering if you still had any family up there.'

'Not in the city centre,' Hendricks said. 'Anyway, I've already called and everyone's fine.'

'That's good,' Thorne said.

'So, they reckon the IRA did a couple of million quid's worth of improvements this morning. Pretty funny, right?' Hendricks smiled, but only for a second, before he took a decent-sized gulp of beer.

'Horrible, though,' Thorne said. 'You must have been worried.'

Hendricks swallowed fast and began to clap when the whistle went.

Forty-five tense and shouty minutes later, it was still nil-nil and there was a rush for the toilets, while those throwing caution to the wind and keen to get more drinks in moved with equal speed towards the bar.

Thorne said, 'So, why all the tattoos?'

'Eh?'

'I mean, I can understand one or two.'

'What, like *LOVE* and *HATE* across my knuckles?'

'There's more ink than skin.'

'They're notches on my bedpost,' Hendricks said.

'Come again?'

'Well, I had a couple when I was younger . . . nothing very fancy mind but lately I've been getting myself a new one every time I get lucky – every time someone else gets lucky, I should say. I get my end away, then I'm straight down the tattoo parlour the next morning for a souvenir. I've got loads, mate.' Hendricks tore open the remaining packet of cheese and onion, grabbed

226

a handful and offered it to Thorne. 'Getting a bit addicted to it, if I'm honest, and I don't mind the pain. Quite like it, as it happens.' He stuffed more crisps into his mouth and grinned. 'Then again, you're probably used to pain, being a Spurs fan.'

'What happened to putting petty rivalries aside?'

'Only during the game, mate,' Hendricks said. 'Half time doesn't count.'

Thorne turned back to the television, having decided that there really were a lot of tattoos and that there had to be some seriously strange women about. Thinking that if the bloke had any other piercings like that vicious-looking one below his gob, it would be like shagging a hedgehog.

Eight minutes into the second half, the pub erupted when Shearer put England ahead. Once things had settled down a little, Thorne stared across towards Boyle's table, hoping the Scotsman would turn round, but he was out of luck. With ten minutes left and England still ahead, the predictable song had just begun to ring around the bar when Scotland were awarded a penalty.

Now Boyle turned round. He got to his feet and shouted, 'Get it up ye!'

The roar when Seaman saved the spot-kick had not yet died down when Paul Gascoigne flicked the ball delicately over a defender's head at the other end and volleyed home what was surely the winner. Boyle was quickly on his feet again, but this time he and his pals were on their way out. A chant of 'Bye-bye, bye-bye' quickly gave way to 'Football's Coming Home', which was still being sung enthusiastically when the final whistle went, and five minutes after that, when Thorne and Hendricks stepped out on to the street.

'Result,' Hendricks said.

'Too right,' Thorne said. They began walking back towards Islington station. 'But it won't do much for my senior officer's mood, so swings and roundabouts.'

'Not a fan of his, then?'

'Put it this way, he didn't exactly go mad for your theory about the heroin that killed Figgis.'

'Well, he's clearly a twat,' Hendricks said.

'That was a pretty smart bit of detective work, you ask me. Best I've seen so far, anyway.'

'What can I say?'

'What do you call it . . . lateral thinking.'

'That's me, mate.' A smartly dressed Asian man in his twenties walked towards them, smiling at something and staring hard at Hendricks as he passed. Hendricks stared right back. A few yards further on, he said, 'So, fancy meeting up somewhere to watch the Holland match next Tuesday?'

'I'll probably just watch it at home,' Thorne said.

'That an invitation?'

Behind them, the volume of singing increased suddenly, as another group spilled out of the pub, determined to continue the celebration.

'When do you reckon we'll get those tox results back?' Thorne asked.

'Yeah, you need them on the hurry-up, I know, so I'm kicking the lab up the arse, but you're looking at another few days minimum.'

It was the answer Thorne had been expecting, but that didn't make it any less frustrating. 'I can't see a murder investigation getting actioned until we get proof about that heroin, that's all. Suits a lot of people to sit on their hands and let everyone think Figgis topped himself. Lets them all come up with a nice convenient reason *why* he topped himself.'

'Couldn't live with the guilt, right?'

'Perfect, isn't it?'

'Two birds with one overdose,' Hendricks said.

They turned on to Tolpuddle Street, the station only a few hundred yards ahead. Hendricks said, 'Even if Figgis *was* murdered, it doesn't mean he didn't snatch that lad, does it?'

228

'*If?*'

'Oh, he a hundred per cent was. I'm just saying.'

'Yeah, well, guilty or not, he didn't deserve that, did he?' Thorne waited, looked at him. 'What, you think he did?'

Hendricks raised his arms. 'Way above my pay grade, mate. I'm just around to cut up stiffs and come up with the odd bit of top-of-the-range lateral thinking.' The pathologist stopped and slowly shook his head, as though something else momentous had suddenly occurred to him.

Thorne stopped, too. 'What?'

'That Gazza goal.' Hendricks grinned. 'It was *seriously* fucking tasty.'

# FORTY-ONE

Dean Meade couldn't believe his luck.

Once he'd found out about the whole Kieron-going-missing business and sold his story to that paper, he'd seen more dosh coming in than he could ever remember, and no shortage of offers that would bring in plenty more. It was like winning the pools or something. All being well, and as long as he wasn't stupid with it, he was looking at enough to sort him out for a year or two, he reckoned, maybe more. Enough to mean he'd already started thinking about telling his boss at the poxy tile showroom where he could stick his hand-crafted ceramics. Most ridiculous thing about it, though: minted as he was, he hadn't needed to put his hand in his pocket for days.

*No worries, mate, I'll get you one.*

*This is on the house, son.*

*She treated you like shit, that boy's mum, but we're not all like that.*

Backslaps from the blokes ever since the story came out, and girls on him like shit on a blanket, like he was some pop star.

That was what happened when people knew your name and your face was in the papers, wasn't it? You were some sort of celebrity all of a sudden. He wasn't daft, though; he knew this stuff didn't last long, so he was determined to fill his boots and make the most of it. If everyone wanted to be his best mate and laugh at all his jokes or some girl was desperate to nosh him off in a car park, who was he to say no?

Like tonight . . . this bloke – he'd said his name, but Dean had already forgotten it – who'd been halfway up his arse and buying him drinks all night, and the two slappers in the corner giggling and giving him the eye.

Fuck it, he was a victim, wasn't he?

He was grief-stricken over his boy and everyone had their own way of dealing with that kind of thing.

The Duke of Richmond in Dalston was livelier than usual after England had stuffed the Jocks, singing and all the rest, spilling out into the pub garden, and even if it was getting a bit rowdy the landlord certainly wasn't complaining. Not with the amount being passed across his bar.

'Got you another one in.'

Dean pulled the new pint towards him, grunted a 'Thanks'.

'Cracking night, yeah?'

'It's all right,' Dean said.

'Just nice to sit and have a natter, isn't it?' The bloke laughed at nothing in particular. 'Even if you've got to shout a bit to make yourself heard.'

The bloke didn't look much like a journo. The ones Dean had met so far all looked fucked, basically: fat sods in shit suits or middle-aged women with long nails and dye jobs. This one was a bit younger and fitter-looking, like maybe the paper or the TV station or whoever it was had deliberately sent a reporter who wasn't like the rest of them and could maybe catch Dean off guard a bit. Only it wasn't going to work, because they didn't know how smart Dean was.

'So, like I was saying, I reckon there's still loads of stuff you haven't told anyone. I'm right, aren't I?'

231

Dean turned slowly on his bar stool, squinted at his new friend. 'Right about what?'

'You been keeping stuff back, yeah?'

'Well, that's for me to know and other people to find out, isn't it?' He raised the glass in salute. 'Cheers . . .'

The bloke touched his own glass to Dean's, though Dean had noticed he hadn't bought himself a fresh pint. He'd been drinking them slowly, one to every couple Dean had been putting away. The bloke nodded then tapped the side of his head. 'Good thinking, mate. You spunk it all away early doors, you've got nothing left anybody's going to want.'

'Oh, there's plenty I haven't told anyone,' Dean said. He swallowed down a belch, put out a hand to steady himself against the bar. 'Plenty.'

The bloke grinned and shook his head like he was impressed. 'I knew it.'

'All the stories about me and Cat at school . . . how I went off the rails when she cut me out of my own son's life. All the sex stuff, obviously, and that's red hot, I swear.' He looked across at the girls in the corner, who were still eyeing him up.

'Bloody hell.' The bloke looked a little shocked. 'People are definitely going to want to know about that,' he said. 'I know I do.'

Dean looked at him. Like the bloke had just happened to recognise him across the pub and decided to spend all night chewing the fat. Like they just *happened* to be talking about this stuff with Cat and what have you.

Like Dean was an idiot.

'How much?' Dean asked.

'How much . . . what?'

'Don't piss me about, mate. Plenty of others in here happy to get my next drink in.'

The bloke raised his hands because he knew he'd been rumbled, then leaned close, sober as a judge. 'Enough.'

'What, enough to get myself a decent curry or enough to buy a new BMW?'

'Somewhere in between,' the bloke said. 'Enough to make sure you don't talk to anyone else. It'll need to be an exclusive.'

Dean took a drink, pretending to think about it.

'We can talk numbers later on, but it'll be worth your while.'

'Yeah, all right,' Dean said. 'What you after?'

'Just the kind of thing you were talking about before. The background about you and Cat when you were at school together, all that. What she was like back then. How things changed when you grew up and how the bitch wouldn't let you see your boy.'

'Cut me out of his life.'

'Exactly,' the bloke said. 'Cut you out.' He downed what little was left in his own glass. 'It's a proper human interest story, Dean. A missing kiddy, that's always going to be popular, and it never hurts if there's a bit of sex thrown in. What readers want, isn't it?'

'So, when do you want to . . . ?'

'No time like the present.'

'Well, yeah . . . I suppose.'

'Your place isn't far away, is it?'

'Ten minutes' walk.'

'Sod that, we're on expenses. I'll get us a cab.'

'Sweet,' Dean said.

The bloke heaved himself off his stool. 'Right, I'm just going to have a quick piss and call my boss to give him the good news.' He snatched two twenty-pound notes from a bulging wallet and slapped them on the bar as he reached for his jacket. 'Drink up and I'll see you outside.'

# FORTY-TWO

It wasn't just his regular glass of wine before bed that was making him feel somewhat . . . maudlin. He'd not been himself an hour or so earlier either, when he'd taken the boy into the woods. Normally he was energised and chatty during their outings, pointing out things he thought might be of interest – a particularly ancient tree, perhaps, or some animal tracks – but he'd been distracted and, in the end, he'd cut it short and apologised to the boy because their walk hadn't been as much fun as usual.

*He* hadn't been as much fun.

This was no long, dark night of the soul, though, and he certainly wouldn't have gone as far as to say he hated himself, because he didn't. It was about a healthy degree of self-awareness, no more than that, about taking stock and admitting that – looked at objectively – what he was doing was not entirely normal. It was entirely *ab*normal, of course it was. It was right, though; he knew that absolutely. Entirely the right thing for him and for the only other person he loved, but he wasn't mad or stupid, so he knew very well that others might struggle to see it that way.

Those who upheld the law.

Those who reported these things and passed judgement.

Those who would cheerfully burn his house down given half a chance, who would sneer and spit and hold their children close, when they weren't slapping them in supermarket aisles.

So, no . . . he was not ashamed of what he'd done, or who he was, but there were one or two regrets, certainly. Or maybe he was being a little hard on himself. It was probably just the wine and the silence and the darkness outside, combining to make some things feel like mistakes, when the truth was there wasn't a fat lot he could have done differently.

His hand had been forced, simple as that.

He hadn't wanted to use that shackle and chain, for heaven's sake. Same as he hadn't wanted to take the TV away. He'd really not wanted to take such drastic action, but the boy had been getting slightly too jumpy and even though everything was fine now as far as the noise was concerned, that busybody postman had made *him* jumpy, too. It wasn't how he'd wanted things to go at all. He'd only kitted out the cellar as a last resort, because he'd guessed there was a chance the boy might play up a bit, but it wasn't ideal. It was always Plan B. On a magic island, the boy would have adjusted to his new situation a little faster, been a bit more enthusiastic all round, and if he had . . . well, they'd be sitting up here in comfort together right now, wouldn't they?

Laughing, playing, whatever.

Yes, he'd been a touch optimistic, but he wasn't going to beat himself up about it. The best-laid plans and all that. He'd adapted, even if the boy hadn't, and it would all be worth it in the end.

His intentions had been good; were still good.

He just wanted to make someone he loved happy and why the hell should he apologise for that?

God, he was tired . . .

He'd always been a light sleeper. Never one of those jammy

buggers who could sleep through a thunderstorm, or a bombing raid. The slightest noise might easily have him lying awake for hours, besides which he often struggled to get comfortable. Top-of-the-range mattress and fresh cotton sheets ... 500 thread count, it didn't matter. He could always feel the smallest lump or irregularity underneath him, any wrinkle in the duvet cover, and he was especially sensitive to extraneous material on his pillowcase.

Grit, feathers, anything.

He was all a bit ... princess-and-the-pea, that's what one woman had said to him once. Shaking her head while he tossed and turned. Laughing at him before she'd turned over and gone to sleep herself, and all the time blissfully unaware that she was what was making him uncomfortable.

*She* was the grit. A hulking great bag of the stuff.

He sat back, feeling a little more relaxed than he had ten minutes earlier, less fretful. The wine tasted better and the silence was comforting. He'd finish the glass, perhaps have another, then call it a night. He'd wander down and say sweet dreams to the boy, then head up and hope that tonight he might get some of his own.

On the street six floors below her, Cat could hear them celebrating.

The incessant honking of horns and the bellowing. *England* chanted with an extra syllable in the middle and that song she kept hearing everywhere.

The night was still and muggy, and the waves of sound floated up easily from the Holloway Road, but it wasn't the incessant racket Cat was finding hard to bear. It was the fact that something so unimportant could make people as happy as this. Yeah, drink had plenty to do with it, but still.

Something so daft, so fucking trivial ...

When she was just a dead thing, shambling around.

236

Fact was, her Kieron would have been every bit as happy as they were; jumping about, singing along with everybody else and getting the words mixed up. He'd been getting excited about the tournament for weeks, looking at the pictures on the backs of the newspapers and putting up a wallchart in his room. Cat had bought him a replica shirt specially and he'd insisted on having one with a number 9 on the back, because Alan Shearer was his favourite player. Little as he was, he'd already had several of the bloody things. Billy had bought him a Babygro with a flag of St George on it, for pity's sake.

'He's a cracking little player already,' Billy had said. 'A natural, I'm telling you.'

Cat remembered shouting at him one day when he was kicking a ball against the lift doors, telling him to stop, because she knew someone would come out and complain. She remembered the look of concentration, his tongue between his teeth, as he ran towards the ball. The glee each time he made contact. She could still hear the echoey slaps of the ball hitting those metal doors; punches to her heart.

She got up and walked slowly across to the window, opened it as far as it would go and shouted at the people on the street to shut up. Screamed her pain into the night. A few seconds later she was answered by a slurry voice from a window a couple of floors below her own.

'Shut up yourself, you miserable cow.'

She stepped back inside and lay back down. She rubbed the soft nylon of that small, brand-new number 9 shirt against her face and wondered how long it would take. The fall from six floors up.

She would never know for sure, of course, not with bits of herself spread all over the place like sick on the concrete, but she guessed that might shut them all up for a while.

# FORTY-THREE

They didn't say a lot on the short taxi ride to Dean's flat on Kingsland Road, which suited Dean fine. He was happy to let the cabbie do most of the talking – the weather, the match, the IRA scum – because he just wanted to lean as close as possible to the open window in the hope that he might start feeling a little less dizzy, and in case he threw up. He'd been drinking most of the day and hadn't eaten since lunchtime. Now he just needed to get home and get this interview out of the way, trouser some more cash and go to bed.

'Neighbours must be excited.' The reporter-bloke was staring up at the darkened windows of the other flats in the house, while Dean fumbled in his pocket for the door keys. 'Living this close to someone who's in the papers.'

'Never seen them,' Dean said.

'London, right?'

Inside, the reporter shifted a pile of dirty clothes on to the floor and perched on the edge of Dean's sofa, while Dean necked a glass of water in the kitchen and rummaged unsuccessfully in the cupboards for something quick to eat. When Dean came back into the living room, the reporter had a notebook and pen in his hand.

He said, 'Just start wherever you like.'

Dean sat down and did exactly that. He talked about meeting Catrin Coyne on their first day at school, how they got on because she wasn't soppy or snotty like some of the other girls, because she was ... sparky, you know? Because she was up for a laugh and would take the piss or whatever. He talked about how they became mates. Yeah, they'd got off with each other at parties a few times, he said, school discos and all that, but they were never a proper couple or anything. Not until later, after Cat's old man had been put away.

'This is gold,' the reporter said. 'Just what we're after.'

When he got to how Kieron had come along, Dean exaggerated the sex with Cat a little bit – how many times they did it, where and for how long – and because he guessed the paper probably couldn't be very explicit, he tried telling it in a way they'd be able to print. *Made love* instead of *shagged*, *passionate* instead of *dirty*. He thought that was pretty clever and showed how he was really getting the hang of these things.

'You were right.' The reporter nodded. 'Hot stuff.'

Dean shrugged. 'Well, you need to know what happened, right? All the ins and outs.'

'That's funny,' the reporter said. 'I might use that.'

'You getting it all, though?' Dean pointed towards the notepad. 'You've only written a couple of things down.'

'Shorthand,' the reporter said.

'Oh, course,' Dean said.

They had been talking for about twenty minutes, and Dean was describing his anguish at being excluded from his son's life. He'd said it all before to other papers, so he tried to find different ways of describing things to make it all sound a bit ... fresh, or whatever. To tart it up a bit. He was just telling the reporter about walking the streets at night in floods of tears, and how

239

upset he'd get if he saw other dads out and about with their kids, when the doorbell rang.

The reporter stood up. 'They wanted to send a photographer. That all right with you?'

'Yeah, whatever.'

The reporter walked over to buzz open the front door while Dean stood to check himself out in the mirror above the electric fire. He was still wearing his replica England shirt, which would be fine, he decided, because he hadn't worn it in pictures for any of the other papers, on top of which he thought it made him look pretty cool.

He turned when the photographer walked in and laid down a shoulder bag.

'This do you?'

'Looks great.' The photographer eyed him up and down. 'Patriotic is always good.'

The reporter put his notebook away and picked up his jacket. 'Right, then, I'm about done, so I'll leave you to it.'

'You sure?' Dean asked. 'You got everything you need?'

'Plenty.'

'Don't forget that stuff about how upset I got seeing other dads.'

'I won't.'

'The crying and all that.'

'No worries.'

When the reporter had left, Dean stood waiting with his hands in his pockets. He nodded at the photographer's bag and said. 'Doesn't look like you've got a lot of gear in there.'

'Got one of these flashy new digital cameras.'

'Yeah, seen them in the shops,' Dean said.

The photographer opened the shoulder bag. 'Cost an arm and a leg, but they're tiny.'

'Cool.' Dean turned to adjust his hair in the mirror. 'So, where d'you want me?'

'What you were saying when I came in about getting upset? Crying or whatever.'

'Yeah. Broke my fucking heart not seeing Kieron.'

'That's really powerful, so I was thinking about a shot of you looking out of the window, out into the night kind of thing. Show everyone just how gutted you really are.'

'Atmospheric, like,' Dean said.

'Right. All moody, like you're upset, but hopeful. Because you know your son's out there somewhere.'

'I like it.' Dean walked across to the window. 'It's a bit different . . . arty or whatever.' He stared out beyond the blur of his own reflection, thinking that a few yards of his shitty patio and the roofs of the warehouses on the other side of the fence were not exactly what *he'd* call arty, but that if offers like this one kept rolling in he might be able to move to somewhere with a slightly nicer view.

'Yeah, that's nice.'

'Looking out like this?'

'Perfect. Stay like that . . .'

Thinking that, whatever the picture looked like in the end, he really had no idea if Kieron *was* out there. If he was anywhere. Yeah, he was milking it all a bit because he needed to and that's what the papers wanted, but honest to God, he did feel bad. A weird, empty sort of feeling, and he knew it would be ten times worse for Cat, and the truth was he had really liked her, once upon a time.

They *had* been mates.

Reflected, he could see the photographer stepping across and moving into position behind him and Dean pressed a hand against the glass because he thought it would be dramatic, which was when he saw that it was not a camera the photographer was holding.

'Fuck are you—?'

Meade turned quickly, but it only meant that the knife went

into the side of his neck as opposed to straight through the back of it. In, *one-two*, then out again, wet-sounding. He staggered back, his hand scrabbling at his neck and his head cracking the window pane, before he dropped hard to his knees, then tumbled on to his side.

He tried to speak, but it was just a silly gurgle.

The photographer did have a camera, but it wasn't remotely flashy. A crappy Polaroid borrowed from a friend, because the pictures were needed fast and they weren't going to be the kind of snaps you could just pop along to get developed in Boots.

*It's not what it looks like. We're making a horror film ...*

The first few came out very well, nice and colourful, especially when they'd been lined up alongside each other on the sideboard.

'Looking good, Dean ...'

Meade cried out, or tried to. His feet pedalled slowly against the floor as he began to drift away. He turned his head and coughed up a thick red mist on to the carpet.

There was an awful lot of blood already, of course, starting to pool beneath his shoulder and pouring through his fingers; spurting between a couple of them like a knackered water fountain and soaking into his sleeve. Still, something extra a bit lower down, just a couple of decent splotches, would really stand out, the photographer thought. A simple red stain or two, spreading nicely against the white of that stupid football shirt. They would show exactly how the fucker had died, bit by bit.

Like a *series*, wasn't that what it was called? The journey of it.

There were people who needed to see these photos, after all, perhaps show them around. People who would enjoy every stage of the proceedings and get a real kick out of seeing just how much poor little Deano had suffered.

The photographer stepped quickly forward and stabbed Meade again twice, short and sharp into the belly, left side and right. Then again, deep into each leg, just because it felt good.

Meade screamed every time, but not very loudly, more like a whimper.

He moaned something as the camera was raised again.

'*Don't*', maybe, or '*God*'. '*Mum*', most like.

'Say cheese . . .'

# FORTY-FOUR

Thorne had been woken by the call just after two-thirty in the morning.

Now, a couple of hours later, he stood clumsily stripping off a plastic bodysuit outside a house in Dalston and, though the adrenalin had chased away the fatigue, he was feeling every bit as disconcerted, as alarmed, as he had been when the phone had rung.

He'd known what to expect, of course. In the dark of his bedroom, scrabbling for the handset, he'd guessed there would be a body. Unless it was a wrong number or a family emergency, a call at that time of night rarely meant anything else.

But he had not been expecting this one.

It had been warm inside the ground-floor flat – the number of people, the arc lights – but now, in jeans and a T-shirt, Thorne shivered slightly as he leaned back against one of the support vehicles and stared around. Satellite dishes clung to the sides of houses like blank-faced gargoyles while, higher up, a ragged line of TV aerials was silhouetted against a sky just beginning to pink. England flags hung in every other window and crime-scene tape was tied off on trees and lamp posts, strung around the house in which Dean Meade had been murdered.

'Not that we really needed to wear these.' Paula Kimmel opened the boot of her car and tossed her own discarded body-suit inside.

'No point making things in there any worse,' Thorne said.

Kimmel wandered across to stand next to Thorne. 'Not sure we could, because I'm damn sure the ladies and gentlemen of the press weren't wearing them.'

Just after midnight, anonymous calls had been made to the night desks of the *Sun, Star* and *Daily Mirror*. An address had been given, along with a promise that the door had been left open and the assurance that it would be very much in their interest to send reporters along immediately. An hour later, a journalist who had not wished to give his name rang to alert police to a murder on Kingsland Road, though by the time officers arrived to attend the scene, the journalist and however many of his colleagues had been there with him were nowhere to be seen.

'Got what they wanted and scarpered,' Kimmel said.

'Whatever our anonymous caller wanted, too.' Thorne turned to her. 'The killer, presumably.'

'You think they took pictures?'

'Why wouldn't they?'

'Reckon they'll run them?'

Thorne thought about the scene inside. The stains and the spatter. 'Well, only if they want people chucking up their cornflakes.'

'Maybe they'll what-do-you-call-it, pixellate them.'

'Or print little stars over the blood,' Thorne said. 'Like some of them put over the models' nipples.'

Kimmel laughed. 'The tasteful ones.'

They waited, then both took plastic cups of coffee from a uniform heading inside with a tray of hot drinks from Teapot

One, the catering vehicle on site even before the forensic team had shown up.

'Could do with this,' Kimmel said.

Thorne slurped his own coffee, needing the jolt, the warmth, every bit as much. He watched as other uniformed officers dealt firmly, but politely, with the predictable handful of gawpers, all seemingly happy to stand and stare from doorways or perch on garden walls, even at this ungodly hour on a Sunday morning. Those of the victim's near neighbours for whom the flashing lights of an emergency vehicle – better yet *several* vehicles – were like a hypnotist's watch; irresistible as a *SALE* sign.

He knew that, inside, the neighbour who lived in the flat above Dean Meade – an elderly and very talkative woman – was still being questioned, though Thorne had already been given the key information.

The woman had heard Dean – she'd been told that was the poor young man's name – come in at around eleven o'clock and she was positive about the time because the football had started on the BBC at a quarter to and she'd not long turned it off. She hadn't been earwigging, she'd said, nothing like that, but she could have sworn she'd heard two voices. Dean and another man. About half an hour later, she'd heard the doorbell and it had all been quiet after that.

'You think it might have been the reporters arriving?' Kimmel asked now. 'When the woman upstairs heard the doorbell?'

'Too early,' Thorne said.

'We can't be certain, though.'

'They didn't even know about it until gone midnight.'

'Maybe the old woman got the time mixed up.'

'She sounded pretty sure, and whoever called the press said they'd left the door open.'

'So, what do you reckon, then? Two killers?'

'It's possible,' Thorne said.

That two murder victims had been directly connected to

Kieron Coyne was clearly more than coincidence, and Thorne could see why Meade, as the boy's father, would have a motive for killing Figgis. As far as killing Dean Meade went, though, only one motive sprang to Thorne's mind, and only one person who might conceivably have it.

Whatever Boyle might have said two days before, now it had to be time to pay Billy Coyne a visit.

With impeccable timing, a squad car pulled up, doors were opened simultaneously and Boyle and Roth stepped out, like bad actors in an episode of *The Bill*. For obvious reasons, the DI had gone to bed the night before in a foul mood and being dragged out of bed clearly hadn't helped.

'When I find out who trampled all over my crime scene, I'll have their cobblers for breakfast.'

'There must be some way to find out,' Roth said. 'Surely the papers have to keep a record of which reporters were on call, or whatever.'

'Do they have to tell us, though?' Kimmel asked.

Thorne nodded thoughtfully, enjoying himself rather more than was probably appropriate. 'Right, yeah. Freedom of the press, protecting sources or something.'

'I'll *make* them tell me,' Boyle said. 'Fucking up my murder inquiry.'

Now, Thorne bit his tongue. *Your murder inquiry? So we're definitely having one this time, are we? You quite sure you don't want to pop inside and make sure the victim didn't stab himself to death?*

Boyle was handed a bodysuit. 'Right, best get in there and have a look.'

As the DI stepped away, Thorne caught movement at the front door and turned to see Phil Hendricks leaving the house, which meant that the body would shortly be making the same journey. Boyle and Roth stared at the pathologist and exchanged a knowing smirk before they began walking towards him up the front path. Thorne was delighted to see that Hendricks had caught the look himself and gleefully gave both officers the finger as they passed him.

Kimmel had wandered away to talk to one of the uniforms by the time Hendricks was helping himself to some of Thorne's coffee.

'Tea wagon's over there,' Thorne said, pointing.

'Only wanted a mouthful.'

'So ... ?'

'Well, just so you know all those years at medical school weren't wasted, I can tell you categorically that he's definitely dead.'

'Hilarious,' Thorne said.

'No more than a few hours. The knife wound to the neck did for him and the rest just looks like someone was having a bit of fun.'

'Jesus.'

Hendricks stretched and yawned. 'I'll have chapter and verse once I've done my own bit of cutting. I shall be incisive with my manly yet delicate hands and then with my remarkable brain.'

'Good to hear.'

'Tomorrow with a bit of luck.'

'Might not be me,' Thorne said.

'Oh? Had enough of me already?'

Thorne looked back towards the house. 'All being well, I'll be talking to the bloke who probably did it. Had it done, anyway.'

'Fun, fun, fun.' Hendricks took Thorne's coffee cup again and drank what was left. 'Right, I'm going to get a few hours' kip. Bit of a backlog to catch up on later today. A pensioners' suicide pact in Golders Green and a drowning in Hampstead Pond.'

'Lovely,' Thorne said.

Hendricks swallowed, chucked the empty paper cup on to the floor and stared at it. 'A seventeen-year-old.'

Today was supposed to have been Thorne's first day off in almost two weeks. Though catching a murder first thing meant that he wouldn't have quite as much free time as he was due, he told Hendricks how he was planning to spend his Sunday afternoon. The little choice he had in the matter.

Hendricks nodded. 'Nice.'

'I'll happily swap you,' Thorne said.

# FORTY-FIVE

Cat could not remember the last morning she'd woken up hungry. For more than a week, she'd not thought about cooking herself a meal of any sort, had been existing on snacks, more or less – crisps and chocolate – and even they were no more than fuel, forced down to keep her on her feet and tasting of nothing. The same was true of the wine and beer, of which she'd drunk far more than she was used to, though without it she knew that even those few hours of sleep to which she gratefully succumbed every night would be impossible. She thought she was beginning to understand how alcoholics felt, what the booze they put away was actually for.

Armagnac or aftershave, it didn't really matter.

As long as it did the job.

She drank her tea at the window, smoked one of the cigarettes Angie had left for her, then went into the kitchen. There was food in the fridge – once again, courtesy of Angie – and Cat knew exactly what she wanted, what she'd woken up thinking about. She took out a pack of bacon, eggs and sausages. She opened a tin of baked beans. She turned the radio on, filled the kettle to make herself more tea and stuck a couple of slices of bread in the toaster.

Suddenly, she was ravenous.

On Radio 1, Kevin Greening talked about how great the weather was shaping up to be. He said something cheesy about a 'quickie' being all he could manage these days, then played 'Fastlove' by George Michael. Cat remembered singing along to the track in Maria's car a few weeks before, on their way home from somewhere or other, and, for a few glorious seconds, while the beans bubbled and the bacon spat, she sang along now and the shoulders that moved in time, the fingers that tapped out a rhythm on the worktop, felt like they belonged to someone else.

A mum cooking a Sunday fry-up, the way she usually did. Something they looked forward to. She would have the full monty, same as always, and she guessed that Kieron would just want a bacon sandwich with loads of ketchup, because that was his favourite, and it wasn't until Cat opened her mouth to call him that she remembered.

She turned the radio off.

She buttered her toast, poured the contents of the frying pan on to a plate and carried it through to the table in the living room.

She had barely managed a mouthful when the phone rang.

'It's Simon Jenner. I came over the other—'

'Yeah,' Cat said. 'The card. That was really nice.'

'I'm really sorry to be calling on a Sunday.'

'No worries. I was just eating my breakfast.'

'Oh, shit . . . sorry. I'll leave you to it.'

'It's fine,' Cat said.

'I got your phone number from the school,' Jenner said. 'From the files. I hope that's all right.'

Cat couldn't think of any reason why it wouldn't be. Parents' contact details were kept so that teachers could get in touch if they needed to, so . . .

'I was just calling to see how you were, really.'

Cat turned and leaned back against the wall, stared across a room that on any normal day should have been littered with toys, abandoned trainers and scattered video cases. A dusty TV screen that, by now, he would already have been sitting in front of. 'Oh, you know, the same.'

'Course.'

Cat took a deep breath, two. 'Thanks for asking though. People stop asking.'

'I'm sure they're thinking it,' he said. 'If they don't ask, it's probably only because it's such a stupid bloody question.'

'Are you going to start apologising again?'

He laughed softly. 'It's just that the other day when I came round, it struck me how good it is to talk in these situations. I mean, it might be the last thing you want to do, of course.'

'Sometimes it is.'

'I'm a teacher not a shrink, but I do think it helps.'

'Yeah, I think it probably does,' she said. 'I'm not much of a talker at the best of times, mind you.'

'Listen, there's something I'd like to give you. Would it be OK if I came over?'

'I'm not going anywhere,' Cat said.

'That's another thing, so better still ... I mean, again, this might sound like a terrible idea, but maybe we could meet somewhere for lunch or something. You probably don't feel remotely like being sociable or anything, but I reckon it would be good to get out.'

Cat said nothing. Her breakfast was probably cold by now. *Sociable?*

'You can tell me to sod off and mind my own business.'

'Well, getting out of here for a bit might stop me going completely off my trolley, I suppose. I mean, doing something that's not going to the launderette or nipping to the off-licence.'

'Yeah, that's what I thought,' Jenner said.

'Just . . . I wouldn't want to go anywhere too far away.'

'No problem.'

'I need to stay close to home, in case there's news.'

'Well, why don't you think of somewhere nearby?'

'OK. There's one or two nice places.'

'Maybe one day next week? I won't keep you out too long, obviously. I do still have these pesky kids to teach.'

Cat felt as though the breath had been punched out of her. She doubled over, as though she might be sick.

He might have heard her reaction or simply realised what he'd said. 'God, what a stupid thing to come out with.' There were a few seconds of silence. He swore under his breath. 'I can't believe I said that.'

It took Cat half a minute or more. 'Listen, it really doesn't matter, so please don't feel bad about it. People shouldn't have to watch what they say all the time. Walk on eggshells or treat me like I've got cancer . . . hide their kids if they see me coming.'

'Still . . . '

'Yeah, let's do it. Let's go for lunch one day next week.'

'OK, great.' Jenner sounded thrilled. 'Which day works best for you?'

Cat found herself smiling when she said, 'Let me just go and check my diary.'

# FORTY-SIX

Thorne sat with his father, drinking cans of Carlsberg in the living room while his mother was busy getting lunch ready. As always, she shouted through from the kitchen every few minutes, keeping them up to date with her progress – 'I'm just putting the peas on . . . the chicken's done, but I'm letting it stand for a bit' – or to check that particular likes and dislikes established decades earlier had not inexplicably changed.

'Tom, I presume you want mash *and* roasties?'

Tom did.

'I'm guessing you'll be wanting the breast, Jim . . .'

In the living room, once he'd shouted back to confirm that his wife had guessed correctly, Jim Thorne shook his head. 'Since when have I ever preferred the leg?'

Thorne nodded, as though the whole thing was daft, but he knew that his old man would have been disappointed if the question hadn't been asked. It was part of the Sunday roast ritual, one of the things they did. Same as how, if his father belched, his mother would always say 'More tea, vicar?' or, whenever his mother couldn't find such-and-such a thing and asked his father if he knew where it was, he would always shrug and suggest, 'Up the crack of my arse?'

His father's insistence on breaking into a terrible Frank Carson impression whenever anyone Irish was on the television.

His mother laughing at it, every single time.

All that stuff.

Fifteen years before, Thorne might have found these tired routines and marital catchphrases more than a little irritating, but now he could see them for what they were. Harmless, comforting; as true an expression of love, he supposed, as diamonds or a dozen red roses. No, truer. He saw that, too, now, and realised it was probably just because he and Jan had never come close to that degree of trust and familiarity.

Or, if they had, they'd both forgotten what it was like.

Jim Thorne had switched on *Sunday Grandstand*, then turned the volume down, because it was Sue Barker talking about tennis, which he didn't see the point of. 'Watch the game yesterday?'

'Yeah, course,' Thorne said.

'It's no wonder our lads are doing so well. Spurs are the backbone of that team, you know.'

'I wouldn't go quite that far.'

Jim Thorne counted off on his fingers. 'Darren Anderton, Teddy Sheringham . . . Sol Campbell when he came on. Gazza, obviously.'

'Gascoigne went to Italy four years ago, Dad.'

'Well . . . '

'He plays for Rangers now.'

Maureen Thorne shouted from the kitchen. 'Just sorting the gravy and we're about there.'

'Yeah, but still. *Used* to be Spurs, didn't he?' Thorne's father rubbed his hands together. 'Right, bring on the bloody Dutch.'

'Should be a good game.'

'Why don't you come over here and watch it? I'll get us a few beers in.'

255

'On the table,' Maureen shouted.

Thorne stood up. 'I don't know what I'll be doing, Dad. Work, you know . . . '

They walked through to the kitchen and Thorne's mother handed the carving knife to his father. He carved the first slice and said, 'Nice and tender,' same as he always did.

As they ate, Thorne's mother twice pointed out to Thorne how many vegetables she was eating, that she was taking on board what he'd said about her diet being a bit healthier. Thorne said that mashed potatoes swimming in butter was not exactly what he'd meant by salad, but told her he was pleased to see she was making an effort.

'You've got to take these things gradually,' his father said.

'Plus, I'll only be having a small portion of pudding,' his mother said.

Thorne's father turned to him. 'So, there you go, then. She's making an effort, like you said.' He stabbed at a roast potato. 'You know we're having trifle, don't you?'

'Mum told me,' Thorne said.

'I put sponge fingers in the bottom,' his mother said. 'You always liked them.'

'Lovely,' Thorne said.

'Could you pass over the . . . stuff?' Thorne's father made a shaking motion with his hand. 'The stuff you have with salt.'

'Pepper?'

'Yeah, pass the pepper.'

Thorne handed the shaker across. He glanced at his mother but she was focused on her food.

'You need to take these things gradually,' she said. 'Not like I'm going to turn vegetarian overnight, is it? And these doctors know sod all anyway.'

It wasn't until they'd almost finished that Maureen Thorne stood up and fetched the *Sunday Mirror* from the sideboard. She set it down and jabbed at the front page. She shook her head.

'Horrible business.'

Jim Thorne peered across. 'Horrible.'

Thorne had seen the paper already, had seen all of them. There had not been sufficient time for any of them to print the story that had broken earlier that morning in Dalston – a story they had been handed on a bloodstained plate – so most had chosen to run with yet more details on what they were assuming was the suicide of Grantleigh Figgis.

A photograph of the body being removed from Seacole House. That leak, still gushing.

### DRIVEN TO IT?

The paper had even managed to track down Kevin Scott, the young man who had accused Figgis of molesting him two years earlier. The caption beneath Scott's picture simply said: *Victim.*

> Whatever the police did or didn't do at the time, this is the man who assaulted me, who took advantage of me. I'm really not surprised he did this to himself, not remotely. He was a very dangerous man and there was clearly a lot of rage bottled up in him. Rage and guilt . . .

'I mean, what are you lot going to do now?' Maureen asked.

Thorne put down his knife and fork.

'About that missing lad?'

Thorne's father looked up. 'Maureen.'

'If this bloke took him, and now he's killed himself, where does that leave you? I say *if*, because, well, we don't know, do we? What do you think, Tom?'

'He can't talk about it, Maureen. You know that.'

It was fairer to say that Thorne didn't particularly want to talk about it, that he'd been looking forward to an afternoon listening to his father chunter on about engines while his mum rolled her eyes at him. To the few hours he would not have to spend thinking about murders and missing children.

'Oh, course he can.' Maureen waved her husband's concern away.

'Leave him alone.'

'Come on, love ...'

Yes, it might be pushing it to discuss an ongoing case with strangers in a pub, but Thorne could talk about the nuts and bolts with his parents if he felt like it. Most of it was plastered all over the papers anyway, and who were they going to tell, after all? His Auntie Eileen? His dad's mate Victor, who was only really paying attention if someone was talking about famous maritime disasters?

'They're going to do a TV reconstruction,' Thorne said. 'Of the boy going missing.'

'Kieron, is it?'

Thorne nodded. 'For *Crimewatch UK*.'

They'd been given the go-ahead that morning, once the team had gathered back at the station and Boyle had asked more or less the same question as Thorne's mother. *What are you lot going to do now?*

'We've got a murder to investigate,' Boyle had said. 'Two murders if that funny-looking pathologist turns out to be right, but as far as Kieron Coyne goes, we're still nowhere.'

Thorne's mother was piling up the plates. 'That the one Jill Dando's doing now?'

'I like her,' Thorne's father said.

'The thing I always wonder, when I see those reconstructions on the telly, is how they find the actors for them. Where they come from.'

'Same place they always come from,' Thorne's father said.

'Not if it's kids, though. And what about those ones where people are supposed to be serial killers or what have you? It's

258

hardly Shakespeare, or *Casualty*, is it? You think those actors put that on their CVs? "Third rapist from the left . . ."'

Thorne helped clear the table, then father and son took care of the washing up while Maureen carried her tea into the living room and watched half an hour of tennis, which she loved. The chat at the sink ran rather more along the lines Thorne had been expecting – the relative merits of BMW's 3.2 straight-six and 4.4 litre V8 engines – and he was happy to have a break before sitting down again to pudding.

The relief was short-lived. As soon as his mother had begun spooning out the trifle, she said, 'So, come on then. What's happening with Jan? With the house?'

Thorne wondered how easily he could steer the conversation back to child abduction. 'I saw Jan the other night, actually. It was . . . better than I was expecting.'

'That's good.'

'Oh.' His father waved his spoon around. 'But you're still . . . ?'

'Yes, we are still getting divorced.'

'Don't be daft, Jim, of course they are.'

'And I was looking at a few flats the other day,' Thorne said. 'In the paper.'

His father pulled a well-filled bowl towards him. 'Oh, so the house is on the market, then. That's good. Anyone been to view it yet?'

'No. Not yet.'

'Well, they will. It's a perfectly good house, that.'

'I mean it's not on the market yet.'

His mother shook her head. 'Oh, Tom.'

'I've been a bit busy.' He pointed to the paper that was still sitting on the table. 'There hasn't been a lot of time.'

'It's just getting a few estate agents round, that's all. Actually, Eileen had a really good one when she sold her last place. I think I've still got his name somewhere.'

'I'll be fine, Mum. I'll arrange it.'

'You say that, but you've not been arranging things very well so far, have you?' Thorne's father licked cream from his fingers. 'Now, me and your mum are more than happy to help, you know that, but we shouldn't really have to, not when you're thirty-five.'

'I'm thirty-four,' Thorne said.

His mother leaned across to lay a hand on his arm. 'He's thirty-five in a fortnight, aren't you?'

'I do know when my birthday is.'

'You haven't told me what you want yet.'

His father grinned, his mouth full of trifle. He swallowed and said, 'I reckon a tasty new girlfriend might go down well.'

An hour or so later at the door, Thorne shook hands with his father then stepped back into the house as his mother marched forward and drew him into a fierce hug. She said, 'I know you've got a lot on your plate, but don't leave it so long next time.'

Thorne remembered his conversation with Hendricks outside that house in Dalston in the early hours. The way he'd made it sound as though an afternoon in St Albans with his mum and dad was a chore, that a post-mortem would be something preferable. Now, suddenly, he wished more than anything that he could go back into the house and simply curl up on his parents' sofa for a while; that he could stay the night and wake up to the noise of his father coughing in the bathroom, his mother singing tunelessly along to Patsy Cline or Loretta Lynn.

His mother stepped away suddenly. 'Oh, I need to give you that estate agent's details.'

'Mum, it's—' She was already heading back to the kitchen.

'No point arguing,' his dad said.

They could hear her talking to herself in the kitchen. 'Now, where's that sodding . . . ?'

Thorne and his father looked at each other.

'Jim . . . do you know where my address book is?'

Jim Thorne shrugged and smiled. 'Up the crack of my arse?'

# FORTY-SEVEN

There weren't too many Category A prisons that did not take security seriously, because there weren't too many prisoners serving time as a result of neglecting to take their library books back. These prisons were home to some of the most dangerous and high-profile prisoners in the system, while a select few, like HMP Whitehill in Milton Keynes, had been designed specifically to house such offenders.

What had Boyle said the week before? Men with issues.

The prison's two specialist units had been constructed with an eye to preventing violence among inmates as well as creating a more humane environment which might encourage them to change their behaviour. They were staffed by specially trained officers. There was air-conditioning to prevent the atmosphere from becoming overheated in any sense and interior walls made of toughened glass to create the impression of space. These two units had, rather unimaginatively, been christened Milton and Keynes, but were known informally by all those working there as Jekyll and Hyde.

It was no great surprise to discover which of these units was home to William Anthony Coyne.

Thorne knew what Billy Coyne looked like, of course. He had seen a picture in the man's file, the day after his name had first been mentioned and his relationship to the missing child established. What they had believed that relationship to be at the time. Like most such photographs – washed-out, utilitarian – it gave something of a skewed impression. A face that was unsurprisingly blank, eyes dead as dolls' and mouth grim-set. Glowering, shaven-headed in black and white above a catalogue of his offences, Coyne looked every inch the man those offences suggested that he was.

Violent, cold, remorseless . . .

The man sitting opposite Thorne now, tugging gently at the ragged cuff of a regulation grey sweatshirt, was a far cry from that, from the majority of those Thorne had encountered with hard time behind them and plenty still to serve. Animated, open . . . baby-faced, almost, with colour in his cheeks and a mop of dirty-blond hair curling across his forehead.

Jarring though the man's appearance was and as comfortable in his surroundings as he seemed, Thorne was making no assumptions. He knew that very few people emerged from a long sentence unscathed in one way or another. He knew equally well that only a particular kind of individual was actually able to thrive in prison.

Billy Coyne seemed relaxed. He seemed *amused*.

He looked at his watch and tutted, as though someone had been keeping him waiting. 'Thought you might have shown up yesterday.' Coyne's voice was surprisingly high and light, the London accent less pronounced than Thorne had been expecting. 'I mean, when did Mr Meade meet his unfortunate end? Saturday night, wasn't it?'

Thorne looked at him.

Coyne flashed a tobacco-stained smile and held up his hands, a picture of innocence. 'It was in the paper.'

It was in several of them and Thorne had seen them all first thing that morning. He had stood for ten minutes or more, leafing through every tabloid on the display and annoying his local newsagent, before climbing into his car and struggling through the Monday rush hour towards the M1.

'Which paper?' Thorne asked.

'Well, there aren't too many copies of the *Financial Times* knocking about in here ... '

No journalist's name had appeared in connection with any of the stories Thorne had read. It was hardly a surprise considering that the stories, and the photographs that had accompanied them, had been obtained by trampling through a crime scene before the police had been called. The photographs were, so each paper had been keen to point out, the least shocking of those that had 'come into our possession'. A cracked window, a patch of bloodstained carpet, a shoe kicked off as a young man had fought for his life.

'You don't seem awfully upset,' Thorne said.

Coyne laughed. *Really* laughed. 'Are you serious, mate? I'm fucking delighted. Why wouldn't I be?'

'Dean Meade deserved what he got, that what you're saying?'

'Too bloody right he did.'

'Because he was Kieron's dad and you're not?'

The laughter died away quickly. 'Because that's what he said. It's a very different thing.'

'What he said?'

'Especially now, after what's happened. It's ... unforgivable.'

'It's not just what Dean Meade said.' Thorne looked at him. 'It's what Cat says.'

Coyne shrugged, folded his arms. 'Not to me, she hasn't.'

'She told me,' Thorne said. 'Told me all about it. Chapter and verse.'

'Yeah, well, she's all over the shop at the minute ... doesn't know what she's saying. Not sure if you heard about it, but her little boy's missing.' Coyne nodded, smiled. '*Our* little boy.'

'So you think Dean Meade was making it up and that Cat's just understandably . . . confused. You still think you're Kieron's natural father.'

'Until I hear otherwise. From Kieron's mother.'

'Have you spoken to her?'

Coyne shook his head. 'She'll call me when she wants to.'

'You could always call her.'

'I don't think so,' Coyne said. 'She's the one needs to pick up the phone.' He had leaned forward and spoken quietly, as though sharing a confidence. As though his position on a delicate subject was one that only another man would understand. For one horrible moment, Thorne had thought that he might actually wink.

'You had many visitors lately?' Thorne asked.

'No more than usual,' Coyne said. 'But I'm guessing you know that. I mean, you'll already have checked, right?'

Thorne nodded. 'I saw the list, but it's just names. Doesn't really tell us who they are.'

'Family and friends,' Coyne said. 'Same as anybody else in here. Go ahead and check them all out.'

'We might well.'

'Fill your boots, mate, but you won't find anything very interesting. I'm not denying that I've got a few mates with colourful pasts, but none of them are hitmen.' Coyne shook his head. 'I haven't even got one of them mad cows desperate to marry a bloke who's inside . . . you know, the ones who think being banged up makes you irresistible. I'm a bit disappointed, to be honest. Feel a bit left out.'

'But you're spoken for, aren't you, Billy?'

Coyne shifted in his seat. Smiled and said, 'That's right, I am.'

Cat had certainly spoken up for him, insisting that the Billy Coyne she knew was not a naturally violent man. That the vicious assault and the attempted murder for which her partner was currently serving time were no more than unfortunate mistakes. Aberrations.

Did she really believe that, or was it a lie she felt honour-bound to tell, to protect herself and her son?

Thorne thought it didn't much matter.

'I think we'd probably be wasting our time checking that list,' Thorne said.

'Up to you.'

'Because it wouldn't need to be someone who'd actually been in to see you, would it? We both know you could have had Dean Meade sorted with a single phone call, or put the word out through someone else in here. Called in a favour.'

Coyne stared at him, sniffed. 'Oh, sorry, are you actually waiting for me to deny any of that?'

'I'm not in any rush,' Thorne said.

'Listen, I *could* have put an advert in the paper and interviewed people who were handy with knives. I could have broken out of here for a few hours, hopped in a cab, carved that little wankstain up myself then broken back in. I could have done all sorts of things.' Coyne rolled up the sleeves of his sweatshirt to reveal a tangle of tattoos on each arm. 'But wouldn't you be better off spending a bit less time worrying about who did everyone a favour by slicing up Dean Meade and a bit more trying to find the animal who took my son?'

'Or Dean Meade's son,' Thorne said.

Coyne stiffened for a few seconds, then leaned back and rolled the tension from his shoulders. 'Yeah, well, maybe one day we can sort all that shit out once and for all. You can find out who someone's real father is with that DNA stuff now, can't you? Just need a bit of blood or whatever and that shouldn't be a problem.' He smiled. 'There was gallons of Dean Meade's splashed all over his front room on Saturday night.'

Thorne stared at him.

*There* were those dead eyes.

'That was in the paper, too,' Coyne said.

# FORTY-EIGHT

Maria's first thought, when the school secretary had called, was that Josh had hurt himself. Her stomach had tightened imagining the blood, or the bone protruding through the skin; a rush to the hospital. Now, half an hour later, sitting anxious and ashamed in front of the headmistress, Maria found herself wishing she'd been right. A few stitches or a plaster cast signed by Josh's classmates would have been so much easier to cope with than this.

So much easier to understand.

'You know already there's been an incident, this morning.'

'Well, I know something happened between Josh and one of the children in his class.' Maria's hand tightened around the tissue that was ready and waiting, that she'd already made use of while she was summoning up the courage to get out of the car, 'I don't know the details.'

The headmistress – a stick-thin woman in her fifties, with a greying perm and oversized glasses – pushed some papers aside, then proceeded, in painful detail, to tell Maria exactly what was what. The poor girl Josh had scratched and slapped, inconsolable in the nurse's room, while Josh remained surly and uncommunicative. A teacher in tears after a barrage of foul language. The girl's parents upset and understandably furious.

'They're demanding that something be done.'

'I don't understand,' Maria said. 'It's his first day back.'

'I'm well aware of that.'

'He was so excited when I dropped him off this morning. He was desperate to come back to school.'

'I'm sorry to say that this is extremely serious.'

'Of course,' Maria said. 'I'm taking it every bit as seriously as you are.'

The headmistress nudged her oversized glasses. 'Because I have the other children to think of, as well as their parents, I'm afraid that I'm going to have to suspend Josh for a while.'

'Come on, is that really necessary?'

'I don't think I have any other choice.'

Maria leaned forward, lowered her voice a little. 'You do know why Josh has been absent from school? What happened to his closest friend?'

'Yes, of course I do. You told me yourself over the phone. I spoke to all the staff about it and I took care to welcome Josh back in front of all the other children at this morning's assembly. To let them know he'd been through a difficult time.'

'It's been incredibly upsetting for him.'

'Mrs Ashton . . . we both know that this kind of behaviour had begun before what happened to Josh's friend. Perhaps nothing as bad as this, but the fact is, he's been disruptive for a while.'

Maria did not know what to say or how to feel. Her fist tightened further around the tissue and she dug her nails into the palm of her hand.

'I was wondering . . . has Josh talked to anybody?'

Maria looked at her.

'Some kind of therapy, perhaps?'

'I appreciate your concern,' Maria said.

'I'm sure the school could help you find someone—'

'We're dealing with it.'

'Oh. Well, that's good to hear.'

The headmistress tried, unsuccessfully, to disguise the curiosity in her expression. She knew that Maria was divorced, that Josh's father had been anything but hands-on when it came to matters such as this, so it was understandable that she might wonder what Maria had meant by *we*.

Maria was asking herself the same thing.

The headmistress stood up and escorted Maria out of the office. They walked in silence past a wall of multicoloured lockers, turned along a corridor decorated with paintings and collages made by children who presumably did not bite or slap or scratch or swear, and stopped outside a classroom door.

The headmistress shook Maria's hand and said, 'I'll put something in writing.'

Inside, Josh sat alone at a desk towards the back. His head lay on his folded arms and he did not look up when Maria walked in. She didn't know if the teacher who quickly stood and put away the magazine she'd been reading was the one Josh had reduced to tears, but Maria mumbled an apology, just in case.

'Josh, your mum's here . . .'

All too aware of the teacher's eyes on her, hating every ounce of pity and judgement in the polite smile, Maria walked across to where Josh was sitting. It wasn't until she'd gently laid a hand on his arm that her son sat up, wide-eyed and shaking as if he'd been woken from a nightmare, and burst into tears.

On the short drive home, Josh stared out of the car window while Maria kept her eyes fixed on the road and tried to cry as quietly as possible. He turned towards her only once, to put on the Babylon Zoo CD he liked, the one with 'Spaceman' on it, that Maria kept in the car for long journeys, that he always sang along to. Maria switched it off. When Josh immediately leaned across to turn it on again, Maria ejected the CD and tossed it into the footwell.

She pulled on to the drive and turned the engine off.

'What's going on, Joshy?' She waited, her hands remaining tight around the wheel. 'Is it because you're still upset about Kieron?'

The boy said nothing. His eyes were squeezed shut.

'You said you wanted to go back to school, so . . . ' Maria shook her head and stared across the perfectly manicured front garden at her perfectly shiny front door, the carefully shaped box trees in aluminium planters and the lush arrangements in pots on either side. The engine ticked slowly for a minute or more and then stopped.

She felt ashamed, helpless and heartbroken.

'I get angry,' Josh said.

Maria looked at her son. He shifted in his seat but would not make eye contact with her. 'Well, we all get angry sometimes,' she said. 'But you have to learn to . . . control it. Talking is always the best thing.'

Josh hugged his school bag tight against his chest.

'What makes you angry?'

Half a minute later, Maria was reaching to open the car door when the boy said, 'Everything.'

# FORTY-NINE

From the front door, Cat walked back across to the small dining table in her living room, sat down and moved a few of the cards around. 'My nan taught me this when I was little,' she said. 'Good for taking your mind off stuff.'

'I don't even know how you play it,' Thorne said, joining her.

'It's easy.'

'I don't think I'm cut out to play any game called "patience".' Thorne pulled out a chair and sat down. 'I haven't got a lot of it.' He watched her turning up the cards then laying them down without a clue what was happening. 'I played a bit of three-card brag at school,' he said. 'For fags at lunchtime. I wasn't any good at it, even then. I haven't really got what you call a poker face.'

'Billy used to play a lot of poker,' Cat said, without looking up. 'He was pretty decent, I think.' She placed the jack of clubs below a queen and grunted in satisfaction. 'Or maybe he just never told me when he lost.'

Thorne watched for half a minute longer. 'I saw Billy this morning.'

Cat glanced up, laid down the deck and nodded. 'About Dean,

I suppose?' She sat back and shook her head. 'Bloody horrible. I mean, he wasn't exactly my favourite person in the world, but why would anybody do that to him?'

Thorne had called her the night before, keen to let her know exactly what had happened to Dean Meade before she read about it in the papers.

'Billy certainly had a good reason,' he said.

Cat stood up, waving away the suggestion as though it was not worth thinking about. She walked over to the sofa, picked up cigarettes from the low table and lit one. 'So, what did he say?'

'Nothing I wasn't expecting,' Thorne said. 'He was over the moon that Dean was dead, obviously, but he had nothing to do with it.'

'Of course he didn't.'

'We don't know that,' Thorne said.

'*I* do.'

'You think you do.'

'Jesus Christ.' She flicked the worm of ash from her cigarette. 'Did you just come round here to wind me up?'

Thorne knew when he was flogging a dead horse, so he turned away to stare down at the playing cards on the table. If he did have any patience, it was starting to wear thin. He was becoming more than a little irritated by this young woman's apparent ignorance, blissful or otherwise, of her partner's . . . capabilities. Her refusal to so much as entertain the possibility of his involvement in an act of violence for which he most certainly had a decent motive. Denial or delusion, kidding herself at best; standing up for her man like some cut-price north London Tammy Wynette.

For a moment he wanted to stand up and shout. He wanted to shake her.

Then he looked across at her again, watched her drawing smoke into her lungs as though the possibility of cancer was a comfort, and remembered exactly who she was. What she'd lost.

The child he had been unable to find and return to her.

And suddenly he no more cared about what had happened to Dean Meade than Billy Coyne had professed to a few hours before. He was being selfish and stupid. *Useless* . . .

He looked at Cat and, more than anything, he wanted to offer her something.

'For what it's worth,' he said, 'things might not be as bad as you thought they'd be. With Billy, I mean. The business about who Kieron's dad is.'

She turned to look at him.

'He seems to think Dean was just shouting his mouth off and that you were a bit confused or something. It's like he doesn't really believe it. So, you know . . . the whole thing might not be such a problem after all.'

Cat blew out a thin stream of smoke and smiled. 'Oh, don't worry, he believes it.'

'That's not what he told me,' Thorne said.

'His sister knows the truth.'

'So . . . ?'

'Trust me, he'll have believed it coming from her. Billy knows damn well I'm not confused about anything. Unfaithful, maybe, but not confused.' She took another drag. 'He'd never have said as much to you, because he wouldn't have wanted to seem . . . weak. Because you're a copper and as far as he's concerned it's none of your business. And because you're a bloke.'

Instinctively, Thorne knew that she was right, and that he should have clocked it at the time. Billy Coyne was as likely to have confessed to Dean Meade's murder, or to nicking Shergar, as he was to have shown his real feelings about not being Kieron's natural father. Far easier to bluff it out than let on to Thorne that he might be upset or, heaven forbid, that he felt . . . unmanned.

'Thanks for trying to make me feel better, though.' Cat leaned forward to stub out her cigarette. 'I'll sort that mess out when the time comes. Other things to worry about now, you know?'

'Yeah, course.' Thorne stood and moved to the window. He stared down for a few moments at the necklace of red lights moving slowly south, then up at the aircraft beacon on top of Canary Wharf, blinking in the far distance. He turned and noticed a large greetings card on the sideboard.

*Thinking Of You.*

'From everyone at Kieron's school.' Cat had seen him looking. 'His form teacher brought it over.'

'Simon Jenner?' Thorne picked the card up, looked at the scrawled signatures inside.

'Nice of him, I thought. Actually ... '

'What?'

'I'm meeting him for lunch in a few days.' She shook her head. 'Don't know why, really. I barely know the bloke. He just said it would help to get out and do something and I thought he might be right.'

'Makes sense,' Thorne said. 'Something normal.'

'Not like I've got a lot on, is it? Nothing that's doing me any good, anyway.'

Thorne put the card back and stepped across to perch, a little awkwardly, on the arm of the sofa. He said, 'We'd like to do a reconstruction.'

Cat looked at him.

'For the TV. What happened in the wood.'

'You don't know what happened.'

'Well, mostly it'll just be you and Maria and the two boys in the playground. Actors wearing exactly what you were wearing. It's about trying to jog people's memories, getting new witnesses to come forward.'

'What about after that? After the playground?'

'Then it'll be what we *think* happened. What our witness reckons he saw.'

'The man with the red car.'

Thorne nodded. 'There's always a lot of calls after one of

273

these things goes out, so I think it's worth doing. You some-times get a few nutters, maybe one or two idiots just trying to piss us about, but if even one person comes forward with new information . . . '

'Right.'

'So, you OK with it?'

'Why wouldn't I be?' She reached for the cigarettes again. 'Anything, you know?'

'Great. Thank you.'

'When?

'If we film it tomorrow, we can get it shown on Wednesday night.'

'OK.'

'It would really help us if you could be there.' Thorne waited. He saw the tremor in her hand as she struggled to pull a cigarette from the pack. 'Make sure we get everything right—'

'No.' Cat shook her head, stared at the cigarette between her fingers. 'No way am I going back to those woods.' She looked at him. 'I can't.'

'It's fine, don't worry.' Thorne leaned down, took the lighter from her and lit her cigarette. 'We'll work around it.'

'Ask Maria . . . ask *her.*' She took a long drag, closed her eyes as she slowly exhaled. 'She'll do it. She knows what happened.'

'OK, that's a good idea,' Thorne said. 'I'll call her.'

They said nothing for a minute or so, the silence only broken by a shout from a nearby flat and the roar of a plane passing low overhead. A sob, muffled by a hand.

'Make sure you get his anorak right, yeah?'

'We will.'

'Tartan with a hood. A furry hood.'

'I know,' Thorne said. 'It's all being taken care of. We've got pictures.'

Cat nodded, relieved.

'Anything else?'

'Well, obviously make sure the actress playing me is properly gorgeous.'

'Obviously.'

'I don't know how big your budget is, but Cindy Crawford would be good.'

Thorne reached down for the box of tissues on the table and passed it across. 'I'll make a call,' he said. 'See if she's available.'

# FIFTY

The day was forecast to be warm, but it certainly hadn't kicked in at a little after six-thirty in the morning as Cat helped unload the van. Wearing a Puffa jacket, fingerless gloves and Billy's woolly West Ham hat, her breath was visible as she and Angie carried the heavy plastic boxes across the road and dumped them behind the stall.

'You know I'm always grateful when you do this,' Angie said, when they'd finished. She was climbing back into the van, ready to move it to the market car park. 'But you really don't have to, babe. Not at the moment.'

'It's good to get out of the flat,' Cat said. 'Feel like I'm turning into a zombie.'

'OK, if you're sure.' Angie started the engine.

Cat nodded, rubbing at the marks that the edges of the plastic containers had scored into her fingers. 'Plus I get a free breakfast, so what's not to like?'

Half an hour later, after tea and sausage sandwiches bought by Angie, the women began unpacking and setting out the stall.

'Where do you *get* all this stuff?' Cat asked. She'd already laid out displays of captioned mugs, hairspray, suntan lotion and a range of household cleaning products. She'd arranged the multipacks of light bulbs, cigarette lighters and felt-tip pens. She'd lined up the VHS films and was now arranging the CDs into alphabetical order while Angie stuck souvenir London fridge magnets on to a large metal board hung beneath the striped awning.

'I've got loads of different suppliers,' Angie said, moving a few of the magnets around. 'I pick up stuff all over the place.'

It wasn't the first time Cat had found herself wondering how Angie acquired her bewildering variety of stock and how – considering the low prices she was knocking some of it out for – the people who sold it to *her* were making anything at all. If it was a step up from *Only Fools And Horses*, she thought, it wasn't a very big one. Cat wasn't going to ask too many questions, though, because Angie was family, more or less, and Cat wasn't an idiot, and if Angie seemed to be making a decent enough living it was probably down to the fact that she had no kids to support and because she worked her arse off.

She worked harder than Cat had ever done, no question about it.

She was popular with the other stallholders, most of whom were blokes on the lairy side; flirting just a little bit when she had to and more than holding her own when it came to the kind of chat that would have made a docker blush.

She had the patter, too.

'Forget the Duracell bunny, love.' She leaned towards a customer who was eyeing up a pack of batteries made by some company Cat had never heard of. 'These'll still be going when that furry little sod's got myxomatosis.' She paused and rolled her eyes, a comic's timing. 'That's a disease rabbits get.' She watched the man pick a pack up. 'Go on, I bet your missus could put a few of those to good use.' Angie carried on grinning until the money had been handed over and safely stashed away, the coins dropped into a metal box beneath the counter and the notes folded into a zippered pouch on her belt.

'You're so good at this,' Cat said.

'Been doing it a while, that's all.' Angie put her arm around Cat's shoulder. 'Go on, you have a crack at the next one. It's just a bit of banter, nothing serious.'

'Not really sure I'm up to that,' Cat said.

'OK, so smile at them.' Angie saw the look on Cat's face and pulled her close. 'Sorry, babe . . . wasn't thinking.'

'I'll just keep everything looking tidy.'

As it turned out, there wasn't another customer for the next twenty minutes. Shepherd's Bush Market was never going to be as busy on a Tuesday morning as it was at the weekend, Angie had told Cat the night before when Cat had called and volunteered to help out, but they'd do decent enough business, she said, come lunchtime.

'What did Billy say?' Cat asked. She'd fetched two more teas and they were sitting together on stools behind the stall, commenting on passers-by as they drifted through the market. Which blokes were fanciable and which women dressed like they didn't have mirrors in their houses. 'When you talked to him?'

Angie looked at her.

'That copper, Thorne. He came round, told me he'd been in to see Billy about Dean.'

'Oh, yeah?'

'After what happened to him, I mean.'

Angie nodded, but looked no more bothered about Dean Meade's murder than her brother had apparently been. 'Fair enough, I suppose. They're not very imaginative, are they?'

'I don't think Billy was straight with him . . . when they were talking about Dean being Kieron's real dad.'

'Sounds right.' Angie slurped her tea.

'But what did he say to *you*? When you told him.'

278

Angie thought about it. 'Not a lot, to be honest. He went very quiet.'

'That's not good,' Cat said. 'That's never good.'

'I said, "these things happen", you know? Told him not to be a twat about it.'

'Right.' It had taken a while, but Cat had come to understand the shorthand between Billy and his sister. 'Thanks, Ange.'

'Don't be daft.'

She guessed that *don't be a twat* meant *don't hurt anybody*.

'I told you, it'll all sort itself out. And anyway, Billy's more concerned about what's happened to Kieron, same as you.' Angie finished her tea and tossed the cup away. 'Besides, who knows what he's been up to inside? It gets a bit ... lonely in there, you know what I mean? Any port in a storm and all that.' She nodded slowly, as though Cat should prepare herself for the inevitable, if unpalatable, truth.

Then they both burst out laughing and Cat flapped her arms, spluttering like she was choking on her tea.

'Can you even imagine?' Angie was doubled over with it. 'Billy doing that?'

Christ, it felt great to laugh, to *really* laugh, like an explosion of sunlight, and Cat's mood lifted as the weather warmed up a little, and then, when business began to do the same, she was amazed to find herself talking easily to the customers. She even managed to sell a few things, much to Angie's delight.

'I should put you on commission, babe.'

It didn't take very long, though, for the guilt to kick back in, hard.

That stone inside her, heavier than it had ever been.

By the time things were every bit as busy as Angie had predicted, Cat could barely string a sentence together. Could hardly move. She hung back, leaning against the fence behind the stall, or sat and let her eyes wander across the pits and stains on the road beneath her feet.

Scraped out and used up, oblivious to the chat around her.

Every few minutes, between customers, Angie would step across to see if she was all right. To ask her if she wanted to go home. To tell her it was easy enough to put her into a cab.

Cat said that she was fine and she didn't want to cause a fuss. She said, 'I'm good here, for now.'

She could not bear the idea of being at home, not then. All her baby's things screaming at her and those woods only five minutes away. So she sat and let the morning slop over her and tried not to think about what Thorne and the rest of them would be doing among those trees, on that road.

The end of her life being acted out.

Two boys, running in a playground . . .

# FIFTY-ONE

Two boys, running in a playground. One wearing a bright yellow coat, the other a tartan anorak with a furry hood. They clambered across the metal climbing frame, jumped on and off the roundabout, then rushed to climb the stairs up to the slide. They shouted and laughed, pushed one another and laughed even louder. They chased one another until they were out of breath.

'Cut . . . '

The director walked across to tell the two young actors how pleased he was with them, before they were ushered across to where their chaperone was waiting.

Thorne turned to see Maria Ashton hovering.

'Everything all right?'

She pointed to the woman who was sitting alone on a bench, holding a cigarette. The actress was now being ministered to by a make-up lady with whom Gordon Boyle had been getting decidedly friendly.

'Do I really have to be smoking?'

'You told us you were smoking.'

'Yes, I was, but it's hardly an important detail, is it? I just wondered if we could get rid of it. It doesn't look very ...'

'We need to be as accurate as we can if this is going to do any good,' Thorne said.

'Yes, of course.'

'Every detail is important.' He looked across at the two boys, who were still clowning around together, even between scenes. The kid playing Kieron Coyne saw Thorne looking and stuck his tongue out. Thorne had to admit, they looked the part, the pair of them almost as alike as the children they were portraying. 'Anyway, thanks again for agreeing to do this.'

Maria nodded and nudged the toe of her boot through a tangle of fallen branches. 'Sorry, that was stupid of me.'

'Are you OK?'

'Not especially,' Maria said. 'I mean, I know it's the last thing I should really be thinking about today of all days, bearing in mind why we're all here. But ... we're having a lot of trouble with Josh and I'm at my wits' end really, so ...'

'It must be hard for him.'

She shook her head. 'He's been playing up at school, so they've suspended him.'

'I'm sorry,' Thorne said.

'They think I should be getting him some kind of professional help.'

Thorne said nothing. The director was waving at Boyle. They were ready to move on.

'I'm starting to think my ex-husband had the right idea.'

'About what?'

'Getting out of London,' she said. 'The pressure and everything. I mean, it's all so ... full-on, isn't it?'

'Tell me about it,' Thorne said.

Maria looked around and shook her head, sadly. 'This fucking city,' she said. 'Forgive my language.'

Thorne knew exactly what the woman meant, even if their

current bucolic surroundings were hardly typical of the city she was talking about. The director was waving again. He pointed, said, 'Sorry, I need to . . . '

'Of course,' Maria said. 'It seems to be going very well, doesn't it?'

Thorne jogged across to join Boyle, who was already talking to the director, then walked with them as they followed the small crew into the woods on the far side of the playground. He watched as they set up for what the director was calling the hide-and-seek shot. A single of the boy playing Josh, covering his eyes and counting before getting up and searching for his friend.

'*Coming, ready or not* . . . '

Leaning back against a tree as the camera operator arranged the light and the sound man fiddled with his boom, Thorne understood exactly why Catrin Coyne had refused to take part. He could only imagine how she might have felt, watching a boy who looked like her son laughing and running into the trees; hearing his name echoing around the woods.

Reliving it.

'OK, we're good to go,' the director said. 'Can we bring "Josh" in, please?'

Half an hour later, when they'd got what they needed, the unit moved towards the road. This would be an altogether more complicated set-up, with multiple points of view needed and uniformed officers stopping the traffic each time they went for a take.

While the unit was getting ready to shoot, Thorne walked across the road to where Felix Barratt stood waiting to be called upon. He was muttering to himself as Thorne approached, breathing heavily and looking for all the world as though he was about to play Hamlet.

'Ready for my close-up.' Barratt smiled nervously.

'Thanks for doing this,' Thorne said.

'Oh, of course. Whatever I can do.'

'Shouldn't be too long.' Thorne looked at Barratt's clothes, a variation on what Thorne had seen when he'd visited him at home. Did the man even own anything . . . casual? 'This is what you were wearing on Saturday, June the eighth?'

'Yes, I think so. I was even told to dig out the same tie. Details are important, I imagine.'

'And this is where you were?'

'Give or take a few feet, yes.'

Thorne looked back across the road. From where he was standing, he could clearly read the number plate on the red VW Polo they were using and wondered again why their witness had not been able to tell them any more than the vehicle's colour and the basic shape. Why he'd been able to tell them almost nothing about the boy and been so vague when it came to describing the man he'd seen with him. A nondescript jacket, a cap. Thorne could not recall seeing Barratt wearing glasses or even hinting that his eyesight was anything less than perfect.

'The weather was the same as this,' Barratt said. 'That day. A perfect June morning.'

'Bit of luck,' Thorne said.

It was due to the vagaries of Barratt's description that this section of the film would be voiced over by the show's presenter.

*A witness describes seeing . . .*

Barratt was playing himself, so he could certainly be shown clearly, but there would be no close-ups of the car or of the man and boy he claimed to have seen getting into it. This was the part they were least sure about, but also the part they hoped would prompt the most useful response. People calling in to say they'd seen the boys playing in the woods would only be of limited use. What they really needed was information from someone who'd seen rather more of what had happened on this road than the man currently straightening his tie and lifting a foot to polish his shoe on the back of his trousers.

The director waved again. They were ready to shoot.

284

'Do they need me to do anything?' Barratt asked.

'You just walk past and look,' Thorne said. 'That's what you were doing, isn't it?' He waited. 'On your way back from the shops, right?'

'Yes, I was.'

Thorne was about to cross the road, then stopped. He said, 'Shouldn't you have binoculars or something?'

'Sorry?'

'You'd been watching birds in the woods . . . earlier. Before you went to the shops, so I just thought . . . '

Barratt nodded, as if he'd just remembered. 'Yes, you're absolutely correct, of course. I did have a bag and binoculars with me, but I dropped them off in my car on the way to Muswell Hill.'

'Right,' Thorne said. They had already checked, of course. The only car they could find registered to Felix Barratt was a blue Audi A3.

'After I'd been in the woods and before I went to the shops.'

'Got it,' Thorne said. 'And thanks again.'


It had taken the best part of two hours to get what they needed and the crew were setting up for the last shot of the morning. The man – medium height, dark jacket and a cap jaunty enough to satisfy Felix Barratt – was driving away having ushered the boy into the red car. They could only guess at the direction, of course, but decided that someone in the process of abducting a child would probably not have wanted to attract unwanted attention by turning round on a busy road.

The director had just called for quiet when Thorne was approached by one of the uniformed officers on traffic duty.

'DS Thorne . . . ?' The officer was proffering the mouthpiece of his radio and unclipping the unit from his tunic. 'I've got Control on the line, with a DS Brigstocke calling through from Islington.'

Thorne thanked the officer, took the radio and wandered back towards the Gypsy Gate entrance to the woods.

'DS Thorne to Control. Am I on talk-through to DS Brigstocke?'

'Control to DS Thorne. Confirmed talk-through is on, but keep it brief.'

'DS Thorne to DS Brigstocke. Go ahead, Russell, over.'

'Tom . . . a bloke called Alan Munro has just walked into the station. Thought you'd like to know. I've put him in an interview room, over.'

Thorne knew that the name was significant, but he was struggling to remember how.

'Tom, did you receive my last, over?'

'I'm just trying to place him, over.'

'A friend of Grantleigh Figgis,' Brigstocke said. 'Well, for one night, at any rate. Over . . .'

A few minutes later, when Brigstocke had told him everything, Thorne thanked Control for the talk-through and walked quickly back out on to the road. The timing was perfect: Gordon Boyle was marching in his direction and looking horribly pleased with himself. Perhaps the Scotsman had managed to wangle the make-up lady's number out of her or simply witnessed an entertaining road accident, but whatever the reason for the DI's mood, Thorne could not wait to piss on his chips.

'That's a wrap,' Boyle said. 'Everyone's happy so we can get the hell out of here.' He looked at Thorne. 'What's up with *your* face?'

Thorne momentarily considered taking a swing at him, then decided there was really no reason to ruin two careers at the same time. He said, 'I've just spoken to Russell and there's been a . . . development. Grantleigh Figgis.'

Boyle nodded, happy to hear it. 'Oh, please tell me those DNA results from his car have finally come back. They've had over a week, so—'

286

'No, but it doesn't matter, because there'll be nothing in his car. Nothing in his flat, either.'

The DI narrowed his eyes. 'We don't know that.'

'Remember the man Figgis said he met at the Astoria the night before all . . . this?'

Boyle said nothing.

'The man he said he went home with that night? The man he was still in bed with the next morning when Kieron Coyne went missing?'

'Yeah, I remember. What's—'

'His name's Alan Munro and he's waiting at the station to give us a statement confirming everything Figgis said.' Thorne enjoyed seeing the blood drain from the DI's face, the Adam's apple jumping in his throat as he swallowed hard.

Boyle shifted his weight from one foot to the other. 'And this bloke's waited the best part of two weeks to come forward, has he?'

'He was on holiday,' Thorne said. 'He got back this weekend and someone at the Astoria told him all about it.'

'Right . . . '

Thorne took a step towards him, thrust his hands deep into his pockets in case the temptation to use them became too strong. 'You never sent anyone down there, did you?'

'Now, hang on—'

'You never checked.'

'Well, I thought I had . . . I'd need to go back through HOLMES.'

'Don't bother,' Thorne said. 'I know you didn't.'

'OK, well, if you say so. I mean, it's a major case and when you've got as much on your plate as I have, things can slip your mind.'

'What, like failing to check the alibi of your prime suspect? Are you serious?'

'You try heading up an inquiry like this and then maybe you can—'

'Only he wasn't a *suspect*, was he?' Thorne let that hang for a second or two. 'You'd already got Figgis marked down as the man we were after. Job done . . . big fat fucking tick as far as you were concerned, so forgetting to check his alibi because you were *so* busy was pretty bloody convenient.'

'I don't know what you're suggesting, pal.'

'Yes, you do,' Thorne said.

A horn sounded as the car carrying the child actors drove past them. The chaperone waved and the boy playing Kieron was sticking two fingers up through the window.

'You're responsible for Grantleigh Figgis's death,' Thorne said. 'You do know that?'

'Bollocks.'

'Is it?'

'Well, as I wasn't the one who gave him those drugs, it might as well be.'

'Let's see what Andy Frankham reckons, shall we?' Thorne watched that big Adam's apple dancing again. 'What the DPS reckons when he passes it up the line.'

'I suppose you knew Figgis wasn't our man all along, that right?' Now Boyle looked every bit as ready to fight as Thorne was. 'You looked in his eyes and you knew. That's how this shit works with you, yeah?'

Thorne shook his head, not wanting to go there.

'You took one look at that freak and you knew straight away whether or not he'd done it. Just like you did all those years back with—'

'This isn't about me.' Thorne leaned closer still, until he could smell the sweat. 'You're the one getting a bit forgetful in your old age. Letting things "slip your mind". So you take the piss all you like, *pal*, because when this is done and dusted, I'm not the one they're going to crucify.'

Five minutes later, walking back towards his car, Thorne could still feel the adrenalin pumping through him. The tang of it in his mouth, like he'd been sucking on an old coin. He stopped, to spit it out. It was only a shame, he thought, that there hadn't been a camera still running. One trained in their direction and able to get a good close-up of the expression on DI Gordon Boyle's face.

When he'd got that first, priceless sniff of the shit he was in.

When he understood just how deep it was.

Now, that was a tape Thorne would have worn out seriously quickly.

# FIFTY-TWO

It was always possible that Jimmy Hill and Trevor Brooking were imparting words of wisdom that would have fundamentally changed his thinking about the beautiful game, but Thorne seriously doubted it. He'd heard the pair of them droning on often enough, so he was keeping the volume down, at least until the teams appeared. Instead, he'd put on *Red Headed Stranger*, having rarely been let down by Willie Nelson's words of wisdom, and spent the time before the start of the match drifting slowly around the house. He'd stood in each room, making a mental inventory of the things he'd be taking with him, if he ever got round to selling the place and moving into a flat.

It wasn't an enormous list.

There would be several boxes of albums and CDs of course, and ... some other stuff, but probably nothing that would necessitate hiring a van. He wasn't sure what else, if anything, Jan would want once the house was sold, presuming that the lecturer already had everything they needed. He had everything *she* needed, clearly. Perhaps they should just bring in one of those house-clearance companies and split the profit. He could use his share to buy new carpets and curtains and furniture that was ... smaller. He flopped back down on to the enormous sofa he and Jan had bought from an overpriced designer-place on Tottenham Court Road, happy enough for now that it was big enough to stretch out on, but seriously doubtful that – if it ever came to it – it would fit into the front room of that place in Kentish Town.

Not altogether sure yet if *he* would.

He was just starting to wonder how much longer the Dutch national anthem was going to drag on for, when the doorbell rang.

Thorne stared at the man who was beaming at him from the doorstep.

He said, 'Oh ... '

'If you remember,' Hendricks said, 'a few days back, you said you'd be watching the game at home, and I said, 'Is that an invitation?' And you didn't say ... no.'

'I didn't say yes, either.'

Hendricks held up a heavy-looking plastic bag. 'I've got quite a lot of beer.'

'Come on,' Thorne said. 'They're about to kick off.'

One hour and forty-five minutes later, after a good deal of air-punching, they opened the last two cans in the bag and touched them together. They shook their heads, still marvelling at the result.

'Bloody hell,' Thorne said.

Hendricks got to his feet, his arms aloft as though holding an invisible scarf, shouting, in what was clearly intended to be a Dutch accent. 'We were comprehenshively shtuffed ... four-one, for heavensh shake ... shlaughtered by a far shuperior team.'

'That was more like a shit impression of Sean Connery,' Thorne said.

Hendricks sat down again, laughing. 'Never said I was Rory Bremner, mate.'

On TV they were showing the goals again. Sheringham and Shearer: the SAS. Jimmy Hill and Trevor Brooking were as animated as Thorne had ever seen them and the England fans were still singing.

'So . . . getting divorced then, yeah?' Hendricks looked at him. 'Someone said.'

'Someone said right.' Thorne turned to look at the pathologist and nodded. 'Miserable fucking business, which I would seriously advise against. I mean, I might be talking out of my arse, because obviously it means you've got to get married first and I don't know your . . . situation, do I?' Thorne wasn't sure why he was feeling so chatty suddenly, but whatever the reason, he felt . . . comfortable. 'You likely to get hitched any time soon?'

'Extremely *un*likely,' Hendricks said.

'Never out of the question though, is it? Right woman comes along.'

Hendricks said nothing.

'Mind you, I thought the right one *had* come along, so what do I know?'

Jimmy Hill certainly thought he knew, at least when it came to England and their prospects in the tournament. Unbeaten, they could go a long way in the competition, he said, if not all the way.

'Wrote up the PM on Dean Meade this afternoon,' Hendricks said.

'Yeah?' By now, thanks to those reporters who'd seen the body before anyone else, half the country knew that Dean Meade had been stabbed to death and Thorne wasn't expecting any great revelation. Still – off the clock or not – he thought he should at least show a degree of interest. 'And . . . ?'

'Well, cause of death was basically being cut from arsehole to breakfast time.'

'You put that in the report?'

'I tarted it up ever so slightly,' Hendricks said. 'Chucked a bit of Latin in there, so it looks proper. Of more interest though . . .

I've seen the preliminary toxicology report on Grantleigh Figgis and I was right. Not that I'm surprised, because I usually am.'

Now, Thorne sat up.

'Shedloads of 6-MAP but, like I thought, sod-all noscapine. So, definitely not street smack.'

'So, he was murdered.'

Hendricks raised his can in salute. 'Let's see what your boss has to say about it, now.'

'I'm guessing he'd rather avoid the subject.' Thorne raised his own can and told Hendricks exactly what had happened that morning. The appearance of the witness whose statement proved that Grantleigh Figgis was innocent; a witness DI Gordon Boyle had made no effort whatsoever to trace. Thorne's confrontation with his senior officer at the woods. The accusation, the denial then the Scotsman's increasingly desperate attempts at justification.

Thorne and Boyle had driven back to the station in separate cars.

Thorne had not spoken to him since.

'What are you going to do?' Hendricks asked. 'What did he say?'

Thorne still had no idea what he was going to do. 'He said that it was an honest mistake, that he had a lot on, blah blah blah. He said these things happen on a major case. Then he got shitty, but I wasn't expecting anything else. Same old digs as always. He said I would've sussed that Figgis was innocent from the off . . . yeah, course I would, because I'd have taken one look at him and . . . *known*. Looked the bloke in the eyes and known straight away, just like last time.'

Hendricks was staring at him. 'I'm not with you, mate.'

Thorne took a drink to shut himself up and let his head drop back. The beer had made him a little more talkative than he'd intended. Or perhaps it had simply forced the lock on a door he'd been needing to walk through for a long time.

Since losing the only person he'd ever really spoken to about it. Hendricks was still staring. 'What happened last time?'

So Thorne told him.

'Ten years ago ... a bit more. Nineteen eighty-five. The Johnny Boy killings.'

'I heard about them.' Hendricks studied his beer can. 'Gay men, yeah?'

Thorne nodded. 'Half a dozen, in eighteen months. The press and everyone else going mental. We'd been interviewing builders, dozens of them, because one of the victims had told his mate the bloke he was meeting was a builder, so ...

'I wasn't even the one doing the interview. I was just a DC back then, didn't know my arse from my elbow ... but afterwards, I was showing this bloke out. This builder, Frank Calvert.' Thorne sucked in a fast breath, then another. 'Francis John Calvert. Just routine, that was all. More to eliminate him than anything else and he was ... helpful enough. We gave him a fag, he signed a quick statement and that was it.

'There was a song playing as I showed him out, I remember that. From the locker room or somewhere, on the radio. "There Must Be An Angel". Nice song ... '

Hendricks nodded.

'He stopped at the door, I said thanks for coming in, something like that, and he made some comment about all the overtime we must be making. Then we shook hands.'

Thorne paused, remembering. He stretched out his fingers, flexed them.

'And when I looked at him, I knew there and then he was the bloke we were after. Simple as that. Fuck knows how, I haven't got the foggiest ... but I *knew*. And worst of all, I could tell that he knew I knew. He couldn't have understood it, but I saw a flash of panic ... thought I did, anyway ... because he knew he'd given himself away.

'This was on a Friday and for two days I didn't say a word

294

about it to anyone. Not for the whole weekend. Not to my guvnor or to my missus ... but it wouldn't stop going round in my head. I was just lying awake every night and thinking about the way he'd looked at me. Hearing that song. Telling myself I was being stupid, then telling myself I was bang on. Backwards and forwards with it all weekend, you know?' Thorne glanced at Hendricks, then went back to talking to the wall above the television.

Taking care to separate the memory from the dream.

'Monday morning, I was outside his house. Just sitting in my car watching the place, with no real idea what I was doing there. His van was still parked on the drive, so I guessed he was inside. Best part of an hour I sat there. One minute I'm telling myself I'm stupid again, all set to start the engine and drive away, then the next thing I'm banging on his door and when there isn't any answer I'm running back to get a truncheon out of the boot and smashing his bloody door in. Long story short.' Thorne swallowed hard, dry-mouthed. He shook his can but there was nothing left. 'They were all dead. His wife was in the kitchen. He'd strangled her. She still had a wooden spoon in her hand. The kids were in a small bedroom at the back. Three of them ... all laid out like they were ready for bed, like he'd put them in nice clean nightdresses before he'd suffocated them. Their feet were all lined up, you know ... ? Lauren, Samantha and Anne-Marie. She was only five ... '

Thorne's voice cracked then, just a little, and he was aware of Hendricks shifting on the sofa next to him; sitting forward and tentatively reaching out an arm, like he was about to stop him. To tell him there was no need to carry on.

'I didn't find *him* until about half an hour later. Calvert. I needed to stay with the girls a bit ... I don't know why, because there wasn't anything I could do, but I just couldn't leave them on their own. That make sense? He'd blown his brains out in the front room. Redecorated the wall above the fireplace. I was sick everywhere and I remember thinking how much trouble I'd be in for messing up the crime scene. I still haven't got the faintest idea what happened that day at the station, when I was showing that animal out. What it was. All I know for sure is that it had never happened before and it hasn't happened since. And that I'm still terrified by it. I think it's happening sometimes when it isn't. I thought it had happened with that poor bastard Figgis, but I couldn't have been more wrong. That one time, it was luck ... that's all. Good luck and terrible luck, because if I'd done something about it sooner, things might have turned out differently.'

Thorne leaned forward to put his empty can on the table and turned to Hendricks. 'So, since then, because everybody heard about it and it got ... talked up, that's been the thing they make cracks about. Some of them, anyway. Little digs about me looking in people's eyes, about *knowing* things. I shouldn't get wound up about it, because that's what coppers do, right? Me included. We take the piss out of someone else because it makes us feel better about the stuff that's screwing *us* up. We look around for weak points to poke at. It's harmless most of the time and I shouldn't let it get to me, but whenever Boyle or anyone else starts on about it all I can see is that bed.'

Thorne said nothing for a while after that. On TV, somebody was interviewing Terry Venables and he watched without really taking any of it in, then got up and went to the bathroom. He grabbed a handful of toilet paper, wiped away the tears and the snot, then came back downstairs.

Hendricks turned when Thorne appeared in the doorway. 'You OK, mate?'

'Yeah, I'm good,' Thorne said. 'Sorry about that.'

'Don't be soft.' Hendricks's sympathetic half-smile widened suddenly, as he thought of something daft to say that might change the mood and make Thorne feel a little less self-conscious. A stupid gag that would get them both off the hook. A gift.

He nodded at the TV. 'A result like that, you're bound to get a bit emotional.'

# FIFTY-THREE

Hendricks called himself predictable names as he walked, somewhat unsteadily, in the general direction of Highbury and Islington tube station. He was happy enough to be a little the worse for wear – though not quite as bad as Tom Thorne – but he cursed himself nonetheless, for the usual reason.

*Spineless twat. Chickenshit. Liar . . .*

By the morning he'd probably have forgiven himself, because he usually did. But for now, until he was home and dead to the world, it would be all about hating the place he'd so carefully staked in it. Being appalled at who he'd become and furious on behalf of the person he still wasn't quite brave enough to be.

More mannequin than man.

*Inked-up idiot. Pussy-arsed fucking . . . disgrace.*

It wasn't like he didn't want to look the way he did. He'd always enjoyed . . . making an impression, standing out a bit. If he was being honest with himself, though, he knew he was only making one statement to avoid another. The piercings, the tattoos, all of it. Because getting stared at because of the way he looked was fine. Because it was easier to answer questions about *that* than about who he chose to sleep with.

Because doctors were no different from coppers, were they?

Looking for those weak points and poking at them, because that was how some of them got through the day. That was how they coped. He spent his days working with doctors *and* coppers, so he'd decided a while ago that when it was his turn to be on the receiving end, he was going to be the one who chose the target they could aim at. He was game for all the piss-takes and prejudice they could throw at him, but on his terms.

'Pinhead', 'Morticia', 'Doctor Death'. Easier, in his professional life, to put up with names like that than a few of the things he'd been called as a teenager. When he'd stood out for very different reasons.

The shit he'd put up with growing up in Blackley.

*You likely to get hitched any time soon?*

Happy to see the sign for the Underground station ahead, he found himself smiling, just for a moment, thinking about Thorne's very stupid question. The genuine interest when he'd asked it. Hendricks didn't know him very well yet, but he reckoned they'd end up getting on well enough, however dodgy the bloke's taste in music and football teams was.

He was a decent detective, too, no question about that.

Hendricks wondered how long Tom Thorne would take to work it out.

# FIFTY-FOUR

It was all about the colours, Maria decided, that's what it would probably come down to in the end, when people came forward. The bright yellow and that gaudy tartan. Distinctive garments which she and Cat had chosen precisely because they stood out and were easy to spot in a crowd; across a busy shop, say, or in a crush of pedestrians on a pavement.

Because they were hard to miss.

She had been well into a bottle by the time the programme started. She had turned up the volume and topped up her glass with an unsteady hand as Jill Dando walked towards the camera past several rows of people on telephones and introduced the item. A nod, a serious expression.

*'And now ... police need your help in the hunt for a child who went missing in London twelve days ago ...'*

People remembered colours, didn't they? Even if they couldn't always remember faces, they were unlikely to forget a nice, bright colour. She'd spoken to one of the police officers when they were doing the filming and he'd said more or less the same thing. That witness they'd found wasn't very clear about the faces, the officer had told her, but he was adamant about the red car.

Birds could remember colours, Maria had read that somewhere. They'd been tested. The clever ones: the crows and the magpies.

'*It was a sunny Saturday morning in Highgate Woods, a popular spot with nature lovers, ramblers and families with young children . . .*'

So, no close-ups of the boys, because they didn't want anyone watching to be focusing on faces that were wrong, did they? That made sense. Lots of shots of the colourful coat and anorak, though, as the boys chased one another around the playground then darted out through the small gate into the woods behind and . . . Maria swallowed hard a minute or so in, when viewers were shown exactly what she'd seen from that bench.

That flash of yellow through the trees, a streak cutting through the green.

While she had simply sat there and smoked. A useless lump, her mind elsewhere.

Now, Maria watched and reached for her glass, because she knew exactly what she was looking at, what she'd witnessed at that moment and failed to understand. Not that she could ever have understood, of course, whatever she'd been doing and wherever her mind had been. Nobody could have known what was actually happening, could they?

Useless, *pointless* lump . . .

Josh tearing through the woods, alone and searching desperately for his friend. Behind trees, deep within bushes. The panic starting to build, that expression he always wore when he thought he was in trouble.

Her son, asleep now upstairs, or more likely wide awake and thinking and worrying and running through those woods again. Tangled in sheets that would be soaked in sweat by the morning, if not something worse.

Still searching.

\*

301

She had known the reconstruction was being shown this evening, because Thorne had told her and because she'd been thinking about it ever since, but that hadn't stopped a helpful journalist calling first thing that morning with a reminder.

'Any message for those who might be watching, Cat?'

Cat had said nothing.

The woman – they'd taken to using women pretty much all the time – had waited a few seconds, then said, 'How do you think watching it will make you feel?'

'Sorry?' If the woman had been standing in front of her, Cat would happily have punched her into the middle of next week.

'I presume you *will* be watching?'

'It depends if there's anything decent on the other side.'

It was the kind of knee-jerk, smartarse remark that she used to make, that got big laughs in the pub, that Billy said he loved her for, and she decided that the woman's stupid question deserved no better. She didn't care that it might be inappropriate. Cat felt as if that stone in her chest was gaining weight with each day that passed, that it might drag her to her knees at any moment, but she refused to let it define her.

She would not let herself become the stone.

She knew straight away that she shouldn't have said it.

Now, while however many millions were gathered around their TVs, wringing their hands and thinking, *Oh, those poor parents* or *Serves them right for being stupid* or *At least it isn't my kid*, Cat lay on her son's bed, surrounded by his clothes and books and toys, and thought about what she should do with his room. Not right away, but maybe in a month or two, when she might just about be starting to come to terms with it. When the press and the police and everybody else had lost interest, because they knew Kieron was never coming home.

She'd read about people who'd lost kids and made a point of never touching their rooms. Keeping them exactly as they were when their son or daughter had last been there, like some kind of shrine. Football scarves draped over mirrors or Madonna posters peeling from the walls. Cat understood why people did that and she wasn't about to start judging anyone, but all the same she thought it was a bit creepy.

Like thinking you were keeping something frozen, when really it was . . . going off.

She would hold on to certain things, obviously – the drawings and cards, the bits and pieces that meant something – but she wasn't going to get sentimental about everything. She would keep what was precious safe and close by, but as long as she had her memories of her son, she wouldn't feel too awful about clearing stuff out and moving forward. She had begun telling herself that moving on was important, reminding herself that however things panned out, she was going to survive this.

Changed, for sure, but still alive and kicking. Stronger even, maybe.

Of course, there was the one obvious thing they could do with this room.

Billy would be out in a couple of years and she wasn't too old to get pregnant again. No child could ever replace Kieron and she would never want it to, but having another one was something worth thinking about, wasn't it? Now probably wasn't the time, but once the dust had settled, she reckoned she and Billy ought to at least talk about it.

She turned on to her side, stared at the picture Kieron had drawn of her, Blu-tacked to the wall above a chest of drawers, and wondered why she had gone from imagining the worst to expecting it. Why what was happening at that moment on live TV didn't make her feel remotely hopeful, even if everyone kept telling her that she should be.

*Having things like this on TV always works, you just watch . . .*
*Someone's bound to have seen something.*

Right, Cat thought, like seeing a child get abducted in broad daylight, which for some unknown reason they'd completely forgotten, but now people were acting it all out on the telly-box it's suddenly come flooding back.

Besides, there'd been something in Thorne's manner when he'd told her about the reconstruction. He hadn't seemed ... excited. Instead, to her, the whole thing felt more like something the police did when they were desperate and had run out of ideas.

The last-chance saloon, whatever.

She checked her watch to see if the programme had finished yet. Still another fifteen minutes and by now they'd probably be showing the picture of him in his West Ham shirt. Cat said, 'Fuck,' and clutched at the duvet, angry because she had promised herself that tonight she wasn't going to cry, but these days it was like telling herself not to breathe, so she closed her eyes and gave in to it.

Thorne had to hand it to Gordon Boyle. The arsehole could certainly turn it on when he had to. He appeared to be totally at home on live television, the accent softened enough to be viewer-friendly, his answers concise and given without fluff or hesitation. He seemed every bit as much of a pro as the woman asking the questions and there was even – during the direct appeal for information – the occasional look straight to camera.

Trustworthy and sincere, when Thorne knew very well he was neither of those things.

In the studio behind Boyle and the presenter, men and women scribbled while talking quietly into phones, and even though Thorne had once appeared briefly on the programme himself – performing with rather less confidence than his boss – he still wasn't sure if they were there for show or were genuinely fielding calls. Either way, watching the numbers for the studio and incident room scroll across the bottom of the screen, Thorne knew that the calls would already be starting to come in.

Plenty of them.

*'I think I saw the boy in a shop in Darlington. The jacket was definitely the same.'*

*'I'm a medium – and before you say anything, I've been right about these things before – and I sense very strongly that the child is somewhere close to water.'*

*'I took him. I took the boy. I took him and killed him . . . '*

There would be no shortage of nut-bags and serial confessors, of those thinking they were helping with their half-arsed hunches or half-remembered sightings, and bar those callers who were clearly acting out of malice or mischief, Thorne and the rest of the team would have to check out every single one.

They had little choice.

They would do what Thorne had always suspected they would end up doing.

They would be thankful they were doing anything besides waiting for a body to turn up, and pray they got lucky.

On-screen, Boyle turned to the camera again. 'If you have any information, however unimportant you think it might be, please pick up the phone now and call one of these numbers . . . '

Thorne did as he was told.

He dialled then waited, a half-smile appearing as he decided that some of his more Job-pissed colleagues might well be right and that a good copper was one who always obeyed a direct order from a senior officer.

'Crimewatch Live . . . '

'Yeah, I've got some information about the copper that's just been on.'

'You mean Detective Inspector Boyle?'

'Right, the pig-ugly Scottish one.'

'I'm sorry, but—'

'He's knowingly perverted the course of this investigation, he might well be responsible for leaking sensitive information to the press and he's indirectly responsible for the death of a man named Grantleigh Figgis. I can spell that, if you want . . . '

There was a pause, a clearing of the throat. Thorne imagined the woman on the other end of the phone waving frantically at her colleagues to get their attention. 'Could I have your name please, sir?'

Thorne pointed the remote and turned off the TV. He let his head fall back. 'I'm the Man from Del Monte,' he said.

# FIFTY-FIVE

These days, he had better things to do in the evening than watch television, but once he'd been told about the reconstruction, curiosity had got the better of him and he'd decided to make an exception. Not *idle* curiosity, of course. The very fact that the police had taken this step at all meant that they were still struggling and in need of help, but nevertheless, he was keen to see whether he had anything at all to be concerned about. If they were even close when it came to the details.

Car, clothes, all of that.

It had been a strange experience, watching this cobbled-together version of himself, of what he'd done. It wasn't a million miles away, he was happy to admit that – the nuts and bolts of it, the actors and the costumes – but they'd made it all appear so much more *casual* than it was. A cosy chat as he and the boy strolled towards the car in the sunshine, like this was something he did every day.

Or even something he might do again.

As if he was one of *those* men.

It was forgivable, he supposed. No witness could ever have

known what was actually being said or come close to understanding just how terrified he'd been at the time. On the day, he'd prepared a cover story in case things had gone a little less smoothly than he'd been hoping; on the off-chance the boy had decided to be awkward. Even now, he felt confident that he could have talked his way out of it if he'd needed to, but still . . .

Once he and the boy were in the car and on their way, things had settled down relatively quickly and he'd begun to relax, but up until then he'd been sick with nerves, shaking with them. It had probably been no more than a minute, two at the most, but he'd fought to keep the tremor out of his voice, because the very last thing he wanted was for the boy to see how frightened he was. He knew just how easily children picked up on that stuff, reacted to it. Walking out of the woods and along the road to where he'd parked the car, it had been an almighty effort to plant one foot in front of the other and to keep smiling, but what he'd seen on the TV, what the witness had seen, convinced him that he must have made a pretty good fist of it.

Relieved, he got up and wandered towards the kitchen. It was mercifully quiet downstairs, so he decided to make himself something to eat while he had the chance. He opened the freezer and pushed aside the stack of pizzas and boxes of ice-lollies he'd stocked up on a month earlier.

He was clearly a better actor than he gave himself credit for, better than the ones he'd been watching, because in the end the whole thing had looked as innocuous, as *everyday*, as he'd intended it to look.

They could have been father and son.


While the man is making himself dinner, twenty feet below him in the cellar, Kieron and Josh are whispering about ways to escape.

'The Hulk would just smash through the walls,' Josh says.

'I know, but—'

'Easy-peasy.'

It was the kind of thing Josh would definitely have said, Kieron thinks, but much as he loves it when they talk about this kind of stuff, he knows it isn't going to help him. 'The Hulk's not here,' he says. 'It's just us.' He blinks. 'It's just . . . me.'

'OK.' Josh squeezes his eyes shut. 'I'm thinking.'

'No superheroes,' Kieron says.

'Copy that, partner.' Kieron is imagining his friend sitting on the mattress next to him, but now Josh stands up and paces around. He walks slowly from one wall to another, like he's seen people do in films and TV shows when they're trying to work something out. He leans down to pull at the heavy chain again. '*This* is the big problem,' he says.

'We need something to cut it with,' Kieron says.

'Maybe he's got tools upstairs. Yeah, I bet he has . . . a big saw or something.'

Now, Kieron tugs at the chain. 'I can't get upstairs though, can I?'

Josh laughs. 'Oh, yeah . . . '

Kieron laughs, too, slaps his forehead. 'D'oh!'

'D'oh!' Josh says.

Kieron tries to concentrate. He breathes slowly and looks around, searching for something, *anything*, that might give him an idea, but he already knows every inch of the room. Every crack in the tiled floor and the shape of every stain on the low ceiling. Each peak and trough in the black spiky-rubbery stuff that the man had stapled all over the walls.

'*So the noise sort of bounces back, and we don't disturb anybody . . . *'

He can feel an ache beginning to build in his stomach, and he doesn't know if he's hungry or needs the toilet.

'What if I pretended to be ill?' he asks.

'Yeah, that's good.'

'Then he'd have to come down and take the chain off.'

'You mean moaning and crying or whatever?' Josh pulls a face. He clutches at his stomach and begins to whimper. 'Like this . . . ?'

Kieron nods, getting excited. 'I've done it a few times when I didn't want to go to school and if I did that, but like . . . times a hundred or something, he might think I need to go to hospital.'

'Of course he would. He wouldn't want you to die, would he?'

'Then, when I get to the hospital I can tell them.'

Now, Josh is nodding, too. 'You just find a nurse or something and tell them and they can ring your mum.'

Kieron thinks about it some more, then sighs and shakes his head. He lifts his hand then lets it fall on to the mattress. 'He might just take my temperature though, same as Mum does, and then he'd know I was putting it on.'

'He might not, though.'

'Yeah, he would,' Kieron says, his head dropping. 'He's really clever.'

Josh says a bad word and kicks at the wall. He trudges back across the room and drops down on to the mattress. After half a minute or so he puts his arm around Kieron and squeezes and begins to nod again.

'So are we . . . '

# PART THREE

## Grandmother's Footsteps

# FIFTY-SIX

She had briefly considered being adventurous and meeting Simon Jenner for lunch somewhere a little further afield, or in a place she hadn't been to before, but in the end Cat had decided to play safe. She had always liked the food at the Turkish café, and was fond of the people who ran it. The two brothers, Adem and Aksan, had always been nice to her and Billy, had gone out of their way to make a fuss of Kieron and given him free Coke and ice cream. These days, friendly faces were even more welcome than usual, and more importantly the café was only a few minutes' walk from Seacole House. Cat didn't want to stray too far from home.

The teacher was waiting for her and stood up when she walked through the door. He was wearing shorts and trainers, a white polo shirt with the school logo on the breast. He said, 'I'm really glad we could do this. I know you need to stay close to a phone.'

'It's fine.' Cat caught the eye of Aksan who was chopping peppers behind the counter and waved. 'It's sorted.'

She had passed on the café's number to the incident room at

Islington station before she'd left the flat. She'd spoken to a nice officer named Kimmel who had told her that they were likely to be very busy after last night's reconstruction. Cat had said that she hoped so, though in truth, she could no longer have said where hope ended and dread began.

'Don't worry,' Kimmel had said. 'I've made a note of the number and we'll call you if there's any news.'

Now, Jenner picked up the menu and studied it. 'Can't be for too long, anyway. I need to be back at school by two o'clock.' He looked at his watch. 'PE straight after lunch.'

'Well, you're already dressed for it.'

'I changed when I got here.' He nodded towards the toilets then pointed to the sports bag at his feet. 'Thought it might give us a bit more time. Rush back, stick my whistle on and I'll be away. Not that I'm looking forward to it.'

'PE not your favourite?' Cat asked.

He laughed. 'Little sods are all so much fitter than I am.'

Cat smiled. 'I know what you mean. Ten minutes in the park running after Kieron and I'm absolutely—' The smile froze and she could do nothing but stare at him, shaking her head.

Jenner leaned across and nudged Cat's water glass towards her.

When they'd ordered – taramasalata and tzatziki, chicken wings and lamb ribs – Jenner laid his menu down and said, 'You look great, by the way.'

Cat thought it was an odd thing to say, all things considered, but that didn't mean it wasn't nice to hear. That she hadn't wanted to hear it. She had spent an hour picking out a dress and shoes to wear, blow-drying her hair and putting on make-up that hadn't come out of its bag for two weeks. She said, 'Thanks,' but was grateful when the waitress arrived with bread and olives, because it meant she didn't have to say any more.

'This a regular haunt for you then, is it?'

'Yeah, well, it's handy,' Cat said. She told him it had been the first place she and Billy had come to when they'd moved to

314

Archway. She told him how nice the staff were and that some-times she'd ring up for a takeaway at teatime and they'd do egg and chips and halloumi specially for Kieron because it was his favourite. She told him that he'd be in no fit state to teach PE after he'd eaten because the portions were so huge and said, 'See?' when Aksan delivered the food, but all the while she was thinking about the last time she'd been here.

Sitting at the very same table a week and a bit before, having breakfast with Tom Thorne.

Telling him all about those few stupid nights with Dean Meade.

Confessing that Billy wasn't Kieron's biological father.

'You were right,' Jenner said, tucking in. 'I think I might have to start coming here, myself.' He gnawed delicately on the wings and then the ribs, wiping his mouth with a paper serviette after each mouthful. Cat was every bit as hungry, if rather less dainty, though once they'd finished she noticed that he was the one with the stain on the front of his white polo shirt.

'You've got ...' She pointed, then leaned across and touched the spot.

'Oh, shit.' Jenner dipped the corner of the serviette into his water glass and dabbed at the mark. Without looking up, he said, 'Did you see *Crimewatch* last night?'

Cat shook her head.

He glanced at her. 'It was really good.'

Cat waited, leaning away from the table while the plates were cleared away. He'd said it as though it was just some new crime drama he'd watched. Like he might start talking about how great the lighting and the music were. She began to wonder what the hell she was doing there.

'I mean ...' Jenner reddened a little as he raised his glass. 'Well, here's hoping.'

'Yeah.' She saw how solemn he looked suddenly, struggling to hide his embarrassment. 'Yeah, of course.'

315

'They were talking about it at school this morning. The TV thing.'

'Who was?'

'Well, the headmistress did this whole bit in assembly.'

'What did she say?'

Now the teacher's embarrassment was rather more obvious. 'She said that anyone who, you know, wanted to . . . could say a prayer for Kieron.'

'Right.' Cat sat back, folded her arms. 'Well, a fat lot of use that's going to be.'

'I know, but . . .'

Cat grunted. 'Whatever.' She shook her head. 'I've done it myself and I don't believe in anything.'

'Maybe that's what God's there for,' Jenner said. 'When we get desperate.'

'Oh, right. Are you religious, then?'

'No, but . . . I mean, the *idea* of God.'

'Well, whether he's an "idea" or some old bloke with a big white beard, it's a bit bloody ironic that we should be asking for his help, don't you reckon? Seeing as, if he makes everything happen, he's the one who took Kieron in the first place.'

'God didn't take your son,' Jenner said.

It had felt good to get out of the flat, no question. She had been looking forward to spending a little time with someone she didn't know very well and it didn't hurt that he was unquestionably . . . fit, but now Cat was starting to feel uncomfortable again. She waved at Aksan to let him know they were ready for the bill. 'Didn't you say there was something you wanted to give me?'

Jenner nodded and reached down to open his sports bag. When he sat up again he slid a bulky cardboard folder across the table. 'I thought these might help,' he said.

Cat opened the folder and took out a thick sheaf of paintings and drawings, dozens of them. Scribbles in pencil on lined paper torn from notebooks, spirals of crayon on coloured squares, and

316

bigger ones, folded in half and stiffened where the paint had dried. She could see straight away that they were Kieron's.

'All the pictures he's done at school,' Jenner said. 'All the ones I could find, anyway. There's loads. Well, you know how much he loves drawing.'

Cat had begun to lay the pictures out on the table, but there wasn't room, so she gathered them up and began leafing through them again.

'Thought you'd like to have them all,' Jenner said. 'To keep them all together.'

'Because . . . ?'

'Because they're Kieron's.'

'Something to remember him by?'

Jenner opened his mouth, but for a few seconds nothing came out. He looked like he'd had the breath punched out of him. 'No, just . . . when I brought that card round, I could tell you were, I don't know . . . *comforted* by it. So I thought having his pictures might do the same.'

Cat stared at the drawings.

Houses and trees and bright, smiling suns. Superheroes of course, loads of them: Spiderman and Ninja Turtles and all six Power Rangers. There were several of Cat, all with that scrawled mop of frizzy hair he always added, and some that were clearly meant to be Billy, with loads of tattoos and muscles like Popeye.

The world inside her son's head.

She reached into a pocket for tissues. It was automatic now, like scratching an itch. She didn't have to think because there were wads of damp tissue or balled-up clumps of toilet paper in every pocket.

Jenner scratched at the tabletop. 'I'm an idiot, aren't I? I mean, now it's so obvious that it was a stupid thing to do and I can see how it might look like . . . a memorial or something, but I swear, I didn't think.' He took out his wallet, reached inside and laid three ten-pound notes on the table. 'I'm really sorry,

Mrs Coyne.' He pushed back his chair and stood up. 'I don't know what to say.'

She looked up at him. 'It's fine,' she said. 'Honestly. There's nothing to be sorry for.'

'I am *such* a twat,' he said.

'Probably. But a twat whose heart is in the right place.' She watched him lean a little awkwardly against the chair, unsure as to when might be the appropriate time to leave. 'Go on, you don't want to be late for PE.'

'Right.'

'Don't forget your whistle.'

He tapped his thigh. 'It's in my pocket.'

The thought came into Cat's head and her mood changed in an instant as she felt the grin building.

This is like being pregnant, she thought. Or insane.

'I thought you were just pleased to see me,' she said.

The expression on the teacher's face – a strange mash-up of horror and relief, like he didn't know whether to giggle or shit himself – made her laugh out loud. She turned to see that Aksan, who had clearly overheard, was struggling to keep a straight face.

Cat was still laughing as the teacher closed the door behind him.

# FIFTY-SEVEN

'Funny old day.' Paula Kimmel lifted her pint and effortlessly downed a third of it.

Thorne had a mouthful of peanuts, but he would not have argued anyway.

At the morning briefing, Ajay Roth had announced that the forensic tests following the searches carried out ten days earlier had now been completed. The results, he said, did not indicate any match to Kieron Coyne's DNA in samples taken from Grantleigh Figgis's flat or car.

'So, we can now officially eliminate Mr Figgis from the inquiry.'

Thorne had stared stubbornly down at the briefing notes, imagined himself jumping to his feet like a pissed heckler at a comedy club, pointing and shouting. *Oh, we can? So, the witness who corroborated the man's alibi wasn't quite good enough, then? The witness our so-called Senior Investigating Officer was too busy to bother looking for . . .*

It was unusual for a DI to ask a DC to deputise when there were sergeants present and Thorne could see that Brigstocke was more than a little pissed-off about it. It came as no great surprise to Thorne though, that Gordon Boyle had asked Roth to run the briefing in his place. The DI knew who his friends were.

'Though we will of course continue to investigate the circumstances of Mr Figgis's death.'

*By 'circumstances', you mean* murder, *right?*

*As the results of* those *tests very* clearly *fucking indicated.*

*Something else your boss chose to overlook, which might explain why he's keeping his head down. Hiding in his office . . .*

'What's up with Boyle, anyway?' Kimmel's question as they'd carried their drinks from the bar, the look on her face as she'd asked it, had suggested to Thorne that he might not be alone in questioning the direction the investigation had taken. Perhaps he was not the only one harbouring mutinous thoughts.

He had to tread carefully, though.

'Boyle just wanted it to be Figgis.' They had taken two chairs at the end of a long table occupied by several other members of the team, so Thorne leaned close to Kimmel and kept his voice down.

'We all wanted it to be Figgis,' Kimmel said.

'I know.'

'You were the one that pointed the finger in the first place, as I remember.'

Thorne did not need reminding. 'Yeah, well, there's wanting it to be someone and there's ignoring any evidence that suggests it isn't. Very different things. So . . . '

Kimmel looked at him across her glass, raised an eyebrow.

*So . . .*

Thorne was not entirely sure what to do next, what to say. He did not know Paula Kimmel very well and guessed that, hard as it was to believe that Gordon Boyle had any real friends on the team, he might well have allies. He knew there were plenty of coppers with an eye on the main chance who believed in loyalty above almost everything else, the truth included.

'*Tom* . . . excited about Saturday?'

Thorne had turned to the young DC shouting to him from the other end of the table. Floppy hair and a well-cut suit, a glass of rosé.

'I reckon we're in with a good chance, mate.'

The quarter-final in two days' time: England against Spain. Thorne was happy enough, for the time being at least, to talk about something other than his piss-poor DI. A little more certain of his footing. 'You never know,' he said. 'We're only three games away.'

'The Spanish are a decent side,' Kimmel said. 'Alfonso, Salinas, Enrique . . .'

The DC shook his head. 'They only won two games in the group.'

'Getting better all the time though.'

While Kimmel and several others argued about 4-4-2 and Christmas Tree formations, Thorne had tucked into his bag of dry-roasted, thought about the rocks Boyle had steered their ship on to and considered the best way forward. He knew that what he should do was go straight to Andy Frankham or even someone higher and voice his concerns, but he also knew what a potentially dangerous step that was. Even back at Hendon, the whispers in the locker room had made it clear that no self-respecting copper would ever set the Directorate of Professional Standards – the 'Rubberheelers' – on a fellow officer.

Not if that copper knew what was good for him.

Thorne had never been altogether sure what was good for him, not when it came to the Job, but he *was* concerned about the practical ramifications. Any ongoing DPS investigation was likely to result in Boyle being taken off the case and, good news though that would be for all concerned, as the complainant Thorne might well find himself reassigned too.

He certainly did not want that.

He owed it to Catrin Coyne, and her son, to stick around for as long as it took.

Once the football chat had petered out, Kimmel had turned back to him and raised her glass. 'Funny old day ...'

That morning, after breaking the news about the elimination of one suspect in the abduction of Kieron Coyne, Roth had done his best to engender a little enthusiasm for finding another one. All those present knew what that meant, of course. The previous evening's TV reconstruction had resulted in hundreds of calls and the day would be all about following up, chasing down, weeding out.

While Thorne had no way of knowing how his own call to the *Crimewatch* line had been received, he and the rest of the team had spent a long and largely pointless shift at their desks, bashing the phones and working at computers, with only a couple of results worth getting remotely excited about.

'Better than bugger all,' Boyle had said, on one of his brief forays into the incident room.

Several callers who lived on Muswell Hill Road had named Felix Barratt, having seen him on the morning in question, and while this was hardly surprising, the information – and in some cases the gossip – provided had revealed him to be even more of a local 'character' than Thorne had suspected. Certainly one who might be worth another look. A good many more callers had confirmed the presence of the suspect car and though nobody had actually seen Kieron getting into it or was able to provide even a partial number plate, plenty had been sure enough of the make for the team to concentrate their efforts going forward into tracking down all registered owners of red Ford Fiestas.

Almost a hundred thousand cars whittled down to eighteen thousand.

'And that's just in London,' Kimmel said, now. 'Me and the woman from the DVLC were practically best mates by knocking-off time.'

'Got to be done,' Thorne said.

Kimmel took another drink. 'Yeah, I suppose.'

'It's what we were supposed to be doing before we got ...
sidetracked. All the Figgis business.'

'A couple of murders, remember?'

Thorne was hardly likely to forget, but he still felt that he
was talking sense. 'It's what good detective work is, right?
Boring, mostly.'

Kimmel polished off her pint and smiled. 'I never had you
marked down as a desk jockey. Thought you were all about ...
I don't know, the gut. The *feeling*.'

There was nothing snide in her tone, but Kimmel had clearly
heard all the stories, same as everyone else. 'I thought I was,
once,' Thorne said. 'But it hasn't done me any favours. Didn't
do Grant Figgis any favours.'

They said nothing for half a minute, tuned briefly in to the
conversation at the other end of the table, then tuned out again.
Kimmel held up her empty glass. 'Same again?'

Thorne still had most of his pint left. 'I think I'll finish this
and get off.'

'Fair enough. Back here tomorrow night, then?'

'Probably,' Thorne said.

'Or we could go somewhere quieter, just the two of us.
Somewhere with a few less coppers?'

Thorne said, 'Oh.' It wasn't that he didn't think Paula
Kimmel was attractive or that he hadn't found himself ... looking around since Jan had left. It was more about feeling like a
player who was unfit and out of practice suddenly being called
off the substitutes' bench. 'Sounds like a nice idea, but I'm going
through this bloody divorce and ... well, you probably know. I
assumed everyone did.'

She stared at him. 'Yes, I know. And I've got a boyfriend.'

Now, Thorne was as confused as he'd been nervous. Was she
telling him she had a boyfriend because he'd horribly misjudged
the situation? Or because he hadn't and she was letting him
know that it didn't matter?

He fiddled with a beer mat. 'Right, well . . . '

'See you tomorrow, then.'

Thorne watched Kimmel stand up and walk away. He stared at the back of her leather jacket as she pushed through the crowd around the bar, then down into his beer, afraid to make eye contact with anyone else at the table in case they'd overheard.

Thinking: Job, life, sex . . . any of it.

He didn't have a clue what was good for him.

# FIFTY-EIGHT

Maria could not remember her ex-husband being on time for anything when they were married. It had been one of the many things she had grown to despise him for. Every other Friday since their divorce, however, when Jeff arrived to collect Josh for the weekend, she could set her watch by him.

Five o'clock, give or take a minute, and usually a few seconds either side of the pips on Radio 4.

In case Josh hadn't heard the doorbell, Maria shouted upstairs to let him know his father had arrived, and as Jeff followed her into the living room, she found herself wondering if this was what happened when couples separated. A change of habits, of *personality*, to go with a new beginning. Or perhaps it wasn't actually a change at all and the truth was that people only behaved in certain ways as a reaction to the partner they were with at any given time. Perhaps Jeff had always been late simply because she was always on time, been sulky because she preferred to discuss things and had nudged the thermostat up whenever he had the chance because she was the one who always turned it down.

Double acts, that was what couples were. Straight man and clown, stoic and flapper. Faithful mutt and horny old dog.

She was most certainly not the same woman she'd been when Jeff had left. Yes, she was more self-sufficient these days because she had little choice in the matter, but she was also . . . kinder and more tolerant. She valued her friends – such as there were – far more, had grown to loathe so much as a minute of wasted time and found herself getting uncharacteristically emotional about everything from the state of public transport to fly-tipping.

Most astonishingly of all, as she had confessed to Cat the last time they'd spoken, Maria had found herself thinking with increasing fondness about the man who had treated her like dirt for so long before abandoning her. Not forgiving him, never that, but making an effort to understand. Remembering the younger man she'd fallen in love with and – she reddened slightly thinking about it – counting down the minutes once a fortnight to those pips on the radio.

'Did you see the thing on TV the other night?' Maria pointed to the coffee machine but Jeff shook his head.

'Need to get off,' he said. 'Traffic's always a nightmare.'

'The reconstruction.'

'Yeah, I saw it.' He perched on the arm of the sofa. 'Boy didn't look anything like Josh.'

'Is that all you've got to say about it?'

'Well, he didn't. Oh, and why was the woman playing you smoking, by the way?'

'Because I was smoking when it happened.'

'Right. Back on the fags again.'

'It's just occasionally.' It had taken less than a minute, but now Maria could only remember the selfish and arrogant so-and-so who'd walked out on her. Annoyed with herself as much as him, she busied herself with the coffee, because she was going to have one even if he wasn't. 'Why am I explaining myself to you?'

'You're right . . . I'm sorry.' He slid slowly down from the arm on to the sofa then turned to look at her. 'Is Joshy ready?'

'Yep. I've packed everything up for him. Including Snowball.'

'He still needs that, does he?'

Maria walked round and sat on the ottoman in front of him. 'He wet the bed again last night.'

'God—'

'So you'll probably need to change the sheets.'

'I can do that, you know. I have done it before.' He stood up quickly, walked to the doorway and shouted up to his son. He seemed irritated suddenly, but by the time he sat down again his tone had softened and, seeing the way his features had crumpled, Maria understood that he was every bit as concerned about their son as she was. That she should never doubt that for a moment. 'Is it about the school again?'

'I don't know what it's about.' Maria let out a long breath. 'I told you, he gets angry.'

Jeff nodded. 'Well, it might not be any bad thing. This suspension.'

'No bad thing for *me*,' Maria said. 'I don't think I can face those other parents at the gate any more. The girl he slapped and the one he bit.'

'Maybe we should look for a different school.'

'Or we could do what the headmistress suggested and take him to see someone. You must know someone, be able to ask around.'

'Yes, of course I could, but . . . '

'What?'

'It's easy for kids to get . . . labelled.'

'I just want someone to help him.'

'Once he starts seeing someone, he's in the system.'

'Not if we go private, surely. Look, you said yourself, what if it's not just what happened to Kieron and it's not the school? Not bullying or anything like that.' Maria leaned towards him, looked at the floor. 'What if it *is* something a bit more worrying?'

'Jesus . . .'

'At least this way there might be a chance of finding out.' The truth was that, ever since Jeff had raised the possibility on the phone a week before, Maria had thought of little else. Imagining, struggling to sleep, and coming close in her darkest moments to understanding what Cat must surely be going through. Dwelling upon.

Worst-case scenarios.

Jeff let out a long breath. 'OK, I'll make a couple of calls.'

Maria nodded, hauled herself up and walked back to where the coffee was starting to dribble. 'So, what have you got lined up for the weekend?'

Jeff turned again and suddenly he was smiling, full of enthusiasm. 'Well, I've got all his favourite food in, obviously, and a few videos he said he wanted to watch. I'd really like to get out and about a bit, though. Into the countryside. Nature, animals . . . there's a farm you can visit. He doesn't get enough of that.'

'Sounds like fun.' Maria poured her coffee. 'Not sure I get enough of it, either.'

'So, move out.' He stood up and stepped towards her. 'Wouldn't everything be a lot easier if we were closer together?'

'Yes, probably, but . . .'

'But what? A new place, a new school for Josh—'

'Not now. Not with . . . Cat, you know?'

'Nobody's talking about leaving the country.'

'It's just—'

'She's got a phone, right?'

'Feels like I need to stay close, that's all.'

'So you're going to stay here for ever because you feel guilty about your friend's son going missing.'

'I don't feel guilty.'

'Good. Because you shouldn't, because it wasn't your fault.'

328

They stared at each other. She sipped her coffee and he leaned against the worktop, wincing as he raised a hand to rub at his neck. When Jeff saw Maria's eyes dart away suddenly, he spun around to see Josh watching them from the doorway. There was no way of knowing how long he'd been there.

'Hey, best boy.' Jeff walked quickly across and Maria followed. 'All set?'

Josh nodded. One hand was wrapped around the strap of a small, blue rucksack and the other clutched his white teddy bear. 'Why is it Mummy's fault that Kieron disappeared?'

'It's not,' Maria said. 'We were just—'

Jeff raised a hand to stop her, then squatted down to fasten the buttons on his son's jacket. 'How would you like to see some animals this weekend?'

Josh shrugged, expressionless. 'What sort?'

'Pigs? Sheep, maybe, and goats.'

Josh lifted the teddy up. 'Can Snowball come?'

'Maybe you should leave him here.'

The boy frowned and shook his head. It was non-negotiable.

'Right then.' Jeff glanced at Maria, said, 'Let's get going, shall we?'

Josh turned and walked away down the hall. They stood together in the doorway and watched him as he stopped at the front door and spoke without turning round, his back to them. 'A man took Kieron, didn't he?'

'Well, we don't really know *what* happened, chicken,' Maria said.

'Yes, we think so,' Jeff said.

'So, if it's Mummy's fault, does that mean she knows the man?'

Without taking her eyes off her son, Maria reached out towards her ex-husband, scrabbled for his hand. He did not move, did not blink, but he let her take it.

# FIFTY-NINE

There were still appeals boards mounted at every entrance, but what had happened in the woods a fortnight before did not appear to be putting anybody off. It would be light for a few hours yet and, in the short time since Thorne had parked the car, he'd sat and watched a good many people ambling happily in and out. Couples, dog walkers, ramblers.

Parents and children.

He could only assume that those who used these woods regularly barely even noticed the signs any more. That despite the flaking notices and the sun-bleached photographs of a child in a football shirt, the disappearance of Kieron Coyne was fading from the consciousness of the general public at around the same rate it was ceasing to be of interest to newspaper editors. The stories were still to be found, of course, every day or two, tucked away on the inside pages. The print that bit smaller than it had been before, and the focus less on the shock and horror at the event itself than on the inability of the police to make any headway in the investigation.

*The Hunt Continues For . . .*

*Clueless Police Still Searching . . .*

Thorne sat and wondered whether the public's voracious appetite for fresh tragedy and scandal made things more or less terrible for Catrin Coyne. The daily reminder – as if one was needed – of what had happened to her son must surely have been unbearable, but was this slow and steady *forgetting* not far worse?

Thorne and the rest of the team had not forgotten, would never forget, but until such time as there was an outcome of some sort, that in itself would be of precious little comfort to the missing boy's mother. Much as he loathed the word itself, he understood the need for closure and the wound left by its absence in those aching for it. Thorne decided that, if there were no significant developments over the next couple of days, he would make time to go and visit Catrin Coyne.

To provide some reassurance, if such a thing was possible.

Some company at the very worst.

On the six o'clock news, they announced that the Greenwich Peninsula had been chosen as the site for the Millennium Dome – whatever the hell that was supposed to be – and Thorne watched a blue Audi A3 cruise past him, slow down, then turn into a driveway a few houses ahead.

A significant development? It was highly unlikely, as Thorne was there based on nothing more than a vague unease, but at least he felt like he was doing something. Working the case. Anything was better than sitting around like a lemon, waiting for—

He jumped at the noise of someone tapping on the window and turned to see Felix Barratt smiling in at him. Thorne did his best to mask the grimace as he wound the window down.

'Why don't you come in, Detective Sergeant?' Barratt leaned down and gave the interior of Thorne's car a disapproving once-over. 'I've just bought a lovely bottle of Meursault and it'll be so much more comfortable if we talk inside, don't you think?'

\*

Thorne was on his way home anyway, so was happy enough to accept Barratt's offer of a drink. He didn't know what Meursault was, but seeing as his host did not keep a ready supply of lager, or beer of any sort, he had little choice but to take the glass that was offered him.

They sat in Barratt's overheated front room. The place stank of wax polish. The carpet bore Hoover tracks and the ornamental birds, perching tidily in their glass case, had clearly been recently dusted.

'I can't say I'm awfully surprised to see you,' Barratt said. 'But why sit there skulking in your car on a balmy Friday evening?'

'I wasn't skulking, I was waiting.' Thorne took a sip of wine. 'This is nice.'

'I'm glad you like it,' Barratt said.

'So, why weren't you surprised?'

'Well, because I watched the reconstruction, of course.' Barratt watched Thorne looking in vain for the television. 'I have a small black-and-white set in my bedroom.' He smiled at the look of disbelief on Thorne's face. 'I hardly ever watch it and the black-and-white licence is a lot cheaper.'

'Fair enough,' Thorne said.

'I guessed that one or two of my more civic-minded neighbours would call in to give you my name. I mean, I was in the reconstruction. I was playing *myself*, so that was hardly going to come as a shock, was it?'

'I suppose not.'

'Not particularly helpful in itself, of course. They knew I was there, because I'd actually spoken to one or two of them on the street that morning. Just in passing, no more.'

'Yes, they told us that.'

Barratt sipped his wine, hummed with pleasure and grinned. 'And what else did they tell you?'

'Well . . .'

'I mean, that's why you're here, isn't it? *Skulking.*' He didn't wait for an answer. 'You see, that's why I'm not surprised to see you, because I know that one or two of the people around here have plenty to say about me and I bet they couldn't wait to share it. I don't know precisely what they told you, of course, though I can take a decent stab at it.' He leaned forward. 'Have a few interesting theories, did they?'

'One or two callers said you were a bit strange,' Thorne said. 'That's all.'

Barratt nodded. He set his wine glass down on a low table, pressed his wrists together and proffered them. 'Well, of course, you must arrest me immediately.'

Thorne said nothing. He was starting to wish he'd driven straight home.

'I am happy to confess that I am most definitely strange.' Barratt widened his eyes and stared at Thorne through his wine glass. 'To those who define it in a particular way, at any rate. I choose not to spend my life with another person, and get all the companionship I need from my cat. I watch a silly little black-and-white television. I choose to dress in a way most people do not, and, among a great many other things, including, but not limited to, antique maps and vintage tableware, I collect ornamental birds. I'm different to most people, I accept that. To *you*, almost certainly.

'It's *otherness* that people really can't stand, Detective Sergeant. Or perhaps it simply frightens them, who knows? A hatred of people with different-coloured skin, a hatred of women ... it's all about a hatred of the other, isn't it? That's always at the root of it. Homophobia is a very good example – and, of course, a sexuality that some people struggle to accept is what probably defined the otherness of that poor man you arrested. The one who took his own life after he was released.' He studied Thorne for a few seconds. 'I do hope *he* wasn't arrested simply because he was ... strange. I can only presume you had a little more evidence than that.'

'Yes, we had evidence,' Thorne said. They had the car, of course, one that broadly matched the description of the suspect vehicle. There was a previous arrest for sexual offences and the fact that he knew the missing boy. But still ...

Thorne could not deny that his initial suspicion had been aroused by little more than the fact that Grantleigh Figgis had been ... unusual. That Thorne had *considered* him to be unusual. Was he sitting sipping this man's wine for no other reason than that was how he considered Felix Barratt, too?

An oddball. A queer fish. A funny strip of piss.

'Well, that's reassuring, at least,' Barratt said.

Thorne was relieved to hear it, though he was struggling to reassure himself. Barratt was wrong, he decided, in the end. Yes, the attitudes of some were almost certainly based on fear manifesting itself as hatred, but when it came to a suspicion of those who people like him found strange, Thorne could not help but think it was simply because they reminded the suspicious of what hopeless and humdrum lives they led themselves.

Reaching for something concrete to justify his presence, to himself as much as Barratt, he said, 'Nobody who rang in saw the man and the boy getting into that car. Not a single caller.'

'Oh,' Barratt said. 'That's unfortunate.'

Thorne nodded. 'It's ... strange, wouldn't you say?'

Barratt smiled. 'If you're suggesting that I didn't see what I thought I saw, wouldn't it be equally strange that you didn't get a call from the presumably innocent party whose car it was? Even if the owner themself didn't see the programme, then surely some friend or relative ... '

'You would have thought so,' Thorne said.

'Unless you think *I* took the boy, of course. That, even though I drive a very different car, I keep a little red one tucked away somewhere, for when it's time to play the child-catcher.' Barratt's glass was empty. He reached down for the bottle. 'That I only came forward in the first place because, even though I'm the one you're after, I'm one of those weirdos who craves attention, who likes to be in the thick of it, deliberately feeding you false information to put you off the scent.' He sighed and began to pour himself a top-up. 'Is that what you think?'

Some version of that scenario had certainly crossed Thorne's mind at one point, had seemed almost feasible after questioning Barratt the first time, but he could hear how ridiculous it sounded, now. 'No,' he said. 'It isn't.'

'I saw that man lead the boy along the road and I saw the two of them get into that red car and drive away. Even if I'm the only one who saw it, that's what happened. As I told you, the boy didn't seem to be distressed or upset in any way and I had the distinct impression that he and this man knew one another. That must be important, surely?'

Thorne had not forgotten, and was more convinced than ever that it was.

Barratt noticed that Thorne, too, had finished his wine. He held up the glass, but Thorne shook his head.

They sat for a while saying nothing. Barratt stood to snatch up a tiny scrap of something that should not have been there from the carpet. When he sat down again, he saw Thorne staring across at the glass case. His ornamental birds. 'Different is good,' he said. 'Different is *liberating*. Who the hell would want to be the same as everyone else?'

Thorne could not argue with the man's philosophy, but he also saw its flaw. He said, 'The man who took Kieron Coyne thinks he's different.'

# SIXTY

Angie had stayed over the night before. As per a fair few Friday nights in the past, they'd gone out to pick up a Chinese take-away and eaten on their laps in front of *Top of the Pops* – 'Not the same,' Angie said. 'Should be on a Thursday' – and *Big Break*, then watched some new American soap on ITV, which Angie loved, but which Cat thought was just a poor man's *Dallas*. They'd shared a bottle, sung along tunelessly with Shaggy and Mariah Carey and laughed at things that weren't particularly funny.

It was a very different atmosphere this morning.

They crept around one another as Cat made tea and fried egg sandwiches which they ate in near-silence, smiling a little nervously or nodding when eye contact was made. They took turns to stare out of the window at the grim, grey ribbon of the Holloway Road below.

Just before eleven, Angie looked at her watch and said, 'Five minutes.'

Cat said, 'Right.' Like she hadn't been thinking about it from the moment she'd woken up. Or hadn't been desperately trying

336

to decide what she was going to say the night before, while she was necking the Liebfraumilch and stuffing herself full of sweet and sour pork.

Angie picked up her jacket and walked to the door. 'I'll leave you to it.'

'You don't have to.'

'Don't be daft. I'll just poke around the shops for half an hour.' She smiled and stuck two thumbs up. 'It'll be fine, babe.'

It had been four days since Angie had spoken to her brother, a few more than that since he'd have found out exactly what Cat had been up to with Dean Meade while he was inside. When Billy had agreed to call her, Cat had been thrilled, but that had quickly given way to something else. Something that crawled around in her belly as she lay in bed unable to sleep or dragged itself up to suck at her chest as she drifted aimlessly around the flat.

*He went very quiet*, Angie had said—

Cat jumped when the phone rang. Billy was ten minutes late, but that little bit of extra time had not done her any favours.

She said his name, hung a question mark on the end of it, then waited.

'So, go on, then.'

'What?' she asked.

'Ange said you wanted to talk to me.' Billy's voice was low, expressionless. 'That you wanted to explain. I'm all ears, Kit-Cat.'

'I'm sorry, Billy.'

'Course you are . . . course you are.'

'What else do you want me to say?'

'Oh, I know what you're going to say.' He left a beat, enjoying it. 'You were lonely, you were desperate, you were pissed. It didn't mean anything and, besides, you were thinking of me when you were doing it. I just want to hear you say it, fair enough, love? Then I can decide if I believe you.'

Cat swallowed and took a deep breath. 'All that,' she said. '*All* of it. It was stupid.'

'Yeah,' Billy said, just a whisper. 'It was.'

There was a crackle on the line, a shout in the background.

'I was missing you, all right?'

'Oh, bless. Poor baby.'

'I miss you all the time, and back then, he was just ... *there*. Dean.'

'He's not there any more though, is he? Randy little bastard's not fucking anywhere.'

'And did you have anything to do with that?' Cat laughed, stuttering and hollow, like she was at a funeral. Like she was walking through a graveyard in the darkness and trying to pretend she wasn't shitting herself.

After a few seconds, Billy said, 'You know they sometimes record these calls, right? They're probably listening in.'

'Are they allowed to do that?'

'Does it make any difference?'

'OK ...'

Billy sniffed. 'I had nothing whatsoever to do with the unfortunate death of Mr Dean Meade. That good enough for you?'

Cat listened to Billy breathing, sucking his teeth. 'So, where are we, Billy? After all this.'

It was Billy's turn to laugh. 'Well, I know where *I* am and I'm not going anywhere any time soon, am I?'

'You know what I mean—'

'Where the fuck are *you*, though, that's the question, and who are you with?'

'I'm here,' Cat said. 'I'm always here ... and I'm not doing very well. I'm struggling, you know?'

'*You're* not doing well ... Jesus.'

'Course I'm not.'

'And how the hell do you think I'm doing? All I had to keep me going in here was knowing you and my son were out there and would still be there when I got out. You knew that. You *knew* it. All the times we talked about it on the phone, all the stuff in the letters. Then, I wake up one morning to find out that my son isn't actually my son at all, that you've been playing me for a mug for years. For fucking . . . *years*. Letting me think he was mine. Letting me love him.' His low chuckle sounded like a growl. 'And what's the only reason I find out?'

'Stop it, Billy—'

'How is the truth finally revealed? Because, would you believe it, it turns out you can't even be trusted to take care of him. To do your one job as a mother. Because, while I'm sat in here like an idiot, bragging about what a top lad he is and showing everyone pictures, you turn your back for a little bit too long, because you're doing . . . Christ knows what . . . eyeing up some stud in the park, most likely, and you fucking . . . *lose* him—'

'Shut up—'

'Like a bag or a set of fucking car keys—'

'I didn't lose him.' Cat sat up hard and glared at the phone, the glob of spittle on it. The fear had given way instantaneously to rage, and she felt something lift as she let it consume her. Had the man she was talking to been within her reach at that moment, she would have punched and clawed and bitten, and she would not have stopped. 'Kieron was taken, can't you get your stupid head around that? He was *taken*.'

For a few moments, she was aware of nothing but the rasp of her own breathing, ragged and wet. She closed her eyes and waited for it to settle.

'Kit-Cat . . .'

She heard something in his voice she recognised. A catch, a change in pitch, a failed attempt to hold it together. She had only seen him cry once, a few years before, clutching an old West Ham shirt and bawling like a baby when Bobby Moore had died.

'Fuck off, Billy,' Cat said. 'Fuck *off* . . .'

He had just begun to sob when she hung up.

# SIXTY-ONE

Thorne and Hendricks stood on a quiet road near the station at Kentish Town West, staring at a house. Thorne turned slowly round to take in the rest of the street, then gazed up at the roof. 'So, what do you reckon?'

Hendricks shrugged. 'Looks all right.'

'It's the ground floor flat.'

'Yeah, you said. I still think you probably need to look inside—' Hendricks stopped and watched as Thorne opened the gate and bowled up the path, craning his head to peek through the front window. 'What are you doing?'

'Don't worry, if anyone's in there I'll just flash my warrant card.' He stepped up to the front door and leaned close to peer through the frosted glass. 'Actually, I could always just tell the owners this address has come up in connection with an ongoing inquiry and that I need to have a look around.'

'Might be a *bit* suspicious,' Hendricks said. 'Not too many coppers are going to be asking what kind of nick the wiring's in or if there's any noise from the railway line.'

Thorne trudged slowly back to the pavement. 'It's fine . . . I've

340

made an appointment with the estate agent for next week.' He turned to get a last look at the place. 'Got another one coming to value the house.'

'Probably the best way,' Hendricks said.

There was a shout from the other end of the street, some cheering, then the predictable song. Hendricks joined in briefly and shook his head. 'Still can't believe it,' he said, clenching his fist. 'We never win on penalties. *Never.*'

An hour before, the two of them had been jumping around in Thorne's front room, having watched the Seaman save that had won the penalty shoot-out against Spain and put England into the semi-final.

They began walking back towards Thorne's car.

'Well, we've broken the . . . what-d'you-call-it,' Thorne said. 'The hoodoo.'

'One game away from the final, mate, that's all.'

'Yeah, but if it's Germany, and if *that* goes to penalties . . . '

Hendricks shuddered, then rubbed his hands together. 'So, what's the plan now, then? Pub?'

Thorne could still hear the singing. 'I reckon the pubs might be a bit rowdy, don't you?'

'*Rowdy?*' Hendricks smirked. 'What are you, gay?'

Thorne unlocked the car. 'There's other places round here to get a beer.'

'Such as?'

'You hungry?'

The Bengal Lancer was unlike any Indian restaurant either of them had eaten in before. The muzak was almost . . . *jazzy* for a kick-off and there wasn't an inch of flock wallpaper anywhere to be seen. Instead, for reasons best known unto themselves, the owners had opted for an arty arrangement of neon lights and – strangest of all – plastic palm-trees, as though this were some flashy seafood place on Coconut Grove, and not a curry house squatting between a post office and a charity shop on Kentish Town Road.

Neither of them had eaten food like it before, either.

'You should definitely get that flat,' Hendricks said, a few minutes in.

'I know, right?'

'This is top of the range, mate.'

They shared a decent selection of starters, then put away dhaba lamb, liver hazri and kalapuri chicken, none of which they'd even seen on any menu before. They each had rice *and* naan bread and, by the time they'd downed a couple of bottles of Kingfisher and finally admitted defeat, neither was keen, or indeed able, to get up and leave immediately.

'I'm done, mate,' Hendricks said. 'Trust me, I know exactly how big a stomach is and I'm seriously pushing it.'

While they'd been eating, Hendricks had, for some reason, decided that Thorne might be entertained by some largely extraneous material regarding the post-mortem on Dean Meade. It was a mark of how delicious the food was that the pathologist's detailed diatribe didn't put Thorne off for a moment.

'Lungs were all but buggered ... twenty a day man, at least, and his liver was more fat than it was liver, so I don't think he'd have had much of an innings anyway. Oh, and his last meal was a kebab, if you're interested ... and I'm talking just the meat. *Just* the meat. I mean, what kind of an animal doesn't at least have a couple of chillis?'

He'd talked with equal enthusiasm about the body of Grantleigh Figgis, and by the time their plates were being cleared the conversation had inevitably drifted back towards the case to which both murders were closely connected.

Thorne told him where they were. What they were doing.

'That's a lot of cars,' Hendricks said.

'That's just in the south-east,' Thorne said. 'We don't know the car isn't registered to someone who lives in ... Glasgow, or the Isle of Man or wherever. Somewhere abroad, even. We don't even know for sure that the car is actually registered at all, because there are plenty of ways to avoid it and, bearing in mind what he was using the car for, he might have done exactly that. All we know for sure at this stage is that no car of that colour, make and model has been reported stolen in the last three months and is currently unaccounted for. That's hardly a surprise, though, because our man's not going to do what he's done and risk getting caught for nicking a car, is he? All we know for sure is ... bugger all.'

'Sounds like you need a bit of luck,' Hendricks said.

'Always,' Thorne said.

'Someone who knows this bloke to come forward.'

'They've had plenty of opportunity.'

'Maybe the bloke himself. I mean, they do, sometimes, don't they?'

'I'm not holding my breath.'

'Or else ... '

Thorne nodded. Nobody was saying it, but it was what he and everyone else on the team had begun thinking. 'Wait until he does it again.'

The waiter was hovering and, when Thorne looked up, asked if either of them would like to see the list of desserts.

'No chance,' Hendricks said. 'I couldn't even manage the *wafferest* of *waffer*-thin mints.' The waiter stared at him.

'We're good, thanks,' Thorne said.

When the waiter had left, Hendricks turned back to Thorne. 'Why do people take children?'

Thorne stared at him.

'I mean, you occasionally read about women who can't have kids of their own doing it. You know, they get desperate because their hormones are all over the shop and grab a pram outside Tesco or whatever. Why do men do it, though?'

'Doesn't bear thinking about,' Thorne said.

'Right, but is that the only reason?'

'Can you think of another one?'

'Mental illness? Voices telling him to do it . . . or a man might take a child to get back at the mother for some reason.'

'This isn't that.' Thorne saw the waiter approaching again. 'Like I said, doesn't bear thinking about.'

The waiter laid down the bill and – ignoring Hendricks's protestations – a small bowl of mints. Hendricks shrugged and popped one into his mouth. 'Might, if it helps you catch him.'

Thorne *had* been thinking about it, of course, but it hadn't got him anywhere. Felix Barratt was convinced that Kieron Coyne had known the man who'd taken him. Or maybe Barratt was wrong and the man in question had just been very convincing with his promises of toys and treats. Weren't children of Kieron Coyne's age naturally trusting, despite whatever warnings their parents might have given them?

Stranger danger.

He remembered his conversation about it with Simon Jenner, and a book with that title doing the rounds, not long after he'd joined the force. Jimmy Savile on the front. A trustworthy face off the telly telling a story about nice fluffy rabbits to make the warnings a little more kid-friendly.

Barratt was probably right, because Thorne knew that strangers luring kiddies into cars with ice cream and puppies were thankfully few and far between; modern-day bogeymen as much as anything. The stuff of horror films and TV thrillers. *Probably*, only because Thorne had been doing the job long enough to know they were out there. To know it wasn't rabbits they were after.

Hendricks picked up the bill and studied it. 'We going to split this, or what?'

When he walked through his front door, Thorne was still thinking about what Hendricks had said.

*Wait until he does it again.*

What he and the rest of them weren't saying, because snatching another child would almost certainly mean that Kieron Coyne was dead.

Thinking about it until he saw the red light flashing on his answering machine and listened to the message.

*'Tom ... you know of course that Jan is living with me at the moment and if we're going to move forward we really need to stop being silly about all this and sort things out. The house ... and so on. The assets. Obviously, Jan is my first priority at the moment and it's upsetting to see her ... in limbo, as it were. So, anyway, I just thought you should know and hopefully you're already taking the necessary steps. Many thanks ...'*

The lecturer. Now the fucking lecturer was sticking his oar in.

Many *thanks?* Christ on a bike ...

Before he'd even taken his jacket off, Thorne had dug out his address book, looked up the numbers and called the two different estate agents he was dealing with in Highbury and Kentish Town.

The offices were closed, of course, so he left messages, cancelling both the appointments he'd booked in for the following week.

# SIXTY-TWO

Kieron and Josh are drawing.

The man had brought loads of paper and felt-tips and crayons down a few days before, because Kieron had told him how much he liked doing art and stuff. The man said that was fine, that he would go out and buy whatever Kieron needed, because he wanted him to be happy. Kieron had thought that was stupid, because if the man really wanted him to be happy he would take him back to his mum or let him talk to her on the phone, but he didn't say anything.

He doesn't want the man to get cross.

Kieron has already done loads of pictures – of himself and Josh, of his mum and dad and the flat – but now he's drawing tunnels. Long swirly ones he thinks they might be able to escape through once they can find something to dig with. He says, 'Look at this one,' and holds his finished drawing up for Josh to see, but Josh doesn't seem very interested. Josh hasn't really managed to draw anything useful at all, because he's crying so hard. Just a few squiggles, and he's making the paper wet anyway.

346

'You need to help,' Kieron says. 'Come on.'

Josh just shakes his head and carries on crying.

'I thought you were going to help,' Kieron says. 'You said how clever we were.'

Josh can't even speak. He's just sitting there rocking backwards and forwards like one of those plastic punching toys and making a noise that Kieron thinks sounds like a dog he saw once outside the Tube that had broken its leg or something.

Kieron pulls the chain as far as it will go, so that he can get as close to Josh as possible. 'That's why you're here, isn't it?'

Josh looks up at him and wipes his face on his sleeve. He shakes his head and then he starts to really bawl. He stands up suddenly and walks quickly from one side of the cellar to the other, running at the walls, bouncing off them and yelling.

Kieron waves his arms and tries to shush him. He whispers. 'We were going to make a proper plan with no superheroes, remember? We—' He freezes when the door opens and looks up to see the man coming down the stairs. '*Now* look what you've done,' Kieron says. 'I told you not to make too much noise.'

'What's all this about?' the man asks.

Kieron beckons Josh across and the two of them huddle close, looking at the floor.

The man stops at the foot of the stairs.

He sighs and shakes his head, like he's disappointed.

He says, 'Oh, dear.'

Josh is still crying, even if it isn't quite as loud as it was before, so Kieron shushes him again. He puts an arm round him to try and make him feel better, but it's all a bit silly really, because now Kieron is making his own paper wet.

347

# SIXTY-THREE

The second quarter-final, between Portugal and the Czech Republic, was the only diversion offered by an otherwise dreary Sunday evening, so Thorne was more than a little irritated when the phone rang ten minutes into the game. He turned the volume on the TV down. He marched out into the hall, ready for another awkward conversation if it was Jan calling, well up for a row if the lecturer had decided to get involved again.

Looking forward to it.

'It's Simon Jenner. From St Mary's . . . ?'

Thorne was thrown for a moment, then remembered that he had left the teacher his card. He leaned against the wall from where he could see the TV screen through the open doorway. 'Not a football fan, then?'

'Sorry?'

'It doesn't matter. What can I do for you, Mr Jenner?'

'Nothing specific. I was just calling to see how it was going.'

Thorne watched a long ball drift out of play and thought how best to sum up an investigation that was, as things stood, every bit as aimless. *Looking for a car, no viable suspects . . .*

'We're making progress,' he said.

'I suppose I was really calling to see how Mrs Coyne was doing.'

'Yeah, she told me you'd been to see her.'

Jenner hummed a confirmation. 'That's right.'

'That was very thoughtful of you.'

'Just seemed like the decent thing to do.'

'She said you were meeting for lunch.'

'Yes, we were . . . we did. A couple of days ago. She seemed to be coping fairly well, but it's difficult to tell, isn't it. So I thought I'd call to check, that's all.'

Thorne thought back to the conversation he'd had with Simon Jenner at the school a week and a half earlier. He wondered if the teacher believed he was *connecting* with Catrin Coyne as well as he claimed to have done with her son. 'Like you say, she seems to be coping. I'll tell her you were asking after her, but it sounds as if you might be seeing her again yourself fairly soon.'

'Oh, I don't know about that,' Jenner said. 'We haven't made any plans.'

'Right.'

'It was very much a casual thing.'

'Have you thought any more about Kieron, Mr Jenner?'

'Thought any *more*? I don't—'

'About anything that might have happened at school. He got upset, you said.'

'Oh . . . that's right. As I told you, he was missing his friend. Or sometimes he was upset just because his friend was upset. I remember him telling me that once.'

'Why was Josh upset?'

'I don't know. Missing Kieron, I suppose. I never met the other boy, obviously.'

For a few seconds there was just a faint crackle on the line, until Thorne said, 'Would you mind telling me where you were on the morning Kieron went missing?'

'Excuse me?'

'I should probably have asked you when I came to the school,' Thorne said. 'Poor police work, basically. If I was one of your pupils, I'd get what . . . an F?'

Jenner took a moment. 'Actually, the kids I teach are a bit young for that kind of grading.'

'Well, anyway.'

'You'll need to remind me. The date, I mean.'

'Saturday, June the eighth.'

'Yes, of course. I think I was away walking that weekend, but let me go and look at my diary . . . '

There was a clatter as the phone was laid down, then silence.

Thorne waited and studied patterns in a hall carpet that was long past its best. He wondered if there was a grade below an F. He looked up and stared through the doorway at the TV screen, and watched as a promising Portuguese attack came to nothing.

# SIXTY-FOUR

Midway through a humid Monday morning, after several less-than-productive hours on phones or at computers – tracing vehicles or trying to find anyone who could confirm Simon Jenner's claim that he had been hiking alone in the Chilterns on 8 June – Thorne and Paula Kimmel stood together at the tea station.

'Good weekend?'

'Not especially,' Thorne said.

'The football, though.'

'Yeah, that was good . . . '

If the conversation felt a little forced, it was only because they had already spoken first thing. A nod from Thorne during the morning briefing, separate exits afterwards, then an urgent exchange of whispers behind a van in the vehicle yard. Out of earshot, but still keeping a weather eye on the pair of uniforms sharing a crafty cigarette by the back door.

A few stolen glances later on; eyes on each other before sliding across to the closed door of one particular office or lifting to the clock on the incident room's dirty-white wall as the morning stumbled forward.

Now, Thorne grunted and stared down, as though he could find what he was looking for in his plastic cup of piss-weak tea.

'I'm sure there's half a bottle of Bell's stashed away in here somewhere.' Kimmel opened a cupboard then closed it again. 'If you want something stronger.'

'I want you to tell me I'm not being stupid,' Thorne said.

'Oh, you're being very stupid.'

'Cheers.'

'Still happy to come with you, though.'

Thorne shook his head, though he was glad of the offer. 'I'm guessing they'll want to talk to you at some point.'

'Fine with me,' Kimmel said. 'I think you can probably count on most of the team. Roth aside, obviously. I'm not a hundred per cent sure which side Brigstocke's bread is buttered on, either.'

'He's sound, I think.' Thorne looked at her. 'I *think*.'

'What time are you meeting him?'

'One o'clock.' Thorne looked at his watch. He took a mouthful of tea and winced. 'I'll just happen to run into him in the place across the road, you know.'

'Come and find me afterwards.'

Thorne told her that he would, took half a step away, then stopped. 'I meant to say . . . the other night in the pub. Sorry if I made you feel awkward.'

'I don't know what you're on about,' Kimmel said.

He smiled, nodded. 'Well, that's a relief, because I didn't mean what you thought I meant.'

'Yeah, you did.'

Thorne leaned against the door, looked at her. 'Yeah, I did. I just came out with that divorce stuff to cover my arse.'

'Not a problem.' Kimmel shrugged and poured what was left of her tea into the sink. 'I haven't got a boyfriend, either.'

*

DCI Andy Frankham was sitting on a stool in the window and stopped eating his sandwich when he saw Thorne jog across the road towards the sandwich bar. He was eating again by the time Thorne had taken the empty stool next to him.

'Not hungry, Tom?'

Thorne was actually ravenous, but there was a good-sized queue and he was keen to get things over with. 'I had something back at the office,' he said.

Frankham swallowed and took a swig from a bottle of water. 'OK, let's have it, then.'

'It's about DI Boyle, sir.'

'You told me that much on the phone.'

So, Thorne told him about Gordon Boyle's failure to follow up on Grantleigh Figgis's alibi, how costly he believed that 'oversight' had proved to be. 'I don't think it *was* an oversight,' he said. 'It suited him.'

'I take it you've checked HOLMES.'

'Yes, sir, and no such actions were authorised. Nobody was dispatched to that nightclub to check out Figgis's statement.'

Frankham was eating again. 'I can see why you didn't want to have this conversation at the office.'

'Sir . . . '

'Obviously you realise that this is a serious accusation and that, whatever the outcome of an investigation, if there is one, you might not come out of it smelling of roses. Quite the opposite, in fact. Something like this can easily affect your relationship with a good many other officers. You need to understand that.'

'I do,' Thorne said.

'You've already got something of a reputation.'

Thorne waited and watched Frankham finish his sandwich. He was happy that the DCI chose not to elaborate. 'Well, while I'm pissing all over my career—'

'I didn't exactly say that—'

'I might as well tell you that I think Boyle's the one who leaked the Figgis story to the press.'

Frankham looked at him, narrowed his eyes.

'And that as good as got Figgis killed, if you ask me.'

'Well, that's something altogether different and rather more serious. So I need to ask if you have any evidence.'

'No sir, I haven't.'

'So, what, then? Just a *feeling*? Like you had ten years ago with Frank Calvert?'

'No—'

'Like you had with Figgis, too, if I remember rightly.'

'Nothing like that,' Thorne said. 'Boyle deliberately chose not to follow the procedures that would have eliminated Figgis from the inquiry, so I think there's every chance he was the one who gave him to the papers.'

'I'm going to need more than that,' Frankham said. 'You know I am.'

Thorne nodded. Paula Kimmel had advised him against making this second accusation and he knew that he should have listened. 'The procedural stuff, though. I mean, surely . . .'

'I'm not disagreeing,' Frankham said. 'We just need to be clear about what can be proved and what can't.'

Thorne nodded, relieved to hear that *we*.

'Now, are you saying that Detective Inspector Boyle's actions are in any way responsible for the failure of this inquiry?' Frankham leaned close and spoke slowly. 'That if he'd done what he should have, we might have apprehended the man who took Kieron Coyne?' He saw the answer in Thorne's face and shook his head. 'I didn't think so, which is why you need to bear in mind that, even though this is certainly gross incompetence, I can't see any grounds for criminal proceedings. Why you need to remember that the people I'll have to take this to will be extremely unhappy about the shitstorm it's likely to stir up in the press. I mean with that lad still missing and probably worse ... we're hardly flavour of the month as it is. Oh, and while we're talking about shit, you should also remember that it tends to roll downhill.'

'I've thought about all this,' Thorne said. 'I've talked to other members of the team.'

'Which ones?'

'I'd rather not say, sir.'

Frankham shrugged. 'Loyalty's good, Tom, though it won't be something people are going to associate you with down the line. Not if you go ahead with this.' He wiped his mouth with a serviette. 'So, I want you to ask yourself an important question before I give you one final chance to pretend this conversation never happened. Whatever Boyle's done, however much he messed things up, deliberately or otherwise ... are you gagging to see him hauled across the coals for it because actually *you're* the one feeling guilty?' He let the suggestion sink in. 'Because Grantleigh Figgis was only ever a suspect in the first place thanks to you?'

Thorne stood up, but Frankham reached out quickly to lay a hand on his arm.

'If you're really being honest with yourself and the answer to that is yes, then maybe you want to think about stepping back a bit. That's all I'm saying. No comebacks, no harm done, and I'm happy to forget everything we've talked about. I mean, we could just as easily have been chatting about the football and how great these sandwiches are, right?'

Thorne moved away and stepped towards the door. He was sweating and he could feel a headache building fast. Frankham was absolutely right, of course. Thorne had known it on the day of the reconstruction, when he'd confronted Gordon Boyle at the woods. His finger busy in the Scotsman's face, shouting and screaming about responsibility and convenience, ranting about the DPS and who was going to get crucified.

Brimful of self-satisfaction and self-righteousness.

And the guilt, boiling in him.

Thorne stopped at the door and turned. He said, 'No, sir. I don't want to forget it.'

# SIXTY-FIVE

As soon as Cat opened the door and stepped back from it, Maria began to apologise and led Josh into the flat as though he were some fragile, yet unwieldy package she was a little embarrassed to be carrying. Cat told her not to be stupid. She said hello to Josh and did her best to smile, though she could not bring herself to look at him for very long. Maria appeared to be trying equally hard, but didn't take her eyes off her son for a moment as he veered away from her and walked past Cat as if she wasn't there.

Like a sleepwalker with better things to do.

'Thank you,' Maria said. 'Really, I can't tell you how grateful I am.'

Cat nodded, thinking how terrible the woman looked, or, at least, how far from immaculate. She was wearing mismatched tracksuit bottoms and a sweatshirt. There was lipstick on her teeth. She looked as though she'd been sleeping about as much as Cat and shed almost as many tears.

'I couldn't think of anyone else to talk to.'

'It's fine,' Cat said, again.

Maria had actually called late the night before, semi-hysterical and begging to come over, but Cat had said no. She'd spent the whole weekend thinking about the phone conversation with Billy, not wanting to move, unable to eat and certainly in no fit state to see anyone, not even Angie. When Billy's sister had come back on Saturday morning, desperate to know how things had gone, Cat had told her she wasn't feeling well and had refused to talk about it. She knew very well that Billy would probably tell Angie about the phone call anyway, because he always told her everything, though Cat guessed he'd leave out the part about her hanging up on him just after he'd started to cry.

However wretched she'd been feeling since the call, that part always made Cat feel a little bit better.

As soon as she was inside, Maria sat down and she and Cat watched Josh walk purposefully across the living room and sink down on to the floor. He leaned back against the wall near the doorway that led out into the corridor and stared into space.

'Do you want a coffee or something?' Cat didn't need to point out that she was talking about Maxwell House and not the fancy frothy stuff she sometimes treated herself to when they were out.

When they used to go out.

Maria said 'lovely', and 'thank you', then carried on talking while Cat went into the kitchen. 'He's not been himself since his dad dropped him off last night. Have you, chicken?' She waited, but Josh said nothing. 'He's been a bit upset. A bit more upset than usual, I should say. He left Snowball at his dad's place, which probably hasn't helped . . . '

Cat came back with two mugs of coffee and she and Maria sat together on the sofa and stared at the boy.

'Actually, it was Joshy's idea to come over.' Maria leaned close and spoke quietly, though they were almost certainly still close enough for Josh to hear. 'He's been nagging me about it ever since he came back.'

'OK,' Cat said.

Josh stood up, suddenly, as though he was aware that the

adults wanted to talk about him. 'I want to go and play in Kieron's room.'

Maria looked at Cat.

'Well . . . ' Cat had tidied all her son's toys and games away and she wasn't sure how she felt about anyone messing with them. Least of all . . .

'I want to go and play in Kieron's room.'

The boy's face remained every bit as blank as it had been since he came in, but Cat could see the plea in Maria's eyes. She said, 'All right, but please don't make a—'

Josh turned and marched out of the room, and the second they heard Kieron's bedroom door close Maria burst into tears.

'I don't know what the matter with him is.' She reached out a hand. 'I don't know what the fuck to do.'

Cat had rarely heard Maria swear, could only remember a handful of occasions. Once, when she'd burned her hand on the hob and another time when she'd had one glass of wine too many and stumbled off a heel. That morning in the woods, obviously.

'The school thinks he should be seeing someone, and Jeff said he'd try and organise it, but he doesn't seem very keen on the idea. What do you think? You always know what to do, you're always so great with . . . ' Maria stopped herself before she spoke the name, her mouth closing slowly and her hand flopping like a dying fish on the sofa cushion.

Cat knew that Maria had been concerned about her son's behaviour for a long time. It had been the thing they had talked about the most for as long as she could remember. In cafés and parks, in Cat's front room while the two boys ran around, or sitting in Maria's kitchen. Some problem at school, that was what Maria had always guessed at, bullying maybe. Or just the delayed fallout from the divorce. Cat had enjoyed being the shoulder this woman cried on, sensing early on that there weren't too many others being offered.

Since Kieron, though, these problems had come to feel almost laughably trivial. Everything had. It was as though the part of her that gave a shit, that felt even an ounce of compassion for anybody else, had simply shut down.

Then she saw the desperation on Maria's face.

A cracked map of it, around her eyes.

Cat took her hand. 'What did Jeff say? When he brought Josh home.'

'He said Joshy had been a bit of a misery-guts, that's all. That he didn't want to do anything. I think Jeff was a bit pissed off because he'd got stuff planned and it didn't work out.'

'Has Josh said anything?'

'A week or so ago he told me was just angry at everything, but now he's not saying a dicky bird.' She was squeezing Cat's hand hard enough to make her wince a little. 'Like he's shut down.'

'It got worse after what happened with Kieron, though, right? You said.'

Maria nodded, struggled to get the words out. 'He was losing his temper and lashing out at school. He started to wet the bed more, was more scared of the dark. More scared of everything.' She let out a long breath then sucked another in fast. 'He told me he thought . . . Kieron was still hiding.'

'*When?*'

'That first night, I think. Just not understanding it, you know?'

Cat swallowed down the jagged fragment that had sheared away from the stone in her chest and risen into her throat. 'So, maybe you should do exactly what the school says and take him to see someone. You can afford to pay for it, I know you can. You don't need Jeff's permission.'

'He's Josh's father.'

'You're the one Josh lives with.'

Maria stared at the wall against which her son had been sitting. 'I swear, I'm at my wits' end, Cat.'

She sounded it, Cat thought. She certainly looked it. But Cat had heard the woman say much the same thing when her local Waitrose had run out of avocados. The rogue, unsympathetic thought must have been briefly visible on her face, because Maria clocked the look and misread it.

She began shaking her head furiously. 'I really shouldn't be here telling you any of this . . . it was Josh's idea to come round, I told you that, didn't I? It's . . . nothing, it's *less* than nothing, because how can it compare . . . ?' She raised her hands and for a moment Cat thought she was about to start slapping herself in the face. 'I was a terrible wife and I'm obviously a shit mother and I must be just about the worst friend anyone could have, because I should be the one sitting here listening to you. I should be the one trying to—'

'Stop it,' Cat said.

'Because I'm the one who made this nightmare happen.' She began to shout, to sob. 'The stupid, selfish bitch who can't concentrate for five minutes and keep her eye on two little boys. I'm the one who should really be suffering. I'm the one who deserves it—'

Cat leaned across and tried to shush her, then they both froze briefly when they heard Kieron's bedroom door open, and moved apart. A few seconds later, Josh appeared in the doorway, his face still a blank. He said, 'OK, then.'

His mother plastered on a smile. 'Did you have fun, chicken?'

'I want to go home now,' Josh said.

'Absolutely.' Maria bent down to pick up her handbag then looked up at Cat, who was already on her feet.

Without thinking about it too much, Cat walked slowly across to the doorway, knelt down and pulled the boy into her arms. Wrapped them around him. He didn't smell the same, but the familiar shape of him – that xylophone of ribs beneath her fingers and the way he fitted so perfectly against her – was intoxicating, and unbearable.

The tears came, of course, because that was what they did.

Cat's cheek was slick against his when Josh turned his head, pressed his mouth to her ear and whispered, 'Kieron isn't hiding any more.'

# SIXTY-SIX

With no more football on TV until England's big game against Germany the following evening, Thorne was reduced to watching highlights of the day's play at Wimbledon. Sue Barker was getting awfully excited about Steffi Graf going for her seventh title, but, superstitious as he was about any German sporting victory at this point, and not really giving a toss about tennis anyway, Thorne was unable to summon up much enthusiasm.

There was bugger-all else on, anyway.

At least it wasn't Henman, and posh tossers shouting, 'Come on, Tim.'

He ate off his lap – a plate of that shepherd's pie his mum had left in the freezer – and thought about a world where he had cause to be grateful to a nineteen-year-old car mechanic called Damien Hunter and to the eight pints of Carling said mechanic had put away the night before. Thorne guessed that the man into whose face Hunter had thrust a glass come closing time did not see things in quite the same way, but such was the way that the fucked-up world turned.

Out of kilter and out of control.

Capable of throwing anyone off, if they weren't cling-ing on tight.

The team had caught the case in the early hours and Thorne, like the rest of them – ground down by two weeks of abject fail-ure – had fallen on it as if it was the biggest case of his career. An attempted murder, albeit one that had been attempted in front of dozens of witnesses and resulted in an almost imme-diate arrest, gave him something positive to do. A reason to be there. It wasn't going to tax anyone's powers of deduction, but it allowed him to move in the right direction.

So Thorne had found himself with plenty to do that day: interviewing witnesses; typing up statements; and assiduously logging pieces of broken, bloodied glass into evidence.

And thinking about Kieron Coyne.

Now, he half-watched Steffi Graf execute what he felt sure would be called a 'peach of a drop-shot' and thought about Dean Meade and Grantleigh Figgis. The individuals still wanted in connection with those murders. Two of them, if the witness at Meade's house was right about how many voices she'd heard that night.

Grantleigh Figgis . . .

One officer in particular had been even more fired up than Thorne when the attempted murder had fallen into their laps, but that was hardly a surprise, as Gordon Boyle had more reason to be grateful for it than anyone else. A nice, easy one, a good result. A welcome distraction – for him and for anyone else paying attention – from the case he'd botched.

It had been a day and a half since Thorne had met with DCI Andy Frankham, and he hadn't heard a word. He should prob-ably have listened to Paula Kimmel. He should almost certainly have given a bit more thought to Frankham's rather more omi-nous predictions about his future.

Did he really care what other coppers thought of him?

Yeah, of course he did, but in the short term, Thorne

reckoned he could live with the occasional spot of piss in his tea, because somewhere down the line he might end up a hero. Anything could happen. One day he might talk a suicidal nun off a roof, or take a bullet for someone, so it would probably all even out in the long run.

He blinked, remembering something Catrin Coyne had said to him, that first time he'd been round to her flat. Barely able to stand, to breathe, the pain tattooed across her face.

*I don't* want *there to be a long run.*

Thorne moved his plate aside and stood up. He turned off the television and walked quickly towards the stairs, because going to bed seemed like the best idea he'd had in a fortnight. Because there were plenty of people he did care about, even if, right now, he didn't happen to be one of them. Because there were those worth ten of him, who clung on to the fucked-up world with broken fingernails, even when there didn't seem a fat lot worth holding on for. Because his wife was better off with the lecturer, because Steffi Graf had won her match and he hoped it wasn't an omen, and because he could put a hundred Damien Hunters away and it wouldn't mean a thing.

# SIXTY-SEVEN

The majority of what would turn out to be the most significant day in the Kieron Coyne investigation had been taken up with routine follow-up procedures on the attempted murder that had come in the day before. Thorne had spent his morning chasing down witnesses who had now sobered up, and most of the afternoon in a tedious back-and-forth with a lawyer from the Crown Prosecution Service, as charges were formally prepared. Then, just before going-home time, uniform in Willesden rang through with a report of a burned-out car, and Thorne temporarily forgot all about Damien Hunter, even if the poor bastard whose face he'd so brutally rearranged would never have that luxury.

'Lost count of the stitches,' Kimmel said, as they climbed into Thorne's car. 'That's what I heard.'

Thorne zig-zagged north-west to avoid the main roads. They drove past Pentonville prison, then tried and failed to dodge the rush-hour traffic between Belsize Park and Primrose Hill. Kimmel winced as they sped past a lorry on the inside, then braced herself against the dashboard as they jumped a light on Kilburn High Road. She said, 'It's probably just kids. This car.'

'Probably,' Thorne said.

Fifteen minutes later, they drove slowly on to a patch of waste ground between the back of the bus garage and the northernmost edge of Willesden Cemetery. Two uniformed officers waved them across, as though the hastily rigged-up police tape, the stink, and the blackened shell of the Ford Fiesta weren't enough to tell them they were in the right place.

'Keen,' Kimmel said, waving back. 'I remember that.'

While Kimmel listened patiently as the officers explained how they'd discovered the abandoned vehicle, and exactly what they'd been doing prior to discovering it, Thorne took a closer look.

Remembering what Hendricks had said.

*Sounds like you need a bit of luck.*

Trying not to get excited.

On the plus side, the number plates had been removed front and back, which would make sense if someone didn't want the car traced quickly, and there was enough paintwork still undamaged to make it clear that, before being torched, the Fiesta had once been the colour they were looking for. What was inside the car bothered Thorne, though. Whoever had set fire to it had been equally keen to destroy the interior, but certain features remained identifiable enough.

A beaded car-seat cover.

A baby-seat in the back.

Kimmel wandered over, while one of the uniformed officers took a call on his radio. She clocked the absence of number plates. 'We can still get the chassis number,' she said. 'Work from there.' She saw the look on Thorne's face. 'Somewhere to start.'

'It's a family car,' Thorne said.

'So?'

'So, what? Dad just borrows the family's runaround when he wants to abduct a child?' He shook his head. 'Doesn't seem . . . '

'It's a very efficient way of destroying evidence, though.' Kimmel was still looking around the car. 'Which is why we should get forensics over anyway, just in case it didn't destroy everything.'

'Why now, though? Why hold on to the car for a couple of weeks and then try to get rid of it?' It was the first question Thorne had asked himself when the call had come through. The fact that there wasn't any answer that made sense should have been enough to prevent him from tearing across town like an idiot. Clutching at straws.

He watched as the two uniformed officers ambled across.

'Do you want the good news or the bad news?' one of them said.

Thorne waited.

'Well, the good news is that we know whose car this is. And the bad news ... well I say bad news, because I know why you're looking for cars like this ... is that it belongs to a nice woman who lives in Dollis Hill.'

Thorne turned away and began walking back towards his car. The other officer continued talking to Kimmel. 'She got home from work fifteen minutes ago to find it had been nicked from off her drive. Just called it in, apparently.'

Kimmel thanked both the officers and followed Thorne.

The officer with the radio shouted after her. 'Kids, I reckon.'

Thorne had already started the Mondeo by the time Kimmel got in. She asked him if he'd drop her back at the station to collect her own car. Thorne said that he would, then remembered a promise he'd made to himself.

He said, 'Do you mind if we take a different route back? Stop off somewhere on the way?'

# SIXTY-EIGHT

Thorne followed Cat into her living room and asked if this was a good time. Cat shrugged, said that it was as good a time as any, and looked at Paula Kimmel. Thorne introduced them.

'I talked to you on the phone,' Kimmel said.

'Yeah, I remember,' Cat said. 'You said you'd let me know if there was any news.'

'Right,' Kimmel said.

'That why you're here?'

Kimmel looked at Thorne.

'I just wanted to stop by and see how you were doing.' Thorne looked around, well aware how awkward he must look, standing there like a spare prick with his hands in his pockets, how ridiculous he sounded. The room was a little too warm, and a good deal messier than the last time he'd been here. A duvet was scrunched up at one end of the sofa. There were newspapers and magazines piled up in front of the TV and clothes strewn across the back of the chair by the door. 'Haven't spoken to you in a while.'

Cat said, 'Right,' and the three of them stood and stared at the floor, the wall, the window.

369

'I would have called.' Kimmel smiled. 'Like I said I would. If there'd been any news.'

'Which there obviously hasn't,' Cat said.

'Actually, we thought we might have found the car. It's where we've just come from.'

Cat looked at her, expressionless; waiting, as if she knew what was coming, but needed to hear it anyway.

Kimmel shook her head. 'Not the one.'

'So, you want some tea or something?' Cat took a step towards the kitchen. 'Got a few beers in the fridge if you fancy one.'

'Tea's fine for me,' Kimmel said. 'Driving.'

'So am I,' Thorne said, 'but one beer's not going to hurt.'

'Tea's good.'

Cat nodded.

'No worries, I'll get them.' Thorne stepped in front of her. 'Two beers and a tea for the lightweight, yeah?' He turned and walked into the kitchen before Cat could argue, happy to leave her and Kimmel to it. Happy to let Kimmel take the lead, dishing out the sympathy while she waited for the tea to go with it. Not because she was a woman, but simply because Thorne guessed that she'd be better at it than he was. With the possible exception of a certain DI, he couldn't think of anyone else in the team who wouldn't be better at it.

He took two beers from the fridge and leaned against the worktop, waiting for the kettle to boil. He could hear the two women talking in the living room; not the words, just the gentle rise and fall of their voices, until the low shush and grumble of the kettle finally drowned them out.

Thorne had delivered the death message a few times. He'd knocked on doors, removed his cap and broken the worst news in the world. He'd looked away respectfully as those on the receiving end – the parents and children, husbands and wives – had fallen apart in front of him, but it was still easier than this.

This ... nothing. This *worse* than nothing.

Chit-chat and fake smiles and Christmas cracker comfort, while you watched someone bleed and bleed. Watched them *drown*, slowly, gasping at each desperate mouthful of hope you were there to provide. Watched them struggle, and sink, because that was your job and because, at the end of the day, it was all you could do. While some shameful, nameless part of you wanted nothing more than for it to be over; for their suffering and yours to stop, whatever that cost, because no amount of training – no victim-relations lectures or seminars or words of wisdom from those with a few more miles on the clock than you – could ever prepare you for it.

However shiny your buttons were.

However spotless those white gloves.

You would never be ready.

Thorne picked up his beer. He wandered out into the hall and took the few steps along to Kieron's bedroom. There were Power Rangers stickers on the door, a picture of Frank Lampard, a peeling keep out sign.

Thorne nudged the door open.

The bed was made, the drawers were closed and the carpet looked as though it had been recently vacuumed. The only thing that seemed out of place was a tattered cardboard folder on the floor next to the bed, a few sheets of paper protruding from beneath the flap.

Thorne stepped inside and picked up the folder.

He sat down on the bed and took out a sheaf of the contents.

'So, your mate making her own tea then, or what?'

Thorne looked up to see Cat standing in the doorway. 'Sorry. I was just ... '

Cat nodded at the folder. 'Those are all Kieron's pictures from school.'

Thorne opened his beer. 'They're good.' He pulled a few more of the paintings and drawings from the torn folder. Cat sat on the bed next to him and Thorne listened while she pointed and commented.

'He's always loved art,' she said.

'I can't even draw a stick-man,' Thorne said. 'Never could.'

She reached for one and held it up. 'Good, isn't it?'

Thorne leaned forward to look and nodded his agreement, though, in truth, he couldn't tell what it was supposed to be a picture of. A lion, or a bear . . . a weird dog, maybe. He took out the next one – a sheet of paper that, unlike the rest of them, had been folded several times.

He unfolded it and stared down at the drawing.

Cat must have seen his face change. 'You OK?'

The drawing was unlike the others Thorne had seen so far. Felt-tip and crayon, with much more detail and heavier colouring-in. It looked as though a lot of time had been spent on it.

A man wearing a cap. A boy standing next to him in a tartan anorak. A bright red car and the letters in black underneath.

DADDY

'What?' Cat said.

Thorne handed the picture to her. 'When did Kieron do this one?'

Cat stared down at the picture, shaking her head. 'I don't understand—'

'Where did you get these?'

'Simon brought them over. When we met for lunch. But . . .'

Thorne's mind was racing. He needed to go back and check Simon Jenner's less than cast-iron alibi. But if the teacher was the man Kieron had drawn, why would Jenner deliver the picture to Cat?

'I've never seen this picture before.' Cat turned to look at him. 'I'm not even sure it *is* one of Kieron's.' She shook her head again and pointed at the folder. 'This definitely wasn't in that folder when Simon gave it to me.'

Thorne's hand moved quickly to the back of his neck and scratched at the tickle. 'Who else has been here, Cat? Since you got these pictures.'

'Angie was round,' she said. 'She's been here a lot . . . oh, and Maria popped in a couple of days ago, because she said Josh was upset and was keen to come over. He wanted to play in Kieron's room . . .'

Then, Thorne understood.

*How many people did the average seven-year-old know?*

*Teachers, neighbours, family members.*

Not *his* family members, though. Not Kieron's . . .

Thorne stood up and reached to take the drawing from Cat. He looked at it again, then walked quickly back into the living room and asked Kimmel for her radio. The moment she'd taken it from her bag and handed it over, he went back out into the hall, passing Cat on the way, and closed the door behind him.

Fifteen seconds later, he was talking to an officer in the control room. He gave them the name and told them that he urgently required a current address. *Any* current addresses.

Thorne waited. He stared at himself in the cracked mirror next to the front door and wondered if he was about to throw a drowning mother a lifeline. Or if he was actually reaching to push her down into the wet dark and finally put an end to it.

A last gasp, either way.

When the information came through, he scribbled the details on the back of the drawing, tucked it into his pocket and walked back into the living room.

Kimmel and Cat were both on their feet.

'We need to go,' he said.

'Where?' Cat watched Kimmel move quickly to join Thorne at the door. 'What's happening?'

'You need to sit tight for a bit,' Thorne said. 'That's all. Is there anyone who can come over and keep you company?'

'Don't tell me.' Cat was breathing heavily, her fists clenching and unclenching at her sides. 'You'll let me know when there's any news.'

'Of course,' Thorne said.

Kimmel walked past him and he turned quickly to follow her out to the front door. This time, whether or not it was the news Catrin Coyne wanted, Thorne guessed that it would not be long in coming.

# SIXTY-NINE

Thorne pointed the car north and, after a couple of minutes with the road atlas on her lap, Kimmel told him to head for the A10.

'It's about the shortest route I can see,' she said. 'It looks like it's a bit further if we go round the A1, but then again, the roads might be better . . . three lanes on the Barnet by-pass.'

'So, which way?'

'It's six of one, half a dozen—'

'This'll have to do,' Thorne said, veering right, making his choice.

The address he'd been given was twenty-five miles or so away to the north-east of them, in Hertfordshire; an area that looked to be largely made up of woods and farmland, between the villages of Hertford Heath and Haileybury. No distance from London in the scheme of things, and not very far from his parents' place in St Albans, but still not an area Thorne knew at all.

Kimmel was still looking at the atlas: tracing the route, using her fingers to measure the scale, calculating. 'Forty minutes, maybe?'

Thorne took the Mondeo hard past two cars before pulling

back into the line of traffic. 'Thirty,' he said. Driving downhill, away from the Archway Road, he accelerated along the edge of Highgate Wood, looking left, for just a moment, beyond the fence into the dark tangle of trees, where all this had begun almost three weeks before.

'Call it in.'

While Kimmel was on the radio, Thorne sped through Muswell Hill and Alexandra Palace, flashing his lights and leaning on the horn in the absence of blues and twos, on through Edmonton and Enfield, towards the M25.

'I've ordered up a couple of two-man cars,' Kimmel said, when she signed off. 'Told them to put an ambulance on standby. They'll call up a forensic unit if and when.'

Thorne nodded and put his foot down harder. He knew that the back-up teams they'd requested would be coming from Hertfordshire Constabulary, but the basic comms set-up meant that, until all vehicles involved had arrived at the target location, he would have no direct contact with any of those units. No idea as to their up-to-the-minute progress or ETA. The Hertfordshire officers could only talk to their own control station, who would then contact the Met, who would, in turn, pass on any necessary intelligence to Thorne and Kimmel via the radio.

It was hardly ideal.

Thorne just wanted to get there.

'Ashton was in front of us all the time,' he said. 'Christ . . . '

'Not really.' Kimmel turned, one hand holding tight to the handle above the passenger door. 'There wasn't any good reason to look at him, was there?'

'Right in front of us.'

She shook her head. 'He never came into it, mate . . . why would he? The missing boy's mother's . . . friend's . . . ex-husband. No way. Not on the radar.'

Thorne stared ahead, bouncing his hand off the steering

wheel as he swore quietly. At the driver of the car in front, at the man they were on their way to see, at himself.

'We didn't do anything wrong,' Kimmel said.

'Kieron would have known him ... course he would, he was his best mate's dad. Right from the kick-off, we should have paid more attention to the people Kieron *knew*. Barratt was saying that all along. Saying the boy knew him.'

Fifteen minutes after leaving Seacole House they'd crossed the motorway, and once they were past Cheshunt – a few minutes and a couple of golf courses later – they were speeding through open countryside.

A bruise of sky rising ahead of them.

Grey fields falling away on one side of the road and the spindly fingers of treetops reaching across the high hedge-line on the other.

Kimmel leaned back in her seat. She said, 'There'll be plenty of time for that later, you know.'

Thorne did not take his eyes off the road. The needle nudging seventy, the lights on full beam. He grunted a 'What?'

'Beating the shit out of yourself.'

# SEVENTY

Angie was there within ten minutes of Cat's call. They sat and drank the beers Thorne had taken from the fridge earlier, while Cat fought to stay calm and told Angie what had happened.

'Jesus,' Angie said. 'So . . .'

'So, Josh must have put the picture of his dad in the folder when he was in Kieron's room.'

'I don't get it.'

'He must have done, right?' Cat was still shaking. 'It's the only thing that makes sense.'

'Why, though?'

'I don't know . . . to tell us?'

'So, why not just fucking *tell* us?'

Cat shook her head. 'He's been acting really weird, Maria said. Maybe he's scared of his dad or scared he'll get in trouble and this was just his way of letting us know. Like leaving a clue, or something.'

Angie swigged and swallowed. 'You reckon his dad . . . ? You know, with *him*?'

'I really don't want to think about it.'

'Sorry, babe. Course not.'

Cat stood up quickly and walked to the window. She leaned her forehead against the glass, the noise in her head not quite able to block out the curses Angie was spitting from the sofa behind her.

'That beast is going to get what he deserves, don't you worry about that. Everything that's coming to him. They'll cut his balls off, wherever he ends up.'

'I know where they've gone, Ange.' Cat turned round. 'I know where he lives.'

'How?'

'Thorne was out in the hall and I heard it come through on his radio, the postcode and all that.'

'Where?'

Cat told her. Said, 'I've got no bloody idea how far that is.'

'It's up past Hatfield.' Angie nodded. 'I've got a supplier lives in that neck of the woods. It's not a million miles away.'

'What if he's *there*, Ange? What if Kieron's there and he's crying for me?'

'I'll drive you.'

'I mean, they told me to sit here and wait, but I'll go mental—'

Angie was already on her feet. She zipped up her jacket and downed what was left of her beer. 'I've got a map in the boot.'

# SEVENTY-ONE

Following instructions from Kimmel, Thorne turned off the A10 and on to the London Road, which wound north towards Haileybury. There was no street lighting, but the road was smooth and wide enough and, as it began to grow darker by the minute, Thorne could see other vehicles coming from far enough away to maintain a decent speed, even into corners. There were fields stretching as far as the eye could see on either side, the tall chimney of a crematorium, clumps of dense woodland in the distance.

Kimmel kept her finger on the map. 'Coming off in a minute,' she said.

They passed several turnings towards what looked like large private houses or country hotels and signs to smaller villages Thorne had never heard of.

Woollensbrook, Spitalbrook, Yewlands.

Just past a war memorial that appeared to have been built in the middle of nowhere, Kimmel pointed, said, 'Here,' and Thorne turned on to a road that was far narrower and anything but smooth.

He slowed down.

There were one or two widely spaced houses or small farms, but within a thousand yards there was nothing. The rutted road twisted for another mile or so, dipping then swinging left suddenly, until it became a track barely wide enough for a tractor. Thorne had little choice but to slow still further, eyes fixed straight ahead, save for an instant when his headlights picked out the eyes of something hiding low in the bushes, and the moment a few minutes later, when Kimmel pointed ahead and to the right.

To a pair of lighted windows in the distance.

'There . . . '

Thorne hit the brakes and looked. He turned off his headlights then began to ease the car forward again.

'Plan of action?' Kimmel said.

'Not got one.' Thorne leaned forward, peering through the windscreen into the gathering gloom as the car crept along the track. 'You?'

Kimmel shrugged. Ten minutes earlier, they had received a message from Control that all necessary units were being dispatched from Hertford. There had been no word since.

She said, 'Suck it and see, then.'


They stopped and got out of the car when they were still a hundred yards or so from the property. Stood and watched the place for a minute or two. It was certainly bigger than Thorne had been prepared for, not quite the quaint, picture-book 'cottage' the address had led him to expect. There were lighted windows on the ground floor as well as the first, a gate to one side, and what looked like a wooden garage attached.

A dark-coloured Volvo was parked in front of it.

'I hate the fucking countryside,' Kimmel whispered. She was smiling, trying to sound jokey, but Thorne could hear the nerves in her voice.

381

It was a relief.

Thorne could *taste* his own fear, metal in his mouth. He could feel it churning in his stomach as he walked to the back of the Mondeo and opened the boot. He had no idea what he was looking for, what might be necessary, but he leaned in and quickly gathered up everything that looked remotely useful.

Torch, crowbar, handcuffs.

'That should cover it,' Kimmel said. 'Oh, hello.' She reached down for the telescopic baton lying next to the spare wheel and tucked it into the back of her jeans. 'You sure you don't want to wait for . . . ?'

Thorne was already moving.

They walked quietly towards the house and, on a signal, Kimmel went through the side gate towards the rear. Thorne moved to the front door, gave Kimmel half a minute to get into position, then knocked.

Waited, knocked again.

He stepped to one side, leaned close to one of the windows and stared through a gap in the curtains into what he guessed was the living room. He could see details of what looked like comfortable, modern furnishings, the edges of well-stacked bookshelves and a top-of-the-range stereo system. He saw just enough of a wood-burning stove to see it was still glowing behind its blackened glass.

Thorne moved towards the window on the other side of the front door, stopping for a moment to look again through its leaded pane. He gasped and stepped back, startled as a figure appeared in the entrance hall and loomed towards the glass.

His fist tightened momentarily around the crowbar, then he relaxed and let the breath out, relieved to see that it was Kimmel.

She waved and opened the door.

'Back door was open.' She nodded upstairs. 'Looks like there's nobody here, so I'll have a poke around.'

Thorne told her to be careful, then stepped back outside

and walked over to the garage. The door was padlocked, so he put the crowbar to good use, and after ten or fifteen seconds of heaving he opened the door and stepped inside. A small car took up almost all the available space. He could just make out a light switch next to a stepladder thick with cobwebs and stepped across to flick it on.

Stared at the red Ford Fiesta.

Just as he was about to turn away, Thorne noticed an odd line just above the sill below the passenger door. He crouched down and ran his finger along the wavy trickle of blue paint.

The original paint.

He remembered what Felix Barratt had said. *Shiny* . . . the car had looked shiny. A nice fresh respray would do that, Thorne thought, even one that was less than thorough, and would certainly explain why this car hadn't shown up on any of the lists from the DVLC.

Thorne left the garage, followed the path that led round to the rear of the property and all but bumped into Kimmel as she emerged from the back door. There was a pond and a small seating area – benches, a barbecue, a slatted table – that, given rather more light than this, would have provided the owner with a spectacular view of the woodland at the bottom of his garden.

'Well, we're in the right place,' Kimmel said.

'I know.' Thorne told her about the car.

Kimmel nodded back inside. 'There's a cellar.'

Thorne waited.

'A chain.'

'Fuck.'

'Toys and stuff, food, drawing equipment. I reckon that's where Josh must have done his picture.' Her voice dropped a little. 'There's cameras down there, too.'

'Christ . . .'

They turned and stared towards the woods, at the well-trodden track that snaked into the trees and disappeared.

Thorne looked at his watch, up at the sky. 'About fifteen minutes until it's dark. *Really* dark.'

'If that,' Kimmel said.

'His car's here and all the lights are on.' Thorne had the crowbar in one hand, his torch in the other. He flicked it on. 'Fire's still warm.'

'Right.'

'And the back door's been left open.'

'Yeah, but this is the countryside, isn't it?' Kimmel was bouncing on the heels of her training shoes. 'It's nice and safe round here.'

'He hasn't gone far,' Thorne said.

# SEVENTY-TWO

He did not usually take him into the woods this late, because there was far less to see, of course, and because the boy was afraid of the dark. So this particular outing killed two birds with one stone. Gave the boy the fresh air and exercise they both needed, but also punished him, just a little, for the disastrous weekend they'd all had to suffer when Josh had been here.

The hysterics, the drama. The spoiling everything.

Josh, too, had been afraid of the dark once upon a time, but Ashton had quickly taken steps to put a stop to that. Whenever Josh was with him, at any rate. It was all well and good to be afraid of something that might actually hurt you, but to be scared for no good reason was ridiculous, on top of which, irrational fears like that did more harm than good. Made a child weak and emotionally stunted. Left him unable to cope. His own father had taught him that very early on and, all in all, Ashton believed that the lesson – one of very many he'd been taught – had stood him in good stead.

'Please . . . '

The boy was doing his best not to sniffle. It was a start,

Ashton supposed, it was something. A smile was probably a little too much to hope for just yet, the boy's hand reaching out for him, but he would have both those things, one day.

'Please can we go back now?'

'We'll go back soon. It's only been fifteen minutes.'

'I heard a noise in the bushes.'

'Don't be silly.'

'Like a . . . scritch-scratch.'

'Just an animal,' Ashton said. 'There are animals out here, you know that.'

The boy nodded.

'Now, come here.' They were sitting next to one another on the same fallen tree they usually ended up at. Ashton had told the boy he could climb up and walk along the trunk if he wanted to, that it would be fun when he couldn't see very much, but the boy hadn't been brave enough. Ashton patted a patch of moss-covered bark. 'Come on, I'll scooch over a bit.'

The boy did as he was told and inched himself a little closer to Ashton.

Ashton put his arm around the boy's shoulders, tried to control his irritation when he felt the boy stiffen.

'See, it's not so bad, is it?' He waited for the boy to shake his head. 'I might do chips for you when we get back, how's that sound? You need to start eating again.'

The boy nodded. He had stopped sniffling.

'That's better. Isn't everything so much nicer when you try to be good and do what you're told?'

The boy swung his legs, a little less tense. 'Yeah . . .'

Ashton tightened his grip. 'Yeah, of course it is. The way it should have been at the weekend when Josh was here. You were supposed to be playing.'

'He didn't want to,' the boy said.

Ashton shook his head. 'You're here precisely so he's got someone to play with when he comes. That's the whole point.

You'd have thought he would have been happy about that and said "thank you very much" instead of belly-aching.'

'I wanted to play,' the boy said. 'It wasn't my fault.'

'I know, but the truth is, I've really got no idea what to do, now. I thought, I *hoped* the two of us could just carry on as we were and that, every two weeks, you and Joshy would have a treat and get to play together. That we'd all be happy. Stupid of me, probably, but that's what happens when you try to do something nice, isn't it? You get let down. I mean ... *you* weren't supposed to have that chain around your leg, and Josh ... ' He shook his head. 'Well, I thought Josh knew better than that. I thought I'd taught him how to be grateful and make the best of things, but clearly his mother has been doing exactly what I told her not to and letting him get away with murder. Spoiling him.'

'I'm not spoiled,' the boy said.

'So ... we'll just have to see, won't we? I only hope that next time things go a little better, that you can both behave and make an effort to enjoy yourselves.' He nodded, held up his hands. 'I can guess what you're thinking. How can there be a next time? Now that Josh has been here, surely he'll rush back and tell someone and you'll be whisked back to your mum and won't all that be lovely? Well, Josh might be spoiled, but I know he'll do as he's told when it comes to telling tales. To not telling them. Yes, I'd prefer it if he loved me a bit more and wasn't scared of me quite as much as he is ... but I can live with it.' Ashton stopped and stared at the boy. 'Look, I know there are things you miss and everything's still a bit strange for you ... but this isn't *terrible*, is it?'

'It's OK,' the boy said.

'I'm not terrible, am I?'

The boy shook his head again, staring down at the ground. 'No ... '

Ashton looked up at the tree-tops, swaying gently in silhouette against the leaden sky. He closed his eyes, as relaxed as he could remember feeling since the debacle when Josh had come to stay; far more confident than he had been for several days that things would be all right. That the three of them could somehow make things work.

That they could all enjoy themselves.

He said, 'Not long now until it's properly dark, so we'll hang on until that happens, OK? Then, it'll be really exciting walking home, won't it? Just the two of us in the pitch black, blind as moles, creeping along together in the darkness.'

He took the boy's head in his hands and turned it until the boy's eyes met his own. Even then, he could tell that the boy was still thinking about what might be in the bushes. Still listening out for that scritch-scratch.

'Then, if you've behaved yourself, and if you can manage to be nice to me, we'll see about those chips.'

# SEVENTY-THREE

While Angie continued to swear and spit curses, railing furiously – at the animal whose address was scribbled on the piece of paper folded beneath the handbrake, at all those like him, at the drivers of every car in their way – Cat sat in silence and kept her eyes fixed on the black strip of the Barnet bypass as it rolled towards her, the blur of white lines as they were sucked beneath the wheels of Angie's ancient Honda Civic. She moved her feet, trying to find a patch of room among the assortment of empty cans and litter in the footwell. She sat on her hands to stop them shaking and thought about the man who had taken her son.

Cat had met him a couple of times, when she'd been at Maria's and he'd dropped in for something or other. She remembered him nodding and grunting a hello while he looked at some spot on the wall behind her. She remembered thinking that he was more than slightly up himself, that he was a bit vacant. Maria had been very happy to put flesh on those bones, of course. She'd talked about her ex-husband all the time. She had plenty of stories.

389

He was selfish and he was arrogant, like a lot of doctors, she said. He was socially inept, whatever that meant, and in their last few years together he'd become very . . . cold. Nobody's idea of a perfect husband, not in a million years, but he was a good father.

Maria had always taken pains to point that out.

A loving father.

The Civic's engine complained as Angie asked more of it and Cat could feel the suspension juddering beneath her, clattering through her spine at every bump or crack in the road.

Jeff Ashton had taken her son . . .

It was all Cat knew with any certainty because she'd seen the look on Thorne's face, the blood draining from it when he'd been handed that picture. She could not allow herself to think much beyond that simple fact. Instead she clung on to the belief that Kieron would have understood what was happening, would have figured it out straight away and tried to keep himself safe until she could get to him. Her conviction that, aside from the thousand and one other amazing things he was, Kieron was a clever boy.

A clever boy, who would have done whatever was necessary to stay alive.

She did not, *could* not dwell on what those things might have been, of course. There had been many times these last few weeks when it had been impossible to think of anything else; thoughts that had inevitably darkened and become unbearable, to the point where reaching for the window latch or the nearest kitchen knife had seemed like the only relief possible.

Not now, though. Not when she was on her way to him, whatever that might mean.

Him, or some trace of him.

Angie said, 'Fucker better hope the police get there before we do. All I'm saying.' She glanced across and nodded. 'He'd better *pray* they do.'

Cat closed her eyes and tried to tune out her friend's anger.

She thought about what Kieron would feel like in her arms, her lips on the back of his neck, thought about breathing him in.

She thought about burying him.

She thought, *clever boy.*

*Loving father . . .*

# SEVENTY-FOUR

Kimmel had found a second torch in one of the kitchen cupboards, so, once she and Thorne had ventured a few yards into the woods, they split up and went in separate directions. Kimmel held on to their only radio, but Thorne reckoned the night was still enough for a shout to be heard a good distance away, if either of them had anything serious to shout about.

They did not want to risk alerting Ashton to their presence before then.

Thorne froze as something skittered through the undergrowth a few feet ahead of him. He pointed the torch but saw only a jumble of exposed roots and fallen branches at ground level, thick bushes and cinder-black earth. He raised the torch higher, but the beam was not strong enough to reach more than halfway up the tallest trees.

He kept walking.

Eyes fixed on the pool of milky light dancing across a wave of ferns a few feet ahead of him, then shifting, every few seconds, to the shadows on either side. Listening for anything beyond the hiss of the treetops above him and the noises he was responsible for.

The crackle-crunch beneath his feet, the wheeze in his chest.

A few minutes from the house, what had seemed to be a path of sorts had petered out and there was no sign that he was following in anyone's footsteps. Thorne had little choice but to keep moving in as straight a line from the house as was possible, veering slightly right or left only when he had to, his choice dependent on nothing save the size of the gap between the trees. Making his choices quickly, hoping his instinct was taking him in the right direction and that Ashton, too, had chosen the path of least resistance.

The man would know these woods intimately, Thorne guessed. He would know where to hide if he heard them coming, how to circle back to the front of the house if he needed to. Thorne cursed himself for not having the forethought to find the keys to that Volvo and pocket them. He should probably just have instructed the back-up units to approach silently and waited at the house for Ashton to come back.

He should probably have done all sorts of things differently.

It was too late to worry about that now.

Thorne stopped momentarily at a fluttering high above him. His palm was sweaty against the rubber grip of the torch. He wiped it on his jacket then ducked beneath a low branch and pressed on into the darkness.

Ashton would have known those woods at Highgate too, of course. The paths and the short cuts, the quickest route from that playground to the second-hand Fiesta he'd bought and had resprayed for the job in hand.

Thorne wondered what Ashton had said to Kieron that morning. A story planned well in advance, or something he'd come up with on the spur of the moment as the boy had stared at him, confused to see his best friend's dad stepping out from the trees?

Smiling and putting his finger to his lips.

A secret . . . an *adventure*.

A surprise for Josh—

Thorne paused, mid-step, as the torch beam floated across something bright, caught in the bushes a few yards ahead of him. A white face and shining black eyes. He moved quickly towards it, reached into the tangle of briar and pulled out a tattered, mud-stained teddy bear.

He sucked in a breath and held it, turned off the torch.

He could hear voices.

# SEVENTY-FIVE

'The thing to remember, that you must *always* remember, is that you can never be weak. Do you understand? Weak is the stupidest thing you can be. I know that some of the time we've spent together hasn't always been easy for you, but nine times out of ten it's the difficult experiences that turn out to be the most important. You might not believe it now, but these last few weeks could turn out to be the making of you.'

They're still sitting on the big fallen tree and the man is talking and talking, so Kieron nods, because he knows that's what the man wants him to do. That's what grown-ups do; he's seen them. When they're having *conversations*. They nod like toy dogs because they're supposed to be listening and paying attention, even when they're not. Sometimes they make a funny noise, too, like a hum, so he does that as well.

He nods and he hums.

'There's an expression,' the man says.

He nods and he hums and he thinks.

'What doesn't kill you makes you stronger.'

Kieron stops nodding. 'Are you going to kill me?' he asks.

'It's just an expression.' The man pulls a face and shakes his head. 'What I've been trying to explain to you, basically. You can let the bad things ... or what seem like bad things at the time ... make you feeble and frightened or you can say, "No, I'm not going to let that happen." It's up to you, do you understand what I'm saying? You can be weak or you can choose to be strong. You can spend your whole life scared of your own shadow, or you can be brave.'

Kieron nods and says, 'I'm not weak.'

The man smiles and pulls Kieron closer to him. 'That's good.'

'I'm going to be brave!'

The man's smile gets bigger and he leans down to kiss Kieron on the forehead. He says, 'Do you know how happy that makes me?'

Kieron jumps off the tree and stands to attention, like a soldier. 'I'm going over there to see what's making that scritch-scratch in the bushes.' He points into the darkness, to where he'd heard the sound that had frightened him so much. 'That would be *really* brave, wouldn't it?'

The man laughs. 'Yes, it would.'

Kieron turns and scrambles back over the fallen tree. He stands behind the man. He closes his eyes and gives the man a little pat on the back, because he thinks the man will want to know he's there, then creeps slowly away.

He takes a few steps, then turns to check.

The man hasn't moved and just sits there looking up at the trees. The man can't see him.

'What do you think it could be?' Kieron asks. He turns again, checks again. 'The thing in the bushes.' He's close to them now, every bit as terrified as he was before, but he doesn't want the man to hear that in his voice.

'I had to do it when I was a boy,' the man says. 'Same age as you, give or take a year or two. I had to decide if all the things

396

that hurt, all the bad things, were going to destroy me, or make me better . . . '

The man isn't listening.

The man is looking the other way.

For a moment, Kieron thinks about running, but he knows the man will hear that and he knows the man will catch him. Then, when he takes his next step, his foot kicks against a log on the ground. A big one.

'I don't really remember sitting down and making that decision,' the man says. 'It was just something inside me. Like an instinct. Do you know what an instinct is? Like something that happens without really thinking about it very much . . . '

Kieron bends slowly down and takes hold of the log. It's very heavy and he can only just wrap his hands around it. He knows there will be a noise when he picks the log up, so he shouts, 'Whatever it is, I'm not going to be scared,' as he lifts it.

'Something hardens inside you,' the man says.

Kieron hums.

'I suppose that's what it is.'

The man carries on talking, but Kieron doesn't really understand. Now, he's only thinking about his mum and about Josh and all the things they talked about, when Josh was there and when he wasn't.

He moves as quietly as he can back towards the fallen tree.

Grandmother's footsteps.

The log weighs, like . . . a *ton*, easy, pressing into his neck and shoulders, his two small hands wrapped around the bottom.

The man says, 'Where are you?'

Kieron starts to run and he swings the log just as the man starts to turn.

He screams when he hits him and he's not sure if the thing he sees fly into the shadows is a bit of the log or a bit of the man's head. It doesn't matter and he doesn't think about it very long, because now the man's on the floor and kicking his legs through the dirt and the dead things, and he's moaning like Josh was doing in the cellar.

Like that poorly dog.

Kieron lifts up the log again.

# SEVENTY-SIX

Cat and Angie were lost.

Angie had bumped the car up on to a verge and now, by the dim light from the vanity mirror, Cat sat staring helplessly down at the tattered map, trying to work out where the hell they were.

'Christ alone knows.' She turned the page, then turned it back again. 'I thought you said you knew where we were going.' Cat was struggling to keep the irritation from her voice. Angie was doing her a massive favour, after all.

'I said I knew this part of the world a bit, that's all.'

'You promised you'd get us there.'

'Don't panic—'

'We could be bloody anywhere.'

'Look, I knew exactly where I was until just after Hertford.' Angie leaned across to peer at the map for a few seconds, shook her head. 'We just took one wrong turning, you ask me.'

Cat looked up from the map and stared out into the blackness. The single-lane road was deserted. There were no road markings, no lighting. Just high hedges on either side and a small wooden gate picked out in the headlights, leading into fields. 'There's not even anyone around we can ask.'

Angie turned the engine off.

'I think we should turn round,' Cat said. 'Try and work out where we went wrong.'

Angie said nothing.

'At least try to find a house or something.' Cat peered at the map again, but it looked like the road they were on didn't even have a name. She slammed her hand against the passenger-side window in frustration, felt the tears coming and let her head fall back. 'I need to get there, Ange, I need to get to him right now. Even when I was telling Billy how I thought Kieron was still alive I wasn't sure I believed it. Just couldn't bear to think he might not be . . . saying it for Billy as much as me. But now I *know* he is.' She clutched her stomach. 'In *here* . . . sure as I know anything, and I know he's somewhere close and that he's calling out for me, and we're sitting here like idiots in the arse-end of nowhere, when I need to be with him.'

Something screeched from a tree nearby.

'It's a bit late for all that,' Angie said. 'Don't you reckon?'

'What?' Cat turned to look and saw the knife in Angie's hand.

'Get out,' Angie said.

Cat stared confused. She couldn't speak, could barely breathe. She did not move, even when Angie leaned across and slowly pushed the knife towards her face.

'Get out of the fucking car.'

# SEVENTY-SEVEN

Thorne was trying to move as quickly as he could, but it was tricky getting anywhere in a hurry without the aid of the torch. The bigger trees and bushes were still easy enough to make out, the dark shapes of them looming ahead of him, but he was repeatedly stopped short by branches that caught him at head height, or by tangles of those lower down that caused him to stumble several times; that sent him briefly – sprawling and swearing – hard on to his arse.

He knew that Ashton – if his was indeed one of the voices Thorne had made out – would hear him coming, but there was nothing he could do about that, or particularly cared to.

One of the voices . . .

Getting there fast was now the only thing that mattered.

Fear had been pumping adrenalin through him since he and Kimmel had taken their first steps into the woods, but now hope had ramped it up still further. His breath no longer rattled. He barely felt the scratches across his face or the pain from the muscle he'd torn when he'd fallen.

A child's voice.

What Thorne had been sure was two different voices had become only one as it had grown louder, then no more than a noise ... or *chant* ... by the time the trees had started to thin out and he found himself on the edge of a small clearing.

A fallen tree, like a footbridge. The shape of someone flat out and face up on the ground in front of it.

A man. Ashton ...

He could see the movement and hear the sounds – a grunt and then a dull crack – but when his eyes had finally adjusted to the semi-dark and it became clear what he was actually looking at, Thorne could do no more than stand and stare.

Once more, the boy grunted with the effort of raising the log above his head, then calmly intoned the same two words as he brought it crashing down on to Jeff Ashton's face.

'Hulk, *smash*!'

The log was huge, almost as big as the boy himself, and he moaned as he bent to lift it up again.

Thorne stepped forward, arms outstretched, and said Kieron's name; shouted it above the noise of the approaching sirens.

Then he shouted for Kimmel.

# SEVENTY-EIGHT

With the knife at her back every step of the way, Cat was marched along the muddy verge for a minute or more, then forced to open the gate before being ushered into the field.

'Keep going,' Angie said.

'Going *where*? Angie, what the fuck—'

Cat felt the point of the blade break the skin between her shoulder blades and cried out as she staggered forward. There was no more than a sliver of moon and, bleak as the unlit road had been, it seemed to grow darker with every step further away from it. A deeper dark. Cat heard the grumble of a car somewhere behind them and turned, then felt the edge of the knife on the back of her neck.

'Don't even think about it,' Angie said.

The ground beneath her feet was rutted and Cat was finding it hard to keep her footing. It made her think that the field had been recently ploughed and that there had to be a farm or something nearby, though she doubted anyone would be out in their fields at this time of night. Even if she screamed, she didn't think anyone would hear.

403

She didn't know what Angie would do if she screamed. What her friend was capable of. Her *friend* . . . ?

Cat didn't know anything, any more.

Why the hell would Angie want to hurt her?

They'd been stumbling across the field for what felt like twenty minutes when Angie said, 'Right, this'll do.'

Cat stopped and stood, breathing heavily. It had been warm all day, but suddenly, wearing only the thin jacket she'd grabbed on her way out of the flat, she was shivering.

'Turn round.'

Cat did as she was told, and waited. It was too dark to make out the expression on Angie's face, within arm's length of her own, but Cat didn't need to. The cold stare and the mocking smile were clear enough in every word the woman spat and snarled.

'Mental, isn't it, babe?' Angie said. 'I mean, knowing you're right's one thing, isn't it? Ridiculous, though, that it takes something like this, something horrible happening, to *prove* you're right.' She hissed out a laugh. 'Means you can't even enjoy it.'

Cat wasn't looking at Angie's face, anyway. Her eyes stayed firmly locked on the knife, its silhouette cutting across the grey sky behind her whenever Angie waved her arm around.

'You never deserved that child. Simple as that. Yeah, I made all the proper noises at the time, bought the toys and the baby clothes and the rest of it, but what else was I going to do? Auntie Ange, right? But you were never supposed to be that lad's mum. Not my brother's little boy. You were never . . . right for it. Like putting make-up on a pig. And I knew you'd make a mess of it, never doubted it for one single second. I just had to hang back and wait for it to happen, didn't I? I never in a million years thought you'd fuck up to this degree, though. I never thought you'd just take him out one morning and *lose* him.'

It felt like the woman wanted a response, but Cat was not going to give her the pleasure. She knew those words had been carefully chosen to inflict the most pain, the maximum damage, but she was beyond that now. She kept her eyes on the knife.

'I'll be honest with you,' Angie said. 'Well, I can't see the point in being anything else, really, can you? Not considering where we are. If I'm being *completely* honest, I don't actually think Kieron is still alive. Sorry, but there we are. Just trying to be realistic.'

She waited, letting her words hit home.

'But, here's the thing. If I'm wrong, and trust me, I hope and pray that the little fella's right as ninepence and waiting for us just up the road ... there is not a chance in hell I'm letting you have him back. How could I? I mean, it'd be irresponsible, apart from anything else. So, there you go.'

Cat saw the knife moving again and, without thinking too long about what might happen, lunged for it. Angie stepped back and slashed hard across Cat's arm, that thin jacket. Now, Cat screamed.

'Don't piss about, babe—'

Cat turned and sprinted headlong into the darkness.

# SEVENTY-NINE

Thorne put the phone down – having listened to his call go unanswered for half a minute – and walked out of the cottage, past local uniforms smoking by the front door and a pair of plastic-suited SOCOs on their way down to the cellar. Now, the small drive was heaving with emergency vehicles and officers. Kimmel wandered over as Thorne stood and watched the stretcher carrying Jeff Ashton being loaded into an ambulance.

'Any joy?'

Thorne shook his head.

'Nipped out for milk, or something.'

'Maybe.' While Thorne had understood Catrin Coyne's frustration back at the flat, the instruction to stay by the phone had been clear enough and he couldn't think of any good reason for her to have simply ignored it. 'Can you radio through and ask them to send a couple of bodies across to Seacole House? Give her the message when she gets back from ... wherever she's gone.'

Thorne would very much have preferred to pass that message on himself, face to face, in a perfect world; to be the one to tell Catrin Coyne that her son was alive. Selfish and stupid, of course, but he felt he needed it. Still, what was most important was that she received the news as soon as possible.

To have seen her face, though . . .

A paramedic waved and Kimmel waved back. They were ready to go. 'I'll do it on the way to the hospital,' she said.

Thorne watched the ambulance drive away, while officers unloaded equipment from the back of a van and began ferrying it around the side of the house. Others were in the woods already, setting up the arc lights and generator, sealing off the crime scene.

No crime had been committed by Kieron Coyne, of course, despite what Thorne had witnessed and whatever the outcome for the man in the ambulance. Not legally, at any rate, not when the boy was still below the age of criminal responsibility.

A uniformed constable strolled over. 'Ready when you are.'

Thorne looked across to the squad car, in the back of which Kieron Coyne sat next to a young WPC. Ten minutes earlier, she had wiped the blood-spatter from his face and tried to hold his hand, though the boy hadn't seemed especially keen.

'How's he doing?'

'Yeah, chatting away like nothing's happened.' The officer shook his head. 'Seems quite excited, really. Asked me if I could turn the siren on for him.'

The scene in the woods was one of several connected to the crimes committed by Jeff Ashton, and no one else. Kidnapping and false imprisonment at the very least. Other things . . . per-haps, though for obvious reasons it would be a while before the necessary facts emerged.

Thorne walked across to the car, opened the door and squatted down. The boy turned and stared at him.

'Do you fancy coming for a ride in my car?' Even as he said it, Thorne found himself wondering if Ashton had asked Kieron much the same question that Saturday morning, three weeks before. Telling himself that he was an insensitive idiot, Thorne looked for some reaction on the boy's face, but saw none.

'Is it a police car?' Kieron asked.

'Not like this one,' Thorne said. 'But I'm a policeman.'

In truth, Thorne's suggestion that he take Kieron in his own car and follow the local team back to the station at Hertford was not strictly in accordance with protocol, but Thorne didn't much care. He had witnessed Ashton alone with Kieron and had not set so much as a bootee-covered foot in that cellar, so there could be no issue with potential cross-contamination of forensic evidence. He'd said as much, a little more forcefully than was probably necessary, only too happy to pull rank when a Job-pissed DC from Hertfordshire had expressed his concerns.

There was no risk at all to any potential prosecution case.

Thorne didn't see that it mattered who drove Kieron to the station.

Besides which, he wanted to.

'Does your car have a siren?' Kieron asked.

'I'm afraid not,' Thorne said. 'But we can make the noise, if you like.'

# EIGHTY

Cat had lost all sense of time and direction. She had no idea where in the field she was or how far from the road, no idea how long she'd been hiding.

More importantly, she had no idea where Angie was.

She'd run until she was out of breath, then lay down, squeezing her body into one of the ruts and trying to keep as quiet and still as possible. For a while, she could hear Angie calling her, telling her that it was pointless to run, that she was happy to search all night if she needed to.

'Nothing better to do, babe . . .'

Just when Cat had started to think Angie had given up, she'd heard footsteps just a few feet away. Angie coughing and muttering. She'd closed her eyes and waited for the worst, but since then – what was that, ten minutes ago? – it had been quiet.

Slowly, Cat pushed herself up with her one good arm, gritting her teeth to stop herself crying out. She peeled off her jacket, but it was too dark to see how bad the cut was. There was plenty of blood though. Her arm was slick with it and her jacket was sopping. She winced as she wrapped the jacket around the wound, sucked in a breath as she tightened it. Had she been stronger she'd have torn off the sleeve and used that, but summoning the strength to stand was hard enough, to get herself to her feet and moving again.

After a few minutes, she could see that she was close to the edge of the field, and she began to stagger towards it when she heard the sirens getting louder. She crashed into a hedge and drove herself forward, branches tearing at the jacket, her hair, her face, as she forced her way through on to the road.

Screaming and waving, Cat ran towards the flashing lights.

# EIGHTY-ONE

The uniformed sergeant – whose squeaky voice and cheery atti-
tude belied a face that looked as if it had been arranged with the
back of a spade – shook his head, much as his colleague had done
back at the cottage. 'Kids are resilient though, aren't they?' He
nodded in the direction of the cells, one of which Kieron Coyne
was currently being shown by a helpful constable.

'Let's hope so,' Thorne said.

'Always amazes me, what they can cope with.'

Thorne nodded, leaning against the desk, but he wasn't
convinced by the sergeant's optimism. The boy's fascination
for the noises a police car could make, the eagerness to try on
a copper's helmet and his excitement about being shut inside a
prison cell for a few minutes did not mean that he was coping.
His behaviour might equally mean that, consciously or not, he
was simply burying what had happened to him.

Disassociating . . . was that the word?

What the hell did Thorne know about it?

'He seems OK,' the doctor had said, after a cursory examination when they'd arrived at the station. 'He's a bit pale,

411

perhaps . . . may have lost a little weight, but otherwise all right.' He'd waited until the boy was out of earshot. 'For obvious reasons, there'll need to be a rather more thorough examination as soon as is feasible.'

Obvious or not, Thorne did not want to spend too long thinking about what those reasons might be, or what *thorough* would entail.

There would be an interview, too, of course, as soon as an appropriate adult could be brought in, but right now reuniting Kieron with his mother was everyone's first priority. Thorne had tried calling Cat again as soon as they'd reached the station, but there was still no reply from her flat. It was almost half past ten. The question of where Kieron was going to spend the night was becoming an urgent one, and if Thorne did not get hold of Cat very soon he would have little choice but to contact social services.

'I'm not saying it'll be easy for the lad.' The sergeant was moving to pick up the phone that had begun to ring at the other end of the desk. 'But they bounce back, don't they?'

Thorne said nothing.

*'Are we going home?'* Kieron had asked in the car. *'Will my mum be there?'*

'*She's going to come and meet us,*' Thorne had said.

Kieron had nodded, thoughtful. '*Will she be cross with me, do you think?*'

Thorne had said, '*Of course she won't,*' something like that. He'd reached across to lay a hand on Kieron's arm, but the boy had shifted away, refusing to be comforted and perking up only when Thorne had turned into the station car park. Had promised him Coke and crisps, and a chance to see inside one of the cells.

'*Josh's dad will be put in one of those, won't he?*'

Now, Thorne looked up and saw that the sergeant was holding the phone towards him. Thorne stepped across.

'Detective Constable Kimmel,' the sergeant said. 'From the hospital.'

Thorne snatched the phone. 'How's Ashton doing?'

'He hasn't regained consciousness.' Kimmel sounded tired. 'It's not looking great.'

'Right.' For a moment, Thorne was back in those woods. Watching as Kieron heaved that log above his head, then brought it crashing down. He blinked, said, 'Listen, I still can't get hold of Catrin—'

'Catrin Coyne's here,' Kimmel said. 'She's at the hospital.'

'*What?*'

'She almost got herself run over by the ambulance, but don't worry, she's fine. They're patching her up right now.'

'Patching her up . . . ?'

'A knife wound, but it's not serious.'

'What the fuck happened?' Thorne glanced up and saw the sergeant look away, trying desperately to pretend that he wasn't hanging on every word.

'I can't really get any sense out of her,' Kimmel said. 'She's on painkillers, which doesn't really help. Babbling about her friend Angie . . . about Kieron, obviously.'

'Did you tell her we've got him?'

'Yeah. Sorry, did you want to—?'

'Tell her he's coming,' Thorne said.


Paula Kimmel was sitting outside the curtained-off cubicle reading a magazine. She nodded at Thorne and smiled at the boy, but he looked quickly away to watch a nurse as she swept aside the curtain of the adjacent cubicle and stepped into it.

'It's like magic.' Kieron grinned and waved his arm. '*Whoosh,* like when they do a magic trick on TV.'

'Do you want to do that?' Thorne nodded at the red curtain, behind which the boy's mother was waiting.

'Can I do a *whoosh*?'

'I think you should,' Thorne said.

'On TV, though . . . sometimes people disappear.'

'I promise you won't disappear,' Thorne said. 'Go on . . .'

Kieron stepped forward, flexing his fingers. He muttered a 'whoosh', threw the curtain aside and ran into the cubicle. He shouted, 'Mum . . .'

'There you go,' Kimmel said.

Thorne looked at her.

'You can stop beating yourself up now.'

Thorne waited half a minute or so, then stepped – somewhat less dramatically – into the cubicle himself. Kieron was lying on top of his mother in bed. One arm was wrapped around his waist while the other, heavily bandaged, was raised, her fingers moving through his hair. Her eyes were closed and her lips were pressed close to his ear, whispering words Thorne could not make out.

It was too raw to watch and Thorne instinctively took a step back, just as Catrin Coyne opened her eyes.

He smiled and shoved his hands into his pockets.

She stared at him.

He whispered, 'I'll come back.'

She mouthed a 'thank you' a moment before Thorne closed the curtain behind him.

He stood for a minute, watching medical staff come and go, listening to a man crying out in pain a few cubicles along, then turned to Kimmel. 'You eaten?'

Kimmel lowered her magazine. 'Not since lunchtime.'

'I passed a twenty-four-hour McDonald's on the way here, if you fancy something.'

'You going?'

Thorne zipped up his jacket. 'God, yes.'

'Just some fries,' Kimmel said. She lifted her magazine then immediately lowered it again. 'And maybe some nuggets. And a large milkshake.'

414

A few minutes later, walking through the hospital lobby, Thorne heard a pair of uniformed officers complaining. There was rioting in Trafalgar Square; windows smashed in and cars getting turned over. They'd probably be down there cracking heads if they weren't hanging about in the middle of nowhere while everyone waited for some paedo to wake up.

'Bloody ridiculous,' one of them said. 'It's only football.'

Thorne walked past the two woodentops and out into the car park. It was drizzling, but he didn't hurry to the car. There would be a good deal more work to do, once he'd eaten, plenty that still needed straightening out, but for now he was content to imagine the look on Catrin Coyne's face when her son had burst through the curtain and run to her.

He climbed into the Mondeo and started the engine.

What was it that annoying magician always used to say on his TV show?

'Now, *that's* magic . . . '

On BBC 5 Live, the pundits were fielding phone calls about the game and the violence that had followed. England were out, having lost the semi-final against Germany. It was always on the cards – the predictable shoot-out – and why the hell had they let Gareth Southgate take a penalty, anyway?

Thorne pulled on to the main road and turned the radio off.

At that moment, he could not bring himself to care.

# PART FOUR

## Poison

# EIGHTY-TWO

'You're pretty cheerful.' Thorne nodded at Angela Coyne. 'For someone who's looking at life inside, I mean.'

The woman on the opposite side of the table appeared as relaxed as she had been since arriving at the station the night before. She smiled, as apparently unconcerned – according to the arresting officers – as she'd been when they'd pulled her car over in Enfield, at the same time Thorne was driving home from the hospital.

'It is what it is.' She shrugged. 'I mean, you make your bed, don't you?'

Paula Kimmel leaned forward. 'Two murders and one attempted. Hell of a bed, love.'

Angie Coyne ignored Kimmel's dig and stared down at the photographs that Thorne had spread out in front of her; a collection seized during a search of her home address first thing that morning. 'These turned out pretty well, I reckon,' she said.

'You think? May I . . . ?' Thorne reached across and turned one of the Polaroids around. These were the photographs Angie

419

Coyne had taken of Dean Meade – dying, then dead – and were rather more explicit than those taken by the journalists she'd phoned when she'd left the scene. Thorne looked down at the close-up shot of the wound in the side of the young man's neck, the blood still pumping. 'Yeah, you've certainly captured . . . something.'

Angie hummed her agreement. 'Funny, because people always told me I could have been a model,' she said.

'That is funny,' Thorne said.

'I mean, maybe I could have made a decent living on the other side of the camera. Probably pays a damn sight better than a market stall.'

'Who was with you in Dean's flat?' Thorne asked.

She looked at him.

'The woman who lives upstairs said she heard two male voices when Dean came in that night.'

'Is that right?'

'And we've found a witness who saw him leaving the pub with another man. Who let you in, Angie?'

'Just someone who was helping us out.'

'Helping? That was nice of him.'

'I'm not going to tell you his name, so don't waste your time.'

'Really? You've been very up-front with us about everything so far. I'd go as far as to say you've been bragging about it.'

She cocked her head as though she was accepting a compliment. 'Well, holding your hand up is one thing, but being a grass is very different.'

'Helping *us* out.' Kimmel looked up from her notebook. 'That's what you said. *Us* being you and Billy, right?'

Angie turned and stared hard at Kimmel. 'You really don't want to go there, babe.'

'Don't I?'

'My brother had nothing to do with this, all right? With any of it.'

420

Kimmel shook her head, said, 'Course not. So, if we were to get his cell at Whitehill turned over, just on the off-chance, we wouldn't find any Polaroids like these?'

Angie raised her hands. *Got me.* 'Well, I might have slipped him a couple last time I went in. Just to cheer him up a bit, you know?'

'That's very thoughtful,' Thorne said.

'He's my little brother, isn't he?' She smiled again and tapped a long, red fingernail against her teeth. 'We're very close.'

'So, killing Dean Meade and Grantleigh Figgis.' Kimmel leaned forward again. 'That was . . . what? A present for Billy?'

'One way of putting it.'

'Most people just send in some chocolate. A good book, maybe.'

'Billy's not a big reader,' Angie said. 'And anyway, Meade got what he deserved. Like I said, I feel a *bit* bad about the Figgis thing, but it's not entirely my fault, is it?' She looked past Thorne, towards the large mirror on the far wall of the interview room, the officers she knew very well were watching from behind it. 'It was you lot that nicked him, wasn't it? Between you and the papers . . . as good as set the poor bastard up for me.' She turned back to Thorne. 'Who's in the other room, anyway?'

Thorne said nothing.

'That miserable Scottish twat in there, is he? The fat one with a face like a bag of spanners?' She raised a hand and waggled her fingers. 'Enjoying the show, mate?'

Thorne did his best to keep his own face straight, imagining Gordon Boyle's reaction on the other side of the two-way mirror. He glanced at the spinning wheels of the twin cassettes in the wall-mounted recorder, delighted that the woman's pithy assessment of the DI had been preserved for posterity.

With any luck, the tape would get played in court.

'So, why Cat?' he asked.

Angie's expression darkened and, for a long few seconds, the only sound in the room was the squeak of those cassette wheels turning.

'Meade I get,' Thorne said. 'Figgis, up to a point . . . but why the hell try to kill her?'

'She can tell you herself.'

'I'm asking *you*—'

'Not that the silly bitch would still be around to tell you anything if I hadn't been wearing heels last night.' The woman sucked her teeth and scowled. 'If she wasn't wearing those hideous training shoes she's always got on.'

Thorne waited.

'Some women should never be mothers. Simple as that. Some of them just aren't cut out for it, are they?'

'Because of what happened to Kieron?'

'Yeah, course.'

'He was *taken*,' Thorne said.

'Accident waiting to happen, you ask me. And if they're stupid enough to let that useless mare have him back, she's only going to fuck it up again. Sit around painting her nails while the poor little sod scalds himself or falls out of a window, whatever.' She shook her head in disgust. 'If Kieron was my boy, I wouldn't take my eyes off him.'

'You think you'd have been a good mother, do you?' Kimmel asked.

'I know I would.'

'Right.'

'I should have been.' She grimaced, swallowed down something sour. 'I *should* have been . . .'

'So, just to be clear . . . you attempted to murder your brother's girlfriend because she was a mum and you're not?' Thorne looked at her. 'That what you're telling us?'

'You don't get it, do you?' Angie leaned across the table. 'Kieron should have been mine. He was *meant* to be mine.'

Then, there was just the faint squeak from the recorder again, until Kimmel muttered, 'Jesus ...'

Angie sat back, smiling again, seemingly happy that they finally understood. 'He was meant to be mine and Billy's.'

# EIGHTY-THREE

The officer on duty outside the door studied her ID for a little longer than seemed strictly necessary, before handing it back without a word. Without cracking his face. No, a big smile and a cosy chat were probably not entirely appropriate, all things considered, but nevertheless, she couldn't help thinking that *some* kind of reaction might have been ... nice. An acknow-ledgement, at the very least, that she was not there in the most pleasant of circumstances.

Maria stepped into the room and closed the door behind her, knowing full well of course what the officer had been thinking; what most people she dealt with these days were thinking, what-ever they said to her face.

*She must have known.*

She walked across and lowered herself into the chair next to the bed. She laid her handbag down gently on the floor. She poured herself a glass of water from the plastic jug and smoothed out her skirt.

Thinking: I *should* have.

She had thought of little else these last five weeks, as she'd

424

struggled to deal with the fallout. Doing her utmost to keep the media at bay. Guiding Josh through the nightmare of seemingly endless police interviews and medical examinations.

Listening to him cry at night.

*I should have known.*

Looking at the pitiful figure in the bed, the machines he was wired up to, she found herself wondering why there needed to be an officer stationed at the door in the first place. It was hardly as if the occupant of this room was going to unplug himself, leap to his feet and make a run for it. She smiled to herself and stared at what was left of her ex-husband, of the thing he'd become.

She tried not to think about precisely when he'd become ... someone different – she could not bring herself to use those words the papers had splashed across their front pages – and comforted herself with the idea that he had only started doing such things since the divorce.

Even so ...

*I should have known.*

Fighting against even the smallest suspicion that something might be amiss, because she was a coward. While the only person who had known had stepped up and done something almost supernaturally brave, found his own super-smart way to get the truth out, and saved his friend. Whatever Josh had gone through at his father's cottage, however much he had suffered, he would always know that much, at least.

Maria would never let her son forget that he was a hero.

As she talked to her ex-husband – her voice low and even – she thought about control. About wielding it and losing it. She thought how strange it was, how funny, that he would never again be able to have the one thing he had valued above anything else, the thing he had set such store by and had used so well and so viciously.

She smiled again.

It was hard to exercise even a modicum of control when you were already dead.

She hadn't actually been aware of that fact and was amazed when one of the doctors had explained it to her. Who knew that once your brain had given up the ghost – well, 'showing no evidence of higher brain function or brain-stem reflexes' was how the doctor had actually put it – you were legally dead? Clogs, to all intents and purposes, already popped.

Maria leaned towards the bed and patted the wrist that lay pale and still against the green blanket.

'So, you know . . . that's why I'm here, really.'

Next of kin.

She sat and thought about the only conversation she'd had with Jeff's mother since it had all happened. The woman's reaction to the news had been typical, priceless. One cursory burst of jagged, mechanical crying before the selfishness had kicked in.

'Well, darling, I hope you know that none of this is *my* fault.'

A second after a sharp knock at the door, a doctor put his head round it and Maria turned.

'I just wanted to see how you were getting on,' the doctor said. 'This is never easy.'

'I'm fine,' Maria said. 'I won't be very long.'

'Well, if you need to talk through things a bit more, you know where I am.' The young man nodded, backing out of the room. 'So, I'll see you whenever you're ready.'

Maria didn't believe that what Jeff had done was anybody's fault but his own. He and nobody else had made those terrible decisions. All the same, she knew very well in whose direction his mother had been pointing her bony finger.

Jeff's father had died several years back. At the time, Maria had tried to comfort Jeff because . . . well, that was what you were supposed to do in such situations, wasn't it? But she had seen very quickly that comfort was not something her husband actually required on this occasion. At the funeral, he

426

had demonstrated a disconcerting mix of devastation and euphoria. He had actually been singing in the car on the way back to London.

She talked for a few minutes more, then sat for a while with her eyes closed, listening to the *drip-drip* of the feeding tube, the *thrum* and *hiss* of the machine that was the only thing causing her ex-husband's chest to rise and fall.

The noises were not unpleasant.

She reached for her bag and stood up. 'Right then, I need to go and do a spot of paperwork.'

At the door Maria stopped and turned. 'Well, this wasn't the most riveting conversation we've ever had, was it? But it was one of the few where I get to have the last word.'

Half an hour later, stepping out of the lift into the hospital reception, Maria was still agonising over the difficult conversation she would one day need to have with Josh about today. The truth would probably be best when the time came, she decided, however uncomfortable that might be. There had been far too many lies already. By the time she reached the exit, the dread had begun to lift a little and she was trying to decide what the two of them were going to have for dinner.

Pizza, she thought. That was his favourite. Pizza with pineapple.

On the pavement outside, waiting for a gap in the traffic, she looked across to see Cat waving at her from the other side of the road.

She nodded and waved back.

A few seconds later, Maria seized her chance and walked quickly across the road towards her friend.

# EIGHTY-FOUR

It's cold and full-dark, the middle of the night it feels like, and the trees are getting closer together, huddling around him as Thorne moves through the woods. He does not hesitate, doesn't pause or stumble. He walks quickly, purposefully, as though his feet know exactly where they are taking him, even if Thorne hasn't got the first idea.

He's not scared, though. It's exciting . . .

Suddenly, the sun punches a hole in the canopy above him and he is standing in a brightly lit clearing.

Thorne sees Kieron waving, and hurries across to join him.

'That's the poison circle,' Kieron says. 'See?' The boy points to the makeshift ring of small white rocks laid out around them. He sounds very serious. 'You need to stay inside the circle, OK? That's the game.'

Then the others are standing with him. Cat and Maria and Josh. Billy, Angela and Jeff Ashton. The eight of them join hands until they have formed a circle inside the circle and Kieron says it's time to start the game.

'Three . . . two . . . one . . . *go!*'

They quickly start to push and pull, to lean and lurch; jostling for position until, finally, Kieron's dad is forced across the line of stones.

He says, 'Poisoned,' and lowers his head.

They start again. Tussling and laughing.

'Poisoned,' Josh says.

'Poisoned,' Angela says.

One by one, each of them is driven beyond the border of white stones and the rest join hands again. The dead grow in number and the circle of safety gets smaller, until there are only two of them left.

Thorne and Kieron.

'Last one left alive is the winner,' Kieron says. 'You ready?'

It doesn't last very long because, although Thorne is obviously far stronger, there's no way he can't let the boy win. They wrestle for a few seconds, then Thorne grunts like a beaten man and steps back beyond the stones.

'Poisoned,' he says. 'I'm poisoned.'

Kieron begins to cry and shakes his head. He says, 'No, *I* am—'

Which is when the siren starts to scream from somewhere close by and a flock of birds explodes from the treetops. Thorne shields his eyes against the sun and watches them beating their way skywards, before they turn back suddenly and begin diving down and swooping around his head. He ducks for cover and shouts Kieron's name, but the siren is getting louder and louder and the boy just stands there with tears streaming down his face and his hands pressed to his ears.

Thorne muttered at Alexa chiming at him from the chest of drawers on which she squatted in the corner of the room, then he shouted, until eventually the alarm stopped.

He lay still in the semi-dark, disoriented, slowly surfacing.

He could not remember the last time he had dreamed about

the Kieron Coyne case; about Cat or Billy or Josh, or the woman who had committed two murders for reasons he still found hard to fathom. Once or twice over the years, no more than that. Certainly nothing like as often as he still dreamed about Calvert.

Old meat and metal and three pairs of embroidered pillowcases.

She might be out by now, he thought, easing himself up and sitting on the side of the bed. Angela Coyne. She'd received a life sentence, begun at Holloway, but, twenty-four years on, Thorne could not recall the tariff. He'd check when he got to the office, just to satisfy his curiosity.

He stood up, pulled on jeans and a T-shirt and padded barefoot into the kitchen. He turned on the radio then leaned against the worktop, waiting for the kettle to boil. Happy enough – happier than he'd been in a while – in the flat he had first seen all those years ago. Standing on the street outside with Phil Hendricks.

*'I still think you probably need to look inside—'*

Just before that first ever visit to the Bengal Lancer.

He hadn't actually bought the place back then, content to be stubborn and hold on to the house in Highbury a while, to piss Jan and her hippy-dippy lecturer around for as long as possible. A few years later, the flat had come back on to the market and he'd snapped it up at a considerably higher price than it had been selling for the first time round.

Idiot . . .

He'd stayed here ever since, living alone for the most part, then renting the flat out for the time he was living south of the river with a woman named Helen Weeks and her son. When that relationship had finally gone the same way as the rest of them, he'd found himself back in Kentish Town.

Single, and fine with that, until a few months before.

He and Dr Melita Perera, the woman with whom Thorne was now involved, had decided not to do anything stupid like move in together, certainly not for a while. When they chose to share a bed for the night, it might be at his place or it might be at her considerably nicer one in Crouch End. It was a suitably grown-up arrangement, Thorne decided, and made a degree of sense considering the chequered history of cohabitation they had in common, and Melita's lack of enthusiasm for music that featured a fiddle or a pedal-steel guitar.

It also meant that Thorne didn't have to tidy up quite as much.

Thorne carried his tea across to the kitchen table and sat, remembering.

Angela Coyne had paid the right price for what she'd done, but she had been pretty much the only one. Any hopes that Jeff Ashton might stand trial were dashed when his ex-wife Maria had finally turned off the life-support machine he'd been on for five weeks.

After that it was just . . . details.

Ashton had kept Kieron Coyne sedated for most of the time, using drugs that, as a doctor, had been easily available to him. He had done other things too, of course, but those facts would never be read out in court and, even though a report was circulated internally, Thorne had not felt the need to see it.

It had been clear enough, in the fury distorting that small boy's face.

*Hulk . . . smash!*

There had been therapy later on, Thorne had been aware of that much, privately and at school. For Kieron and for Josh. Talking and drawing and structured play.

'Result,' Boyle had said at the time. 'No trial means a damn sight less paperwork and no titting about with the CPS. You ask me, Ashton got what was coming to him, anyway.'

It was more than could be said for Gordon Boyle himself who, after the most cursory of DPS inquiries, had been quietly transferred to a force at the other end of the country. That Boyle's mishandling of the investigation should be swept under the carpet was hardly surprising, considering the flap once it

431

had emerged that DCI Andy Frankham had been the source of the mysterious press leaks.

The Rubberheelers had been on overtime for weeks.

A swift early retirement, pension frozen and deferred until he was sixty-five.

Not that it had done Grantleigh Figgis any good.

Thorne stood up and took what was left of his tea back into the bedroom.

'Alexa ... shuffle songs by Merle Haggard.' It was music he enjoyed while he was getting ready in the mornings, but sometimes Thorne could not help but wonder if whatever algorithms made the song choices for him had a dark sense of humour built in.

'House of Memories' ...

Only a week or so earlier, Thorne had driven past Seacole House – or at least the block of swanky, overpriced apartments that had replaced it a long time ago – and wondered, as he had many times before, what had become of Catrin Coyne. In the back of his mind, he had an idea that she'd struck up a relationship with her son's teacher, but he couldn't be sure and he was struggling to recall the man's name.

Jennings? Jensen? He couldn't remember ...

He liked to think that she *had* found somebody else and hadn't simply taken Billy back when he'd come out of prison.

Wherever she was and whatever she was doing, Thorne hoped she had been able to leave what had happened that morning in Highgate Wood behind her. He hoped she was happy and ... settled, though he had good reason to doubt it.

He had recognised Kieron Coyne's name on an arrest report, a dozen or so years before; as many years after he had seen him burst through that curtain in hospital and run to his mother.

Disturbing the peace, assault on a police officer, possession of Class A drugs.

Thorne had not been surprised.

He was leaning down to tie his shoelaces when the text alert sounded on his phone.

*We still on for tonight, big boy?*

Phil Hendricks and his partner Liam were coming over for dinner with Thorne and Melita. Their first time together as a foursome.

Thorne texted back: *As long as you behave yourself.*

He briefly wondered if he should tell Hendricks about the dream when he saw him that evening and imagined the pair of them trotting out one of their many war stories after a bottle or two. He quickly decided against it. Kieron Coyne's story was not one fit for sharing over the dinner table, besides which it was rarely a good idea to talk about your nightmares when your girlfriend was a forensic psychiatrist.

Anyway, he knew what Melita would say, that she would be supportive, as she always was.

*You've got nothing to feel bad about, Tom. You* saved *him ...*

Thorne wished he could feel the same way. He walked out into the hall, thinking about that old arrest report. He had seen enough damaged souls to know that for some people drugs were not a choice. He knew that, for those desperate enough, they were taken every bit as easily and with as good a reason as the rest of the world gobbled down antibiotics or statins or vitamin pills.

Painkillers ...

Thorne picked up his leather jacket and opened his front door.

He hadn't saved Kieron Coyne from anything.

# ACKNOWLEDGEMENTS

Writing a novel set twenty-five years ago has much to be said for it – it is certainly a joy to write about a crime being investigated without your cops being almost wholly reliant on email trails, mobile phone cell-site triangulation and CCTV – but it was also a somewhat bizarre experience. I remember the mid-nineties well (most of it, anyway) but quickly realised that I was actually writing a piece of historical crime fiction, albeit one that features A-Zs, video recorders and smoking in pubs, as opposed to hansom cabs or Roman vases. As history has never been my strong point, it will come as no surprise that I needed a great deal of help to combat both the vagaries of memory and my all-but-total ignorance when it came to matters of police procedure a quarter of a century ago.

Sometimes, old episodes of *The Bill* are simply not enough.

I am far from being the first crime writer to be grateful for the advice and expertise of retired detective Graham Bartlett. His help has been incalculable, and if you want proof that Graham knows what he's talking about, I can thoroughly recommend his own non-fiction book, *Babes in the Wood* (co-written with

Peter James). The very different expertise of forensic pathologist Dr Stuart Hamilton was equally valuable and I am indebted to him for providing fictional colleague Phil Hendricks with his revelatory moment of lateral thinking. Professor David Wilson's book, *My Life with Murderers*, was enormously useful and the prison scenes in *Cry Baby* – including the nicknames of the special units – were largely inspired by Professor Wilson's writings about his work at HMP Woodhill.

This is my twentieth novel in as many years, and among any number of things that make me realise how lucky I have been over the past two decades is the fact that so many of the people I need to thank have featured on the acknowledgement page of almost every single book. So, thank you, yet again, to my amazing agent, Sarah Lutyens (and Juliet, Francesca and Hana), my eagle-eyed friend Wendy Lee and my partner in crime Mike Gunn.

Thank you, Hilary Hale and David Shelley, for so much.

Thank you to the team at Little, Brown which has been my publishing home, and *family*, for twenty years: Catherine Burke, Charlie King, Robert Manser, Hannah Methuen, Callum Kenny, Thalia Proctor, Tom Webster, Gemma Shelley, Sean Garrehy, Sarah Shrubb and Tamsin Kitson. Thank you again to Nancy Webber for a brilliant copy-edit, and for the stickers!

Thank you to my brilliant editor Ed Wood and to Laura Sherlock, the best publicist in the business.

Thank you to all those at Grove Atlantic who continue to fly Tom Thorne's tatty, beer-stained flag on the other side of the Atlantic – Sara Vitale, Morgan Entrekin, Justine Batchelor and Deb Seager – and to all those at assorted publishing houses worldwide who keep my children in shoes. *Danke sehr, Toda, Grazie, Tak,* ありがとう。etc . . .

I want to thank all those writers whose friendship and support has meant and continues to mean so much. The only reason I'm not going to list them is that I'm bound to forget someone and several of them can be touchy, not to say extremely vengeful. But I hope they know who they are. I *will* name the five who, as fellow Fun Lovin' Crime Writers, have made the last couple of years so much more fun than they would otherwise have been. So, thank you Val, Chris, Stuart, Doug and Luca. We will *always* have Glastonbury.

Lastly but not leastly, I need to thank those without whom I would not be sitting down to write these stories at all. I'm talking, of course, about . . . Nando's, Brewdog and Cadbury's. Please forgive a cheap joke, made solely in an effort to undercut what some may regard as the cheesiness of this final acknowledgement. I don't care. Those familiar with my love of country music will know I'm a sucker for the cheese, so just imagine my beloved George Jones breaking your heart, his backing singers in perfect, angelic harmony and the strings swelling behind him as I say a heart-felt *thank you so bloody much* to all those readers who have stuck with me, and with Tom, for all these years.

Seriously, without you, there wouldn't be any point.

437